BOOK ONE

# FORGOTTEN RUIN

## JASON ANSPACH
## NICK COLE

# WARGATE

An imprint of Galaxy's Edge Press
PO BOX 534
Puyallup, Washington 98371

Paperback ISBN: 978-1-949731-49-1
Hardcover ISBN: 978-1-949731-48-4

www.forgottenruin.com
www.jasonanspach.com
www.nickcolebooks.com
www.wargatebooks.com

# TECHNICAL ADVISORS AND CREATIVE DESTRUCTION SPECIALISTS

Ranger Vic
Ranger David
Ranger Chris

Green Beret John "Doc" Spears

Rangers lead the way!

# CHAPTER ONE

WHEN I began to dream in Elvish, it was then I knew I could speak it. And it was when the orc horde overran one of the fighting positions along First Platoon's sector on the east side of the island the Rangers were defending that I knew we weren't in Kansas anymore. The US Army had sent us someplace no one had ever gone. And it was looking like the kind of place no one was ever coming back from either. Back then, we had no idea where we were. And by *we*, I mean all of us lowlies in the Ranger detachment tasked with defending the grounded C-17 and her complement of crew, Deep State, and science and tech personnel.

I was attached to the detachment, which was part of a larger element known as Joint Task Force Tarantino.

Also, I've never been to Kansas.

It was just after 0300 when the enemy came through our defenses along the west side of the big island in the middle of a river in a lush green valley. I was down close to First Platoon's command position, or CP, just before the whole line of First's fighting positions and foxholes got hit. Corporal Brocker, whose machine-gun team's position anchored the north end of the hundred-and-fifty-meter line of the platoon's fighting pits, had the tactical forethought to launch an IR pop flare well out in front of the line and a few hundred feet high. The comically small parachute

1

attached to what could be described as a road flare came down in slow motion out over the sluggish river and off into the dreary wetlands on the other side. This had the effect of bathing the entire scene in soft light invisible to the naked eye, but as strong as direct sunlight inside the dual-tube night vision devices we all had mounted on our helmets.

Someone in our pit swore in the darkness. I think it was Tanner. Everyone else just hunkered there for a brief moment. Assessing the situation. Too stunned by what we were really seeing out there in the river and along the wetlands on the other side to react immediately.

What were we seeing? Sometimes, after long hours of using night vision, NVGs, IR light can play tricks on your eyes. But not like this.

Not. Even. Close.

A real live orc horde was storming across the river bottom, making for our fighting pits along the shore. Coming straight for us.

Why do I call them orcs, you ask? Because that's exactly what they looked like to us. Our patrols had spotted them in the days leading up to the attack, and we'd even seen them on the ISR feeds being pushed from the Raven drones we'd sent out. Hairy, misshapen brutes in ancient Bronze Age armor carrying swords, wicked-looking axes, and feather-laden spears. Fangs and eyes that seemed alive with menace in the ghostly night-vision feeds.

Now, along the river, in the shifting, almost supernatural glow of the falling IR pop flare, the orcs looked blue-black as they waved spears and swords, gave battle cries, and rushed for us. They looked to me like monsters. But a guy in our platoon—Kennedy—who knows about orcs and wizards, who loved all D&D and all that stuff, he said they were more like the orcs in Ralph Bakshi's animated version of *The Lord of the Rings* than the ones in Peter Jackson's mega-blockbuster epic. They moved fast and silent through the gentle river. If someone over in one of First Platoon's forward observation posts hadn't spotted them barely splashing as they entered the river, swords, scimitars, and spears ready to go... they would have been a lot closer before we opened fire on them. Things would've been much worse than they were about to get.

The weapons squad leader had been busy improving the fighting position that consisted of a two-man pit and a defensive berm. He worked like a man possessed in the middle of the night, but that was Sergeant Kurtz. Rangers are highly motivated as a rule, but they don't like to dig. Kurtz, the heavy weapons squad leader, didn't care what anyone liked.

Sergeant Kurtz swore at Private Watt for not spotting the orcs coming to kill us sooner. We were only running one active pair of NVGs to a fighting pit to conserve battery power. The Forge inside the C-17 back at the CP was busy cranking out as much ammo as it could gin up. Guys who understood the tech said we couldn't use it to charge batteries at the same time. Go figure. It was made for the government.

We expected to get hit hard and no one knew how long we'd be in a fight. The Forge had been on ammo crank since the captain made the decision that this *horde*... yeah, he used that word specifically, and yes, everyone—you could just about feel it in the TOC—thought the usage was a little... grand. A little too geeky for the tactical operations center aboard the grounded C-17. Call it whatever, but this *horde* was coming right for us, no doubt about it. The captain had overridden the Baroness and the Deep State guy and demanded we switch our Forge over to ammunition production.

*They* wanted to "parley." The Baroness's word.

She's a scientist, not an actual baroness. It's just that the Rangers think she looks a lot like the villainess from the *G.I. Joe* cartoon they all grew up watching. The other guy, Deep State guy, who's here as a "civilian adviser" actually said, "Slow down. Let's just see what they want first before we start shooting at them."

The captain ignored both Deep State and the Baroness and ordered his detachment to dig in and prepare to repel.

All of us who had boarded the C-17 were carrying a basic combat load of ammunition, plus some. And though I'd never been to war with the Rangers, nor combat at all, I was aware that every Ranger around me in the task force knew a basic combat load probably wasn't gonna be enough to go properly medieval on what we were facing.

"Never is enough," said the only guy in the detachment with a beard. The only tabbed Ranger who is generally tolerant of my non-Ranger presence. Everyone calls him Thor, and not just because it's what's on his issue nametag. The man could probably go to Hollywood and get cast playing Thor's double in one of those super hero movies. That is, if he weren't here with us about to die in the big mystery that is this bizarre place of orc hordes storming the sandy beaches along the riverbanks in the night. Now Thor is looking through his scope at the approaching horde. As far as Rangers go, Thor's one of their best snipers. And that's really saying something in sniper world.

One of Kurtz's two-forty gunners opened up from their pit with tracers in the mix. A hot streak of 7.62 slammed into the forward line of the orcs coming across the water, cutting down a bunch of spear carriers at the front of the swelling mass. A tribal leader of some sort went down too. He had dangly teeth-necklaces and a big horned helm, and generally acted more elite than the rest of his command currently being ventilated by the two-forty's traversing fire cutting across their front ranks. The light from the falling IR flare made the monsters suddenly, horribly, startlingly clear to everyone as the machine guns tore them to shreds right there in the middle of the river.

Then as the flare fell over that first lot, we began to see really just how many orcs there were out there. There were hundreds, if not a thousand, coming straight at Bravo to our left. My mind didn't want to accept a number like that. How could so many have moved swiftly and silently, en masse, right up on the elite fighting troops known as US Army Rangers?

That's pro. It requires a certain amount of cunning.

That burst from the two-forty should have stopped their advance right there. Stopped 'em cold, in fact. *Hajis* in the third world who got caught like that out in the open would have scattered and ran. But. Big full-stop *BUT* here. These guys didn't. All of a sudden, the rest of the swarming, snarling, bellowing pack of orcs forward of the main horde, which we didn't quite see yet, surged at us, ululating horrible tribal war cries and waving their blackened scimitars as they came on.

Horns. Tribal battle horns rang out, I kid you not. *UROOOO UROOO UROOOOOOOOOOOOOoooooooooo.*

That's what it sounded like. I won't lie. It was like the realest surreal thing that's ever happened to me. Ever.

All that didn't stop anyone in First Platoon from continuing to unload into the face of an oncoming flood of nightmares straight out of a nightmare's nightmare rushing right at them. These are Rangers, after all. The opportunity to inflict hyper violence upon a determined enemy was not one any of these men would pass up. Ever. The machine gunners timed their individual bursts and "talked" their guns along the platoon's defensive line, answering the enemy's battle horn calls with their own staccato of unrelenting fire to teach our attackers the error of their ways. Fanged teeth gnashed while claws still holding cruel black-steel swords were shot away. Outgoing rounds slammed into tattered leather armor and faded gray cloaks, dropping foul bodies into the waters of the slow-moving river or blowing open misshapen skulls in sudden bloody sprays. By the time the IR pop burned out in the sky we could see more orcs entering the water from the far side of the river. Slinking out of the wetlands in the thin silver moonlight. Pushing through the silhouettes of the reeds along the far bank like predators coming out for the late-night hunt.

"Rico!" bellowed Second Squad's Alpha Team Leader. "Shift fire to support Third Squad's holes! Make 'em talk!"

Specialist Rico, with the help of his assistant gunner, lifted the entire machine gun, tripod, and ammo bag, then settled it down reoriented on their new target.

"Gun Two up," Rico called back while landing the machine gun's sighting laser into the flank of the orc element that was attempting to mass directly in front of Third Squad's holes.

"Engage!" was the sergeant's only response.

Before the word had fully left the NCO's lips, Rico was pouring cyclic fire into the group pushing through the water towards Third Squad's position.

*That should do it*, I thought stupidly. Now the orcs were being hit by intersecting fire creating not only more death, but more confusion for the enemy as they tried to figure out which position was shooting at them.

Spears launched at short range volleyed into Third Squad's pits, but it was hard to see if anyone got hit. No one screamed, at least.

A short burst from Specialist Rico, followed by a *ka-thunk* sound, signaled to all of us in the hole that Gun Two had just malfunctioned.

"Gun Two down!" erupted like a bitter indictment out of Rico's Copenhagen-filled lip.

"Weak!" called out Tanner, who was already engaging with his MK18 carbine. Single fire. Good marksmanship. At the same moment Rico began to clear the malfunction, Sergeant Kurtz grabbed his M320 grenade launcher and began to fire into the mass of orcs now surging forward on Bravo.

Specialist Brumm, the SAW gunner supporting our position, came up and called out to Sergeant Kurtz, "Switching to on!" Then he unloaded with the devastating squad automatic weapon in short, staccato bursts as he kept the barrel down and made sure the damage was as brutal as it sounded to my ears.

I actually felt sorry for the orcs at that moment. Second and Third Squads were slaughtering them as they tried to cross the river. It was like, and this is a stupid thought I had in the middle of it all, but I think a lot, so excuse me, it was like the orcs didn't realize they'd just stepped into a writhing pit full of deadly vipers and now they were getting taught a fatal lesson by the best in the business. To a Ranger assault platoon… what can I say? The ultimate truth is that they are the physical manifestation of the First Horse of the Apocalypse as far as the enemy should be concerned. Sure, there may be some resistance, but those efforts will ultimately prove futile.

In hindsight, now that I've been afforded the time to think about it—I'm sure everyone else who survived thinks about it too—in that moment we should have been concerned. They were getting slaughtered. So why didn't they break?

Brumm, crouching behind the berm at our rear for a better angle, continued dumping fire into the dark mass of orcs off to the left in front of Third. Rounds tore through the monsters and created sudden silver plumes in the river currents.

That was when Third Squad's gunner, Corporal Brocker went black on ammo. That is to say, he used it all up and had nothing left with which to dissuade the orcs from continuing their onslaught. They were being overrun.

The orcs were now halfway across the dark river and pushing for the bank where our first line of defense along the eastern side of the island was set up. An M240 Bravo fires roughly six hundred rounds per minute from hundred-round belts that can be linked belt to belt. Basically, you've got two thousand rounds. More than enough for a few seconds of combat against insurgents in brush-fire conflicts.

Except in those first few seconds we didn't realize this horde attack was something more than that. It was something ancient. Something dating as far back as Marathon and on through history. Gettysburg. World War

I. Everywhere men had been fated to die in droves and bleed out in anonymity.

There were easily six hundred orcs in the water now. Probably more. Hard to say in the darkness and chaos of the sudden firefight. More still came out of the shadowy woods on the far side of the river.

We had no mines in place yet.

Space had been limited on the last flight out of Dodge. The Forge was supposed to pick up the slack once we were on the ground, wherever that happened to be. We'd only been here in the valley, wherever here was, for a little under three days.

Granted, these were Rangers who'd fought in the Middle East, Venezuela, and a couple of hot spots in Latin America in recent years. But no one, and I guarantee you now as I write this, *no one* in that early morning, halfway to dawn darkness, had ever faced a mass wave attack similar to something straight out of the Chosin Reservoir during the First Korean War. That's what we were facing .

Except it was orcs instead of humans. On that we all agreed.

It was Tanner who'd first said it during the ops briefing after the initial recon drone footage came in. Of course it was Tanner. For a Ranger, he was actually pretty funny. And friendly.

Ever the low man on the totem in the detachment, the perpetually-serving-extra-duty PFC Kennedy counted Tanner as his only friend. Or at least the only Ranger who would talk to him. It was actually Kennedy who first said they were "probably orcs." But it was Tanner who relayed that to the rest of us.

So, orcs it was.

"Get to work, Talker!" bellowed Sergeant Kurtz as the fight dialed up to desperate. Bellowing at me in the middle of the onslaught.

He meant for me to join the fight. Which wasn't why I was there. At least not until that moment.

It's true. I did have a rifle with me. And I had Ranger gear. Back at Fifty-One I'd been issued the RLCS kit. But a tricked-out MK18 and Ranger gear don't make one a Ranger, as I'd told myself on more than one occasion. Yes, I'd done an abbreviated RASP just to get ready for this mission. Ranger Assessment and Selection Program. But the truth is, I'm just a linguist.

The scroll patch on our left shoulder that identifies us as Rangers still means something though, even for a just-a-linguist like a me. As Sergeant Thor put it to me the first day with the detachment, "The Ranger tab is just a leadership school. The scroll is a way of life."

He had both a scroll and a tab.

I had been placed here as augment, really. So even though I had trained enough for this mission that on paper I was to be considered a Ranger, I had too much respect for what they did, what they'd earned, and how they lived it, to just assume I was one of them.

That's why they call me Talker—because I do languages—instead of Walker. Which is my real name until I went through RASP.

I'm also only a PFC, and Kurtz is a real live staff sergeant weapons squad leader. And in the Ranger batt that actually counts for something. Word is, Kurtz was some kind of scout sniper in the marines, except he got thrown out for being too violent and offensive for the marines. Or maybe he didn't like the taste of crayons. That was another Tanner joke said  only when Kurtz was nowhere to be seen.

I went prone next to Brumm, who yelled "Get some!" while spraying the orcs now surging up the bank onto and all over Third. At the same time Kurtz called for his team to shift fire back out into the river for fear of hitting the Third Squad guys in their now-overrun holes.

"Engage second wave coming into the water now."

Specialist Rico said something about the situation being dumber than a bag of hammers.

"Steel Eight One, this is One Four. Request fire mission on TRP oh-eight-zero." Kurtz was both calling in fire support and directing fire where he wants the two-forty to concentrate. "Say again…"

"Loading!" Brumm said calmly as he knelt and dragged a new drum of ammo for the SAW from over near the pit. Hot brass flew everywhere and I fired into the orcs, never really aiming for anyone. You didn't have to. They were so thick you couldn't miss. There was this surreal moment when it felt like I wasn't actually doing anything to help. Because the orcs weren't reacting to the 5.56 rounds coming from my rifle. But I still tried to hit them.

"Brumm, you're with me," yelled Kurtz. "We're going QRF to relieve Third. Talker, you too, you worthless slag. Follow me and don't shoot anyone dressed like us."

I did Basic with a bunch of other support types. Fort Leonard Wood. Cooks. Truckers. Telephone repair specialists. But as the Army says, everyone's a rifleman. And I was pretty good at it. So much so that I qual'd BRM first time through and ended up doing KP so that those who couldn't shoot got some extra range time.

But when Kurtz told me we were forming a quick reaction force to relieve the pit next to ours along the riverbank, I realized I had no idea what I was doing. As the first mortar rounds from the top of the small hill at the northern tip of the island began to fall out there on the far side of the river, near the trees the orcs were swarming from, I at least had the presence of mind to put a new mag in my weapon. I pulled it from my chest carrier, and the look of pure contempt Brumm gave me as he lugged the SAW up to get ready to counterattack—I guess my mag pull wasn't slick enough for him— was palpable.

Kurtz was in front of us as we pushed out of our fighting position, hunkering low as if we were flanking jihadis in Honduras. The orcs were frightening, hairy beasts bristling with fangs, claws, leather armor wrapped in dark rags, and literally wicked-looking scimitars they tried to slash us with. But swords as deadly as they appeared, couldn't shoot back at us. They didn't have AK-47s or PKMs. So we had that going for our three-man counterattack to relieve Third.

Then the arrows started to fall and Brumm took one right in the plate carrier. I heard it land with a loud *THOCK*. Not a *Thunk*. But a *THOCK*. I don't think it penetrated because Brumm started to laugh and just snapped it off. Yeah, we were wearing full battle rattle. Plate carrier. Knee pads. Combat helmet. But there were a lot of places an arrow that big, and it was huge and dark in the half-light provided by the falling explosions out there on the far riverbank, could find a home in a body.

I wasn't scared.

I gotta make that clear, because I'd been worried for a long time leading up to this that I was going to be afraid when I actually got into combat. *When does a linguist ever see combat* was a phrase I couldn't get out of my head. Sure, I knew that someday-probably-never, combat might go down somewhere in my general vicinity on some garbage-littered third world street against jihadis or Chinese irregulars. But orcs? Nah. I hadn't planned for that. Who would've?

And yet there I was. Supporting Sergeant Kurtz with live rounds. Arrows rained down through the willows and slammed into the muddy bank all around us, but Kurtz kept us moving forward. Then one went right through his forearm and he swore once. Violently.

Not a blue streak.

Just once.

He snapped it off and moved on Bravo's pit. The orcs were in there and one of the Rangers was fighting hand-to-hand, swinging a rifle like a club. I noticed another one on the bank, hammering a tomahawk straight into the chest of a prone orc he was straddling. His helmet was missing.

"Push right, Brumm. Clear forward!" shouted Kurtz and then started firing his rifle into the orcs in the pit with blood streaming down his arm and onto the overturned earth we were crossing.

I raised my rifle and drilled an orc warrior with bright eyes like some twisted devil in the dark. Eyes gleaming cold malice. He wanted me dead. I shot him twice in the chest and he just backed up along the pit, snarling and taking the rounds. Gnashing his broken teeth at me. Not sure what to do or why this was happening, but enraged that it was. Slick as a snake he flung a black dagger that came from out of nowhere right at me. The aim was true, but I twisted out of the way at the last second. When I turned back, Kurtz had blown that one's head off and was heading down into the pit to retrieve the two-forty.

The surge from across the river had abated as mortar strikes rained down along the far bank. Tanner was probably adjusting fire from our fighting position.

"Find out who's still alive!" shouted Sergeant Kurtz raggedly as he dragged an ammo can up next to the pit's two-forty and fed a belt into the receiving tray.

Brumm swore.

Swore to the effect of *What in the hell is that?*

I looked up from the bodies in the pit. Side note. It's impossible to tell if someone has a pulse when yours is firing like a jackhammer. I had no idea who was dead or alive in there. But there was a lot of blood and there were dead orcs bleeding down there among our guys too. They don't bleed green or black, if that's what you're thinking. In the dark it was red as near as I could tell. And it was all one big bloody mess of limbs and arms. Plus, the orcs stank.

Here's what I was doing. And this is my account of the Battle for Ranger Alamo. I was basically asking the bodies of Rangers on the ground, "You okay, buddy?"

Pathetic.

But I was doing my best.

Did I mention I speak eight languages? I can get by in a lot of others, too.

And when Brumm expressed some sort of dark wonder at what he was seeing off to our right out across the river, punctuated by the fact that the normally trigger-happy SAW gunner, who preferred the music of gunfire to anything else found on his iPhone, had suddenly stopped firing, I involuntarily looked up to see what had captured the Ranger's attention.

Even hard-core Sergeant Kurtz paused.

And this is what we saw.

Walking through the night mist and clearing smoke of the mortar strike, striding across the field and heading toward the dark river and straight for us... was a real live giant.

A goliath. Easily twelve feet tall but built like it was hewn from a mountain. Thick and wide. All muscle.

Later, PFC Kennedy, who plays a lot of D&D, would say that it was maybe a hill giant, and then he added a bunch of other geek stuff no one could stand to listen to.

At that moment, as it tromped across the river shallows toward us, it didn't look like one of those friendly giants in Disney cartoons. Or even the sort of misshapen cave trolls from the Jackson films.

"Talker! Inside the pit! Brumm, find me the Carl Gustaf!" Then Sergeant Kurtz ran a line of bright fire up the torso of the menacing giant in the flowing dirty gray kaftan with an iron cap across its head. The rounds spat out and streaked across the water as Kurtz tried to find his range. The giant wasn't lumbering, and it carried a massive spiked mace. From its wrists dangled heavy chains. It began to laugh, bellowing angrily as it came on at a smooth, fast stride that would have it all over us in seconds.

That was the scary part. How fast it moved.

The 7.62 from the M240 just made it angry. I knew that because it began to charge across the river, raising a massive mace over its head with both of its fat swollen fists, river water gushing to get out of its way. I was in no doubt that the mace would crush us in a single blow within the next few seconds.

I may have said, "I think you made it mad!" while Specialist Brumm called out at the same time, "Loading HE!"

Sergeant Kurtz ignored me and silently burned through an entire belt of ammo, teeth gritted, as he tried to kill a thing that would not die. On the other hand, if looks could've killed, Kurtz's glare would have done the job easily. That man is pure hate.

You always know where you stand with him.

He just hates you.

I find that refreshing. It's one of the reasons I walked away from my old life and chose the military. I like people who don't play games. And yeah, I asked for a chance to become a Ranger, but all they would guarantee me when I signed up was linguist and Airborne. Also, my recruiter said there was no way in hell he was letting me join the infantry with an ASVAB score like mine. And wasn't I "good at languages or something" the big E-6 Samoan had asked intently on the day I walked back into the recruiter's office. Now that I think about it, there must've been some kind of bonus in it for him if I was.

Yeah. Eight languages plus some usable pick-up lines in a dozen more, buddy. Maxed the DLAB. And that's just a made-up language.

So anyway, I'd just said "I think you made it mad" to Brumm. Which I hope I really said, because from a screenwriting point of view that's perfect for what happened next. I want to be a writer someday on the other side of this.

*I think you made it angry.*

That's what I said.

And then without missing a beat or even looking over at me, Brumm shouted "Firing HE!" and fired a round out of the Carl Gustaf launcher. A recoilless, direct-fire, 84mm weapon that is for all intents and purposes a miniature shoulder-fired artillery piece. It took off like an invisible hornet that was late for a drive-by.

It wasn't an explosion. There was no kick that I saw. Just Brumm rocking back a bit as the round disappeared from the Gustaf. My ears were already ringing from the gunfire, but somehow the low *whooomp* of the weapon rose above the blare of gunfire and the battle cries of the orcs swarming in the river.

The round went straight through the looming giant and out its back, tearing away guts and bone in the half-light of the battle. I would find out later that the round was anti-personnel and that after ripping a hole in the giant it shotgunned eight hundred tungsten pellets through the giant's back, effectively shredding the behemoth's insides. It was like making a shotgun explode inside him.

The giant twisted, groaning titanically, and fell back toward the far shore, hitting the water with a terrific splash and crushing a bunch of his buddies.

In the darkness and sudden quiet Brumm muttered, "Carl Gustaf don't care."

# CHAPTER TWO

IN the aftermath of the night slaughter along the river-bank, the orcs faded into what remained of the cold and mist out there on the other side of the dark, murmuring river. We weren't the only ones to face down that horror. Other defensive positions along the Ranger line had been probed at various points across the island we'd found ourselves on. As PFC Tanner remarked right about the time Command Sergeant Major Stone and Chief Rapp showed up to assess the situation at our CP, "If that was a probe, I'm pretty sure I don't wanna know what it feels like when they commit to a serious relationship."

Nearby, while the wounded were attended to, Brumm, with a mouthful of dip and standing watch with the strapped 249, spit off into the damp woods. "More than enough Carl Gustaf to go around for anyone else who wanted to try."

Brumm was like a Kurtz-in-training. He'd dare the suck to come at him just to see if it would blink. And then be happy when it did, because that meant something in Ranger Brain. I don't know. Maybe they just train 'em that way.

Or find them under rocks.

Chief Rapp, a Special Forces medic assigned to assist the unit in getting patched up and the detachment commander regarding Special Operations doctrine, went through the wounded who'd been pulled out of the pit. There was one with a serious slash to a forearm where the Ranger had managed to get his arm up to defend himself against a sword. Better than the way it could have gone. He took the cut there as opposed to getting hacked in the neck.

"The human body do love to defend itself no matter what else you try to make it do," chuckled the good-natured Rapp. "Ain't that the way Mike?"

Rapp called everyone by their first name or tag. Even the Command Sergeant Major. No one corrected him because he was a warrant, and chiefs held no allegiance to anyone but their own. And because he was also Special Forces, that made him an even higher order of the mystery operator voodoo.

But maybe that was just surface reasoning. Maybe the real reason no one ever corrected him was because he was six foot six, and built like a pro wrestler. If you're asking me to pin it down I'd say it was because he was nice and Rangers don't understand that strange and foreign emotion. I'd like to think that I do. I've found that Green Berets tended to be positive and upbeat while Rangers preferred a sort of enthusiastic fatalism that required tall odds and small hopes. So they either memory-holed his friendly behavior or evaded it with their version of HardMan/Asperger's.

Corporal Brocker was also injured. No slashes to the arm, but he had been knocked clean out. A big old crack ran right down the center of his combat helmet where one of the orcs had tried to split it with an axe.

"He is concussed, as they say," mused Chief Rapp in the pre-dawn darkness. He had the man led back to the rear for rest and observation.

As sunrise drew nearer, we started to get a better picture of all that had happened. Apparently Third's two-forty had run dry after the eight hundred rounds of belted ammo was used up at an almost cyclic rate of fire as they tried to weather the oncoming orc wave rushing directly across the river and straight at them. No barrel change either—there'd been no time before the orcs were all over them. It was that close. And then the orcs were hacking and stabbing and the assistant gunner was trying to connect another linked belt to the two-forty as the rest of the team switched over to secondaries to engage at the last second.

Looking back, the attack had happened faster than I remembered it. Faster than I thought possible. In several places all at once along our island. But no one got hit as hard as Third Squad's sector. Later I'd learn it didn't just get close... it got downright weird, at several points. Strange things had happened. And that made everyone, even the Rangers, a little nervous.

But no less resolved.

It was dawn by the time Chief Rapp finished up with the injured. By that time, I'd been ordered by Sergeant Kurtz into the pit to take watch with him while the rest of the team either got patched up by Chief Rapp or ran back to the C-17 for more ammo. Kurtz got a full round of antibiotics and his arm wrapped. The arrow had taken a chunk of flesh, but the muscle and bone were intact. If it hurt, Kurtz didn't bother to say.

I bet it hurt. It *looked* like it hurt.

Just before dawn, it was dark out there on the river. You could hardly see anything because the moon had gone down by then. Sergeant Kurtz just sat there in the quiet with his NVGs on, scanning the other side of the river for any sign of the enemy. Like he still owed them something. As though he wasn't just expecting them to come back; he, in fact, *wanted* them to come back. He had something for them.

I could feel it in the cold air between us.

The hostility that radiated from him felt dangerous, so I said nothing because he'd probably figure out a way to smoke me while we waited for the next attack. And that's saying something for me, because I'll usually try to make conversation with anyone. They call me Talker for more than one reason. But the Do Not Disturb sign was permanently hung out on the heavy weapons squad leader.

Kurtz was that way.

Fine. That was probably for the best. I'm sure everyone was pretty wired by the fight and not getting hacked to death and all by things that until now had only been in games and old novels written by Oxford linguistics scholars. Monsters. Orcs. Axes and swords.

But part of me wondered...

What would have happened if they'd gotten through? What would they have done to the prisoners? Cannibalism, I'm betting. They'd eat us. But it wouldn't be cannibalism because they're not human. They're orcs.

Does that make it any better?

These are the things I thought about in the dark waiting to get my throat cut by some misty night goblin or any of the other ridiculous imaginings PFC Kennedy had been freaking everyone out with. What might be here. Where we may have possibly ended up.

None of it made sense. And yet there we were. Watching our sectors and waiting for the next attack.

Ten minutes before dawn Kurtz looked over at me as though assessing my gear and finding every piece of it, and me as a whole, woefully lacking for a warrior who finds himself among the Army's premier fighting force, the Rangers. He took my MK18 and stripped off some of the equipment I'd been issued as part of the SOPMOD upgrade package we'd been handed back at the Fifty-One armory. In the end, after going through the rest of the gear I'd been issued, he took off the Specter telescopic sight I'd been rather proud of getting attached and zeroed all by myself.

"Just use it this way," he said not-so-angrily-as-he-looked and shoved it back into my hands.

Now I would use the holographic reflex sight. Like a pro Ranger, even!

We sat there in the dark for a little longer, and even though it had been a horrendous battle in the middle of the night and the bodies of the orcs were still floating slowly down the river or hung up on rocks or branches, or along the shore, the first birds of morning began to test their songs. Tentatively. Cautiously. Just a few notes. As if to say… *We're still here. You guys finished yet?*

Vonnegut's *poo-tee-weet* sprang to mind.

The sun was coming up in the east, but for now, along the river, it was all quiet and you could see a soft, forgiving, kind of light in the sky to the west. And the dark shadows along the near-silent river we were watching.

Maybe it was beautiful because we were still alive.

That's me practicing at being a writer with this journal and Mont Blanc pen my mom gave me when I graduated Basic. Every so often I still try to figure out whether that was a nice gift, or a sarcastic one. A comment at me having turned my back on what I'd worked so hard to attain for something as mundane as serving one's country. That had been her opinion.

Knowing her, it was sarcastic.

Sergeant Kurtz got a comm telling me to report back to the TOC. He told me to "shove off" with little fanfare even though we'd killed a bunch of bad guys together. Well, technically *he* killed them all. I was just there. Helping. By then Brumm and Tanner were back with more cans of ammo for the two-forty.

Later, when I got back to the C-17 that served as our tactical operations command post, barely clearing the river and setting down in a long field the pilot was some how able to get it down onto, the morning light among the thin, skeletal trees on the island was gray and wan. It was silent out in the woods and the field. All I could hear was the sound of my own boots snapping dry deadfall and tramping through the dewy grass.

I boarded the C-17 and found a full-blown meeting in progress with all the high muckety-mucks of detachment command and power in attendance. So, being a nobody, I sat in one of the seats and listened in. If they wanted to know how to say *screwed* in one of the languages I spoke, then maybe I could chime in and be helpful.

Command Sergeant Major Stone was busy briefing the captain of our detachment. The sergeant major was riding with us when we left Fifty-One. Our colonel and three other detachments were on other flights, parts of the larger overall joint task force. The plan had been for us to all link up wherever it was we were going when we got there. Instead we ended up here, wherever here was.

Information about the *where we were supposed to have gone* part had been woefully lacking in the week-long run-up to this operation. And since I'm a PFC linguist, no one is really obliged to tell me much of anything anyway. But still, I'm always curious. I knew it was something out of the ordinary when I'd signed on for two to five years in the future back at Fifty-One. But I was thinking Iran at the time. Not freaking Gondor.

The captain here on the ground was in what would normally be considered a Major slot for Ranger company command, and the command sergeant major with all his years of experience killing people overseas in exotic places was effectively acting as staff for the captain. Supply. Planning. Intel. Having the sergeant major was probably our luckiest break. Everything we didn't know, he did. And he'd probably forgotten a lot we'd never know. That kind of guy. Y'know?

"… we won't get hit, sir," the sergeant major was saying. He had a deep voice and hadn't quite managed to get rid of a Texas drawl. "At least not for the rest of the day. That's my guess, sir. These… forces we're facing… they've proved they're night-fighters of some kind. I estimate we'll have the day to prep, but they'll be back after dark. Until then I suggest… in lieu of not being here altogether… we fortify, deploy the hi-ex, and get some Reaper teams together to respond asymmetrically. Something more creative than what those things saw last night. Rangers defend by offending, sir.

"This was a probe. Clear and simple. They'll be back tonight like they mean it. You're the ranking ground force commander, Captain, and you have my recommendation. It's your call. I'm just here to make sure they shave and don't roll their sleeves up too high, sir."

Then the command sergeant major sat down and picked up a paper cup full of coffee to indicate he was done with everyone. He had a Kindle on his knee, but he wasn't reading it. His stare was so downrange you couldn't tell if he was here or somewhere in Iraq twenty years ago killing everyone.

The platoon leaders were there too. The captain was there. The first sergeant was there. And so were the Baroness and the Deep State guy. And the Forge technician. I hadn't caught his name yet. The pilot of the C-17 was around. But his first officer, a really cute LT with a blond ponytail, wasn't. Which was too bad. I'd gotten a smile out of her a day ago and I was looking to improve my position with some witty turns of phrase in Italian.

I locked eyes with the pilot instead. If anyone felt more useless than me, it was probably him. Getting us on the ground alive was the extent of what he could meaningfully contribute to our situation. We'd smashed a landing gear coming in, and the fact that the plane wasn't spread all over the river rocks and burning in pieces in the tree line was to his credit. There was no getting off this small river island in the C-17. This was home for now. The Forge weighed about six thousand pounds, so until we figured out a way to move it without the plane, we were stuck here.

The captain is someone I have no idea about. He's always busy and he looks like his stomach is upset all the time. His hair has gone prematurely gray, but he's tabbed and has a Ranger combat scroll on his right shoulder, and that makes him somebody around here.

The scroll, according to Sergeant Thor, is a way of life and a culture of success, every day, at all things—it never ends. Every day is a selection in the regiment. The easiest day in the regiment, as explained to me, is the day you graduate RASP; after that it gets real hard to keep up. If you don't produce results, you are fired. For junior enlisted, going to Ranger School and getting your tab is the standard—if you fail, you're out. Sergeant Thor told me his young studs were great kids, but until they were tabbed, they were just "renting space." You cannot be a "landowner" until you get your tab. After that you can take your first junior leadership spot as a gun team leader, and then, again according to Thor, "They start to figure out what this stuff is really all about."

Everyone who's been through the various Ranger orientation programs, throughout the ages, is a Ranger. But if you earned the Ranger tab then you're considered Ranger-qualified. Tabbed. And like I said, that's something.

But the captain was more than something. He was an officer, had a combat scroll, and was in command of a company-sized element, in a slot usually reserved for majors. And if that's not enough, let me just add this. Company commanders can only be officers who have already had successful tours as platoon leaders in the regiment—a very small pool. If fifty guys are successful platoon leaders in the Ranger regiment (and that in itself is like .0001 percent of the infantry platoon leaders in the Army) then less than ten of those will be asked to come back and be a company commander. There are less Ranger company commanders than there are NFL quarterbacks.

In short, to be a company commander means someone is literally as good as the Army can produce.

The captain thanked the command sergeant major for his assessment and was about to issue orders when the Deep State guy in his L.L.Bean adventure-golfer-I'm-not-CIA-no-really gear stood up to speak.

"Hey, Captain Harwood," began Deep State.

"Go ahead, Volman," Harwood said.

"I'd like to jump in here right now and just… y'know… contribute a few things before we get started. Just some… contributions. I hope I can improve the overall atmosphere and synergy we need to achieve in this next phase of the… ah, well… the operation here on the ground and all. I think we've gotten off to a bad start with a… ahem… the locals. One of yours, a PFC Kennedy I believe, one of your Rangers, told me he thinks these are… orcs."

"PFC Kennedy," interrupted the command sergeant major, "is a wretched child who I will turn into a first-class killing machine unless it destroys him in the process." Statement of fact. More like an ancient truth carved in granite.

In the short time I had been part of the detachment, I knew as gospel that whatever came out of the command sergeant major's mouth was like some unbreakable code written in granite law that was the basis of all our existences. Even the Deep State guy, Volman, seemed to flinch as the senior-most NCO in the detachment interrupted him and began to fire words like the slow sure boom of distant artillery headed your way. Falling on your head directly. Meteors falling from the heavens. Giant space rocks that could crush you flat.

Stone was a good last name for the command sergeant major because it *was* him. A hard ass thing that was there before you showed up with all your agendas and ideas. And would be there long after he kicked the dirt over your shallow grave on the other side of the firefight you just got yourself killed in. The one your fancy ideas and agendas got torched in by the cold reality of expended brass, timing, preparation, and just plain old bad luck.

The command sergeant major made you feel temporary. *Unless*. Unless you adhered and knew wisdom. And then... maybe. Just maybe. You might see the sun rise tomorrow.

Maybe.

The Deep Statie barely recovered from the command sergeant major's sudden destabilizing verbal attack. Allowing emotions to cross his presidential appointee face that had been beaten out of the rest of us during Basic. Drill Sergeant Ward would have smoked this guy like a cheap cigar until Ward got tired. Just for nothing more than letting his face react the way it did to what the command sergeant major had said.

And as Drill Sergeant Ward was fond of telling us, "I don't tire easily."

Nonetheless, Volman persisted, despite seeming completely unaware of the situation and the kind of people he was dealing with. He continued, a sick smile, but a smile nonetheless, pasted on his sallow civilian face. Like he was gonna turn all this around and close the deal on a brand-new BMW. He just needed you to sign on the dotted line. Will you be financing at twenty-four percent interest?

"Be that as it may," continued snake oil salesman of the month Deep State Volman. "They... whatever they are... let's call them orcs. They're the locals and we're here as guests. In their territory. Don't you think we should try to... you know... talk to them first, Captain Harwood?" He was speaking to the captain directly now. Not playing to the crowd as had been his first instinct until the sergeant major tactfully rained down verbal fire on his rhetorical position and caused him to doubt the footing of his not-so-firm foundation.

The captain just stared at the Deep State man like some town sheriff might regard a local village idiot who's just gotten himself up to some new drunken indiscretion involving pants down around ankles. Raving that two plus two was steak and that he, the village idiot, was indeed the Grand Czar Nicholas the Second's long lost great-great-grandson while the deputies got ready to cuff another lunatic for the drive out to the mental asylum.

Volman opted to nod to himself in a long-suffering saintly fashion when he realized his grand play to manipulate the low IQ losers he thought we all were didn't go over like he'd planned. Rangers are screened for motivation and aggressiveness. They also, like all Special Forces, test high on the military's intelligence test, the ASVAB. They just prefer to act stupid because they think it's tougher. And tough is a kind of cool regardless of what some beta-male website says about letting other men sleep with your girlfriend.

Then, and for me this was the fun part, the high point of the whole trip, Volman decided to try, active word *try*, to pull rank. On a Ranger captain.

*Oof.*

"Listen, Captain," said Volman anew. "I don't want to go over your head. But the calls you're making here, right now, in this situation. Armed soldiers out there on the line... out there playing with explosives and indiscriminately killing anyone who comes near them. Locals. Most likely a minority or even a victim group of some kind. We don't know. And here your guys are, acting like they're making up the rules of engagement as they go. And forcing the... the uh... the kid who runs the Forge to start making more *bullets*. That's your first call on the ground, Captain Harwood? Correct me if I'm wrong. But we don't know... orcs or whatever those things are... we don't know if they started out as enemies or if you just turned them into enemies when they came out to communicate with us. And now we'll probably never know thanks to you and your Rangers.

"But maybe... maybe... maybe we still have a chance to do like I said and try some parley. Encounter them on their level. Get to know the leaders. See what they need. See what we can give them to be our friends and allies. No different than how Lewis and Clark won the favor of the Native Americans. This kind of thing worked in Afghanistan and Iraq, and it can work here. We are guests in their country, wherever this country is. And to be brutally honest... I'm a direct appointee from your commander-in-chief. So you should just consider that, Captain. In other words... what I say..."

I think he was about to say... *goes.*

But the captain had had enough at that point.

He held up his hand and looked like he was fighting down sudden indigestion. The hand held up was knife-edged, and you had the feeling as you watched it come up and stay there that it could probably slam a carotid artery and just kill you right there on the spot. And that it wouldn't be the knife hand's first rodeo in carotid artery slamming.

"I'm going to stop you right there, Mister Volman," said the captain, using concise clipped speech. The rage was controlled. "This is a military operation. No Tomorrow Rules in effect. So until a lawful government is established... *I* am the government. I am your commander-in-chief. The one you're referring to... that commander-in-chief, Mr. Volman, sir... he died about ten thousand years ago if our pilot is correct in his celestial navigation calculations regarding our current position and how many years we've gone forward."

Deep State's face drained of all color.

The captain put his knife hand down and came around the desk he'd set up near the C-17's rear cargo deck door.

"So, here's the situation..."

# CHAPTER THREE

I probably need to stop right there and tell you how exactly we got here, wherever here is. Surrounded by orcs. Trust me, an explanation of what Captain Knife Hand had to say next will sound a lot more rational and sane if I give you that much. Otherwise it would all just sound crazy.

And believe it or not, things still weren't as crazy as they were gonna get. Crazy was gonna be an easy and good day in comparison to what was coming for us.

So there I am before I join the army. I just wrapped my sixth master's degree in language, this time in Farsi. It took me seven degrees to finally realize that I hate academia and... I've got this crazy desire to be a soldier. I want to have an adventure. A real adventure. Not just travel to another country, take a few selfies, eat the local food, and record it all on Instagram.

I want to do something with my life before the day comes when I can't do anything but wish I'd done something. So I start talking to the recruiters, and yeah, when they find out I speak a lot of languages they're excited and offer me all kinds of fun things that may or may not be true. Bonuses. Choice of station... "How'd you like to go to Hawaii?" None of which really matter to me. I don't think the recruiters really understood what they had in me. What I can really do with languages. They just get me into

Basic Training and then I'm off to the Defense Language Institute at Monterey.

It wasn't until Monterey that someone figured me out. I showed up at the Chinese School, an eighteen-month course, and tested out two days later. To be honest, it wasn't fair. I already knew Chinese. Then we played a fun game where I ran through most of the other languages they offered and tested right through those, too.

It became kind of a game-show atmosphere for a couple of weeks after that. A general even showed up to watch. I should have known something was up then. The guy was from SOCOM and covered in badges and tabs and he looked like Captain Knife Hand's older, angrier brother.

I'd already been to Jump School after Basic. And after the teachers at DLI were told in no uncertain terms they could not have me, I was sent off to learn how to Ranger on the introductory level at an abbreviated three-week RASP course designed especially for me and a few other intel monkeys who were needed late in the game. Then a two-week intel school that was completely off-book. It was basically me and a guy who told me I could call him John but that that wasn't his real name. I kid you not. It was in an airport Best Western out in Las Vegas. And not the good part of town. Then he drove me to Area 51 and dropped me off at the Ranger detachment's temporary headquarters along the airfield.

And though I'd been in an isolation bubble of training for the previous six months, I knew a little bit about what was going on out in the world. Things were coming apart at the seams, and you could tell it was for real this time because the news networks weren't saying a lot. It was their guy in the White House and they didn't want him to look bad.

But thanks to Twitter and the internet you can source your own news if you don't mind digging around and you follow the right people.

Strange stuff was happening outside my little military bubble. Everywhere, but mainly out in the third world along the edges. If you weren't curious, you wouldn't have connected the dots at all. But I'm good at pattern recognition and I was curious. Something wasn't quite adding up for me as I began to look at the whole.

Machines were starting to come apart in China. And not from the usual shoddy manufacturing from the state-run factories. Cars. Airplanes. Brand-new airplanes, too, just crashing or disappearing out to sea with all lives lost. The Indians and the Pakis had gone to war but managed not to use nukes on each other. In fact, there was an early video of the two forces attacking one another with clubs and swords and one guy even using a bow and arrows. All of it during a border flare-up in Kashmir. There were lots of unexplained murders everywhere. And then there were the Mothman, Bigfoot, and aliens-type sightings and conspiracies. Oh, and blood-sucker cults. Stuff that sounded crazy and honestly too weird to be true. The kind of stuff that has been in tabloids, late night radio, and whispered over campfires for years. And sure, there were videos, but there's also Deep Fake and people with too much time on their hands who get a thrill out of hoaxing other people. So what was true? And what wasn't? Everything had to be taken with a grain of salt. Or just disbelief. Or... not wanting the pandemic to be what it was clearly shaping up to be. Something worse.

There was a collective creepy factor happening, though. People were starting to use the word *monsters* to describe what other humans were driven to do.

In the US for the most part, things were still pretty cool. But not what you'd call normal. There was a general low-grade anxiety going around. Violent crimes were way up, and there were reports of those small towns in the northwest just going ghost. The people disappearing and someone showing up after two weeks to find a modern-day Roanoke Colony. If you don't know what that means, look it up. It's a slice of Americana that's been memory-holed. But then again, anyone reading this probably has no idea how to look anything up anymore. That level of civilization is no longer available at this time. Please try again.

Markets were tanking and rich people were suddenly jetting off to private islands and pulling up the runway behind them. Movie productions slowed to a crawl. In other words, people were getting out of Dodge. Celebrities didn't have time to make movies. They were aboard those planes heading toward those islands no one who wasn't someone could get to.

It was clear the powers that be knew something was headed straight toward them. Toward all of us. A civilization-killer. They just didn't know what it was. And they didn't care about the rest of us if they did.

So there I was, along with the rest of the Ranger battalion and all the other elements that made up the JTF, Joint Task Force, along with several other special operations groups consisting of almost every branch you could think of. We were all gathered in one of those massive super-secret hangars out in the desert at Area 51. Yeah, *that* Area 51.

It was getting so surreal it just started to seem real.

Then we got the truth. With both barrels. Whether we liked it or not.

There was a plague sweeping the world. There was no way to stop it. So we were going forward in time.

Yup.

Forward in time with Forges and science teams to re-establish the government.

"How long?" someone asked.

"Indeterminate. We're aiming for two to three years."

"How?" someone else asked.

"It's called a quantum singularity tachyon gate. QST for short. We're going through that into the near future."

"Does it work?"

"It works… ish," said the briefing lady in charge. The Baroness was up there next to her. She was part of that team. "We know it goes somewhere and we're able to get a safety signal before the singularity window collapses on the other side. There's no way to come back after that." She didn't try to soft-pedal it. It was a one-way trip. "But if you stay here, you'll likely become a victim of the plague."

"What exactly is this plague, anyway?"

"It's a nano-plague. It destroys machinery and technology. It can also alter DNA, or even kill."

"What do you mean by… alter DNA?"

*Monsters.*

"Classified."

"What about our families? What if we don't want to go?"

"Then you don't go. You stay here and face the music. But if you want to save this country and everything it stands for, then we need you to go forward and re-establish the government and the rule of law. Because that's precisely what you'll have to do. We estimate that in six months, the world will be a lawless ruin. Being able to re-establish there, on the other side of the plague, may be the only chance your family and loved ones will have, if they've survived that long. The same goes for this country and the world. This is the only chance they'll have for a better tomorrow. The only chance."

*C'mon, lady. Don't make it easy on anyone.*

"You are capable of performing this mission. But it's your choice. Stay and face the consequences. Go and try to save what's left. Either way the plague is coming, and there's nothing that can be done to stop it or we would have already done so."

"Will the plague be over in two years?"

"Our top people say yes."

Everyone in the hangar who was wearing a uniform was the type who really believed in that sort of stuff. The self-sacrifice and service to your country stuff. And they didn't only believe… they lived it. I could tell. Normal people would have started crying, getting angry, blaming everyone, denying that all this was really happening to them. I believed it too, though the lay-your-life-down-for-your-country element had never been required of me so far. At least, I was pretty sure I believed in it, and now I knew why they wanted a linguist who knew a lot of languages to go with them. Space was limited going through the QST. They wouldn't want to waste it on a bunch of linguists when they could just bring one who knew a lot of languages along for the ride. Plus, a lot of spec ops types have excellent language training already. I was most likely a redundant catch-all.

And I was surrounded by people of the been there, done that type. The saved countless lives, if not the world, type. This was just Tuesday for them. Granted… it was a pretty big Tuesday. But they were the kind of people who go where normal, safety-loving, non-risk-taking people don't want to go. The kind that gets dropped off by little black helicopters on garbage-strewn streets outnumbered but determined to try to pull some downed pilot back to safety. Heading toward the gunfire, when everyone else is running away.

I'm sure they all thought that way.

But later, one of the high-speed low-drag operator types explained it to me a little bit differently. He said it was the "Addiction of the Edge." A kind of lure. Once you got to that level of operator operating, you were always looking for a new edge to jump off of. Or just *any* edge, because you were kind of addicted to it now. To the jumping.

It sounded cool. Except it was a problem. Because what happened when you weren't required to save the world anymore and you still found yourself opening the hotel balcony door late in the night and standing on the railing? Looking at the drop and daring yourself to just jump, not because you wanted to kill yourself, but because that too was a kind of edge regardless of whether you had a parachute or not.

You'd been trained to jump off edges. For your country.

So you're always looking…

There are all kinds of edges in civilian life. Addictions. Crime. Law and order. Revenge. Relationships you shouldn't be in and places you have no business being at. Edges abound if you're always looking.

Places to jump from.

He told me he had to be careful around cliffs. Because there was this haunting siren call to just go for it. A voice inside telling him to jump. To take that first and last step into the void to see... to see if there's an other side. Something waiting that no one's found yet. I guess jumping out of enough planes makes you think this way after a while.

Door kickers call it the fatal funnel. You might live, you might not. The feeling of making it to the other side is something no pharmacy can match.

And this was the biggest edge of all. The sharpest edge, the sheerest of drops, the potentially fatalist of funnels. The super-secret Area 51 hangar briefing couldn't undersell that point enough to the junkies standing all around me. The edge of all edges. Go forward in time and save a ruined Earth. I don't think anyone in the room hesitated for a second in that deep-down-inside super-raving lunatic self we all are that no one else knows about. That place where you're completely honest with yourself about all the completely nutty stuff you want to do. Most of the highly trained and highly motivated people in the briefing were just trying to figure out how they were gonna tell their wives they were going.

That it was just another Tuesday, babe.

Also, there was PFC Tanner and probably a whole bunch more like him. He said that neither of the two strippers he'd married and had been divorced by in the last year would miss him much if he went. And there was a DUI pending at Joint Base Lewis-McChord that the command sergeant major was "pretty hacked off about." So... why not?

We were all going. No one asked me if I wanted to go or not. Maybe that's how clever they were about telling all of us there in the hangar. There was no one you could report to in the back of the room and say, *Hey, this isn't for me. I just signed up for some college money and to maybe see the world. Good luck with the future and all. Hope it works out. I'll just take off and let you guys get to saving future Earth without me holding you back. Thanks for the offer.*

Again, this was not that kind of people.

Not even the air crews. They were highly trained too and had learned a lot of fun stuff. The cute co-pilot assured me of that.

There were fifty teams of this kind of people. Fifty C-17s going forward in time to restart the government. How? I'll tell you about all that in a moment. It's fairly underwhelming until you understand that you've violated mass, energy, and time. Somehow.

For the next week, I drew gear, got shots, trained with the Rangers, and got assigned to the command sergeant major who asked me, "What is it, exactly, that you do, PFC?" He had my thin little records jacket in front of him. I told him I was just a linguist. He nodded. Then said in his gravelly, quiet drawl while picking up his Kindle to go back to his reading, "Try not to get in anyone's way, son."

He turned me over to Sergeant Kurtz for a day, who smoked me and the rest of his team by running the airfield three times just to show everyone that he hated everyone equally. And the day after that I went to the snipers to get to know them, and they were pretty chill about things. They didn't think running fast made you a better shot. Sergeant Thor told me about surfing in Patagonia. I think the command sergeant major was sending me around to the rest of the sections to get familiarized with them when it came time to work with them two years in the future, doing whatever it was we were supposed to be doing when we arrived there tomorrow night.

And what was it we were supposed to be doing? We didn't know. But if you had *fighting an orc horde to the death* on the Doomsday Bingo Board… well then, you turned out to be the grand prize winner.

There would be no grand prize winner. Not even that geek PFC Kennedy had predicted that one.

The next night all fifty C-17s were on the tarmac and we were loading in, ready to go. To me, this was what an invasion looked like. D-Day or something. And way down at the end of the longest runway was what, for all intents and purposes, was a stargate. Like the one in that movie, Stargate. Except this one was merely some arrays that interconnected and then there was nothing in between them. And I mean nothing. No night sky. Just null space. It actually hurt your brain to try and look at it directly. So you didn't. Eventually we were hustled inside and then we couldn't. Apparently, we were going to take off and fly right into it. And then arrive two years from now less than a second later.

Tanner was next to me inside the C-17. We were in Tier 4 posture with our overloaded rucks between our knees. That meant every Ranger was wearing their tactical carrying system, ESAPI armor plates, soft armor inserts, ballistic combat shirt, shoulder pads, and combat helmet, with weapons and magazines loaded with all the ammunition we could ever wish for. And then some. We were going forward in time, and we were going to take as much as we could. There was not an ounce of room left in the aircraft. Of course, the Forge took up a lot of it.

We'd gotten a briefing on the Forge and what it could do. Mostly, it could make a lot of things on the other side. Tanner called it a "perpetual taco machine." Still, we took what we could. Captain Knife Hand decided to take a lot of ammunition for every weapon system we had. He felt killing things might be immediately important once we got to the future, and he didn't want to come up short in that department. The killing everything department.

I felt good about his choice.

I felt even better about it later. We all did.

We were taxiing toward takeoff, warm and comfortable and imprisoned within our gear, when Tanner said to me, "I saw a test of the QST last night. They sent the first bird through with a SEAL team. It just faded into nothing as soon as it went through."

One of the other Rangers asked how come the SEALs got to go first.

"Their publicity agent probably arranged it for the film deal with a tie-in motivational speaking book tour," Tanner quipped.

Everyone laughed. Because it was true.

Going through the gate after the takeoff roll was… nothing. Like literally. We were maybe only just wheels off the ground in the middle of night when there was a sudden strobe light flash that seemed to go right through your whole body down to your very cells, and then it was harsh daylight coming in from the windows, where there were windows. Of course, none of us could get up and look out those windows. But we knew. We knew that whatever we had just done… we had thoroughly done it.

We flew for about six hours and then they told us we were making a soft field landing and that it was going to be tricky.

The engines constantly changing in pitch and urgency was the most unsettling part about almost getting killed trying to land. Then we were down and it was rough. My guess is we landed on an exposed part of the riverbed before rolling onto the island and coming to a stop in a field lined by trees. There was one massive jolt when, apparently, we smashed the landing gear probably for forever. But we'd made it. We were here.

Wherever here was.

# CHAPTER FOUR

"SO, here's the situation…" Captain Knife Hand was saying before I needed to go back and explain what we're doing here at what was officially called Forward Operating Base Hawthorn. Ranger Alamo. No one else was calling it that, but it was beginning to feel that way if you had a spare moment to dwell on current events. We stood on the cargo deck of the C-17 serving as the detachment command post. "This operation was always to be a joint services JSOC bridgehead. Those orders are still in effect even though we have yet to contact other elements in the task force. Our mission still stands. We came forward in time to establish a secure position from which to re-establish the government. Currently…"

The captain aimed this next bit right at the Deep State guy. Center mass of course, because right between the eyes is for optimists and show-offs. Not that he couldn't have.

"… our position is not secure," continued Knife Hand. No one was calling him this except me in my head. But I bet they were thinking it. "Once it is, and once we link up with other elements and command, those with a higher pay grade than mine, then they can determine just what will be done next and how we'll respond to the current imperative threats. Until then… this is a military operation, and this is what we're facing. Our last drone recon as of two hours ago is tracking massed irregular infantry forces, and I use those terms very loosely because what we're seeing is like nothing we've dealt with before.

"All enemy elements are currently heading straight for our position from several points on the compass. It would be naive in the extreme to think they are not going to hit us in the next twelve hours, and hit us hard with everything they've got. The enemy force is numbered at upwards of five thousand. We are two hundred rangers and special personnel plus a highly trained flight crew and three civilians.

"I don't have to tell you, but I will because often government and science specialty civilians don't completely understand military capabilities, but these are not good odds regardless of what you think special operations troops can achieve. This is not a movie, and my men, and this flight crew, are not action stars with unlimited ammunition to do all kinds of ridiculous things with.

"Furthermore, Rangers are raiders. We are not primarily defensive troops. We execute raids. We hit hard, and we disappear. Yet due to the nature of this mission and the high-value asset we are charged with protecting— the Forge—we have been forced into a defensive role. And we will execute that role to the best of our abilities. Make no mistake about that. Rangers were given a mission, and it will be done or we will die doing it. That's the best I can offer you, and that's our objective until the situation changes."

He turned on a small projector and displayed the latest drone recon of the island against a screen that had been erected along one side of the aircraft's interior.

"For the next eight hours we will continue to improve the forward fighting positions along the island's edge. We will concentrate on cover to protect from enemy arrow fire. Platoon leaders, I need you to salvage what the sergeant major and the air crew decide is expendable and use that to better cover your troops in their positions."

He pointed to the waterways that had so recently been visited by the marauders seeking to ford the river. "We are going to place punji sticks along these water approaches across the shallow points in the river and along the sand bars on the east and west sides. Claymores will be used on the western sand bars. They hit us from the east this morning, chances are a significant number of elements will come from the opposite direction after dark.

"Sniper and mortar teams will continue to improve the hill on the northern edge of the island. That will be our last line of defense if we need to evacuate our positions around the aircraft. Once the main attack commences, two squads will go Reaper under the direction of the command sergeant major. One will be tasked with eliminating an identified high-value target. The other will attempt to destabilize the main body of the attack by hitting the enemy rear and conducting hit-and-run operations along the flanks. My intent is… we are going to fight for our lives tonight. Priorities are to protect the CP here at the aircraft and, failing that, to fall back, on my order or that of the sergeant major's, to the hill and retake the island at dawn."

The captain left the projection going and stepped into the light to stand before it, the images making ghosts on his features. He peered at the men he was leading, dark shadows sitting outside the brilliant projector light.

I couldn't tell if he was satisfied or not. The captain wasn't easy to read. He gave his final words on the pending battle.

"We're not doing kill chains. We're not working 'near certainty.' If we determine that anyone approaching our defensive perimeter is our enemy, we are going to kill them and make the people they knew afraid we'll come for them next."

# CHAPTER FIVE

THE briefing cleared and the sergeant major made straight for me. I should have known better than to stand around looking like I had nothing to do.

"Come with me, son," he muttered, not breaking his long-legged, mile-eating stride for a second.

We left the C-17 and made for the hill at the north end of the island. He moved through deadfall and wet grass near silently. Me, not so much. Once we were out of earshot, he let me know what we were about.

"Talker, you're goin' Reapin' tonight, son. Sergeant Odinson will be taking a squad out beyond the perimeter after dark. They're going after a high-value target. I'm sending you along because you're my only intelligence asset, and when they hit that target, I need you to collect anything you find and bring it right back to me. Roger?"

"Roger," I managed.

Eight hours later, me and the six other rangers that formed the sergeant major's Reaper Team would slip into the dark waters of the river and cross to the eastern shore. It would be dusky and quiet and the woods along the water would be a black tangle that felt like swimming in a nest of snakes.

Sergeant Thor the sniper, or Sergeant Odinson as he was officially known, led our team of personnel pulls from various squads. Each squad had given up someone for our little Reaper Team. The only person I knew among them was Brumm. The other four were Sergeant Kang, Specialist Lucke, and Privates Brasher and Gomez.

But I'm going to rewind three hours before that, when we did the op order and briefing around a sand table Sergeant Thor had put together from various MRE wrappers and eating utensils. The afternoon sun was just beginning to sink down toward the high trees, and strange and forlorn birds called out through the forest, agitated at something. We could hear faraway drums rolling out in the distance, and there was that strange tribal horn sounding intermittently.

*Urooo Urooo. UrUrooooooooooo.*

Our enemy was preparing for war.

Sergeant Thor had helped me get ready, going through my gear and making sure I was down with basic patrolling, verifying my gear was quiet and that I could move in it without making too much noise. We ran a refresher course on patrolling techniques and hand signals. And now, with the full team formed up on top of the hill where the snipers had set up their observation points and hides, Thor ran through how we'd approach the target and the actions on the objective once we got there. Rally points and command and signal.

And then he told us about the target.

Remember when I said things were getting crazier? Here's where they really began to finger-fiddle their lips like the lunatic in the padded cell next to yours...

I probably need go rewind a little bit more. I should explain that the night before, I had been sent out to the Third Squad pit because in the minutes leading up to the attack, the command post had lost contact with the heavy weapons section along the line at that specific point. The sergeant major ordered me to go out there, find Sergeant Kurtz, and tell them they had bad comm. Then I showed up and of course everything went pear-shaped as the orcs tried to cross the river and cut everyone's throats.

So how the hell did we lose comms in the first place? Good question. It seemed that our HVT was somehow responsible for jamming our comms in those moments just before the attack. Or so everyone believed enough to send a Reaper team out to nab them.

Because apparently, when the enemy probe orc-swarm was hitting the Bravo pit along the eastern edge of our defensive line, one of our drones—not a hunter-killer but really just a tactical high-speed model airplane the air crew was handling—picked up something interesting out there in the dark. The air crew and the sergeant major had been shown the video capture. What they saw was strange enough that the decision was made to show it to PFC Kennedy, the only one who seemed to know what was going on, or at least had an idea of what to call things. .

And then we saw it too, on Sergeant Thor's smartphone. It was taken from the drone's thermal feed and showed the main enemy force attacking across the river as the drone redirected and circled out over the forest beyond the bank where the enemy was attacking from. It even picked up the giant whose carcass was by now no doubt starting to stink up the eastern bank.

The drone circled out over the forest, and as it did it picked up a single figure out in a lonely clearing well away from the main assault. The figure was waving his hands and almost seemed to be throwing something at the island.

Something invisible. The way a football crazed kid tosses touchdown passes with an imaginary football in the living room. For a moment the thermal feed scrambled as these invisible balls left the lone figure's hands and pitched off toward the island where our defenses were.

The figure danced around in circles, holding up his arms in an almost ceremonial fashion, and then began to gesticulate even more wildly as he summoned more... who knew what... that when thrown, disturbed the drone's thermal feed at points. Each time the HVT waved his hands, and they were clearly the hands of a human, not orcish and misshapen in some monster-like way, each time he scrambled the feed for just a few frames. So slight that if you weren't paying close attention you wouldn't even notice it happening.

According to Thor, this coincided with the jamming bursts along the line at Alpha and Bravo pits.

"Now watch this," he said as we all gathered closer around his phone atop Sniper Hill. By now it all had the distinct feel of listening to frightening stories by a campfire. What in the world was out there?

The video started over, this time showing the night-vision feed. The gray-green of the forest was pretty clear and the resolution on the images was a cut above anything I'd seen in night-vision mode previously. Leaves and tree trunks had separate textures. The ground could be identified as either dirt or grass. When the drone circled over the orc horde crossing the water you could even see the ripples on the surface, and the beast's gear visibly stood out. Daggers and axes. The twisted masks of their snarling faces looked even more frightening in night-vision hues than they had up close. Seeing it now from this angle I was surprised at how many of them there had been out there and coming for us last night. The bright tracer rounds from Corporal Brocker's two-forty streaked across the water, slamming into recoiling monsters or skipping off to the far side of the river to get lost in the trees there. The drone's night-vision feed again caught the giant hunkering in the darkness with another force. Ready to move forward and get killed all over again.

And then the drone was over more trees. Trees shifting gently in the gray-green and black of the image. Drifting in the night's cold breath. Like I said, the resolution was epically good. Then the clearing in the woods came into view. Where the lone figure waving like a madman and playing a game of invisible catch with no one else… should have been.

Except he wasn't.

I swear on everything. He wasn't there.

Thor stopped the feed. "Pretty cool, huh?"

"He's… invisible?" I asked.

Thor shrugged. "Whatever he is, you can't see him without thermal. Anyway, the captain and the sergeant major along with the air crew think this target is the indig equivalent of a jamming device. That's why we lost comm right before the attack. So Sergeant Major wants us to go out there and hit this guy tonight when the attack begins. Rest up. We leave just before dark."

In the quiet afternoon silence that followed, Private Brasher forlornly said to no one, "PFC Kennedy says it's a wizard. Probably casting spells."

"What? Like Harry Potter?" asked Kang.

"That's what I asked. He said worse than that." We got two hours of sleep and time to eat an MRE. Sergeant Thor decided to hold a pagan ceremony before moving out. He wanted to know if I or anyone else wanted to participate. I opted out, and I suspect the privates only participated because he was their sergeant. Over a small fire—mortars and snipers got to have a fire—he made cakes out of some of his MREs, mainly the chocolate and peanut butter mixed with creamer, and then baked them on a piece of dry smoking dead wood he'd found. While they ate the "cakes"—they were essentially cookies—Thor held both of his tomahawks up to the darkening sky and inhaled the smoke of the tiny fire like he was performing some ancient cleansing ritual. Afterward he came over to his ruck and began to assemble the rifle he'd need for tonight.

I watched as he attached a CNVD-T thermal optic to his MK11 and checked the suppressor.

"Thermal sights are good up to three hundred meters, but I'm thinkin' I gotta use this thing up close," he said, talking to himself happily as he played with his gear. He was tabbed, but unlike every other Ranger he seemed to enjoy himself no matter what he was doing.

"You think that's crazy, don'tcha, Talker," he said after a moment, nodding toward the smoking board over the firepit and the couple of cookies still waiting there.

"I officially have no opinions about anyone's religion, Sar'nt," I replied.

Normally I couldn't pass up a cookie, but I had a little case of the nerves. We were heading out beyond the wire, the defensive perimeter. Where Rangers lived, right there in the heart of the enemy. As a linguist I was best suited for staying here on this side of the line and shouting through a megaphone that they, the enemy, might want to rethink their position before some Rangers went over there, broke their stuff, and killed them. But now I was going out there with the Rangers to do exactly that. There was an impending realism to all this, along with a question I'd been concerned with since the day I'd walked into the recruiter's office.

Could I hang?

*Embrace it*, I reminded myself, and I tried to push nerves away that wouldn't easily go. It was turning into a not-so-fun game you couldn't win.

"I officially have no opinions about anyone's religion, Sar'nt." That's what I said and how I said it. I'd started saying *Sergeant* like the Rangers said it sometime about the middle of RASP. But only to E-7s and below. I had no idea why. Sometimes I don't think I understand things or know as much as the tests indicate I should. Sometimes I think I just act like I know things. Even things I actually know.

Leaving the defenses that night had me questioning everything.

Sergeant Thor looked around. When he was satisfied no one was listening to us, he leaned in close.

"Back there... y'know, before Fifty-One and the Gate... I only did it, became a pagan, so they'd let me grow a beard. Was just somethin' to do. A laugh that, if I played it straight, they'd let me get away with, right? So I looked up all kinds of Viking crap and made them think it was my thing. Even changed my name last name to Odinson. And they had to let me. Listen, chicks dig the beard, Talker. No way am I gonna pass up the trifecta of being a Ranger, a sniper, *and* having what all would agree is the most epic operator beard ever. No way. So I converted. Makes sense, right, man?"

I agreed it did make a certain kind of sense.

"Except… this place…" And Sergeant Thor Odinson looked up from his work on the rifle he'd carry out into the dark to kill things with. He stared out across the darkening gloom of the forest below and the late afternoon shadows we'd be going out into. "This place is… me. I don't know… how. But…"

He inhaled deeply and shook his head. There was a pleasant, satisfied smile on his face like he didn't need to fully articulate how he felt. It was good enough for him that he knew it. Like it was something new and unexpected, but familiar all the same.

He put the rifle down on his poncho and picked up the two tomahawks he'd used in his ceremony.

"This place is something older than anything we've ever known. I know it's supposed to be the future, Talker, but it's like a lost age of legends and myths and… and heroes. Know what I mean?"

When the blue-eyed killer with two tomahawks in his hands and dozens of notches indicating kills on the anti-materiel rifle he called *Mjölnir*… when he asks if you know what he means…

The answer is, "Yes. Yes, I do."

You're the new guy, you remind yourself. What'd the command sergeant major say? *Try not to get in anyone's way, son.*

I'm trying.

Later, as darkness came on, we made our way down to the river carrying the poncho rafts we'd constructed. We were going into a deeper part of the slow-moving currents north of the island. The main over-water access points were now mined and no doubt watched by enemy scouts out there in the murky gloom of the woods, but north, the river was heavily forested on both sides. It was a quick, cold paddle, pushing our poncho rafts across the river, and then we unpacked our gear, broke down the rafts, and had mission-essential items distributed and comms checks completed.

As we sat in the dark tangle of trees and branches where we'd come ashore, we could already smell the smoke of their fires and torches drifting through the near-dark forest. The drums were reaching a fever pitch, and the tribal horns were ringing out from every corner of the forest.

They were coming.

We sat there, acclimatizing and listening to the hostile environment we were about to move through. Then Sergeant Thor nodded, and without a sound we were off in a patrol column, heading toward our hit. Sergeant Kang bringing up the rear. Specialist Lucke on point.

Eyes wide open in the dark and looking for monsters to slay.

# CHAPTER SIX

SERGEANT Thor was on comms with the drone operator. The target was back in the clearing and up to the same thing again tonight. We were well inland now and moving slowly through a dark forest. Meanwhile, back on the island the orcs were hitting the eastern edge of our defenses, and from the west, out in the wetlands opposite the heavy weapons team, hundreds of hidden archers were filling the night sky with arrows. Arrows arching in the moonlight and then raining down. We could hear them whistling, a chorus of mournful high-pitched shrieks shooting off into the night, and through the gaps in the trees, off to our right, we could sometimes see their swarms unexpectedly cross through the cold early evening sky. If we turned off our NVGs and flipped them up, that is. Which I admit to doing. The rest of the Rangers kept their NVGs "down" or "on" as we continued the patrol.

We followed the bottom of a small, barely moving stream, our pace not much faster than the water's, because we had no idea if these orcs had their own version of IEDs. Something they might have left lying around for us to get stuck with. Best to move slow and safe as we closed on our target.

"Slick and silent, smooth and quiet," Sergeant Thor periodically whispered into the comm as we followed our course to the hit, tactically problem-solving and navigating different pieces of terrain as they presented themselves, addressing each situation along the route. Chokepoints. Open fields of fire. Lines of drift. Places that looked ripe for an ambush.

As we were getting ready to climb a steep dirt-and-overgrown-root embankment to move up into the trees that surrounded the clearing, Specialist Lucke held up a fist, freezing the patrol in place, signaling that he'd ID'd the enemy's presence. They were working their way down the same narrow stream the patrol was working its way up.

"Hasty ambush," said Thor quietly over the comm and pointed quickly with numbered fingers where he wanted us, roughly moving us into an L-shape along a slight bend in the streambed with Brumm and his SAW anchoring our attack. I was placed with Brumm, and the two of us hunkered behind a dead log lying in the burbling water while the rest of the team faded into the brush off to the right.

It felt like forever as we just lay there and waited. And then, peering over the log through my NVGs, I saw them coming straight at us. They weren't orcs. I mean, they were similar, but smaller. They had large, flappy ears that twitched and flicked. Wide luminescent eyes mischievously scanned the dark as they slowly padded along the stream bottom. No torches. No lights. They muttered one to another, and from what I could pick up it sounded familiar. Like maybe there was something in its construction that was similar to a few of the languages I knew, or knew of. They carried curved bone daggers and feather-laden spears. They wore little clothing beyond ragged loincloths and toothy-teeth necklaces, like some Bronze Age group of hunter-gatherers from the long ago had mobbed a shark at one point.

Brumm was waiting on the signal to open up and start the ambush when abruptly, before they reached the leading envelope of our kill zone, the twitchy little creatures headed off into the forest to the north, falling to all fours and climbing up out of the streambed like fast-moving spiders, snooting the earth of the forest. In seconds they evaporated into the dark trees, it was as if they hadn't ever been there at all.

Thor let them go, and we waited for a long moment in the new silence, listening and trying to hear them over the distant gunfire erupting back at the island. A fresh round of mortar strikes began to *whump whump*, and the tribal battle horns, farther away now, seemed to call up more forces to the action.

Ranger Alamo was getting hit hard tonight.

"Patrol up," said Sergeant Thor softly once he was sure we were safe to move. "Continue to objective. CP says the target is still active and affecting the battle."

What happened next went exactly as it was supposed to... until it didn't. Then it got wild. Real sideways, real fast.

We made our turn up onto the embankment and into the woods that surrounded the hidden clearing and the location of our HVT. The trees there smelled damp and rotten, with branches twisted among each other like snakes frozen in their embraces. This was a forest that had been wild and tangled for a very long time. And it was cooler here than it was down along the stream bottom, and that didn't seem right.

"Feel that?" Brasher asked as I followed him toward the hit.

I didn't reply.

"Don't feel right, do it, Talker?" he said regardless.

"I don't know what you're talking about," I said, pretending to myself that it was the truth.

Brasher gave a grunt in reply.

Maybe the air temperature, I confessed to myself. But at the time I didn't want to admit that what we were heading into simply… didn't feel right. Like Brasher said. I suppose it would have meant a loss of control of some sort if I had admitted that things weren't making sense on a basic level. And if I did admit that, if I admitted something as simple as *things didn't feel right*, then things like *up is down* might be the new normal. It would be like opening a gateway to dark stuff you might not be able to stuff back in the bottle no matter how much you wanted to.

A moment later, Specialist Lucke halted us along the approach to contact. Through the woods ahead the trees began to thin, and the space was so filled with silver-blue moonlight it created a swirling column of dusty-light, fireflies, and dancing motes. A pillar of soft, otherworldly glow leaving us here among the murky trees in a state of otherwise near pitch-black darkness.

I had to remind myself that this was where the predator preferred to be. In the dark, unseen and watching. And the Rangers were the predators tonight. We had come out to hunt. The darkness was our world now.

"Wait one…" said Thor, who had his MK11 up and the thermal sight active, scanning the darkness ahead of us. I watched all of this completely unsure what was actually happening. The rest of the Rangers were scanning their sectors, watching the gloom all around on one knee. I took off my comm headset and listened.

I could hear something.

I held up one hand and whispered into the comm telling them what I was hearing. Someone muttering in low monastic tones. I didn't add that it sounded ominous and extremely creepy. But it did. The advanced hearing detection mounted on our helmets, and in our earmuffs, should have picked it up. But it didn't. And that had been my hunch. Just like the guy being invisible on everything except thermal. He was silent, electronically speaking.

"Not even picking this guy up on thermal now," Thor muttered through gritted teeth. "Anyone have visual on Jackpot at this time? Anything on night vision?"

"Jackpot" was Ranger for an HVT.

Negatives all around.

Since the drone's thermal imaging system had detected our target, the thermal scope Sergeant Thor was carrying should have done the same. That was the plan. But Thor's bitter oath indicated that the scope he was running was high-priced junk. Now he sat there, staring into the darkness ahead, searching the empty moonlight with his cold blue eyes.

"He's there," he whispered. "Drone has him."

I knew what he was thinking right at that very moment. He was thinking we were supposed to hit the equivalent of an invisible swordsman. Yeah, it made no sense. That didn't matter. Right now, the main body was fully engaged with a horde of savage orcs trying to overrun them and slit their throats for bonus points. Apparently reason, logic, and things that made sense hadn't come through the QST gate on the ride we'd taken into the future. This—fighting orcs and giants and invisible "wizards"—this was what reality was here. Which meant the sergeant had to figure out a way.

"We'll frag it," he muttered in the darkness so low you could barely hear.

No one said anything. After a moment he outlined the change in plans over the comm.

"Gomez and Lucke. Take the right and move up slow and close. Right to the edge of the wood line over there. Once you're in position we'll move forward in a firing line. Deploy your grenades on my signal. After they've detonated, Specialist Brumm will lay down suppressive—full pouch with the SAW, Brumm. Then the firing line will sweep the clearing. We should get it via overwhelming firepower. If I had mortars, I'd tell them to just delete the grid square, but we don't, and that's why we're here. Roger, Reapers?"

Affirmatives all around.

Three minutes later, Lucke and Gomez were in place and ready to toss grenades into the clearing in order to kick things off.

And that's when the plan went completely off-rails.

Gomez tossed the first grenade, and it was a good throw—according to him later—right into the dead center of the clearing. Except as the tossed explosive neared the top of its arc, it just bounced off an... invisible shield. And came right back at them.

Bounced off an *invisible shield*.

Say again. It. Bounced. Off. An. Invisible. Shield.

Yup. Crazy town.

Lucke, who had lightning reflexes and a cooked grenade ready to go himself, grabbed Private Gomez and fell on top of him. They had no idea where the tossed live grenade had gone. A moment later it detonated in the woods nearby, and in the moment we had no idea if either of them were hurt. Lucke had the presence of mind to take the cooked grenade he'd intended to deploy and toss it off in a safe direction away from us and the clearing. He threw it back toward the river, and it detonated harmlessly.

The plan had called for them to toss at least two more apiece before Brumm opened up with the 249. But instead Lucke was telling Sergeant Thor over the comm that there was some kind of invisible barrier up.

"A what?" asked Brumm, listening in. Then he swore and opened up with the SAW anyway. "Switching to on!" he shouted.

A blur of bright fire streaked out into the moonlit clearing as the specialist dragged the chattering weapon across the small open space, raking it with bursts of fire. The barrier shimmered from dozens of impacts, then collapsed with an audible *pop*.

Sergeant Thor shouted, "I have visual. Engaging!" and pulled the trigger on his target. A second later he was staring through the thermal sight mounted on his MK11, scanning the field of fire. Then, "Wait! What...?"

I was on pins and needles as to what all this meant. That was what I'd learned about combat so far. It was really confusing to pay attention to what was important because everything was important. And there were lots of loud explody things going off all around me.

I looked out into the moonlight. There was indeed a man out there in the center of the clearing. No—there were now six men out there in the clearing. All of them wearing those bamboo hats you find all across southeast

Asia. In Chinese it's called a *dŏulì*. Which literally means *bamboo hat*.

This is how linguists contribute to pitched battles between Rangers and invisible sorcerers in the dead of night. Identifying the enemy's haberdashery.

That was when my mind locked in and remembered that the muttering I'd heard had sounded vaguely Chinese. Like a Hui dialect with some Persian and Arabic.

Sergeant Thor fired the suppressed MK11 again. It was still loud because I had my hearing protection off, trying to hear what the muttering guy was saying that wasn't being picked up by the electronics. Which was impossible what with the grenades detonating and the M249's roar. Brumm was changing over to a drum now as the rest of the team began to try and hit the man, the men, in the clearing. They, the men in the *dŏulì* hats, were blinking from place to place, shifting in and out of existence, here one second, over there the next. Y'know... to make things easier for us.

The men in the clearing were all the same man. We all saw that. The same Chinese peasant in bamboo hat and dark robes. Hands weaving in almost balletic movements. All six of him blinking in and out of existence as the Rangers tried to acquire and fire. Did I mention the blinking out of existence? Because it was the weirdest thing I'd ever seen... up to that point.

Ask yourself... how many times have you seen something like that outside of a video game? *Teleporting*.

The men, the man, they were weaving their hands around, most likely about to do something that would vaporize us all in an instant. The feel of wild energy loose in the night air was palpable, and suddenly the trees were alive as though something invisible and angry was up there and moving through the treetops.

It was at that moment I realized everyone should probably have been paying more attention to the nerdy and ever-punished PFC Kennedy. Absorbing his geek knowledge a lot more than we had been. Instead, the sergeant major had been keeping him close to the C-17 doing every lowlife task there was to do. Which mainly consisted of digging a latrine pit near the aircraft. It had been three days of nothing but MREs since we got here. Eventually that sanitation pit was gonna be much-needed.

Fog suddenly swirled up from the ground and all six blinking men, like figures on a cycling slot machine, began to slow their roll until there was only one. But by that time the fog had choked off the moonlit clearing and we were facing a wall of solid mist through which we could see absolutely nothing at all.

"Cease fire!" yelled Thor, swearing. He was scanning the fog, mumbling that the thermal should work despite smoke, fog, or dust.

"Mag up!" shouted Brumm. "Want me to spray the clearing again, Sar'nt?" He was just hefting the M249 up when sidewinders of burning comets rocketed out of the fog and found the SAW gunner. They slammed into the ESAPI plates he wore in the plate carrier across his chest, scorching like white-hot phosphorus, and Brumm was shucking out of his gear just to get clear of the tiny hellfires burning there.

A moment later I felt the worst sinus infection I've ever had. All at once and suddenly out of nowhere. The kind that abruptly clogs your nose and ears and makes you feel stupid all at once. I felt like someone had just added a five-pound weight to the brain inside my skull.

Not only was there fog everywhere now, my brain was covered in a mental wool blanket. Thinking back about it now, if you'd asked me what my name was at that very moment, I probably couldn't have told you. Couldn't even have guessed what it might have been.

To my right I could see the rest of the team firing into the clearing. But everything was slow. Like when the footage of a camera is undercranked. Like I was seeing only every other frame of the movie. The explosions of the weapons seemed far away and distant, and somewhere else not here.

Farther to the right—where later I would remember Lucke and Gomez had gone, though at that moment such a thought, any thought really, was hard to hold on to—I saw a sudden streak of lighting race through the fog, crooked and sharp. And then a massive thunderclap.

As if my brain were catching up to thoughts it had already had, I told myself, "Hey, this guy is some kind of wizard!"

"Cease fire!" shouted Sergeant Thor on my left, not concerned in the least if the high-value target was a wizard or not. But he said it in slow motion, underwater, covered in syrupy dripping molasses. Or at least that's how my mind processed the whole thing.

I looked to my left. It took forever to get my head over there and see what I wanted to see. This wizard had definitely done something to me. Thor had dropped his rifle and drawn his M18 and one of the tomahawks he carried. I missed a few frames of what happened next because my mind was so scrambled, but I knew he was heading into the fog, pistol leading and scanning the terrain in front of him, tomahawk down and ready to come up to play. In my completely stoned state, I thought he really did look like an action hero striding out to do battle. The pagan warlord he'd lied to become just so he could pick up chicks off post. He really could make it in Hollywood.

That's what I was thinking as we almost got killed.

Or maybe it was what he'd tried to tell me back on the hill when we were prepping for the op. That this place was weird. And that it was him, too, in a kind of way. I thought that, because at the same moment, another Sergeant Thor appeared off to our left. Coming suddenly out of the dark trees there. I turned, willing my eyes to see our Sergeant Thor's back just disappearing into the fog bank ahead. Then I snapped my head back to my left, except that it took forever, and I could feel my tongue and open mouth trying to catch up. Like some actor playing the village idiot in a comedy of manners about exits and entrances, lords and ladies. I was just the simple village idiot in this one.

An action hero I'm not.

And there was Sergeant Thor again over to my left.

He walked right past me, a strange and evil smile on his face as he headed straight toward Brumm, who was up and out of his armor, the 249 ready once more and scanning the right flank into the fog.

It was at that moment that I thought it strange for New Sergeant Thor to have big long demonic claws hanging down below his knees. And that his stride was... rather robotic. Like something wearing a human skin... but not really knowing how to human. Or even walk like one.

New Sergeant Thor was saying something to Brumm, and the voice was a dead ringer for Thor. But there was no way this was the sergeant. I didn't want to believe that.

That was when the fog lifted from my brain. Just like that. Like stepping suddenly from darkness into light. Except your eyes didn't have to adjust. They just had to remember what seeing was.

I immediately saw New Thor for what it was. And what it wasn't was the sergeant, or even vaguely human beyond being basically bipedal. It was tall and demonic. Its skin was a mottled mixture of pale and red like some utterly poisonous spider you don't want to mess with. Topped off with a throbbing exposed brain and horror-show eyes alive with a mindless hunger.

I could feel Brumm's mind tagging the approaching creature as Sergeant Thor regardless of what I was seeing. I could hear Brumm's thoughts inside my head. Or maybe I was just reading them on his face. He wasn't even thinking on a conscious level that *This is the sergeant*. His mind was just accepting that the thing coming toward him was Sergeant Thor.

And as I did nothing, like action heroes never do, I thought... *That ain't the sergeant, Brumm.*

And...

*That thing's going to attack and rip your throat out with those claws that are already opening and closing like the mandibles of some vicious predator from a pit no one should've ever gone looking in...*

I heard Brumm's mind hear my thoughts, and I felt him think *Whoa* as he recognized the creature for what it was. His mental eyes had opened.

Maybe he'd read the look on my face?

With zero hesitation Brumm dragged his right arm back, bringing to bear the heavy weapon he'd picked back up after getting hit by the shooting comets, and he fired a single burst of fire right into the hideous brain-headed creature. The flurry of speeding bullets tore the thing's bulbous rib cage to shreds. The monster flung up its long demonic arms and screamed like a shrieking spoiled girl, but it was already falling to the dirt in the night.

Brumm, unfazed, just stepped over and shot it a bunch more, hosing it like some shopkeeper spraying last night's filth off the sidewalk. The thing twitched and flopped, and the Ranger filled it full of lead, perhaps to make sure monsters died just like everyone else.

In the silence that followed, staring into the fog, we heard nothing. And then the shooting started. It sounded like someone was rapid-firing their sidearm, and accompanying that sound was Sergeant Thor roaring like the Viking warrior he'd convinced the chain of command he was just so he could get an epic beard going.

We waited in the silence that followed and heard someone grunting and heaving.

"Sar'nt Thor!" Brumm called out. "What's your location? I'm up and can support with fire!"

There was no answer.

But a moment later, Sergeant Thor came out of the dissipating fog bank carrying the bloody head of the wizard, sans the bamboo hat. The whites of the sorcerer's eyes were rolled up into his leathery skull. A drooping gray mustache hung down along tattooed cheeks scrawled with meaningless symbols and numbers. The mouth hung agape in horror at what had been done to its owner.

Or so I thought.

Later, in my mummy bag, I knew the horror written on that face wasn't at what had been done to it, but at what was coming.

# CHAPTER SEVEN

WE crossed back over the river and onto our island before dawn. For much of the rest of the night before we did, we watched enemy attacks come and go against our defenses along the water's edge as the strange dark force hurled itself out of the midnight forest and into walls of intersecting and accurate fire put up by the Rangers from inside their fortified positions. From our vantage point just within enemy-held territory, it seemed like we were winning. That the defense of the tiny river island was easy and that our side effortlessly repelled these titanic assaults that broke against the dug-in Rangers.

Three different elements of the orc horde did manage to get close enough, despite the overwhelming fire, to engage in hand-to-hand combat. But they had to literally trample their wounded and dead just to push forward across the dark river and through the bright lines of intersecting tracer fire to attack with spears and axes. To take the fight right up onto the shore and straight into the face of the Ranger-manned pits. Only to be pushed back.

And all the while mortar teams were busy dropping fire all over the staged masses out there in the forest, no doubt spotted by drone recon, and the booms of the snipers' powerful Barretts could be heard from the hilltop at the northern end of the river island. With each shot Sergeant

Thor would wistfully remark to the rest of us hiding there in the dark tangle near the river's edge, "Got another one." As if he could see the shot in his mind's eye. As if he was watching the geometry of fatality and finding it beautiful. Like some benched athlete playing the game from the sidelines.

It *seemed* like we were winning, judging by what we could see and hear of the battle out there in the dark. But based on what we heard over the comm, revealing the portions of the battle we could not see, it was clear we were *not* winning. We were holding, at best. Not letting the do-not-cross lines get crossed.

Then again, "not losing" was a win on that long night.

The Rangers would tell you "surrender" is not in their vocabulary. So that wasn't gonna happen.

On the western side of the island, the defenses we could not observe from the tangle of our hide were getting hit hard. Real hard. They had wounded. Two KIAs just after midnight, and that was a portent of all the bad things to come. A promise from the snarling orcs that their horns and war drums would win and overwhelm us in the end. They had the numbers. And the willingness. Three pits were overrun toward 0200. The Rangers, led personally by the captain, violently retook them. One of the platoon leaders was killed doing so.

No one made any LT jokes as we sat there in the dark and waited.

We didn't make our poncho rafts until the last moment in case we needed our gear and weapons, but when we did, and they were completed, we slipped back into the dark, cold water and tried not to look down along the drift of the southern current. Down there where the waters were clogged with the bodies of dead orcs in the half-light before dawn. Where the rotting giant still lay against the far shore. Large wolves had come out of the forest to tear at him.

I spent much of that night just thinking about the "intel" I'd secured off the dead sorcerer. Our high-value target. That's what PFC Kennedy had called the man we killed out there in the night. No—Kennedy had said "wizard." Not "sorcerer." Where was the line between such things? I pondered word meanings and roots, usages and origins. My happy place that was not here.

Maybe it was time to embrace what the little geek PFC Kennedy was trying to tell everyone from the bottom of the latrine slit trench that people kept throwing current events down into for him to digest, comment upon, and illuminate. Like a character from a Joseph Heller novel. A dark comedy about war and battle and the opinions of someone who didn't count in the big scheme and would get killed in the end, and was right about the whole mess all along.

The fool in any Shakespeare play.

PFC Kennedy was trying to say that somehow we'd ended up in another world. A fantasy world of monsters and goblins like something out of *The Lord of the Rings* or some mega-budget MMO. That we should wake up and smell the witch's cauldron of boil and toil and trouble. That maybe this was something more dangerous than insurgents and hajis with RPGs. That even though it seemed fantastic, it was best to be honest about things before we got ourselves killed by not knowing what we were going up against.

*Double, double toil and trouble;*
*Fire burn and caldron bubble.*
*Something wicked this way comes.*

*Open, locks. Whoever knocks.*

I'd sometimes used translations of Shakespeare in other languages as flash cards to improve my comprehension. In the night, inside the enemies' world, those lines stuck out and seemed to echo in my mind as I listened to the battle and the dark all around us alongside the river. As Rangers died. Overrun by "fantasies" with snarling fangs, sharp knives, and hard-swung axes. To those dying Rangers in their last moments, it probably didn't seem like much of a fantasy. Not like any book or game.

To them, it was all too real.

And so I turned my mind to what intel I'd managed to find on the headless corpse of the wizard of Oz, or mad sorcerer of the Purple Tower, or whatever he was here in whatever this place was. The one Thor had gone completely Viking on and decapped.

*Join the Army. Rifle the bodies of dead sorcerers in the bare moonlight,* I'd told myself as I searched the corpse. I guarantee you that would have beaten every Army recruiting slogan ever dreamed up as a marketing tool by the DoD and Fifth Avenue. Probably even *Call of Duty,* too.

The most obvious piece of intel was a book. A... *sigh.*

Stop it, I told myself. Embrace it.

*A spell book.*

Or at least what I would imagine a spell book would look like. I'd never played any of PFC Kennedy's games with strange little dice or on a computer screen in some internet café. Never much of a gamer. Wasn't my thing, and I'd never even met PFC Kennedy before Fifty-One. But I knew people in college who did those things, and they were always trying to get me to join their imaginary adventures.

I guess they figured the books I always had my nose in were some kind of common ground. That if I wasn't part of the tribe, I was at least a distant cousin.

Languages and the histories of them, the origins and roots of words and the civilizations that employed them, that was my thing. My little game. My worlds to explore. I didn't know I needed anything else until one day I did. That's how I joined the Army.

So I always declined. Never played those fantasy make-'em-up games.

I'd seen movies though. Movies like the remake of *Evil Dead*. There was what I assumed to be a spell book in that movie. The Book of the Damned. And this thing I took off the headless corpse in the dark clearing somewhere after midnight, it was pretty close to that prop from the movie.

It was bound in the skin of something—something that didn't feel like supple leather from the Ralph Lauren Home Collection my mother had furnished her "barn" in back in upstate New York. If you had told me it was pixie skin or minotaur flesh, or some other mythological creature skinned for dark and thaumaturgic purposes, I would likely have believed it. It was something other and not sane, and I just sat staring at the thing in the wet grass of the clearing while Gomez gave me a red-lensed headlamp for me to inspect everything. The fog was still dissipating along the ground, and Sergeant Thor and the rest of the Reaper Team were still securing the objective's perimeter.

Those goblins that we'd almost ambushed in the stream—that's what we'd decided to identify them as, goblins; we didn't need PFC Kennedy's help with that particular designation—should have been close enough to hear the fire of Brumm's 249. And drone recon was down for the moment, according to comm. So while the others established perimeter security, Gomez was tasked with me to assist with the SSE. Sensitive site exploitation. Or collection of intel.

Anything I could find on a dead, headless, wizard's body was intel.

*Join the Army, kids.*

Embrace it, I told myself. Like the special operators are always saying. About embracing "the suck," as they call it. Now I was telling myself to embrace the situation, "the suck," as presented. Whether I wanted to accept it or not, I was in it to win it. We all were. This was "the suck."

Embrace the fantasy, I told myself.

"Think he's booby-trapped?" whispered Gomez as we crouched over the headless body in the wet grass.

*No*, I thought. *Not until just now when you reminded me he might be booby-trapped.* And a wizard's version of a booby trip would probably banish you to the nth dimension where time has no meaning and hell is every day. Basic Training forever, in other words.

I was already freaked out having to search a headless corpse in the middle of the night on a dark otherworldly battlefield. Now I also had to worry about magical IEDs exploding in my face and burning my flesh off or turning me into a newt. Great. Fun. I'd like to re-enlist now, if you please.

"I don't think..." I began, not really sure if I did *think* but trying to reason out whether this strange headless man could be rigged with magic explosives. "I mean, Thor cut off his head," I said finally, muttering low, so the goblins with bone daggers and spears, wearing shark-tooth necklaces, couldn't hear us. LOL. "Any... explosives... would have detonated then. Right, Gomez?"

Like Ranger PVT Gomez was suddenly an EOD expert.

In my head I heard myself explaining why I hadn't completed the mission. *Sorry, Sergeant Major. Couldn't bring back any intel because I was afraid of magical IEDs. You know how it is and all, dawg.*

About a minute later I'd be digging slit trench latrines with PFC Kennedy. Being all that I could be.

"Dunno," said Gomez with a shrug, and I watched the circumference of the red light Gomez was holding grow and become thinner at the same moment. He'd wisely backed away a step or two.

Fine, I said to myself, and I started to search the body, convinced I'd get blown up or have my hands suddenly torn off by something like that thing from the old John Carpenter movie where the guy's chest caves in and a giant fanged mouth cavity just bites the other guy's hands off.

Fun stuff. I wasn't even sure if, ten thousand years in the future, I was even getting paid to do this. Would someone give me a medal?

Embrace. The. Fantasy.

I found the spell book in a large messenger bag type thing the sorcerer kept around his body, though I'm sure he didn't call it a "messenger bag" like he was some metrosexual film critic who'd picked it up at an haute store on Fifth Avenue in NYC.

Ten thousand years ago.

Inside the worn "messenger bag" the first thing I found was the spell book made of dried dragon flesh leather, or whatever. Dried dragon was probably what you made these things out of, right? I put the book to the side. I'd recovered it, and nothing the command sergeant major said indicated I had to look inside. I was curious but I wasn't stupid. That was how you end up turned into a toad or something worse. Is there a worse? Yeah. There probably is.

So I didn't look.

I put the book aside on the poncho square I'd laid out and then found some sheets of parchment. That's old-timey fantasy paper if you're playing along. Yellowing. Crumbling. Ancient. Put that aside too. I did note that on one sheet there was a fairly accurate map of the island but no clear markings indicating our defenses. Just some scrawled symbols that seemed vaguely familiar.

That was interesting.

Next, I found some disgusting stuff. Orders were orders, so I took what amounted to eye of newt and bat's tails and jars of foul-smelling dust. One small crystal bottle was filled with what looked very much like blood that hadn't congealed, and a few pouches contained what I guessed were either the dried brains of small animals or spongy dark mushrooms that would probably fry your mind.

The dead guy had a staff, too. Because of course he did. Gomez found that in the dirt nearby. It was made of dark wood, like the mahogany I'd seen in some of my father's high-priced lawyers' offices. One end of the staff had been carved into the head of a dragon, its snout wide and toothy and malevolent, its carved eyes glittering with dark destruction. Even the wood itself was unsettling, its patterns and whorls seeming more like other places than mere textures in the grain. Worlds and hidden rooms if you looked close enough. I had that thought, and then at the same time, I had another thought. Namely, *That doesn't make sense.*

"It's heavy," said Gomez when he picked it up.

I looked up only briefly from my work on the body. Which by the way was still drooling blood and gore into a congealing puddle in the wet grass. I had my issue Oakley Assault Ranger gloves on, but it was impossible not to get things bloody. A lot of the Rangers wore Mechanix gloves. Gomez handed me some rubber surgical gloves he kept in the calf pockets of his assault pants.

There was a pouch full of strange coins, all with different stamps and words on them. Some were shiny like gold. Others dull like copper and silver. I was pretty sure I could read some of the languages on them, but I would need better lighting to inspect them closely. NVGs didn't nail that level of detail. The images stamped in relief on the coins were human. And that... that was somehow comforting. Like somewhere in this crazy world we ended up in there were still other human beings who existed. Better yet: humans who charged each other for stuff. Basic commerce can be very comforting. Especially when you thought the world ended while you were off leaping through time in the back of a C-17.

So, humans existed, or had existed. Once.

Then I remembered that this headless corpse I was groping had been a human too. Or at least human-looking. But so had the thing that had gone for Brumm. The lookalike that disguised itself just to get close so it could tear out our throats. I didn't need PFC Kennedy to know what that particular monster was called. *Doppelgänger.* Doppel meaning *double*, gänger for *goer*. German word. Common literary device in certain literatures and old wives' fables.

They were never well-intentioned beings. Real monsters. A myth preying on the human fear that something known and familiar might not be what you think it is. Might be something else. Something with bad intentions. And maybe, I thought, kneeling there in the grass, maybe this wasn't so much the future, but more the past reasserting itself once again after a brief and inconvenient interruption by our modern civilization. The one we'd left. The one that had been getting overrun by a technological plague gone wild. Something that got away from a defense lab in China. Something that never should've been made, much less thought up.

There should be a special place in hell for the real monsters that sit around thinking that stuff up. *Whoops, my science experiment just croaked the world* is a pretty poor excuse.

I checked the sorcerer's hands, remembering the low-hanging claws that dangled from the doppelgänger killer's frame. No claws. The dead sorcerer had human hands. But… there was a ring on one finger.

I pulled hard, dislocating the finger in order to remove it from its cold, stiff host and studied it. It was made of a dull silver, but like the staff, it felt heavier than it should have. Much heavier.

When I'd patted down the rest of the body, we notified Sergeant Thor we were good to go. A minute later we all withdrew from the objective, taking a different route back. We went farther upstream, away from the battle, cognizant we might run into flanking forces out there in the dark.

It was while we were on the way to our crossing point that the orcs back at the island really pushed the eastern defenses hard. They hit the emplaced mines on the sand bars and pushed on through by sheer numbers, never minding the steel balls and flechettes from the mines, nor the flying body parts of their victims. IR flares went off from our lines, throwing spooky shadows and changing the colors within our NVGs. The illumination shells started going up so often I switched from NVGs to plain old analog human night vision. We sat for twenty minutes acclimatizing to the shifting darkness and then continued along the animal track we were using to get to our new crossing.

Off in the distance the 240s chattered death. Talking to one another above the bellow and roar of the swarming orc horde pushing once again like they had all the numbers in the world to burn just to take ten more meters. Their tribal *Uroo Uroos* urgent and insisting that now was their moment to be seized.

It was do or die, lads, some orc NCO might've been bellow-barking in orc tribalese. Like this was their Little Orc Roundtop. Their finest hour.

I wondered... What if they take the island? What if there's nothing for us to cross back to? What then? What do the seven of us do after everyone else has been killed?

The mission would seem to be over at that point. We'd be down to just doing survival. And how long could that last? What exactly was the high score we'd need to beat?

We sat in the dark for a long time near the crossing. Hidden in the wet mud and tangled trees, listening to the battle out there in the dark across the quiet river. It grew and faded sometime around three. An hour later there was one last push by the enemy, but it petered out pretty quickly. Like those orc NCOs' hearts just weren't into it this time. Or they'd all been killed, and the last assault was just for form rather than meaning. Then it was time to cross back over. We constructed our poncho rafts and eased back into the cold water. The current had picked up and we got carried downriver a bit as we paddled and pushed to make the crossing back inside our line. We were paddling and pushing hard when Brumm gasped, "Look at that down there."

The first light of distant morning was in the sky, coming through the skeletal trees to the east. To our left, south along the eastern defenses, a horse and rider all in black, or maybe that was just how the bare pre-dawn light made them look, were easing out across the mined shallows where the bodies of dead orcs floated and drifted away. The rider had one hand up and was calling out something to our forces. I could barely hear him from here.

"Sounds like," said Thor, pushing and paddling with me, "sounds like he's using the original operational countersign. From day one."

Now I could hear someone from the weapons section down there, bellowing out the challenge in that Ranger-pit-bull bark. No doubt more than willing to light up the dark rider after a night like the one that had just passed. Probably jittery with spent rage and bottoming out as the adrenaline of combat disappeared in the first dawn light. Piles of expended brass all over the pit. But the challenge must have been met with the countersign, because as we pushed onto shore, we could see the rider walking his dark horse ashore as well, hands up, the Rangers coming out to cover him with their rifles.

# CHAPTER EIGHT

WE reported back to the sergeant major, and he made sure we got to heat up some MREs at a station he'd set up near the casualty collection point. Then he told me to hang on to the intel and we'd link up later to review the SSE material. The rest of the Reaper Team heated their rations and took off back to their assigned positions in the defense, but I just sat for a while, not really as interested in the Chicken Chunks as I could usually work myself up to be. I was still covered in wizard blood, and even the small Tabasco bottle didn't make it any better. Considering the blood... it kinda made it worse.

Nearby, Chief Rapp was sewing up slashes while Rangers groaned at the first-rate care they were being given. They roared and swore when whatever the chief was using for a disinfectant got liberally splashed around to clean out the wound first. After that they grunted and tolerated. I guess everything after the sudden fire of the cleansing felt like a picnic. One guy was probably going to lose a hand. So, there was that.

Fun times at the CCP.

The sergeant major came back from somewhere, moving swiftly in that long-legged road march stride he had, and scooped me up in his wake with a terse command to "Follow." Once we were clear of everyone else he added, "Need you to listen in on something and assess."

What? Was I actually going to do languages? Had the insight and forward planning of someone at the Pentagon finally paid off? I could hardly contain myself. It was a good thing I was dead tired, or I might have been too excited about getting to do the special thing I did.

"Capture a bad guy, Sergeant Major? What language? What's it sounds like?"

Yeah, I couldn't help myself. I still hadn't mastered Ranger Tough. Which basically meant brooding with a mouth full of dip and staring off into the forest while either thinking up all the ways you could get killed or thinking up new ways you could kill those who were trying to kill you before they killed you first.

Basically, hit some dip and think about revenge. That was how you looked like a Ranger.

But on the way to the briefing I was just hoping the language was one of mine. Though even if it wasn't, I could most likely get an anchor on anything anyone spoke given enough time.

"We did get a subject to interrogate, Talker," said the sergeant major, moving swiftly ahead of me through the trees back to the CP in the C-17. "But this ain't that. Guy from another one of the detachments came through the line this morning 'bout the time you guys came back over. I want you to say nothing and just listen to what he has to say. *Comprehende?*" he said in Tejas-English. As a party trick I could've told him within a two-hundred-mile radius exactly in which border town he'd picked that up in. But not important right now.

I was learning.

Ten minutes later the brief started in the CP. Except it wasn't a brief. It was a debrief. We were listening to information instead of disseminating it. In attendance was the captain. The XO, who'd I'd never really seen. The sergeant major was there of course. And the pilot. Chief Rapp, who was more than just a medic, arrived a few minutes later. The Green Beret, or what Rangers liked to call a Green Beanie, was an operational detachment advisor.. And now I was going to see him doing work that didn't involve doling out stitches, water bottles, and motrin.

Oh, Captain Knife Hand had dried blood on his forehead. I was betting that was someone else's. Just wanted to point that out.

And then they introduced the person we'd be debriefing: Chief Petty Officer McCluskey, Naval Special Warfare Operator... or what most people call SEALs. Apparently this was the dark rider we'd seen cross the sandy shallows along the river just before dawn as we came back across ourselves.

Turns out it wasn't just the light that had made him dark. He still cut a dark figure there in the gloom of the cargo deck of the C-17. If it weren't for the otherworldly blue in McCluskey's hooded eyes, his face would have been nothing but white stripes and black grease. A kind of night camo he'd applied. His hair was dark and curly. And long. Definitely not Ranger short. I guess SEALs are different. I'd only ever seen them in the movies, played by actors. So, not actual SEALs.

He wore supple high black boots and armor fashioned of black leather and dark rings. Like some thespian might wear at the local Renaissance Faire. The guy playing the rogue villain at the four-o'clock fencing demo near Ye Olde

Timey Mead Hall. I'd dated a girl who went in for playing mead hall wenches and other wonderfully bawdy waifs. It was a scene. Wilder than I'd guessed for a bunch that was into playing dress-up and make-believe and talking funny. Using words like *sheweth* and *thine*. It didn't last between us. She made me nervous. She slept with a dagger and had night terrors she could never remember.

A dark cloak was wrapped around Chief McCluskey's body, the hood only barely pushed back over his thick hair. But I could see a silver hoop, like a pirate might wear, in one ear. I guess the Navy is cool with that too. In the Army there'd be no end to the smoking you'd get if you showed up to morning formation with something dangling from your ear. It would be like asking the first sergeant to have a stroke right in front of you while you did grass drills for the rest of your life. The silver hoop was formed of two twisting snakes intertwined, and it caught the light in its dangle.

Now correct me if I'm wrong, I told myself, but there had been no one who looked like this back at the doomsday briefing on the Fifty-One airfield. Less than two weeks ago. But, y'know, also ten thousand years or so ago. So how this guy was with one of the detachments but practically looked like he belonged out there with the rest of the *I-am-Gondo-of-the-Gondori* lunatics didn't really add up in the first seconds of the debrief. No one looked more the opposite of Ranger than this guy.

Chief Rapp examined a big sword still in its fancy duelist Ren Faire Ye Olde Leather Shoppe scabbard. He held it in his hands like some mythic sword of kings. Almost reverently. Black leather with silver ornaments and moon charms. I guess they'd taken it off this guy before letting him into the command post. It was like something out of a movie. A real pro-level prop.

I shifted my focus back to Chief Petty Officer McCluskey. SEAL.

*How?* I sat there wondering in the back of the briefing inside the captain's little CP. I had a lot of *How* questions about the SEAL. Plenty of *Whys*, too.

"Twenty years ago," began Chief McCluskey to everyone as I sat there and wondered. "That's how long we've been on the ground, fellas. Since I know you're asking."

*Fellas.* Uh, there were three officers and a sergeant major here. And a chief warrant officer. Rangers most of them. Things were indeed different in the Navy. If someone had called Sergeant Kurtz a *fella*, Kurtz would have killed him with a brown MRE spoon regardless of if we were in a combat zone or not.

The SEAL's voice was easy. Friendly. He was the good-timin' guy in the squad everyone liked and was easy to get along with. The bad kid in school who wasn't really bad so much as just a rebel who liked to have a good time. He could score beer long before fake IDs. Chicks dug him. But you could tell, he was the mistake those same girls shouldn't make, but did anyway. He was the kind of guy who probably had a muscle car and a couple of dirt bikes he dragged around from post to post. He followed a football team like a Catholic priest reciting the tenets of faith. Pretty much unlike anyone I'd met in the Language Arts departments of any of the ivory towers I'd studied in. He could probably rebuild a carburetor.

That was my initial assessment, probably not what the command team was looking for. Nor would it be of any use to anyone. But hey, that's me. Why fight it?

"We came in twenty years ago off the coast of Normandy," continued McCluskey. "That's where you guys are, if you haven't figured it out yet." He stared around at us, daring us to call him a liar or present evidence to the contrary. "This is Europe about ten thousand years in the future as near as I... *we* can tell. There're some things that have changed. Like..." His eyes searched the roof of the grounded aircraft. "Like England and the continent are now connected by a land bridge. But this is future Europe for sure. Took a while for us to figure that out. And before you ask... I have no intel on America."

"And you were with?" asked Captain Knife Hand. He was writing all this down like it was McCluskey's job interview at the DMV. Like the mysterious SEAL had come in for a low-level GS position, or to report a crime, or to give a final interview to the parole board. Completely administrative.

"First Group, Team Five. Lieutenant Commander Rudd commanding. But... he got himself killed first year out. So I guess that QST ain't as accurate as they thought it was, right guys?" He laughed. No one else did. Rangers and SEALs have different senses of humor. SEALs probably know regular-people jokes that everyone would find funny. Rangers tend toward the horrifying for their amusements. The jokes they know would cause people to switch seats on an airplane.

"We only left the night before you all were supposed to take off," McCluskey continued, "but we showed up twenty years earlier. Go figure. Time travel's wacky. Way-above-my-pay-grade stuff. Anyway, we go through the QST and we're over water when we come out a moment later. Pilot decided to fly east, and we link up with the French coast at Normandy, though of course we didn't know that at the time. Set down right there on the beach like it was a second invasion and all. Anyway, like I said, all that was twenty years ago, and things have developed since. A lot of things. Don't worry. We ain't gone native or nothin'."

He laughed and seemed not to notice that no one else found this amusing.

"And what have you been up to, Chief?" asked the captain as though there were a question on the form he was writing on that desired exactly that information and needed to be filled out properly or the world would fall into the sun or something.

"Doing what we do. SEALs. First in, last out. Strategic reconnaissance operations. Trying to figure out the situation on the ground. I personally have been as far east as a region north of Turkey they call Umnoth now. Bad place. Real bad in fact. Oh, and by the way, there's no Black Sea anymore. Big meteorite broke apart and scored a direct hit there and a bunch of other places a few thousand years ago. A lot of topography got changed in the interim."

In the interim.

He paused for the captain to write all this down. No one said anything. Chief Rapp shifted in his chair. It groaned and cried out in anguish because his legs were the size of tree trunks. I'm not kidding. Even his muscles had muscles. He was *jacked*, as they say.

The captain wrote like an administrator whose passion was the smallest detail. Exact detail. Focused. Sharp. Complete in studying the world in the words he was putting down to make sure he had it all as it was supposed to be. Not concerned in the least by the uncomfortable silence in which he worked. I had no doubt everything was going down on that paper precisely as it was being relayed.

That bothered me about Captain Knife Hand. He could go completely Roman on the enemy, and then write it all down like it was just some bureaucrat's report on labor statistics. *"Subject made gagging noises and cried briefly while I strangled him from behind. Hyoid bone broken twenty-two seconds into strangulation. Death followed one minute later. Assassination complete."* I could imagine him writing that kind of report. He was the epitome of cold-blooded. He was that kind of machine. The kind that kills you and then subtracts your number from the global equation.

The tough guys in the squads aspired to be the captain. They were lucky. They'd gotten the kind of officer they wanted.

I allowed myself to consider what would have happened if instead of going enlisted linguist I had taken the recruiter's offer to go off to OCS. Officer Candidate School. Yikes. Everyone would be dead or feasting on one another for a decent meal by day three if I was in charge of this operation. I have no faith in my ability to lead anyone into anything. Everything would be Mad Max by the end of the week. I gave the captain at least a month before we resorted to the cannibalism that would have marked my administration from the get-go.

You have to be honest about these things.

The captain sniffed and muttered for the SEAL to, "Continue."

McCluskey obliged.

"Three days ago, I hear tell among the tribes that a big bird came down out here in the western end of the Loire

Valley. That's where we are. We, humans, used to make wine here. But they call this river the Low River now, and the tribes call the valley the Catch. In their language. Orc. That's what we call them, the guys drifting dead in the river out there. Orcs. Because... well, you've seen the movies. Spitting image. Am I right, guys?"

So it wasn't just PFC Kennedy who saw it. Funny how things often just name themselves. No one has to decide— you just know it when you see it. Orc. Giant. Washing machine. Truly new words, pure neologisms, are actually far less common than you might think, outside of marketing departments. Mostly we just reuse and repurpose the words we already have. Or they repurpose themselves. Evolve on their own.

I wondered what McCluskey called the goblins.

"Anyway," he continued, "I knew what that meant. The *big bird* part. Knew one of ours had finally come in through the QST. Or at least that's what I hoped. So I hopped on my horse and tore out for you guys. By then the orc tribes already had scouts all out in the woods looking for you. You were surrounded within twenty-four hours. I captured a few and found out what I needed to know after conducting a short interrogation. Then I took my time and got through the lines just hoping the operational countersign from day one was still good. I never forgot it. Never ever. We knew you'd show up one day, and we wanted to be ready for you. And now... here you are. Know what I mean, fellas?"

*Fellas.* The nerve of this man!

"Where's the rest of your team?" asked the sergeant major bluntly.

McCluskey leaned back. Up until now he'd talked fast. Eyes sharp. Train of thought clear. Now he leaned back and looked off to his left like he was considering what to say next.

*John*, the guy whose name wasn't really John, had spent three hours of our two weeks in the cheap hotel in Vegas telling me everything he knew on the subject of lie detection. And if the things not-John had taught me were true... then this guy was about to tell us all a big old lie.

"Team's gathering," replied McCluskey. "Sent word using a communication system we've set up. If they get it soon enough, and remember, things are a little Bronze Age here in the future... but if they get it, they'll be ready to come in and assist. I can signal near nightfall and we can find out if they're out there yet."

"What weapons and assets does your team still have?" asked the captain.

"Well," said Chief McCluskey, leaning forward as if to think, letting his hands dangle between his leather-clad legs. "We ain't got this fine gear you got. Ain't seen an MK18 or an MP5 the way I like it rigged in a very long time. And you won't either, not much longer. Weapons, equipment that is, everything machine-made and technological beyond a certain level... it all breaks down here after a while. You'll notice it first when your optics go offline. Then about a month or two later the weapons'll start malfunctioning regularly. Get so bad you can't go five rounds without clearing a jam. That's what got Stillwater killed up around the western edge of the Crow's March. That's old Germany, FYI. I can draw you a map once we're clear of this fight. Point some interesting things out for you. So yeah..."

He looked around. Spotted the sergeant major.

"I'd start trainin' your Rangers to learn to fight with axes and swords here. Because that's what it is from here on out. Once your weapons go sideways, it's all over. You gotta go savage or end up in the pot, know what I mean, guys? That's the way the world works now. Only way there is to it."

He laughed about this to himself but didn't expand on the subject.

"What's the geopolitical situation like, Chief McCluskey?" asked the captain, matter-of-factly.

The SEAL laughed again and slapped his knee. Gently. "Ain't none."

Now I realized what was bothering me about this guy. And it might just be me, so I didn't know what to do with what was itching in my brain. But… here it is. I'd been in training for basically most of my very short military career, and I might not be too familiar with how the various branches treated one another. But even for a newbie like me, I couldn't help but take note of the fact that at no point did Chief Petty Officer McCluskey of the SEALs ever use anyone's rank or address superior officers with respect of rank. Stuff that had been drilled into me from day one of my military service.

Everyone in the debrief—everyone except me— outranked him. But Chief McCluskey seemed not to notice, and no one took a moment to correct his egregious breach of protocol.

And that was odd to me, too. Them not correcting.

I was just waiting for the command sergeant major to lock the SEAL's heels and rip McCluskey's spine out so he could show it to him and how it should look when addressing Captain Knife Hand with the respect due his commander's rank.

But maybe things are different in the worlds of darkness that are the special warfare groups. The Rangers certainly had a passion for rank and respect. If there were modern-day Spartans filled with nothing but hate and coldness and a grim fatality despite all odds, it was the Rangers. Even lower enlisted Rangers at the E-4 rank got addressed as such. They'd earned it in the miserable suck that was the Ranger batt, and it would be noted. Every time. Unless perhaps you reached some inner circle that was entirely beyond my experience as of yet.

But hey... I was new in town. So I continued to listen. Keep my mouth shut.

If I'd said something like, *But Sergeant Major, he didn't use your rank,* Kennedy'd have help digging latrines one minute later.

There was something else. Something I saw and heard in McCluskey's manner that stuck out as odd. Out of place. Maybe the thing that counterattacked us when we hit the HVT out in the woods had messed with my head, but... for just a second... I was reminded of the thing that looked like Sergeant Thor.

The Doppelgänger.

I looked around to see if anyone noticed anything else odd. Later, I'd realize the captain had. He'd been subtle about it, repeatedly prompting McCluskey by using the man's rank as if to remind him how things ran ten thousand years ago back when we'd all sworn to support and defend. But Chief Rapp, the command sergeant major, and even the pilot were like Easter Island tourist attractions watching the whole debrief go down. They just sat there listening, giving away nothing.

So I made like a rock and just listened too. Filing my bit away for later in case everyone was so out of ideas they actually came to me for anything.

"So no other detachments have come through since you and your team arrived, Chief McCluskey?" the captain asked.

"Negative. We have not made contact with anyone in the last twenty years, nor have we encountered any evidence that any other friendly task force element has come through the QST." Then he added *sir*. For the first time. Like he'd read my mind and everything I'd been thinking in the seconds before. Or like giving an official report and using the word *negative* had awakened something ancient within him. Something he'd forgotten during twenty years of Robin Hood Outlaw. Some memory of what it was like to still be in. In his defense, I posited how often he'd been called upon to use actual military courtesy in the last twenty years.

Probably not often.

Maybe that *was* his defense, and it had to be considered. If just to be fair and keep an open mind about things. Perhaps he had gone native despite indicating he hadn't. Maybe he didn't even know he had. What do they always say? Crazy people don't know they're actually crazy.

It was to be expected. Going native, that is. Hell, he was the one who sat here looking all Game of Thrones. This was the new normal. *We* were the ones out of place. Out of time. Out of our element. He'd said it himself. *You gotta go savage*. That, or die.

"Ain't nothing left, if that's what you're asking, sir," said the new McCluskey, suddenly conscious of rank. "No human civilizations or kingdoms anywhere. Nowhere. Or at least none that we ever found, sir. Just a few villages and enclaves in very, very inaccessible places, and more often than not, there ain't much human about 'em anyway anymore. Everything you knew... all of you," he looked around at us as though challenging us, his blue eyes looking into and past us, "it's flat-out gone now. Long gone, long, long time ago. And this is gonna sound crazy. Even I know it does..."

Like I said, his manner was so friendly and easy, intoxicating in a certain way, you wanted to believe him. Wanted to be his buddy. He was capable. He radiated capability in that way operators do. You wanted him to be on your side. Especially when your back was to the wall. And Ranger Alamo was starting to feel like some kind of wall we had our backs to. If not tonight, then some night.

"This world..." continued McCluskey softly. "It's filled with nothin' but big bad real-life monsters now. Nothin' but evil. Humans are all gone now. You'll find the occasional, but we have nothing in common with them. They're used to what we would call the monsters and magic of this place; what's foreign to them is us with our high tech and weapons and old-fashioned mores and culture. They don't have rules of engagement here, sir. If you're an enemy, they try to kill you with everything they got. All of you. Prisoners of war? Conventions? Cease-fires? Nah, they don't do that here. Best you can hope for is a chance at being a slave until they need the calories one tough winter. And... spoiler alert, as we used to say... all the winters here are tough. Then it's the pot."

He paused. "Closest to us, in values and civilization... maybe... and they're still weird... is the elves. If—and it's a big if—you can find them. Which you never can when you need to. They're all underground and hiding out in the woods and caves. There are also dwarves, we call 'em. They're not like midgets, but more like the ones in the movies with Frodo and Sauron. The dwarves aren't allies, but they don't like orcs any more than you do right now. And the orc tribes comin' at you are going to be only your fourth biggest problem here in the Ruin. That's what they call the whole world. The Ruin."

The SEAL seemed to relish the brief dramatic pause, all eyes locked on him. "So let me tell you about problem number three. That's the Crow's March. Vampires. Werewolves. Ghosts. I kid you not, sir. And yes, I know it sounds crazy. But it's like..." He searched the darkness above his head. "Think of it this way. It's as if the old Soviet Union went all Nazi Germany, but with boogeymen in control. Very, very, dark place. They're ruled by a character who calls himself, you'll like this... the Black Prince."

*You're dressed in black, psycho*, I thought, and then watched as McCluskey's serial-killer blue eyes flicked over toward me for half a second. Like I'd said what I'd thought out loud, instead of thinking it all quiet.

"That's problem number three for you. The Crow's March. Problem number two is the Saur. They're a race of—and believe me, even if I sound real casual about this, or... what's the word... blasé ... it's only because I've lived it, here on the ground, for so long. But the Saur are a race of lizard men. They've ruled this whole place starting about a thousand years after we departed the scene and the plague wiped out human civ. Okay? Got it? The Saur keep to the south, like down around Old Eygpt. Let's just say they're asleep right now. They're into some dark stuff and they got designs and prophecies about enslaving the whole Ruin forever and ushering in a whole Dark Millennium. Bad stuff.

"But your Problemo Number One-Oh... is a being. And I use that word specifically because I don't think he's from this world if half the stories we've heard are true. Think of this being as more of... well, a lot like that Sauron character. I think he's like an alien from another dimension or something. In the tales and records of the various shamans I've encountered, he starts showing up about the same time as the 'sky fell,' as they say around here in their oral traditions. That's when that meteor broke apart and slammed into Western Europe and North Africa. Anyway, this being—problem number one for everyone here, including me—is called the Nether Sorcerer. And these boys, the orcs trying to cut your throats out there in the dark tonight, the ones trying to wipe you out, they basically work for the Nether Sorcerer. Though I'd say most of them don't exactly understand it that way."

The captain began to write once again, and we all sat there listening to the scratch of his pencil against the sheet of paper he worked on. The form he was filling out. Preventing time as we know it from suddenly reversing course and flinging us all off the planet.

McCluskey leaned forward, his black leather armor creaking softly in the silence.

"And there's one other... thing... and I should be honest about this with you, up front and all... but that plague that was changing all of us way back then, ten thousand years ago, that's what it did. It changed the very fabric of... everything. It still does things to people. But I think... in a way it's done its work, mostly, or... run out of juice. But you should know something about me if we're gonna work together from here going forward. I ain't evil or nothin'. I'm no monster like the things out there trying to kill you. I'm still just Mike McCluskey from Michigan. Joined the Navy and went to Special Warfare School at Coronado, BUDS class 299. Fought in Iran and Iraq. But... well... I'm what you'd call a vampire now."

# CHAPTER NINE

"WHAT do you mean… a vampire?"

It was the pilot who asked the question everyone was thinking about asking. The rest of us were just Easter Island statues. Even me.

Hey, I'm learning to Ranger!

So I just sat there as the command team had throughout the entire insane-sounding debrief. Except it wasn't really insane given current events. Or… was it what crazy sounded like in a world that had lost its marbles, and humanity, ten thousand years or so ago? Hard to say. And that's not an understatement. But for everyone else sitting around me it was like they'd heard this sorta thing before. Or shades of it. In all the other dark places they'd been sent off to die in across their careers. They knew crazy because they'd seen it before. And they knew that if *crazy* was the set of rules you were supposed to play by… then it was best to embrace it sooner rather than later.

Chief McCluskey nodded to himself and launched into the story of how he became a vampire. Half of me felt like an idiot for just sitting there and listening to it, and the other half couldn't resist hearing it. So much so that at certain points I had to wipe my sleeve across my mouth just to make sure it was closed.

And still… it felt like it was a performance played for the thousandth time one too many. The SEAL turned escaped Ren Faire lunatic knew all the beats of it a little too well. All the jokes too pat. And I couldn't help myself from thinking, as I listened to him, that it was little more than a bad script read I was sitting through for a bad B movie I'd never admit to watching.

Long story short. He and his team had been crossing into "the Crow's March." The place he'd told us was old Germany. More specifically, Bavaria. They, his SEAL platoon, had gone into an alpine human village high in what was now called the Giant's Teeth. You could say this much for the new world order: the location names were more colorful. Three of their team took injuries during exfil, or getting out of the village of the living undead. Yes. They did indeed suffer bite wounds. Within thirty days of walking away from the place they'd left in flames on a snowy dawn morning, the three with injuries began to show signs of some sort of virulent infection their on-hand meds couldn't lick. They got weaker and weaker by the day. It became clear in pretty short order that they were dying of some kind of wasting disease.

The team medic diagnosed it as extreme anemia. Massive iron deficiency. And the infected SEALs couldn't tolerate daylight. They broke out in severe burns, almost third-degree, even when exposed to the wan winter light the team was struggling through. Then came the hunger for what they thought, at first, were just animal proteins. Soon it became apparent that it was blood the dying SEALs wanted. The team figured it out, adapted, and overcame a bad situation.

"But there were some benefits too," said McCluskey.

"Such as?" asked Chief Rapp from the shadows of the briefing area. Interested. Probably because he was doing a mental health evaluation. That was my guess.

"It's really, and I mean really, hard to kill me," McCluskey replied. "Don't know if a stake to the heart'll do it. But I've been hacked, slashed, and stabbed just about every which way you can cut somebody. I've been what the team medic called 'dead' a couple of times. I go into a kind of stasis, and if you keep me outta daylight then I come back after a while. Feel like roadkill though… but it's better than being permanent dead, know what I mean? I can see in the middle of the night, even with no moon, clear as day like it's straight-up noon. And I'm stronger than I ever was back at Coronado. I don't know how much I can bench, but one time I picked up a warhorse and threw it over a stone wall because we were being chased by grave trolls down in Skeletos. Greece, I mean. Skeletos is Greece now. Man, haven't said that word for… a long time. Greece. And I'm fast, too. Faster than I ever was… before. It's been a long time since I've broken down a weapon and put it back together, but back on the teams, with an MK18, thirty-four seconds was my best. In pieces to rock and roll. I haven't used a firearm in about twenty years, but given time… I bet I could beat my old record now easily. I'm totally sure of that. Here—hand me my sword. I'll show you a trick if you're all up for it."

Chief Rapp looked unsure. But Captain Knife Hand nodded once for approval, his eyes wary and tired at the same time. The command sergeant major just sat in the back, motionless. Seeing, and not seeing, everything. I couldn't tell if anyone had completely bought McCluskey's story as of that moment. If these were their poker faces, then I had to wonder what they were doing in the Army. They could've cleaned up at tables in casinos around the world.

Then I remembered that the world we'd known was dead now. And that there were no more casinos or endless shrimp buffets. You wanted shrimp, you were going to have to get a rowboat and kill them yourself. Then figure out how to make butter. And there were probably sea orcs and lobster trolls all down in the ocean now. The possibilities of how one could die expanded geometrically each time I stopped to consider the mess we'd ended up in ten thousand years late for our mission to save the world. This... this was losing its luster fast. And there were a whole lot more troubling and unasked questions looming and hiding that would surface once immediate survival wasn't a factor. What were we fighting for? Were we still under the terms of our enlistment, which should have expired, at the outside, nine thousand nine hundred and ninety-six years ago?

Did coffee still exist?

Granted, that last question was personal more than big-picture stuff. But no less dire, in my opinion. I was currently sitting on thirty-six packets of instant. In the land of no coffee I was the king of the blind, or something. All I knew was, I had that much, and it wasn't enough as far as a real coffee junkie was concerned. I needed all the coffee. Only then could I relax and try not to get killed by the sea orcs, or something equally bizarre.

Chief Rapp half stood and handed McCluskey's sword, hilt first and scabbarded, to the self-professed vampire in our midst. The SEAL was just sitting back in his chair with his hands between his spread knees like the most unconcerned and relaxed Ren Faire tragedian dude in the world.

What happened next was fast. Lightning-fast. Faster than anything I'd ever seen happen up close and personal.

Chief Rapp, being a big man, and tired, had barely stood to hand the sword over and across the table to Chief Petty Officer McCluskey. The giant Special Forces medic had clearly had the intent of just sitting back down in his chair and watching whatever happened next. The trick McCluskey was promising to show us. You could tell from his posture that that was Chief Rapp's next move. He was tired from two nights of combat and a lot of meatball surgery. That was to be expected.

But in the next second McCluskey had somehow shot out of his chair like a blur, drawn the sword from its scabbard so fast it didn't make even the slightest sound, and thrust the blade forward again like a streak of lightning, landing its razor-keen edge right against the chief's neck with incautious precision.

Or at least that's what had to have happened by looking at the final result and using inductive reasoning to figure out how we'd arrived at a conclusion wherein with the slightest flick of his wrist, McCluskey could open a vein in Chief Rapp's neck.

No one said a word. The silence was stunning. And McCluskey just stood there, blade resting against the chief warrant officer's neck. A hungry smile on the SEAL's face, his eyes casting about for approval because he knew the trick he'd just pulled was pretty slick and neat to boot. And it was clear he liked the adoration of being the best at something. This was his big move.

Then, in the stunned silence, Chief Rapp began to laugh. Because what else could he do? He really was a good-natured man even though there was a dark black sword with a pretty sharp edge held right to his thick neck. He rumbled with laughter and sat back down.

Oh yeah. It was a black sword. Black armor. Black horse. Black sword. McCluskey definitely had a thing for black. Add to all this that apparently he was a vampire, and we had ourselves a real live *character*.

This is the truest thing I can tell you about Rangers. They. Do. Not. Like. Characters.

It makes them uncomfortable. And things that make Rangers uncomfortable have a tendency to end up dead. A sergeant in RASP, a sergeant who made sure I got through, explained that to me. He saw my effusive and outgoing personality and the problems it might present in a Ranger batt, and he took me aside and told me what was what. I heeded and knew wisdom.

McCluskey, on the other hand...

It was like he wanted to play the villain even if he was on the wrong team to be cast as such. He was gonna do villain anyway.

"So," said the SEAL easing back down into his chair. "I'm quite fast." He casually re-sheathed the sword, leaving it on the table between everyone where he could pick it up quite easily again and kill us all real fast if he wanted to. It wasn't like we could stop him. He was really that fast. Message received. Because that's what it felt like. A message. Even more so later.

I'd felt a lot more confidence in Captain Knife Hand before this meeting. I'd seen him as a competent soldier and a no-holds-barred killer who would get us through this by any means possible. Whatever it took, he'd do it. I also had no doubt the command sergeant major had gone exciting places and killed interesting people in horrific ways more than anyone else in the detachment. But now... I wasn't sure about what I knew. Not about them. Not totally. Not like they were false idols and my phony personal security religion based on them had been exposed for the fake that it was. More... I was unsure about the thing in the briefing with us. McCluskey. Like there was a shark swimming nearby in the dark waters you found yourself in. You really didn't know where it was, but it was there all the same. Have fun.

You never think about that when you go swimming in the ocean. But that's where sharks are. That's where they live. The first time you do think about sharks swimming in the same water you're swimming in, it's hard to stop yourself from thinking about it forever after. You find yourself swimming a lot less once that picture gets into your personal hard drive.

McCluskey was a shark. And he was sitting right across the table from me. Swimming.

I guess we, or maybe just me, were hoping he was a friendly predator. Because he was definitely a shark of some kind, and we were in his ocean now. Even with all our Rangers and weapons and gear, this world was his. He'd been swimming in it for twenty years. Hence the dark armor, wicked sword, and vampire-enhanced skills.

What would *we* all look like in twenty years? If we survived.

"So... how do you... sustain yourself... if you need blood or plasma?" asked the chief, in his seat once more.

McCluskey was back in his seat too. Same easy-going helpless posture of hands between his leather-clad thighs. That was for show. He was trying to teach us. Or convince us. Or lie. To us. That he wasn't really a shark.

It's just that he couldn't help being one.

"Blood of my enemies," he murmured with a knowing smile. "Topped off on my way in. Now all I need is some sleep until dark. And then I can either stay and help you—if you'll let me—or I can slip back through the attacking force and link up with the team. Gather some useful allies and start hitting the enemy rear to relieve the pressure on your line. It's your call, fellas. What's your situation? Exactly."

He looked around at everyone and landed on the captain. Then, so fast maybe only I noticed, he flicked his eyes off toward the front of the aircraft where the Forge was busy cranking out more ammo for us to burn through tonight when the orc horde came back to finish the job.

And he'd also caught me noting that I'd caught him noting where the Forge was. His eyes flicked to the staff I'd been carrying since returning from the mission, a quick appraisal and then back to the audience before him.

"So..." began the chief again. "Daylight burns you but... you were out in it this morning when you came inside the wire. And there's the light still coming in through the rear cargo door and a few of these windows. How isn't this bothering you right now, Chief McCluskey?"

"Well," said the SEAL, running his hand through his thick curly hair. "Truth is... it's killing me. But you're gonna find out that, even though this world takes away your weapons, well, there's all kinds of fun prizes it gives you to make up for it. Magic being the number one, Chief. Real live magic. This…"

He pointed to the intertwined serpent hoop in one ear. The piece of jewelry that made him look like a pirate. To me at least.

"This here is a magic charm. It mitigates some of the more serious effects of daylight. My redundant backup protection system is this cloak. The elves of Charwood call it a Cloak of Darkness. Basically, with the hood up, it's midnight for me. Even in broad daylight. And this…" He tapped the scabbarded blade on the map-covered table. "… this is *Coldfire*. Took it off the Shadow King down in the Underworld beneath what we used to call the Italian Alps. Blade is the sharpest I've ever felt. You get cut with this, it doesn't heal, and it hurts like you wouldn't believe for a long time afterward. Like you're freezing and burning up all at once. It's a real party. Believe me."

He smiled, and it was then we could see the pronounced canines. Like he'd learned to hide them and then show them when needed. Now he was showing.

"But even with these tricks, I gotta stay out of the daylight. Sick as a dog when I'm in it. These just help me move around like I'm fighting off the worst flu ever. But come nighttime… hell, I'm ready to party, know what I mean, guys?"

He looked me right in the eye, no doubt wondering what in the hell a PFC was doing here in the CP. Why I was getting to listen in? What was my deal? That seemed to vex him for a moment. A look that said so crossed his face.

The captain declined the subtle invitation to lay out our disposition of forces to the SEAL. So that told me I knew the trust and love wasn't mutual on both sides so far.

That Captain Knife Hand was still a cagey animal. And I sensed that wasn't lost on the SEAL either.

"Grab some rest, Chief," said Captain Knife Hand. "Sergeant Major can get you settled somewhere that meets… your needs. We'll discuss what to do next later and then I'll let you know what we need from your element. We appreciate the cooperation."

The meeting broke up, and the sergeant major nodded at me to stick around while he took the SEAL off to a space between some stacked clamshells that would be dark enough, apparently.

I waited around outside the grounded plane for a few minutes and tried to wander away when the Deep State guy came up out of the quiet woods. He looked like he was coming from Sniper Hill. Or he'd been out along the line along the river's edge. He was looking inside the plane now, but not going in.

"What's going on in there, Private?" he snapped at me.

I shrugged. It's a special skill PFCs have. One day I'd join the E-4 mafia and learn all new powers of shamming. But right now I thought it best not to divulge what I'd heard. Best not to have anything to do with this guy. He was stupid. You could tell that from a long way off. He was smart stupid. Someone had made the mistake of treating him like he was special because of his big brain and right schools he'd gone to. And that had promptly gone right to his head. He actually did think he was better than everyone else around him. I'd seen a lot of that in my old life inside academia. Smart stupid people. Combined with a sense of certainty and ego, it made them very dangerous to everyone.

My E-3 shrug didn't deter him in the slightest. You could tell he didn't really see people whom he considered lesser than himself. They weren't there. He only saw the people above him, the ones he could suck up to for goods and prizes. Everyone else was just a thing to be used by him, for him, to advance *him*.

"Hey, PFC," he said earnestly, as if actually seeing me now, though he clearly didn't.

This is another skill those types possess. They're convinced they can relate to "commoners" like he perceived me to be. He turned back from trying to see what was going on inside the aircraft and faced me in the woods, putting on a friendly-buddy face. Maybe Captain Knife Hand had thrown him out before the meeting, citing the debrief as a military matter?

"That's a nice, uh… walking stick. How are the men?" asked Deep State faux-sincerely. No longer Deep State Volman. More… Comrade Buddy.

But seriously?

*How are the men?*

Who was he kidding? This lame attempt at concern was laughable. The *men*. Why not use *fellows*, or *mates*, or even *chums*. Each of those would have been as off-putting and out of place to a real soldier as the word choice he'd just employed. *The men*. I should know; I'd been masquerading as a soldier ever since I'd raised my right hand during enlistment. Someday, if I didn't get killed by an orc werewolf or troll dragon, if I kept doing Ranger stuff with the Rangers, I might become a real soldier. Or at least that's how I felt.

This guy never would.

"No idea, sir," I told him. "I'm just the linguist, and there's no one to talk to in any of the languages I speak. So, *Auf Wiedersehen.*"

That means *take a hike* in German.

He faked a laugh like he understood what I'd just said.

"That's the Army for you, huh, PFC?" he said with his mouth and not his eyes, like he was relating to common old me. His new working-class buddy comrade. Not really a statement. Not really a question. Nothing really. That was probably his skill. Managing to never say anything he could end up being hung out to dry for. You could tell he was pure political animal, and that was an alien thing in the military. I'm sure it existed somewhere. Higher up. And there was a kind of politics here for sure. But not this kind. Not so far in my training experience. And definitely not in the Ranger batt.

By his eyes I could tell he was done with me. I hadn't been recruited to inform and be on his "side." Plus, I couldn't do anything for him. I was just some extraneous piece of the Ranger company he had no idea what to do with. Useless to him and the power games he was no doubt up to. What was he gonna do, have the captain impeached? I had no street cred with the men for him to use. I watched the math in his eyes add up as he turned and walked away, barely throwing a goodbye over his shoulder as he went. He definitely looked like he was off to find more busy to body.

*Auf Wiedersehen* off a short pier, dude.

A few minutes later the sergeant major came off the cargo deck walking right past me and dragging me along in his wake once again as he muttered through gritted teeth, "C'mon, Talker. We got work to do. Now, son."

# CHAPTER TEN

THE sergeant major led me off through the woods to a little place out among the trees he'd set up for himself. Sort of his unofficial command post where the NCOs and none of the junior officers knew to find him. There was a tiny smoking fire and a blue camp percolator of coffee still sitting among the ashy orange coals.

This place was the opposite of the whole island.

"Coffee?" rumbled the senior-most NCO.

I gladly got out my canteen cup in giddy anticipation. You'll never need to ask me twice regarding the sacred brew. I'm an avowed coffee addict, though I tell people I'm merely just an enthusiast and pretend to accidentally "find" craft coffeehouses doing the latest pour-overs or whatever. That's all an act. Like an alcoholic who pretends they know something about wine. Truth is, I'll even hit a government vending machine like break room doughnuts left out three days too long if I'm desperate enough. I don't judge. Coffee is a dark mistress that must be served, and I'm not too proud about where I have to find it. I'd been ignoring a creeping terror that told me there was no more coffee in this world, and my thirty-six packets of instant and whatever else we'd brought along in the MREs was all that was left. Forever. That's real terror. Like waking up and realizing you didn't survive the plane crash and you're all in hell now.

So what I'm saying is, I'm not particular about where I find it. Especially not now.

We sat down on some rocks around the fire.

I watched as the command sergeant major listened to the sounds across the island. To his Rangers cutting down more trees for defenses. Chainsaws growling and screaming so as much work  got done as possible before nightfall. Then silence after the thin leafless giants collapsed with loud rustles and a final *whumph* into the dead grass.

"They'll be back tonight," observed the sergeant major as he blew on his coffee and held the tin cup close to his gray eyes, watching the silent woods and seeing the battle we'd find again there tonight.

He wasn't inviting my opinion on the matter. He was telling me what was going to happen. To be honest I'm not even sure I was part of the conversation. More than likely he was talking to himself. Steeling himself what was coming next. So I didn't say anything. Either because I didn't know whether what he was saying was true, or… and this is what I really suspected… I didn't want it to be true.

"All right, son," said the sergeant major, looking at me after scanning the work and positions he could see from his little campsite observation post. "Let's see the intel you pulled last night."

I produced the wizard's messenger bag. The spell book. The gruesome "ingredients," for lack of better words. The documents, and by documents I mean sheets of brittle parchment covered in strange scrawlings. The staff I'd been carrying around with me ever since we'd crossed through the forest and back over to our side of the river. Through the entire debrief with the SEAL McCluskey. I'd held on to it like I'd been ordered. When I told the sergeant major it was heavy, heavier than my rifle, he said I should put it down, but he didn't make any move to touch it himself. Instead he got out a Benchmade folding knife and began to probe the spell book. Opening the cover carefully with the blade. I laid the documents out too. We sat there for a long moment just looking at everything. Or rather, the command sergeant major looking at everything. Me just sitting there and trying to think up something meaningful to contribute. It was all pretty... crazy. Truth was, none of anything made sense. The writing inside the spell book wasn't recognizable. It looked to me more like a code based on strange symbols and what had to be numbers, though they defied my ability to give them values. Occasionally characters in Chinese would pop up, and these I knew. Earth, Wind, Water, and Fire. And then a fifth one that I didn't know, but which seemed to stand as a unifier, a combination of all of these essence characters. A quintessence, if you will.

None of this was of use, militarily, regarding our current situation. Situation Ranger Alamo as I'd taken to calling it in my head when I allowed myself a moment to think about just how deep we were into this. Given time—and a nice warm room with a fire like the library at any ivory tower university would have on a winter's day of research—I could probably unlock this stuff and translate. No. Not probably. I could. Definitely. I was just being modest. But I didn't have those things right now. No fire. No unlimited coffee. No ivory tower. No time.

We had something trying to kill us all from every quarter, and the ticking clock of nightfall hanging over us. That's all any of us had.

There were no plans, orders, command, and signal... nothing. Even the wizard's map was just a rough sketch, geographically speaking, of what the enemy had been sent to attack.

One of the loose pieces of parchment might have been a letter to someone. Just a guess. But there was definitely an official-looking seal at the bottom of that one. Black wax. A pitchfork and the letter T. Not like official as in government, but clearly someone with some kind of authority in this crazy messed-up world. But the body of the enigmatic letter was in code and there was no easy way to crack the text with daylight burning and another battle coming with the night.

Eventually, after a long quiet pause, the sergeant major told me to bag it all up and hold on to it.

"Oh," I said, remembering one last thing I'd forgotten to show him. "Guy had this ring... on... his finger..."

I dug around in my cargo pockets for it.

Then I found it.

And without thinking I slipped it on as I pulled it out, past some Carmex I carried in that pocket that had made everything waxy and slick.

"Uh... Talker," drawled the sergeant major slowly. In Texan. He stood. "Where'd you just go, son?"

"Uh... right here, Sergeant Major," I answered brightly. Y'know, like the guy trying to have a positive attitude before the doctor tells him the very bad test results he knows are coming.

I took the ring off my finger and held it out to the sergeant major for inspection.

The command sergeant major jumped back and swore.

"What the hell'd you just do, son?"

"I'm... not sure what you mean, Sergeant Major. I didn't do anything." I looked around. Everything seemed normal. The thin sunlight was getting down in the trees. The Rangers had started on another clump of spindly spruces over by the water with their chainsaw. It ripped and roared and began to cut down another tree.

"You just disappeared and reappeared, Talker. Either that or it's my old head injury from Kandahar."

"What?" I shrieked, my heart suddenly jumping off a cliff. I'm not sure if I actually did *shriek* like a frightened child. But I probably did. This was exactly the thing I was afraid of happening here. Disappearing. I hadn't visualized that *particular* fate, but I'd been sure something completely unexpected, and having to do with the unexplainable, supernatural stuff, bad, terrible, would happen to me despite my best efforts at self-preservation.

Then I remembered I hadn't addressed the senior NCO by his rank. "I mean... uh... Sergeant Major. I... what happened? Sergeant Major."

I stammered for a while until he stopped me.

"Talker. When you went fishing for that ring you just held out... you disappeared. I could hear you, and if I tried real hard, I could see you move a little. Or maybe it was just the light shifting. But it wasn't you. It was like that Schwarzenegger movie about the team down in South America. *Predator*. The alien that hunts 'em."

I hadn't seen that particular masterpiece. But I wasn't stupid. A cold sweat had broken out across my body despite the chill in the afternoon air. And... I knew what I had to do next. I took the ring in one hand and slipped it back on the finger I had unconsciously slipped it onto while trying to get it out of my cargo pocket in the first place.

The sergeant major gave a low whistle.

"You just did it again, Talker. You just disappeared, son. Well... I'll be a..."

"I'm still here, Sergeant Major." Then, *oh crud...* What if this was like the ring in the Frodo movies? I looked around. I didn't see a netherworld of spirits and wraith riders coming for me. Or a burning giant eye in the sky. Everything looked exactly the same as when I hadn't had the ring on.

I took it off and realized I'd been holding my breath. And that my heart was racing like a freight train.

The sergeant major held out his hand. I handed the ring over and he looked at the metal circle. Turning it over and over again as he studied it.

"So..." he began slowly. "This thing kinda acts like a cloaking device. But on a personal level." He spoke almost to himself like he was thinking about something. "I don't suppose it matters much now, but we had something similar to this in Delta. Not this simple. Not that good. But... given time... DARPA mighta cooked something like this up. I could see that."

He was still staring at it when he asked me, "Did you feel okay, using it, Talker?"

I didn't respond. I was still trying to differentiate between fear and well-being. My heart was racing, but I was pretty sure that was just fear.

"Did it mess with your head or anything, son?" he continued.

"Nah," I said, trying on Ranger Tough for a second and then remembering I was talking to the sergeant major. The command sergeant major of a Ranger batt. Yeah, I'd gained some kind of special inside confidence role, but best not to take that for granted. "Negative, Sergeant Major. Good to go."

He stared at the ring a moment longer, his weather-beaten face frozen like some statue as his eyes searched its surfaces and he studied the dull silver of its composition, musing to himself about something. He pushed the thing back to me.

"You hang on to this for now, son."

And that was that. I had a ring that made me invisible. Like Frodo, or one of the hobbits. The other one first. Frodo later. I hadn't read the books or seen the movies in a long time, but I knew colleagues in the Language Arts who spoke and communicated to one another in one of the made-up languages Tolkien had created. I knew a few words. I'd always meant to play their little game but...

"Boys over in the weapon section caught one last night," said the sergeant major, shifting to a new topic. He drained the last of the coffee in his canteen cup. "Need you to go over there and talk to it. See if you can understand it and find out what it knows about the enemy's disposition of forces."

He scanned the forest once more like it was full of invisible enemies just waiting for him to go kill them. Just looking at the sergeant major looking for enemies made me nervous.

"Uh... Sergeant Major," I began.

The sergeant major said nothing. I was used to, after the last year of introductory military training, waiting for permission from NCOs to speak to NCOs. I guess we were beyond all that now.

"I'm not really an interrogator, Sergeant Major," I said.

The old NCO put his empty tin cup down on a rock near the blue camp percolator and leaned in close.

"I know that, Talker. But... *John*. He taught you the basics. Gave you the course, right?"

How did he know that? I'd looked at my records jacket, and the two-week stay in a cheap Vegas motel had been designated by only an alphanumeric string of numbers and letters. Meaningless and indecipherable even to someone in personnel and admin. Somewhere in some government computer it meant something to someone who could read that particular language. Knew what it meant. But me, I had no clue. I knew what it stood for only because I knew what had happened during those two weeks in Vegas at a hotel no one would ever think twice about. Most military schools noted in records jackets on the appropriate line said something like *Basic Training. Eight Weeks Completed.* Or *Airborne Training. Three Weeks. Fort Benning. Completed.* The sergeant major had looked at my records jacket and had been able to determine what that mysterious string of numbers and letters had meant? And he knew...

"He still call himself John?" asked the sergeant major.

I nodded that he did.

"Good," drawled the sergeant major. "So... you know what to do. How to interrogate for intel."

I nodded again.

There was a lot of nodding going on. We'd entered that world. A world I'd been told about by *John*. He'd told me about that world one time in a conversation I thought was just a break between lessons. But later I realized it had been just another lesson. Sometimes, he'd told me, when you were talking about stuff that didn't openly get talked about, you ended up just nodding a lot. Using words that didn't seem to mean what they were supposed to mean, to stand in for the meanings of the dark words you needed to use to communicate valuable intel.

I'd had no idea, at the time, what I was being trained for, but apparently this kind of behavior was part of it. Intel stuff. I'd read a couple of spy novels, and I was pretty sure I was being groomed to either "run joes"—a John le Carré term—or be one. Very low-level spy stuff, I was sure of that. Observe and Report. Not James Bond, if that's what you're thinking.

I remember John and I were eating eggs at a diner one evening. South side of Vegas. No one else there in that cheap diner. I kept looking for the waitress to have some horrible scar around her throat where it had been slashed once, long ago. But she didn't.

John said, low in the quiet while some jazz instrumental version of the song "Goin' Out of My Head" played over the bad speakers, he said, "It's like this…" He put down his fork. "If the mob asks if you kill people, professionally, the way they ask you is, they say, *Do you paint houses?* Like that. That's how they ask you. And sometimes, if you ever do get asked to do some work, I'm not saying assassination, I'm just saying… to employ some of the skills I've taught you, then it will be requested indirectly using a code phrase, some of which I'll teach you. Because these are things that can't be reported. Can't be official. Can't be known. Understand? This is what you signed up for."

I sure, kinda, did. At the time. I thought I did.

I mean c'mon. I was in Vegas, in a diner, on the absolutely wrong side of town, getting an off-books intel course before being told to go who knew where and do who knew what. It was all very not real and very exciting at the same time. Probably because it wasn't real. And if you thought I had Area 51 and then ten thousand years in the future on my dance card then you're giving me way more credit than I deserve. I just thought I was headed off to some embassy in Germany where I was gonna pick locks on government file cabinets, which is what we'd spent most of our time on during the two weeks in Vegas in the cheap motel. The other stuff had been along the lines of *Oh-by-the-way-if-you-do-happen-to-need-to-interrogate-someone-here's-how-you-do-it*. Y'know... like that. Like I'd probably never need to actually do it.

Or maybe that's just what I told myself the whole time throughout those two weeks because there were some things being taught that... let's just say... required one to be morally flexible.

I nodded across the wisps of campfire smoke, and the sergeant major folded his large weathered hands together as we just sat there. Hands that had probably murdered people and left them out in deserted forests similar to my current surroundings. He stared into the fire and I couldn't tell if he was thinking or just watching the dying orange coals turn to gray as the afternoon moved into its decline.

I decided to change the subject.

"Hey, that State Department guy..."

The sergeant major's gray eyes came up fast. But nothing else in his tall and powerful body moved.

"He asked me how we were doing," I finished.

I waited for the sergeant major to react. He didn't. So I clarified.

"Used the word... *men*. As in *How are the men doing*. Know what I mean, Sergeant Major? Seemed... odd. Like he's up to something."

The sergeant major thought about that for a moment. His eyes seemed to see, and not see, the drifting smoke in the coals.

I drained the last of my coffee, indicating I wouldn't mind more if there was any.

"Lemme see your sidearm, Talker," rumbled the sergeant major abruptly.

*Okay*, I said to myself, wondering if I'd just committed some error that was about to get me buried in a shallow grave close by. I put my empty canteen cup down and drew my weapon, ejected the magazine, cleared the chamber, and then handed it over.

The sergeant major put my weapon aside on a rock and drew his own sidearm. It was the same as mine. M18. We'd all been issued M18s as our secondaries at the Fifty-One armories. He handed his over, and that was when I saw the difference between his and mine. His barrel was threaded. Mine wasn't.

John had covered a little bit of this. One day when we took a long drive out into the desert east of Vegas.

The sergeant major reached into his ruck and took out a wrapped bundle. Green cloth and then bubble wrap. He handed it across the fire to me.

"Clean him," muttered the senior NCO as he sat back. "Can't have that going forward."

I unwrapped the cloth knowing what I'd find. Knowing the sergeant major had understood exactly what I was saying about Volman. Even though I hadn't. Or I had. Maybe I'd just expected a different solution. A talking-to. Even a punch in the face.

Instead I was looking at a silencer.

"Back in the old days, Talker, we called it R&R. John probably used 'clean' like they do in the Agency. We'd say take a guy out to R&R. Some thought it meant Rest and Relax."

I'd really been waiting to pick some locks on file cabinets. I'd gotten really good at that. But I also knew the code word the sergeant major had just used and what it meant. I just never thought anyone would use it.

"R&R don't mean that, son. It meant Roughly Retire. Just so we're clear. Know what I mean?"

*Clean him.* That's code for assassinate. In Russian it's *ubiystvo*. In Korean it's *amsal*. In American it means kill him. R&R.

Silly me.

# CHAPTER ELEVEN

ON the way over to talk to the prisoner Kurtz's heavy weapons team had managed to capture, I ran into two Rangers from one of the rifle squads. One was the typical age of the average Ranger. Early twenties. Maximum rage and physical prowess intersected at around that point. Plus, youth could absorb the constant damage of Rangering. But the other was a man on the far side of middle age. Not typical for a line Ranger. And other than the command sergeant major and the captain, no one was even remotely that old. Not even the first sergeant. I'd never seen this guy around. No one with gray hair and hunched over, limping like an old man. Not at Fifty-One or here on the island.

They were sitting on opposite logs along the trail I'd been following out toward that area of the defenses. Like they'd been coming the other way and had stopped for a chat. But not to chat. The old guy looked like he was having trouble breathing.

I stopped to see if I could help.

"You guys all right?" I asked. "Anything I can do?"

The older one held up his hand before he spoke. His hand shook and the skin there was wrinkled and liver-spotted like he'd worked in the sun all his life and thought sunscreen was a conspiracy by the government to control our minds. He'd either ditched, or lost, his assault gloves.

Or any of the other kinds some of the Rangers preferred to use when sticking their hands into nasty places. Like I said, a lot of them liked a brand called Mechanix. I just had the issue gloves that came with the RLCS loadout. And there was probably never gonna be another store where I could buy the other kind ever again. So...

"He ain't doin' so good," said the other Ranger. He was carrying both of their MK18 rifles.

"What happened?" I asked.

"Most messed-up thing I ever saw," said the younger one. "Last night about zero-three-thirty we'd just been repositioned to support a machine-gun team. Bravo got hit hard earlier. So, we're in the LLC waiting to go forward, and this... I don't know what you'd call it, but this is what I'm callin' her... this *witch* is what she looked like, she just comes out of the darkness along our flank and points right at Sims there..."

Sims, the old man, began to cough, and his lungs gave their best performance of an actual death rattle.

"She's shriveled up and old and she's got a big crooked nose, nothing but a sack on," the other man continued. "But her eyes were like nothin' I ever seen before. Like looking into an ocean that ain't got no bottom to it... know what I mean?"

I did. And that creeped me out. But go on...

The one telling the story fumbles for some smokes he's got in one of his cargo pockets. He lights one and hands it to Sims. Rangers never smoke in the field. Only when they're drinking. It's always dip when they're operational. So these guys are pretty shook if they're breaking out the pack they brought along in hopes of finding a bar somewhere in the post-apocalyptic future.

Sims is hacking up a lung but he's gonna smoke anyway. Ranger gonna Ranger as they say. Personally, I don't think Sims needed a smoke so much as an iron lung. Or a full team of geriatric specialists at this point.

Sims takes the offered smoke and inhales weakly, coughing, forcible coughing like he's trying to hack up something that won't come unstuck. I'm pretty sure he's gonna die right on the spot there at the worst of the coughing fit. But he doesn't.

I notice the other Ranger holding a smoke out for me.

I take it. Why not try to fit in, I tell myself. I quit two years before I joined the Army. But hey... it's like ridin' a bike and all. Or falling off one, as they say.

"Ain't had one since Honduras and that was the real deal down there," said the one handing out smokes. I notice his hands are trembling a little too. The forest around us is all quiet. I'm guessing some of the Rangers are sleeping in shifts while they can catch it. It's been two nights now without sleep. Three is the accepted Ranger maximum.

The cigarette calms down Sims's fit, but he just keeps his weathered old face toward the ground. After a moment he takes off his bucket and I can see his hair hasn't just gone gray. It's stark white. Pure bone-white. Like he saw a ghost.

"I'm Sims and this is Matthews," the old man tells me, and we just sit there smoking in the quiet woods. Occasionally Sims coughs softly. Then he mumbles, "I'm dyin', man."

"So this... lady...?" I prompt. 'Cause I'm curious. And afraid. And I've found knowledge is a good cure for fear. I always restrain myself from asking a survivor or loved one about the symptoms someone they knew had before they died. Even I know that's selfish. As in self-interested. I don't ask. But I gotta admit it here... I wanna know.

"Ain't no lady," mumbles Matthews. "Was a witch fer sure. I'm from Appalachia. I heard enough about 'em down in them hollers ya ain't supposed to go to, to know one is right in front of me and all. Reyes was right. Confirmed. Except he called her a *brujita*. That's Rican for witch, y'know?"

By *Rican* I assumed he meant Puerto Rican Spanish. *Brujita* I knew. Surprise. I speak Spanish too. That one was easy. Italian, French, and Spanish all unlock each other, more or less.

*Bruja*. Witch or sorceress.

Old Man Sims picks up the story from there. "She comes outta the darkness," he wheezes. "One minute she ain't there and we got NVGs on and everything. Next minute she just appears out of the dark and points right at me..."

Sims indicates himself by stabbing his bent and bony finger into his plate carrier.

"I open up on her, but she's gone in the next second." He coughs. "I'm firing into nothing but smoke. And..."

He takes a long drag on his cigarette and mumbles something I can't hear. Like maybe he was just swearing.

"What was that?" I ask.

Sims looks up at me sharp and angry.

"I said... I can still hear her laughin'. Thought it was out across the forest and over the outgoing fire last night, but... it's still there in my mind, man. I can hear her laughin' like she's up in the attic of my head. In some old rocking chair. Just slow-rockin' and laughin' at me. This is really jacked up. I didn't enlist for this, man. One more and

I was gonna get out and go to Cali and maybe become an actor or somethin'. That's…"

He starts coughing again.

"That's what I say," he finishes once the fit is done.

The forest is silent, and some crow flaps off moving from one tree to another. Its wings make a leathery *hush* and when it lands in a tree nearby it just watches us like it knows what's going to happen and there's nothing we can do about it.

Okay. I officially have the creeps.

Sims looks at me, not angry this time, but like he's asking me to believe him. To understand. To say something like, *Oh yeah. That's happened to me, man. That's nothing. It'll clear up.*

The emotional equivalent of when the doctor tells you to just put some cream on it. Nothing to worry about. It'll clear up.

That's what Sims needs to hear right now.

But I'm just sitting there with my half-smoked cigarette. Listening. And thinking about witches who can curse you and make you old. Just like that. That's gonna really cut down my chances with the cute co-pilot. Getting turned into an old man and all.

"She said…" coughs Sims, who flicks the butt of his cigarette off into the wet forest. "*Para… malda City* or something. Then… *Hilly po-yahss*. And then, all of a sudden, I felt like I got the flu and had a heart attack all at once."

Matthews chimes in. "We didn't see what happened until first light. When Kurtz made us stand watch until his guys got more ammo. That's when we could see that Sims got turned into an old dude. So now I'm takin' him back to the chief for a look. What do you think's wrong with him? Ya think they got somethin' besides Motrin for somethin' like this? I mean, this is messed up, man. He's only twenty-two!"

Sims starts to hack up a lung.

Both of them look at me.

Unlike them, I know what the old woman said. *Para... malda City or something. Then... Hilly po-yahss.*

*Para maldecirte, gilipollas.*

*Curse you, bastard.*

# CHAPTER TWELVE

I didn't tell them what it meant. What the witch had said. The *brujita*, another Ranger had called her. *Little witch.* I just stood there in the quiet forest and considered the implications while we finished our smokes.

Sims the old man and Matthews the young one didn't need to know. Didn't need that on their plate along with the double helping of Ranger Alamo we just got served. What was coming at us next, by all indications, and even just by the feel of the air, was going to be a junkyard dog fight for our lives in the night hours ahead. They didn't need to think about curses and witches that turned into smoke when it came time for round three.

Another helping.

I told them Chief Rapp probably had a shot that would make it better. That didn't make them happy. Rangers felt that every time someone had to get a shot it was probably pretty bad. I could see the look in their eyes. It verged on superstitious paranoia. I added that maybe just a drip would straighten Sims out, and they seemed to grab onto that like it was a piece of drifting debris in the river of fear they were currently in.

For me, the details bore more significance than what was just on the surface. First off… Spanish. A witch, human-like and mixed in and supporting the attacks of these orc monsters as assault infantry, was using Spanish. And Spanish from Spain, not Latin or South America. She didn't use *bastardo*, which was far more common.

She'd used *gilipollas*.

The Spanish from Spain version of the word *bastard*.

Combine this with the HVT sorcerer speaking some kind of Hui dialect, and things were starting to get interesting for my particular military occupational specialty. Languages. The Chinese characters on the recovered documents and tattoos on his severed head also stood out.

Yeah, I get it, we were all about to get our throats cut here at Ranger Alamo, but still, the language thing was fascinating. To me at least. Probably not to Captain Knife Hand or the command sergeant major. Or the rest of the Rangers.

But me... I was practically riveted. Pins and needles.

Maybe PFC Kennedy would appreciate the nuances...

Stepping back now to view the larger picture as I was doing, making my way once more toward Sergeant Kurtz and the heavy weapons squad, the really exciting part about all this was there might be something more for me to do here ten thousand years later than we'd intended. A way for me to be of use in this waking nightmare of a fantasy world that was out to kill us as fast as it could. Until this moment I'd wondered if maybe we'd gone some other place not our own. If the languages here were so different that all my available ones were made useless. No problem, I could learn a new one. It's all just code and there are tricks. And that was exciting in its own way. But...

"Talker," Sergeant Kurtz barked. Like my acquired tag was a slur reserved for the unclean who were not Ranger or even Airborne. To be used on the great unwashed of Leg Infantry.

"Yes, Sergeant!" I replied as fast as I could jerk myself out of my reverie about how I might possibly spend the rest of my life here in the future. I have to admit, I was pretty excited about being useful.

"He's down there in the gully!" shouted the sergeant before turning back to his work at the firing pit. They were dragging trees and deadfall across their position to improve it in the time that remained to them. "Tell Tanner to stay with you and don't get too close," he barked over his shoulder. And finally, "Thing's got a set o' teeth that'd probably take a chunk out of someone. I'm telling you..." He turned back to face me and pointed his own version of the knife hand at me. I guess he was practicing at one day being as matchless a killer as the captain. "He's dangerous, Talker. Watch out. You been warned."

That sobered me a bit.

I went off toward the gully behind the squad's machine-gun pit. It was nothing more than a dry portion of the riverbed that had been cut off from the river at some point in the past. It was filled with loose sand and rock, and a giant hunk of dead wood lay in the middle of the open space. Tied to that hunk of tree, with paracord and then zip ties and some chain... was a goblin.

Just like the ones we'd seen the night before.

Smaller than the orcs. Green-gray skin. Large ears. Eyes like half-moons. Claws opening and closing and scrabbling about as I approached. Worrying one another. This one didn't have the loincloth and spear the others had. This one wore a sort of crude armor. A leather cuirass. A tattered kilt. Over-large boots. He eyed me fearfully as I came down into his space.

Tanner, who'd been leaning against the embankment a little farther down the gully, weapon ready, moved on an intercept course to cut me off before I got too close.

"He's..." began the Ranger private.

I held up a hand. "I know... dangerous. Kurtz shouted at me."

Tanner stood back and watched the little thing try to hop and move about defensively as we gathered near it. It couldn't have been more than five feet tall. If.

I said hi. In Spanish at that.

The thing cocked its head and looked at me quizzically. But it was clear it didn't understand even though I repeated this five or six times.

Then I tried Chinese several times. I was working with the languages we'd encountered so far. I figured that was a good starting point.

Tanner looked at me like I was a lunatic, and frankly, for a moment, I felt like one standing there and trying to talk to...

Just embrace it, I told myself.

... to a... goblin.

It was either that or *hairless little malevolent monkey*.

I attempted a few other languages, but it wasn't until I tried some phrases in Turkic that I got a recognition response from the thing.

The positive response came when I asked it, "What's your name?" I said it fast because I was just trying out a bunch of stuff and the thing wasn't responding to anything. But when I asked it that, when I asked it what its name was, in Turkic—*Isminiz ne?*—it answered without guile and seemed just as surprised as I was.

Apparently, its name was Jabba. And using some German, some Turkic, some Arabic, and a language I just was beginning to discover as... well, Jabba's description for it was *Orc War Talk*... we were able to have us a big old conversation.

# CHAPTER THIRTEEN

ROUGHLY translated, here's what was said between the little goblin and me. At first it was slow going, but things picked up fast once he understood I could understand him and what was being said, and once I let him try one of the precious Cokes I'd smuggled on the flight. I had a case of thirty-two minis in the bottom of my duffel. After speaking with the sergeant major, I'd picked up three to bring to the interrogation.

John whose real name wasn't John had told me this simple technique often worked better than expected and should be used before the rubber hoses and sleep deprivation fun got started.

Do goblins even sleep?

"What's your name?" I ask it. Him.

Strange look but dawning realization. The thing croaks more than it speaks, like it's part frog somehow.

"Me Jabba. Me Jabba. Me Jabba. You know Jabba. Me Jabba," he replies. Repeatedly.

I'm writing this down verbatim. Because of the record, and it's kind of funny.

"Your name is Jabba," I say.

"Me Jabba. Me Jabba. Me Jabba. You know Jabba. Me Jabba. Jabba is me."

It was at this point I was really hoping it knew something more than *Me Jabba* and permutations thereof. I paused. The sergeant major said interrogate and find out what it knows. I received a short course in interrogating at a cruddy motel in East Vegas ten thousand years ago… so I'm totally qualified for this. Monster interrogation.

Not monsters.

Embrace the fantasy, I had to remind myself. Embrace it or you're all gonna die at Ranger Alamo, and apparently there're things you can do here in this forgotten ruin of a future so start doing them. Start being useful. Languages. You do languages, and languages are nothing more than the coded exchange of information. So do that. Get some useful information from this thing. Start talking, Talker. Start helping.

"Why you…" I began. I stumbled here when I discovered he didn't entirely understand the language we'd started off in. Through trial and error, I fell into some German and Arabic to complete the communication. "Attack me. Us."

"Why you attack us, Jabba?" ended up being a mix of three languages.

The goblin looked genuinely hurt when we finally got a clear translation. Or maybe like he wanted me to think he was genuinely hurt by what I'd just asked. I had no grounding in goblin body language to operate from. But I had the feeling he was playing me a little.

As best he could, he pawed at the ground with his claws and mewled like a sick cat. Humbling himself by getting his head lower than his butt. I assumed it was humbling. I'd seen something similar in a nature documentary once.

"Why you attack island, Jabba?" I asked.

Jabba nodded energetically all of a sudden.

"Attacka…"

Okay. His word usage wasn't academically perfect. Far from it. And for purposes of the translation I'm adding the pidgin patois to approximate how he spoke in other languages. C'mon, people, these things are important. Or at least they're important to me.

And yeah, I know: who am I to criticize how this goblin spoke its own language? I was the foreigner here—that doesn't even begin to describe it—patching together bits and pieces of dead languages, using ten-thousand-year-old pronunciations. My *academically perfect* was Jabba's *pigeon patois* and vice versa. But this is how he sounded to me, and I'm sure it's how I sounded to him.

"Attacka eye-land cuza big orc from Guzzin Hazadi say so," babbled the little goblin. "He says… Jabba, all Jabba kind… sneaky sneak on eye-land. Cuttah throats and make fire to burn you. So no attacka… you. See… attacka eye-land," finished the little fiend all wide-eyed and innocent.

They hadn't attacked me personally was what he was saying. They had attacked "eye-land."

Apparently this was a serious point of distinction for him. We went round and round about this and I got kind of angry because he made no sense. If the orders from "big orc" from Guzzim Hazadi, which seemed to be some kind of uber-orc tribe, had told them to slit throats, then how did you slit an "eye-land's" throat?

Jabba shrugged his bony shoulders at this logic and just played dumb for a while. And that made me even angrier.

Then all of a sudden I remembered I was arguing with a goblin who even by his own accounting seemed to be some kind of low-grade idiot in the hierarchy of monsters of this world. That's when I pulled out my Cokes and showed them to Jabba. I gave one to Tanner and kept one for myself, and we each opened a can and drank right in front of him. Of course Tanner didn't spit out his dip first because he was a Ranger and that's what they do. I hadn't acquired that habit. Yet. And I wasn't looking forward to it. But if that was what it took to go to Ranger School, and yeah I wanted that tab, then I was going learn to dip.

I like to collect achievements and skills.

That should be obvious by now.

Jabba watched our every movement. I got the impression that he thought what we were doing—opening a soft drink can and drinking from it—was the most amazing thing anyone had ever done. He tried to jump up and down, but he was still tied to the giant piece of driftwood that must've weighed a couple thousand pounds.

"Do it again," he croaked in low German.

I took another sip.

And then he barked and laughed, and that was a hideous sight to behold.

I opened the third can and placed it in front of him. As I got close, he shied away.

"Be careful, man," Tanner warned.

"I am." I placed the Coke on the ground and backed away.

Jabba eyed the can suspiciously and tried to circle it as much as his restraints would allow. Every time he sniffed at it, we took a long slow drink to make sure he knew it was safe. Finally he got down on all fours. His armor, for all its ragged condition, didn't make a sound. I was pretty sure he was some kind of infiltrator. Or his kind were. There was no way they were going to do what the bigger, more ferocious orcs were doing out there. Charging wave after wave into the solid walls of gunfire and mortar barrages. But somehow his little crew had slipped in during the chaos and had gotten close enough to the pits for him to get captured.

I needed to ask about his weapons and how he was captured. But now was not the time.

Jabba sniffed the can and then, quick as a snake, he swiped it up with one claw and downed all of it in a go. His thin neck worked and a massive Adam's apple bobbed up and down, gulping the soda quickly. Then a slithery long tongue appeared and swept up the bits that had managed to splash across his face.

His expression was caution for a moment. He was looking upward but not really looking *at* anything. More… waiting for something to happen. Then Jabba belched… and that's an understatement.

It wasn't so much a belch as it was the roar of a small and ferocious predator from the Pleistocene era.

The goblin croak-laughed and again tried to jump up and down, straining at the cords he had been secured with. He laughed manically and tried to bust the zip ties, like the soda had given him some incredible surge of strength and good vibes.

"Is it possible?" I asked Tanner as we watched the thing struggle. "To break the ties?"

"Nah," said the Ranger, watching the little thing jump and shake. I noted that he flipped the selector on his MK18 off of safe.

Then Jabba busted the tie around his wrists and waved both knobby arms wildly about, claws flexing, opening and closing on nothing in some sort of weird goblin triumph.

Jabba was screaming about being the Moon God. In Arabic.

Tanner had his MK18 pointed at the creature now that it was getting erratic and dangerous. When Jabba came to his senses a few minutes later and saw the weapon, he threw up his hands as if to plead sudden surrender.

He indicated, through several languages spoken a mile a minute, that he'd never felt so alive. And could he now please have more of... what was the wizard's potion called? Jabba's word for wizard was *sahir*. From Arabic.

"More potion. Jabba wanna more potion. Potion! Potion! Potion! Jabba moon god now!"

"I don't think givin' him a soda was such a hot idea, Talker," remarked Tanner, following the dancing goblin through his MK18's sight.

I had no doubt that if the wild Jabba managed to break one more zip tie, Tanner was going to splatter his little goblin brains all over the river rocks.

"Maybe," I said to Tanner, keeping my eyes on Jabba. "Or maybe... Jabba. Jabba! Jabba! Jabba want more potion?"

What happened next was not seemly. Basically, Jabba wheedled and pleaded and begged like a dog for what he called "more moon god potion!"

I indicated he could have more moon god potion if he'd settle down and tell me what I wanted to know.

He agreed and started telling me before I even asked any of the important questions. Like *How many of you are there? Who are your leaders?* And *When will you attack next?*

How many?

"Bigga-more than all the stars!"

Who were the leaders?

"Skorum leader of gob people. Azar leader of orcs. Many other and poooooor thirsty Jabba not know the witch people or the Trollen and all the others of Crow who come-uh now to take and kill Potion Giver. More potion now, please. Jabba moon god want! Jabba moon god need!"

When would they attack next?

"Night blanket comes then we come for you again. Killah all. Killah ye. Jabba sorry. Moon god want more potion before you die." Then it caterwauled and collapsed into a dispirited lump that was just pathetic.

I thought about this and swirled the last of my can of soda. Jabba watched this with one open eye like any junkie watches the last of the dope being passed out, cooked or cut, made ready to take and disappear. His open eye was large and hungry.

Sergeant Kurtz had come over the hill and stared down into the gully to see what was going on a few minutes earlier when Jabba had been in the full throes of his first encounter with a corporate soft drink. I wondered if the Forge, which we had been told could make anything, could gin up more Coca-Cola for interrogation purposes.

It was afternoon now and the dim sunlight was heading west through thin and skeletal trees. A mournful bird called out and I could hear the river on both sides of the island.

*Night blanket comes then we come for you again. Killah all. Killah ye.*

How long could the Rangers hold out? Jabba said they were *as many as the stars* and who knew what that meant. Was that an accurate count, or just tribal hyperbole? Bronze Age propaganda.

And what were we holding out for? Who was going to come rescue us? There were no other known detachments to assist. No air cav for support. No artillery to call in. No rear to pull back to. We were five days into this and two days into a battle that didn't show any signs of being over soon. Ammunition requirements were soon going to outpace what the Forge and our reserves could keep up with. What then? Sharpen our entrenching tools and keep your tomahawk ready.

The Rangers lived for that.

But did they really?

I was actually afraid we were going to find out soon if that was indeed the case if we didn't find some way out of this relentless attack from all sides.

"How long, Jabba? How long do they attack? What goblin and orc and witch and troll come for?" I asked.

*And how long can Ranger Alamo hold out?* Which I didn't ask but couldn't stop thinking about.

Jabba just smiled slyly and croak-whispered the answer.

"Triton say *never never never never never* stop. Triton say. So... is," whispered Jabba.

# CHAPTER FOURTEEN

I hustled back from the interrogation through the deepening gloom of late afternoon. The air on the island surrounded by the river was tense and quiet. Not many Rangers were moving around as the day finished up and we headed into what would probably be a long, violent night.

I was bothered.

Something the little goblin called Jabba had said was bothering me like an itch that couldn't quite be scratched, and believe me, I was the first to admit that what was bothering me sounded stupid. Real stupid.

But let's just say evidence and reason were insisting that I needed to start playing by PFC Kennedy's game's rules and fully embrace the fantasy. And try to scratch the itch. There were goblins and orcs, a giant, magic. If those were the rules... then it was time to learn more about them.

It was less than an hour from full dark when I made it back to the plane. Inside the aircraft they'd already switched over to tactical operations red lighting, and I found the command sergeant major before I should have done what I first needed to do just to make sure what I was about to say wasn't as completely stupid as it sounded to me. Because it probably was. But he wouldn't let me speak until we'd moved away from the plane and stood under the outboard engine on the right side of the grounded C-17. Back in the quiet of the forest and field on that small river-locked island. The gloaming coming on out there to the east. Blue fading to purple. The air getting colder. A chill. Breath turning to steam as we spoke.

"What'd you find out, Talker?" asked the sergeant major once we were out of earshot of everyone else.

I relayed Jabba's conversation and stuck to the intel John had taught me to identify and disseminate. Even then, as I think about it now, there wasn't much when I laid it all out. They, this horde of darkness, were coming for us. There were a lot of them. They were never gonna stop.

No real surprises or game-changers.

I'd left Jabba secured and had hustled back before Sergeant Kurtz could find something for me to do. Like police spent brass and build IEDs out of leftover MRE utensils. Some last-minute make-work project that might buy us a few more seconds before all our throats got cut by dirty knives wielded by green scrabbling claws.

By monsters in the dark.

"There's something else, Sergeant Major," I said, interrupting my own report.

The sergeant major asked me to clarify.

I stopped myself from saying, "This sounds dumb, Sergeant Major." I decided to own my hunch. A gut feeling had started during the debrief with the SEAL Chief McCluskey. And when I got a vague confirm out of something the little goblin dropped near the end of the interrogation, that gut feeling became a hunch that wouldn't stop itching.

Trust me, it was stupid. But you know how when you read novels and some character gets a hint about who the real villain is in the story or what the big twist is gonna be and the writer was hoping it was vague enough that you would miss it, but you, the reader, you spot it from a million miles off and the rest of the book is just flat-out ruined and you hate the characters because they're all stupid for not spotting the obvious dangling plot hook even though it's not their fault because the writer had to make them practically blind not to see it…

You know how that is? This felt like that.

So there I was cutting to the chase and acting on the not-so-vague implication itching the back of my brain. I was telling the sergeant major what my hunch was. Who it was. If I was wrong, then I was a bigger dork than PFC Kennedy. And it was the slit trench latrine pit for me. Probably forever.

"You know how we both had a… bad… if not strange feeling about the SEAL… McCluskey, Sergeant Major?"

The sergeant major scanned the darkening forest and then looked back at me, merely nodding once to make it clear he understood what I was saying. Where I was going.

We were back to nodding again.

"Okay," I continued. "In the prisoner's debrief he mentioned only one named figure. Identified their commander, as far as I can tell. What we're facing seems to be a joint effort by different entities to hit us. Why? No idea there, Sergeant Major. It was above his pay grade, so to speak. But the name the subject used during the interrogation was 'King Triton.'"

I actually used air quotes and it was at that moment I felt that *yes, what I was saying was indeed pretty stupid.* But sounding stupid had never stopped me before now. Ask any of the girls I've asked out.

"Okay…" I took a deep breath so I could explain Greek and Roman mythology to the command sergeant major and thereby indicate that Chief McCluskey had indeed gone native and turned himself into a warlord probably masquerading as King Triton. My stupid hunch. I know. Here goes…

"McCluskey's a SEAL, son," interrupted the sergeant major just as I began. "If a SEAL was gonna call himself something I could see Triton being one those nutjobs would go right for." His voice was low and confidential, and he cast his gray eyes about the silent clearing at the edge of the field we'd barely made our landing on. "Follow me."

I did.

I knew it was serious when the sergeant major drew his sidearm as we boarded the rear ramp, passing the two SAW gunners assigned to protect the plane. "Follow me, boys," he growled through gritted teeth at both gunners. It was clear he was in a mood to bring some hate.

We were heading right to the clamshell nest the sergeant major had made for the chief to wait out the daylight due to his self-confessed state of vampirism. I wondered at that point if I should draw my M-18, but what with the two gunners and all, I felt my contribution to the shooting about to ensue would either be superfluous, or not enough if it was just me left.

Surprise, surprise—we found the clamshell nest empty with McCluskey and all his gear gone. Horse missing out in the woods. No one had seen him go.

A few minutes later we'd find out only one of the fighting positions had seen him crossing the river upstream of them just as the sun went down through the trees in the west. Twilight coming on.

Outside it was dark now. The air was getting cold. And the island and the forest were dead silent. No drums. Not even the smell of smoke from out there in the woods.

But you could feel something coming. Feel the length of the long night already stretching out into a never-seeing-the-sun-rise-again moment.

You could feel that they were coming now. Coming for us. "King Triton" was ordering his forces into battle, marshaling and telling them where to hit us exactly. A dark man on a dark horse, riding here and there in the shadows of the night out there to make sure all was as he wanted now that he knew what he needed to know.

Now that he had us right where he wanted us.

# CHAPTER FIFTEEN

I was ordered to the meeting that took place in the hour after we'd discovered Chief McCluskey had taken himself off outside the wire. The sergeant major and the platoon leaders got a change of mission from Captain Knife Hand thirty minutes later. Then I was sent down to the river to find out exactly what happened when the SEAL rode his horse across the water.

There wasn't much to find out. The rifle squad, still improving their fighting positions and working on their MREs, told me Chief McCluskey just walked his black horse down to the river's edge, crossed over, and disappeared into the gloom under the trees over there.

When I got back to the C-17 to report this, I was then tasked with standing by and waiting to see just where I'd be needed tonight. For a while I listened in on the general murmur inside the tactical operations center of the command post and I began to understand what the new plan of action would be to meet tonight's threat. The sergeant major and the captain, with Chief Rapp listening in and commenting where he felt he could contribute, didn't trust Chief McCluskey in the slightest. None of them did. They hadn't liked him, and they'd picked up on everything I'd noticed too. Though their critical assessments were probably much more insightful than, "*But Sergeant Major, he didn't use your proper rank.*"

The general consensus was that most likely the naval warfare special operator was somehow compromised. Or he'd just gone crazy. It was noted by Chief Rapp that McCluskey had been specifically non-forthcoming with regard to useful details from a tactical assessment side of things. He'd obviously been on the other side of the wire and had passed through enemy-held territory. Why then no disposition of forces or plan to disrupt enemy operations? Also, what happened to the rest of his team? What happened to their Forge on their C-17, which was, according to the Forge technician, Josh Penderly, specifically hardened against the nano-plague here in the future? Unlike all modern technology—weapons, smartphones, and Ninja blenders—it should still be operational. Why, then, was McCluskey geared up like a Bronze Age warlord?

That was someone else's assessment, by the way. The *Bronze Age* part. Mine would have put his tech cap at somewhere around late Dark Ages, not Medieval just yet. But *tomato tomah-to.*

They'd also noted that McCluskey had been very interested, without being conspicuously overly interested, in the Forge's exact location aboard our grounded aircraft. Long story short, he'd left a pretty bad vibe in everyone's *chi* and no one much trusted him. Given time… maybe the command team could have developed faith in him. But instead, in the face of an imminent enemy attack he'd left the defenses and moved right back into enemy territory. Therefore it was agreed he was most likely working with the enemy currently harassing us for reasons unknown.

"He's a bad guy now and is to be treated as such," saith Captain Knife Hand.

So, it has been spoken, so will the Rangers snuffeth on sight. This was the safest route forward and it was just considered by all a bonus that he was a SEAL.

When dark came, the captain went forward to the southernmost fighting positions along the island's edge. This was where the command team was expecting us to be hit tonight. It was the last direction the enemy had left that they had not come at us from. The first night had been the probes along the eastern side. Last night a full-scale assault from the west. The northern tip of the island, just beneath the watchful gaze of what we were calling Sniper Hill, was guarded by a fork in the river where the water was swift, dark, and deep. The enemy couldn't cross effectively from the other side to there. Plus, Sniper Hill was too steep to easily ascend from the river's edge. Or from any other direction for that matter. We'd had to cut trenches into it to make a path to the top to carry gear and ammo up there.

With the platoon leaders, platoon sergeants, and squad leaders in attendance and me somewhere in the back, the captain laid out our new battle plan just before he left.

The command sergeant major would take the CP. The two civilians, Volman and the Baroness—the latter of whom just watched everything and now and then shook her head with a bewildered smile before returning to her work on her notebook—along with Forge Tech Penderly, the flight crew, and the two SAW gunners, were tasked with CP security around the aircraft. And me. But I was going to be used as a runner in case comm went down for any more unexplained reasons. PFC Kennedy had been relieved from latrine pit construction and was sent off to fill one of the KIA slots in the line rifle squads.

Volman objected to all this and indicated he would feel much more comfortable if a general vote by all "survivors" could be taken in order that "a Leadership Steering Committee might be formed" to navigate this current crisis.

His words.

The sergeant major, upon hearing this from Deep State Volman, looked utterly blank, allowing the bureaucratic buffoon to actually stop the meeting and hector Captain Knife Hand for a few minutes in front of everyone as the op order was being given. I was pretty sure the blank look was the sergeant major's murder face. Blank. Nothing personal. He was just going to murder you as soon as possible.

Then I remembered he already had.

Rather, he'd ordered me to do it. I was supposed to murder Deep State Volman with the sergeant major's sidearm and silencer. *Retire. Clean.* Call it what you want. I felt for the silencer in my cargo pocket, because I'm super cool like that, just to make sure it was still there, and when I looked up, the sergeant major was staring right at me as Volman continued to run his mouth on and on about how the vote he wanted taken should be conducted and who should tally the results so that a new government could be formed here on the island.

He felt that bloating enemy corpses floating in the river were a big problem and a clear indicator that things were going badly.

The captain stopped him suddenly and said, "That won't be happening right now, Mr. Volman. We're fighting tonight. I suggest you find a way to make yourself useful with the chief and the medics. There will be wounded." Then the captain continued on with the plan.

That shut Volman up. He turned to his iPhone and started furiously tapping in notes. No doubt preparing some kind of report that would indict everyone who disagreed with him when "the government" was formed. I had no idea who he'd give his secret report to. Nor did anyone else. But he seemed confident that almighty bureaucratic order would soon be restored, and that Captain Knife Hand would be hung from the nearest tree in the judicial aftermath.

Some people want to watch the world burn. That's true. Others want to organize a committee to watch the world burn—and to make sure everyone goes up in flames right along with it.

When the meeting was over, Deep State Volman made a big show of sweeping his super-expensive Sharper Image messenger bag up and rushing off to something important. Instead of offering assistance to Chief Rapp as had been suggested. I wondered exactly what he imagined was an "important" place to be. Because this was it. The cargo deck of the grounded C-17 was the only place of importance. The tactical operations heart of the command post that would be the center of a fight for our lives tonight. The rest of the island was fighting positions and Rangers with murder in their hearts.

He'd be real stupid to go and try his *Hey, let's all overthrow the captain, guys* act out there on the line. No one was that stupid.

But then I remembered he seemed stupid enough to try.

Now would probably have been a good time to *retire* or *clean* him. But when I got outside the C-17, he was gone, off into the forest dark. I stood there for a long moment, alone in the cold and the deepening twilight. Knowing I should hear some soft little night bird calling out, trying its first song of the night. But I heard nothing. And somehow, that made what we were about to face in the coming hours even more ominous.

There were three body bags laid out a short distance from the aircraft and I found myself just staring at them as night covered the island and the drums began to roll and chant to one another across the river. Deep and way off in the forest on the other side. They were coming for us now.

I watched as the flight crew came out and sent their humming little drone up into the sky a short while later. Then it was quiet and I thought about not dying tonight as I watched the dark motionless shapes in the body bags over there. Out of the way. Done with the fight. But not forgotten.

# CHAPTER SIXTEEN

THE battle we'd fight that night would be a retrograde. The Rangers were tired of being where they were supposed to be and just taking it from the enemy. The swarming orcs and other messed-up beasts and monsters that made up the OPFOR hitting us whenever, and wherever, they wanted.

OPFOR. Opposing Force.

As Captain Knife Hand said, that wasn't the Ranger way. If Chief McCluskey had gone over to the other side, and again we had no idea what that side was exactly, other than that they'd just shown up and decided to relentlessly attack our positions every night, then chances were they were here for something specific. And the only thing specific they could possibly be after was me and my vast knowledge of languages. Obviously. I was an incredible treasure trove of most likely dead languages. C'mon... what's not to covet?

Just kidding.

Had to be the Forge. McCluskey and whatever cabal he'd established here in the fantastical future knew the value of a Perpetual Taco Machine that could churn out endless amounts of explosives, weapons, and tech. It had templates for everything. I'd even asked Penderly if it could make a nuke.

He'd just nodded, not looking very happy about it.

So the captain had decided to let the enemy horde pay the heavy price of getting onto the island. We'd even let them actually take the C-17 close to dawn. The Rangers would cede ground grudgingly, falling back by squads to pre-established phase lines, setting off claymores and other explosive devices dreamed up by the Ranger master breachers in the face of the hordes. Indirect fire support from the mortars would make the dark army pay a dear price just to get close. The Rangers would then turtle around Sniper Hill and detonate body bags filled with chlorine gas the Forge had cooked up. With the enemy having only one avenue of approach to assault from the south, and the gas... and then add in all Ranger elements firing into the kill zone at the base of the hill, overwhelming firepower concentrated in a tight space... well, it was hoped, by Captain Knife Hand, that the enemy would be severely weakened. There were a whole bunch of other dirty tricks we could get up to, but time was of the essence and the Forge didn't crank stuff out particularly fast. Filling the gas bags had been a tricky operation for a group of Rangers in MOPP gear already.

The issue of night attacks, or the enemy's sole usage of them, would also come into play. Maybe the orcs were only good at night fighting. Maybe, like bats, they were also blind during the day. Or weakened somehow, like the vampire McCluskey. Twice now they'd withdrawn in the predawn hours, ceasing their attacks. If we forced them to commit to holding the objective, the Forge, then once they got weak we'd have a combat multiplier. At dawn tomorrow, the Rangers would counterattack and sweep the island, pushing the orcs back into a wall of walking mortar fire starting at the southern end of the island. The island and fighting positions would be retaken, and the Rangers would live to fight another night. The Forge once more back in possession of the home team.

There was no way an attacking force could get that massive chunk of equipment off the island without heavy equipment. So the Perpetual Taco Machine's excessive weight mitigated some of the risk of letting it fall into enemy hands for a brief few hours.

Night fell. Two hours later the drums in the forest beyond the river reached a fevered thunder pitch. It was clear some kind of final conclusion had been arrived at by the swarming masses out there in the shadow lands beyond the body-bloated river. Like some blessing or permission to attack us had been given. We could see them moving toward the river like a dark mass that wouldn't stop multiplying and spreading. Ever.

The end decreed.

The means justified.

Then the night sky was filled with falling flaming stars. The enemy out there in the darkness was putting up walls of fire arrows that arched up and then fell fast down onto the island and all across our fortified positions.

I went inside the aircraft to shelter from the rain of fire arrows that fell along the outskirts of the island's defenses out there. It looked like the captain was right: the majority of the flaming missiles fell on the southern portions of our defenses. They'd hit us there in the next few. The comm went live with reports and then fell silent as the Rangers prepared to repel the expected assault.

The drone feed, or what the Rangers called "Kill TV," captured what happened next.

As the rain of fire continued in the gray-green night vision of the drone's camera, the first enemy troops came across the swift waters at the southern end of the island from two points along the far bank. These first two surges were orc warriors. Curved and gleaming scimitars in the moon's silver light. Spears with long leaf-shaped blades, dangling with small skulls and feathers, stabbing up and down as they waded out, and then rushed, through the current. Heavier armor for these. These orcs were heavy assault troops. They entered the shallow crossing points and were promptly torn to pieces by command-detonated SLAM mines ignited from the firing pits. Massive water plumes sent the shredded bodies of the orcs in every direction. Tossed in the spray and the bare moonlight out there.

I was listening to the comm coming back at the CP when the captain, who was forward, told the mortars to hold their fire even as more orcs swarmed into the river, crossing shallows to take the place of those who'd been devastated by the submerged explosives.

The first Rangers to open up with their weapons were on the left-hand side of the southern edge. The orcs were halfway across when tracer fire streaked into the front ranks. A few bursts. Then the pit on the right flank opened fire. Tearing into that flank. This wasn't two-forty fire. These were SAW gunners and riflemen. Someone was firing from their grenade launcher, dropping rounds back along the bank as more orcs poured into the water to sustain the momentum of their assault.

The drone feed circled out over the island and we got an expanded view of what the Rangers on the line were facing. I'm not good at estimating crowd size, but in that first wave it looked to be in the high hundreds. The pilot, who was watching the drone feed while the co-pilot flew it from the handheld controls she was operating, said it was well over a thousand. At the top of the drone's circling flight path over the action we saw the ogres coming next.

At that moment we didn't know they were ogres, but later that was the generally accepted term for these heavier combat types now entering the battle against us. And of course, the name was blessed by the ever-wise-in-geekdom-lore PFC Kennedy, who asserted, "Oh yeah, definitely ogres.".

The ogres stormed out of the trees and into the roiling body-laden waters. Pushing aside the trunks of stout trees or hacking at them with vicious double-bladed battle axes. Single impossible strokes slashing through the meat of trees along the riverbanks. There was no stealth in these angry behemoths. They had come to war and battle. Even via drone feed it was pretty awe-inspiring. Impossible to believe such gigantic brutes seething with rage were real. Fangs gnashed. Broad muscled chests heaved like bellows, head and shoulders above the orcs and ten times more frighteningly vicious.

But it was time to believe in all of it. It was real, and real wanted to kill us all dead. There was no other choice now.

As I write all this down it's important to note something my mind has since tried to forget. The smell. Two nights of carnage and heavy enemy losses had left a reeking stink across the tiny river island. The waters were choked with bodies and drifting gore. Bloating orc corpses had created small dams along the western side of the island. Along the eastern bank the bodies had collected on the far shore, but their stink still contributed to the general miasma that had become pervasive in every inhalation. For much of that last day before the last night of the battle, Rangers had taken to wearing their shemaghs up around their faces just to keep out the wretched stink of the enemy dead. Vicks VapoRub was being used with abandon and had even attained a traded commodity status at some point. Ten thousand years in the future and the Ranger economy was now based on dip and Vicks. Candy bar futures were trading lower, but they were still trading. A base PX would have been a treasure trove of endless wonders here in this unholy far future front of madness and darkness.

I had none of these things: dip, Vaporub, or candy. I was looking to quietly corner the instant coffee market during most of my contacts throughout the day. I knew there was a shortage coming. I didn't want to get rich because of it; I just didn't want to be on the wrong side. The wanting side. I wanted coffee and I would do anything to get it. Anything. As a fellow caffeine junkie once said to me, *Coffee will get you through a time of no money. But money will never get you through a time of no coffee.*

True. And I was afraid of what that meant in the coming days. Very afraid.

He'd said this worked for all other addictions too.

So the smell was bad, and that was from the carnage of the previous two days of fighting. And already, within the first few minutes of the third night of fighting for Ranger Alamo, the numbers the enemy were putting up to dislodge us were looking to put the previous two nights to shame.

This is another important point: there wasn't an unlimited supply of ammo. The Forge made stuff, but it didn't make it fast. And it was at that moment, watching the massive ogres charge into the river, that I realized there was a very real chance the enemy could wear us out on sheer numbers alone. Run us dry on ammunition and get close enough to hack us all into a thousand pieces. Had McCluskey's recon been enough to provide that much intel? I didn't know and I bet no one else did either. In the quiet of the afternoon when he was supposed to be sleeping and avoiding sunlight... had the SEAL overheard even one of the SAW gunners mentioning his ammo count during an ACE report conducted by one of the NCOs? Or had he heard the blue sky reports coming in to the first sergeant at the CP that told him exactly what we had and where we were committing it?

Because if McCluskey was this King Triton, then he knew he could wear us out on sheer numbers. He knew where to hit us. And that if he kept hitting us, we'd soon be dry on ammo.

Especially with the howling nightmares that were these giant ogres pushing forward out onto the river. What did we have that could put them down? These things made the giant from night one seem small. Like we were too hasty in labeling it that. Here were the real giants.

I was fascinated as I studied the ogres via drone feed. They were basically larger, giant versions of the standard orc foot soldier we'd been facing. Huge heads and saber-tooth fangs. Massive bulging muscles over green scarred skin. Not just the patchwork leather and occasional beaten armor of the orcs, but finely worked cuirasses like old Roman legionnaires might have once worn. Except made of dark metal. Battered and unpolished. Sometimes covered in black grease. We could see there were designs in relief, stamped into their armor, but in the drone feed, to see the details of these designs was asking too much. They carried their impossibly huge battle axes with one hand as they thundered forward, spears like vault poles in the other fist.

And I mean they *thundered* forward. They moved fast like rolling thunder on a hot August night loose in the hills. For things so huge they were incredibly fast. Enormous strides, their swollen bodies rippling with muscle and fat pulling their bulk through the dark waters as they trampled the bodies of the smaller savage orcs to reach the near shore as fast as possible, hissing and bellowing murder.

If the outgoing fire was doing anything, it was only telling on the orcs, who were being cut down in clusters by explosive bursts of Ranger gunfire from the heavies down there in the fighting positions. Misshapen heads exploding and bodies flung away into the water to drift a dead man's float down the river and away from this battle. But the ogres, and I could see the ghostly streak of tracer fire hitting them, they didn't seem to mind the incoming at all. I saw one ogre take a tracer round right in the head and keep moving. Either it had been a graze that would leave a hot trail in the side of the thing's lumpy skull, or the ogre continued on fury and madness alone. It was incredible.

The ogres, who were now less than a thousand meters from the aircraft, launched giant spears into the first Ranger defenses along the riverbank. The drone was now circling to the south and all we could see was river for a few seconds. We had no idea if the spears found their targets among the defending Rangers in the right-flank pit. But the captain was already ordering that pit to pull back and for the left-flank pit to provide cover fire in the interim. Then the drone came back over our portions of the defenses and I could see outgoing fire from the center, the captain's squad, and the left-flank pit. Ghostly white Rangers were evacuating the right flank in the drone's feed as the hot white glowing ogres, made that way by night vision and thermal overlay, swept up onto the riverbank and charged the fighting pit, giant axes pulled back to strike. Fire arrows were still burning in the trees and along the sands of the beach all around. Glowing and phosphorescent as they gushed clouds of oily black smoke.

And then suddenly, someone said something over the comm to the effect of "firing," and an entire pit about to be overrun and cleared of Rangers belched a gout of flame out across the swarming ogres and into the river, covering more of the orcs following on to support the assault. The flaming fuel spread like iridescent vomit across the enemy front.

Apparently a few of the Master Breacher–qualified Rangers, with the help of the C-17's crew chief, had mixed up some avgas and other industrial fluids to create the gel that, when ignited, turned into a living unquenchable spreading fire. *Napalm.* And when the shape charge was detonated on the improvised napalm canister, the ogres were covered in burning fuel that crawled greedily across their armor. Melting it and roasting the scarred skin beneath.

One of the burning ogres swung a flaming axe and crushed the overhead protection of the fighting position.

But the greedy gel-ignite fire that couldn't be put out easily made any living thing rethink its personal motivation to do harm. To do anything at all other than to transform its state of "on fire" to "*off* fire."

Right?

Wrong.

Not when it came to the ogres. Mindlessly, covered in living fire, they continued to swarm fighting positions, hacking and slashing at the defenses with their massive axes even as they burned alive. No wonder the outgoing fire hadn't stopped them. They were crazed. *Berserk*, I think the term is. They were hit and burning and maybe even some were dying, but their rage and anger kept them slashing and hacking in hopes of taking some Ranger off to Ogre Valhalla.

One finally collapsed as the flames crawled over and consumed it. Probably strangling it through sheer oxygen deprivation. The others gradually lost steam and were raked by fire from the Ranger center, until one of the Rangers finished off the initial ogre assault with a well-placed grenade. But the fighting pit had been destroyed. It was covered in burning napalm and roasting ogre carcasses.

"More entering the river," announced the co-pilot operating the drone. I looked over at her. Her mouth was open beneath the VR goggles. And it was true, more wild ogres were indeed hitting the water with no less fury than the first. More orcs too. Weapons waving and dancing wildly, just looking for someone's body to serve as a resting place for their axe. I had no doubt death would be very unpleasant at the hands of these vicious and stabby things. There would be no quarter. No surrender. No prisoners of war. No mercy. Just hacked into pieces and stabbed to death more times than were probably needed. Or maybe it was the other way around. Stabbed and *then* hacked into pieces.

And in the next instant something... somethings... even taller than the orcs and the ogres, though not as bulky and not armed with any weapons, joined the assault. Later Kennedy would tell us these were called *trolls* in his imaginary game world. In the real world they were freaking walking nightmares with a guaranteed bonus round of night terrors for the rest of your life.

The right flank group of Rangers, a rifle squad, had already pulled back to the next phase line in the retrograde that would bring us all back to the hill. Now the left flank was being pulled back while the captain and his squad hit the collapsing front from the center. Tracer fire went in a semicircle, outbound in every direction. Tearing up orcs, raking ogres, and doing nothing to the advancing terrible trolls, looming up in the smoke and firelight. Someone in the captain's squad was carrying a two-forty, and this opened up on the orcs who were holding the shoreline along the river's edge for the moment. The sudden burst of fire found the huddling orcs and tore them to pieces.

By the drone's feed we could see the enemy covering and lobbing hand axes at the Rangers not more than twenty meters ahead of them. More orcs were coming through the waters as the next wave of ogres swarmed for the evacuating left pit and got the fresh and patient attention of the Ranger gunners. One ogre went down and the rest pushed on. The two-forty could hurt them, but the blitzkrieg of the ogres advancing was so fast, faster than we'd expected or could be expected to have expected, that the two-forty team was already being pushed back.

*Blitz* is German for lightning.

*Krieg* means war.

And these monsters were the living embodiment of that concept in ways the Nazis could have only ever dreamed of.

Even from inside the aircraft, the explosion was deafening as another napalm canister cooked off and detonated, spreading more burning fuel across the river waters and the swarming orc horde trying to force its way onshore.

Some of the ogres were hit, and a lot of the orcs were covered in greedy flames, but more ogres made the shoreline to support the beachhead. One deployed a massive bow and began firing at the Rangers just ahead of it. The bow was the size of a man and the ogre flexed and fired arrows the size of rebar poles into the forest and the Rangers.

"Pulling back," said the captain calmly over the comm. "Weapons sections, shift fire and cover as we establish the next line to our rear."

Captain Knife Hand's calm matter-of-factness was the opposite of every muscle in my body. Coiled and rusty-tight. I was holding my breath as I watched the swift enemy assault overwhelming our front line just hundreds of meters away. Out there, up front, it had to be pure, barely managed chaos. With gunfire and explosives and monsters that wanted to hack you to pieces in the dark. It was like…

… there is nothing I can compare it to. A living nightmare. Maybe you could compare it to that. Something that should only have been a bad dream. But wasn't.

I was glad the captain was in charge of it all.

The weapons sections who had the eastern and western side of the island would get ready to pour fire into the advancing horde as the other elements passed through the next phase line. From the comm in the CP I could tell they were engaged with enemies coming into their sectors. Small bands hitting the river from different points along the other banks. We were getting it everywhere all at once. But the southern front was the enemy's focus. That was clear.

Meanwhile, the captain ordered detonation of the claymores that had been planted just a few meters in from the southern beach. A string of them tore the clustering orcs and ogres staging there, still thrashing at the pits they'd overrun and launching spears and arrows at the retreating Rangers, transforming the attackers into fleshy bits flying in every direction. The deafening puffs of explosions ruined the attackers. More pressed onshore and into the bushes.

At this point the easternmost weapons section, run by Sergeant Kurtz, opened fire toward the south, raking that end of the island with fire. But the western weapons team didn't fire at all. The command sergeant major was on the comm and trying to get through to them, but they weren't answering. And that was when I started to get a bad feeling in my stomach.

Someone would have to leave the CP and go out there to find out what was going on. And that someone was almost certainly me. My hand found the high-value target's ring. The invisibility ring.

Everything was happening all at once and I couldn't tear my eyes away from the drone feed as one of the tall lurching trolls with long claws and a flat, almost Frankenstein head attacked the phase line and a group of Rangers firing at it with everything they had available. Nothing stopped it in the least as it suddenly picked a Ranger up and flung him off into the river. It swiped wide with its long demonic claws and knocked two more Rangers down. One of the team sergeants was firing point-blank into the twisted thing as it bore down on him. Later we'd find out that 5.56 did nothing to trolls.

Almost zero penetration.

At the same time one of the snipers from the hill fired, the spotter informing the CP they were engaging. I think it was Sergeant Thor and *Mjölnir* who took the shot. *Mjölnir* was an M107 anti-materiel sniper rifle. A deadly weapon that fired heavy fifty-caliber rounds at extreme ranges.

Again, we're watching a twisted lurching thing that looked a little like an ugly tree swiping and hammering at the Rangers trying to get out of its way. It's humanoid. But only just. It's lean, and rangy, and very tall. Greedy and hungry eyes glow in the night vision like a deadly animal's might while out hunting. It feels sickening to even look at the thing over drone feed. Like it's got too many joints where it shouldn't have any at all. The Rangers who can get back are firing burst, dumping ineffective rounds into the horror at near point-blank range. Nothing is slowing this monstrosity down in the least.

Until Thor fires *Mjölnir*.

Maybe the fast-moving round appears in the feed, it's moving at roughly 2800 feet per second. The bullet has broken the sound barrier. The shot is like a streak of sudden heat lightning. The sergeant major can't help but whisper to all involved that the sniper is using the Raufoss Mk 211 round. One of the SAW gunners standing at the back tells me that's an expensive armor-piercing incendiary tracer munition used against bunkers. It's a fifty-caliber round that's explosive, with a tungsten penetrator core. And it's incendiary to boot. It has a little dollop of explosive in it that makes things "interesting." His word.

The rampaging troll has warranted the extra-special attention.

We can't see details, but the round knocks the troll down onto one misshapen and oddly jointed knee. The hit flared in the night vision when the round struck. I can tell Sergeant Thor fires again because there's a second flare right in the troll's huge flat skull, and then the menace flops over, clearly dead. What it had for brains leaks out into the dirt. The brains are on fire.

The Rangers have enough room and distance to fall back to the next phase line as someone pops smoke to cover their retreat.

"Talker!" shouts the sergeant major, who's been trying to get through to the team that's out of communication on the western bank.

"Roger, Sergeant Major."

I tell my stomach to shut up. I'm needed to do a thing.

He stands and tells the first sergeant to take over as he walks me toward the rear cargo ramp. Just as we do, the drone feed goes wild and for a moment we see every angle of the battle, and then—a vulture's horny claws and the half-naked torso of a woman, a shrew, a hag, a harridan, screeching into the camera as the drone is destroyed. We hear her cawing like a crow with a slashed throat.

"Son," says the sergeant major, focusing me away from the incomprehensible terror we've just witnessed, a horrid, flying bird-woman who knocked out our drone intel. "Son, I need you to get out to Sergeant Jasper's team. They're not responding. Could be enemy interference again. Get in contact with them and tell them we're pulling back to Phase Line Charlie. Don't come back here. We're pulling out. Stay with them and link up at Charlie. Then connect with me on the hill. Copy, Talker?"

I copied and got myself ready, checking my MK18 and making sure I had a mag loaded and a round chambered. Keeping the safety on.

"Talker," he said to me as I turned to exit the cargo deck.

I turned back to the sergeant major, sure I was white as a ghost despite the war paint we'd applied to break up our outlines.

"Son, you don't know everything about combat there is to know. Not even by half. Sorry about that. This ain't your thing. But in the Rangers, everyone's a killer. This is current events and I need ya right now, out there, where it's all going down. So here's a piece of advice from one soldier to another, Talker. You get into a fight with anything out there..."

He paused to make sure I got this part. Because this was the important part. Not the getting into a fight part. Any idiot can do that in a bar most nights of the week. But this part, this was the part that might let me survive if I listened and knew wisdom.

"Be meaner than it, Talker."

# CHAPTER SEVENTEEN

THE distances we're talking about here aren't long. I'm not on a twelve-mile road march into unfamiliar territory. This river island is only about three thousand meters long and a thousand wide. Over the last three days since we arrived, I've walked most of it. There's the big field we barely managed to come down in, ringed by spindly trees on the east, west, and north. Poplars, I think. The center of the island is covered by clumps and stands of other trees with a few small dry streambeds running through it all. The northern end of the island is a tall and steep hill. I'm not good with elevation, but up there the island's highest point reaches about as tall as a six-story building.

As I leave the aircraft to link up with Sergeant Jasper's section, the one that's out of comm contact, the entire Ranger force is falling back. The perimeter security SAW gunners are getting ready to lead the civilians and flight crew along with the company's two senior NCOs back to the hill. Everyone is humping ammo. As much as they can. A lot of the available ammunition and explosives have already been shifted up to the top of Sniper Hill, but not everything. There wasn't enough time. So they're carrying what can be taken. We're leaving a lot behind.

Volman looks none too happy about having to carry a crate of grenades. He'd returned suddenly from his "important" mission. But it's been made clear to him that if he wishes to survive, then everyone needs to pull their weight right now. Immediately. The Baroness has two stretchers under her arm and a computer notebook slung in a messenger bag across her shoulder. She regards me for an instant with that quirky sexy smile as I take off into the dark and look back over my shoulder toward the plane. Wondering if I'll see it again. Trying to convince myself I'm not heading toward my death.

It's not dark-dark. But dark enough.

The forest is filled with small fires that can't quite catch because if this really is France, the Loire Valley as Chief McCluskey indicated, then it's winter or late spring here and the woods are wet from the rains. But fires still smolder and the air is filled with that drifting gray haze wet wood produces.

Therein lies the extent of my woodcraft. Wet wood will burn gray smoke.

The sound of Rangers fighting with automatic weapons and explosives to my south in the field we landed in, pulling back from the collapsing line, is erratic. Sudden explosions rock the forest and echo like large things moving out there in the dark. The detonations drown out the sounds of the enemy's shrieking tribal horns and advancing thundering drums. Amid the battle roar, their ground forces bark and call to one another as they swarm forward.

It feels real easy to get caught in the wrong place at the wrong moment right now.

I enter the woods just as the Rangers down there use a Carl Gustaf on one of the big trolls. The round cracks off, hissing away into the trees and slamming into a dark looming figure in the background. I have no time to pay attention to the effect. I just need to reach Sergeant Jasper's team and get them up on comms, and also make sure the phase line doesn't get behind me.

Because that would be bad.

It would mean I'm forward of anyone on my side. It would mean I'm currently inside enemy-held territory. Right in the middle of a bunch of monsters who would probably just as soon eat me. Regardless of how many languages I can speak. No amount of talking was gonna talk me out of that situation. I was sure about that. So best not to get caught.

I see the dark river ahead, and the heavy weapons section off to the right of Sergeant Jasper's team is intermittently engaging dark figures out there in the water and across the bank. More orcs trying to cross the river there. Tracer rounds streak off into the forest on the other side of the water, illuminating the tree-lined halls of the dark forest and the faces of the snarling beasts swarming down toward the bank. The enemy numbers on this side, the western side of the island, are nowhere near those hitting the southern bank, but it's enough to keep the two-forty busy and working.

The real question of the hour is... Why isn't Jasper's team hitting the enemy elements coming from the south along the western bank? Why aren't the two-forties "talking" to coordinate their defensive fire? Covering the Rangers at the center as they pull back to reach Phase Line Charlie. The second line of the Ranger defenses.

I take a knee in the woods and scan the riverbank ahead. In the dark I'm having trouble finding Sergeant Jasper's team's pit. I switch over to night vision, bumping my head forward and letting my NVGs fall down over my eyes. Neat trick Tanner taught me. That way I can keep my hands on my weapon.

Night vision comes on and it doesn't disorient me anymore like it used to. I'm comfortable here in it now. We're supposed to conserve battery power and so I don't activate the targeting laser or the illuminator. I focus out toward engaging distant targets, instead of working more up-close like in CQB. Not that I'd ever be involved in room clearing. But I might have to follow a group in and talk to captured bad guys. I trained enough in RASP to understand the basic concept.

Now, via night vision, I can see the trail to the fighting position where I should see Jasper's team. I see tracers streaking across the river and down in front of their position coming from another team. The weapons section farther up the bank is attempting to cover this portion of the river. The rounds are hitting the water and the dark figures moving through it. The plumes of outgoing rounds hitting the water are iridescent and white in the NVGs. The two-forty shuts down and I can hear someone calling out for a barrel change. Five seconds later the M320 gunners are dropping grenades into the water and along the far bank to cover the gunner and his AG.

Then one of the bushes ahead turns and looks in my direction. Bright eyes glitter within its mass in the dark of night vision and I realize I'm looking at a hunched orc directly ahead of me and along the sandy little trail leading to Sergeant Jasper's squad.

Without moving I switch from safe to semi as I bring up my MK18 and press down with my left thumb on the forward pressure pad that activates the IR laser. I can see a lot of other lasers dancing across the field and out along the river ahead. But because I'm not with too many others it's just my laser revealed in night vision here along the trail.

The orc spots the laser immediately. He stares at me inside night vision and cranes his lumpy head forward, fanged jaw opening and closing as he tries to figure out what he's seeing. Following the laser right to me. He stands up, throwing out his chest and weapon-carrying arms wielding two daggers, and begins to bellow some warning to others of his kind that I can't see yet. The targeting laser dances on his chest over a necklace made of small bones. Center mass.

The orc bellows a war cry and I squeeze off three shots in rapid succession. I know I hit him in the chest with at least one because he drops the dagger he's carrying in one hand and sinks to his knees. I close quickly, following the laser and pulling the trigger on him several times more. At the time, I don't know how many shots I've fired. Later I'd tell you I fired at least five more times before I was satisfied the clump in the bushes was just a dead orc. But I was caught up and engaging. I was surprised I was getting the important parts right while at the same time knowing I was missing some steps.

I can hear the sergeant major telling me to "be meaner than it" because there's a part of me that's telling myself that if this orc is behind the pit I'm headed toward, then that fighting position has been overrun. And that means I'm walking into an area the enemy is already all over. In other words... I'm in it now. Common civilian sense, the thing I used to measure every action by, is telling me to back off and go get someone competent to help me deal with this emergency situation. Y'know... maybe call the police or something.

"Hi, I'd like to report a suspicious band of orcs in the neighborhood. Yes, you heard me correctly. Orcs, officer. Mean ones. They look like they're up to no good. You'll send a car around? Great. I'll just stay inside and peek through the curtains occasionally. Thanks, officer."

But that isn't now. That isn't here. Right now isn't just an emergency... it's war. And I'm here as a soldier even if I am just along for the ride as a linguist hanging out with a bunch of Rangers. I've been sent out here to find out what's happened to some of the Rangers I'm hanging around with. Clearly, by the looks of the situation, something is not good.

I keep my weapon on the dead orc, lowering it to stay on target as I approach and thread through the bushes to see the hill twenty meters off where Sergeant Jasper's team dug their fighting position. It's not so much a hill as it is a simple rise along the riverbank. They probably placed it there for elevation and a greater field of fire.

Other orcs are there around the fighting position and they're dragging the bodies of Rangers out of the pit and I don't know if anyone is dead or alive. There are three orcs lugging one of the Rangers with their claws. Or they were, except now that they've heard the bark of their sentry and the gunfire, they're frozen. As if waiting for something to happen. Wide-flared nostrils twitching and tasting the air. They're using their other senses to find the danger. To find me.

Looking back on this, as I write it all down, I realize orcs must have some kind of natural night vision that dips down into the IR spectrum, letting them see our lasers. But right now, the dancing beam of my laser is covered by the dense brush I'm just barely trying to push through, scanning ahead with the NVGs to see all three, along with a fourth who's standing over the pit making motions with his hands like someone trying to calm down a bunch of drunks at a comedy show. That sort of soft bounce with both hands out, urging everyone to calm down now for the next act. Be quiet. Get ready for tonight's special guest coming on the main stage.

This one, the one trying to quiet everyone, isn't a warrior. No scimitar or other hacking weapon. No spear or bow to stab either from close or far away. This one has a short gnarled staff. Instead of armor it wears a crude kaftan like a Taliban mullah might.

In the gray-green of night vision all their eyes glitter evilly. The three others searching the dark for me are like hunting animals scenting prey. Wide nostrils continuing to twitch, tasting their air with their other senses, trying desperately to find me so they can start baying for the kill. But the fourth, and let's just call him the orc equivalent of the high-value-target sorcerer we hit out in the woods, maybe a tribal shaman type, his eyes are pure malevolence as he glares into the darkness like it's an old and very familiar friend.

There are three Rangers lying on the ground outside the pit that was Sergeant Jasper's fighting position. Again, I don't know if they're dead or alive.

I fire on the shaman because he's the only one I can shoot without maybe hitting one of the Rangers. I'm operating on the assumption they're not dead until I can confirm that.

The torrent of fire hits the shaman and ragdolls his kaftan-wrapped body away from me along the fresh dirt of the riverbank. He twists and tries to stumble for the river to get away from me, hit in the gut and doing the orc snarl equivalent of gagging as he clutches his blood-soaked belly.

The other three see me fire and drop the Ranger they're trying to pull out of the fighting position. I eject the mag and get a new one in, hit the bolt release and fire at the leader who has decided to rush me. Axe upraised. I'm still on full auto and I drag the weapon up the length of his body, spraying rounds into his misshapen face at the last second.

Then I feel the bolt lock back to the rear, empty. I just blew the whole magazine.

My breathing is fast. And my chest feels tight. One of the orcs has run off and the other is circling me to the left, axe out and running through the bushes to get behind me. Predator hunting party tactics. These things are pack hunters on some basic animal level. One charged me. One circled to drag me down from behind. The other ran for help.

I can see the remaining orc clear as daylight for a moment, but he doesn't know that. I didn't know that at the time. It's just now in the hindsight of writing it all down that it's revealed to me that I had the advantage of night vision. But then again, these things have a kind of night vision too if they can see the targeting laser in the dark.

And there's one other thing.

The mistake that's easy to make is to think they knew what modern weapons are. They didn't. Reviewing everything I'd seen so far, and would see that night, the enemy at times had no idea what kind of impossible magic was being hurled at them from out of our barrels.

The one circling had no idea that if he had just rushed trigger-happy me, I'd be wearing his axe in my chest.

Circling gave me all the time in the world to eject the spent mag, get a fresh one out, slam it home, and release the bolt, loading another round into the chamber, ready to fire. Even time to flick back to semi. Except I'd lost him in the dark of the bushes that clustered along his route.

I didn't switch from full auto to semi though.

I was still wired.

And if all that sounds like I did it the way I just wrote it down... forget it. My breathing was rapid, my fingers were trembling and numb, and the magazine didn't go in smooth. Under night vision it's harder. You don't realize how much you use your eyes until you don't have them. Because the night vision is dialed up for ranged engagement, close-at-hand work is just a blur.

I activated the illuminator on my barrel and caught sight of my target. *Now* he was charging straight at me, small axe raised and ready to swing down into my chest. I fired. Not everything in the mag. But enough to put that one down too. In RASP the instructors said, "Shoot them until they change shape, or catch fire."

I stood there knowing I should chase the one that had run off back down to the river. I was breathing hard and feeling, honestly, like I was gonna have a heart attack right there.

This was CQB.

Yeah. I'd done range time and assault courses in Basic and RASP. But Basic was always with a bunch of other people who'd end up being truckers, cooks, and telephone repair people. Some of them were pretty good. Skills learned back on the block or out in the woods "getting their buck" the year before. But most soldiers in Basic were clueless, and that was good because you learned the army way of shooting, moving, and communicating, with good marksmanship to boot, from scratch. No bad habits to get rid of. That was me.

I'd never seriously expected to be in what is known as close-quarters battle. CQB. I got the introductory course at the Shoot House in RASP. I remember thinking I'd never get to do it again. The real Rangers would do that stuff. I'd just talk to the captures. Sure, I'd *imagined* being in it. Imagined being attached to an infantry unit and ending up close enough to a fight to actually start needing to engage because it was that close. But even then all my fantasies included me and forty of my heavily armed best friends, properly trained infantry who did it for a living, covering my butt.

I'd certainly never imagined being out here and in it all by myself.

*Be meaner than it, Talker.*

"Yeah," I mumbled, shaking in the darkness.

I could feel sweat breaking out all over my body. The battle was raging across the island now. More explosions and chattering heavy-weapons fire to the south and closer than it had been just a moment before. Mortar strikes landing out in the water, this side and to the south where some new enemy force was trying to flank and come ashore. The pit off to my right firing everything they had into the dark shapes out there on the water. Star-shells falling through the forest in other sectors. Dancing illumination shells, the dying light they made causing the shadows of the trees to move like living things all around me.

I flipped my NVGs and just stood there. Trying to control what seemed uncontrollable. Impossible. My heart, and my breathing. Knowing I had stuff to do.

And then… it all just stopped and I felt myself take a big breath. And let it go. My fingers were ejecting the magazine in my MK18 and getting a new one out of my carrier. Smooth. Easy. This was the next step. This is what was done and I was fine with that now.

This was what I was supposed to do.

I felt calm and I knew the answer then. I didn't need to think about it and figure it out later to put it down in this record no one will probably ever read.

Ever since I'd walked away from those Ivory Towers of Education that would have become fusty old prisons I'd grow doddering and old in, I'd wondered about this moment. Even if I hadn't known it. CQB. Wondered if I could really Ranger. *Ranger*—it's a noun, a verb, a personality trait, a thought process, et cetera. No one had ever said I couldn't. They'd been too busy being bewildered by the fact that I was walking away from everything I'd worked so hard for to do something they considered beneath…

… beneath me?

No. Beneath them. They'd thought that way. In their ignorance.

My reasons are my own for why I joined the Army and got my chance to hang with the Rangers. Maybe I'll write them, those reasons, down someday. Here. But I never considered that being a soldier was *beneath* anyone. If anything, I'd always considered myself beneath what it took to become one. And I wondered if that was true. If I could. Until this moment, with dead orcs all around me, I'd wondered if this was just some little game I was playing at that I wouldn't be able to pay for when the bill came due. When it came time to put all my chips on the table and go all in. When it really came time to pay with my life.

When the lives of others were on the line. When it wasn't just assault lanes and warrior faces. When it wasn't me and forty of my heavily armed best friends supported by an M1 Abrams tank, artillery on demand, and air cav in the skies all around.

In other words... when other people were expected to do the fighting that needed to be done. Not just me contributing with a few rounds downrange and where the enemy might maybe be.

But CQB. In it.

*Be meaner than it, Talker.*

Running into a room with nothing but a weapon and the training you had and the attitude that you were gonna be the winner today.

Because that's what a fight is. Winners and the dead.

There are no participation awards.

There are just winners. And the dead.

I was breathing normal now. The sweat felt good. Cleansing. Like I was sweating out all the doubt that had been with me from the day I walked into a recruiter's office just to see if I could.

I won this one, I told myself.

Okay... rinse and repeat, as Drill Sergeant Ward liked to say.

Do it again.

Just like the sun. Every day.

# CHAPTER EIGHTEEN

THEY weren't dead. Staff Sergeant Jasper's squad wasn't dead. No wounds. Or at least no fresh ones gushing blood from hacks and slashes by small curved swords or long daggers. Or blunt trauma and broken bones from massive war maces. All the first aid I'd learned in Basic Training had consisted of identifying wounds and putting a bandage on them, or even applying a tourniquet when necessary. But that was it. Sword slashes and concussions and fractured skulls were going to be a bit beyond my ability to repair.

Chief Rapp had been training, and using, some of the air crew as medics to support his casualty collection point. I'd told myself I probably needed to get that training so I could be of some assistance when things got serious. But I'd been busy, and so now I fell back on the basic stuff I knew, which seemed woefully inadequate right at this current moment of seriousness.

Evaluation. That was the first step.

The first guy I checked wasn't dead. I shook him, and slowly, like he was shaking off a three-day bender, he came around a little. I chanced a glance across the river and saw that the tracer hurl of the two-forty to our north had stopped. I tapped back into the command net and heard the first sergeant ordering all units to pull back to Phase

Line Charlie now. Phase Line Charlie was to the rear of our current position.

There were clusters of dark shapes out there on the river, crossing directly for us. Orc shapes. Even the mortar fire had stopped, and it seemed like there was a lull in the battle as both sides reloaded and took up new positions in order to recommence killing one another. The problem for us was our position was in front of the forward line of friendlies, other Rangers. We were now in what would be, for the next few hours, enemy-held territory.

I went to work on the next soldier laid out outside the pit. Yeah, this one was sleeping too.

"C'mon!" I wanted to shout at them all. "Wake up!"

But I didn't say anything because I was too busy trying to hustle and hunker and get to each of them. Still, they began to stir. As if they'd heard what I'd been thinking. Just like McCluskey seemed to have during the debrief.

Was that a thing here? Could people hear your thoughts? Or was it just me? Because I could see that going really badly for me the next time I tried to advance my cause with the cute co-pilot of the C-17.

"What the..." began SSG Jasper when he sat up. His primary wasn't at hand, and fast as he could he had his M18 out and pointed into the darkness all around like he'd just woken from the worst nightmare ever, mixed with a case of the DTs for bonus terror.

He then, not politely I might add, asked me who I was. When I told him I was the linguist and that that wasn't the most important thing right now, he asked me what was the most important thing at that moment. Exactly. Again, not too politely.

"Sergeant Major says we're pulling back to Phase Line Charlie, Sergeant Jasper," I said. "We lost comm with your section and he sent me out to reconnect with you. Also, still not the biggest problem, Sar'nt."

"Yeah. Then what is?" he raged accusingly.

Rangers were going for their weapons. Scrambling through the dirt and the sand to find them near and around the fighting position.

"We got bad guys coming in from all directions, Sar'nt." I pointed toward the river where what looked to be at least a company-sized element was wading ashore as stealthily as a company-sized element could possibly do.

Sergeant Jasper swore and hissed his orders. He wanted the SAW up and working them. Grenadiers were to start dropping smoke to cover our retreat.

Then I pointed toward the three trolls tearing apart trees directly to our immediate south. Surrounded by teams of orcs on foot. They were moving slow. Apparently Captain Knife Hand had left a bunch of explosive surprises for them to find and they were getting leery about advancing too fast. One of those booby traps detonated and ripped into a troll who staggered from the hundreds of tungsten balls that zipped through its leathery hide. But then it just continued on. The dead orcs around it continued to be dead, torn to pieces by the explosive's fast-moving shrapnel. Lying about like the victims of a massacre.

"Gotta boogie!" hissed the sergeant, changing plans. Everyone in the section grabbed as much as they could and a minute later we were headed down the trail toward the center of the island to follow the path back into the one lane clear of explosives that would take us to Phase Line Charlie.

Sergeant Kang was on point and SSG Jasper brought up the rear. The rest of the section carried the SAW and the extra cans of ammo. I was with Kang and pointed out which way we needed to go when we emerged at the edge of the field the C-17 had landed in. Off in the distance I could see the shadowy bulk of the plane. Someone was retreating out of there and we could see the two SAW gunners laying down suppressive fire on some element out there in the woods threatening to come in close.

A moment later the three trolls stormed into the position we'd just left behind. They tore large trees right out of the ground and pounded the dug-in fighting position along the riverbank. The heavy weapons section to the north engaged them, slowing them with outgoing fire.

It was an ominous sight. The towering creatures moving through the tall trees, their mean yellow eyes blazing with fury as they scanned for something to rend limb from limb. Trying to dodge the bright tracer-laden fire of the two-forty coming at them from the north.

Sergeant Kang was watching forward, trying to find the trail we'd take next, when I spotted a line of orcs racing across the field around the plane. They'd cleared the southern defenses and were now storming forward into the CP. There were other creatures, strange and bizarre, mixed in with this enemy infantry force. Misshapen, twisted freaks. I had no idea what they might be called in PFC Kennedy's games.

Kang was on the comm and talking with the platoon sergeant. Trying to figure our next move. We couldn't go back because we'd run into the trolls. Forward was someone driving the command team out of the CP. And to our right was the main body of the enemy's attack from the south.

And there was one more problem with our movement to the rear. We didn't want to run into anyone's ambush or booby traps.

"Streambed to our northwest. Take that, Kang. Watch for tripwires," ordered Sergeant Jasper.

Kang sighed, shrugged, and hunch-walked underneath the burden of his overloaded ruck into the bushes, leaving the trail we'd been following back to Charlie. The twisting sandy-bottomed streambed that ran through the center of the island was just off to our left. It didn't fill with river water unless the river got high enough, and that hadn't happened in the three days we'd been on the island.

Twenty meters into the brush we found the bed and dropped down into it one by one. Kang and I set up security while the rest of the team came down in and Jasper advised command of our situation and position. They noted our loc and told us to hold.

A minute later mortars started sweeping across the front just behind us. The first few indirect strikes landed out in the field the orcs were moving through. That should have checked any enemy troops and sent them for cover or pulling back. Not orcs. These warriors ululated, war-whooped, blared their tribal horns, and charged right into the raining maelstrom of death being dropped down all over them. The snipers atop the hill were engaging the huge trolls who were getting weirdly crafty about not getting hit by two-forty fire. For things so large and menacing, they somehow hunkered and ducked behind stands of trees and even slithered like giant snakes on their bellies to get closer to the line.

Here now, it's just words I'm writing down for no one to ever read. At the time, there in the dark and already behind enemy lines shifting forward faster than we could move, it was one of the freakiest things I'd ever seen. And if I thought I was close to death in that firefight I'd pulled not ten minutes ago, seeing those trolls get crafty to avoid sniper and heavy machine-gun fire made me feel even closer now. They seemed unstoppable. One even pulled up a huge boulder half-mired in the earth and overhand threw it like a big-league fastball pitch straight at the hill. It snapped off the tops of trees along the way and rocketed right into the raised earth.

One of the Rangers down along Phase Line Charlie replied with a Carl Gustaf round. It didn't kill it, but it went straight through the thing's chest. That troll stumbled off toward the river. To die or recover, I had no idea. Kennedy told me later that in his games, trolls could regenerate hit points.

Then he had to explain what hit points were.

So, that could be a thing here.

Or not.

Who knew?

But right now, the front line turned into a battle all around us as we hid in the streambed. We were only three hundred meters from Phase Line Charlie. But we might as well have been a thousand miles and all out of gas away.

# CHAPTER NINETEEN

THE forward elements of the enemy were hitting our line at Phase Line Charlie along several points now. Sergeant Jasper was in communication with the captain and we were being told to continue to hold our position for the next few as the outgoing fire got heavier. Orcs were streaming through the forest above our heads as we hunkered down in the gully.

"Suck dirt!" shouted the sergeant as a sudden line of mortar strikes landed across the enemy front to both sides.

Down in the streambed we were ducking below the plane of outgoing fire from our teams along the line to our rear. Fire was being directed away from us toward the flanks, but we were still keeping our heads down. The SAW was being carried by Specialist Mercer, with PFC Soprano acting as the AG carrying reloads. Sergeant Kang was with me at the rear, and Jasper and one other Ranger were on opposite sides of the gully watching our flanks.

When the enemy came at us under a minute later, we were effectively fighting what's called a "Reverse Slope Defense." Before joining the Army I read a few primers on military tactics just to better understand what I was getting involved in. What I'd be a part of. Yeah, it was above my paygrade, but I've found a little knowledge can vanquish fear of the unknown. Now I was watching what I'd learned come into play.

It looked a lot different in the book.

Because we couldn't poke our heads up beyond the gully for fear of getting hit by our own outgoing fire from friendlies, we had to defend the gully and kill whatever came into it until it was time to pull back to safety. The SAW was positioned toward the front of the gully where we expected the enemy to come from as they advanced along their axis of attack. We'd switched to night vision and were ready to go as, overhead, tracer rounds streaked and zipped off into the night beneath the crystal blanket of the universe night vision always showed you despite the mess you found yourself in down below. Sergeant Kang had placed his rucksack facing outward toward the perimeter with a Claymore mine mounted atop it.

We concentrated on our assigned sectors. Of course, I was watching everything as I was pretty sure I'd been given the least important sector to watch: our escape route to the rear and back to Phase Line Charlie.

The SAW opened up in a short burst and I turned my head around to see the targeting laser dance along fast-moving rounds in night vision, ripping into five orcs carrying wickedly curved swords and small shields. Hot 5.56 rammed into heavy-browed orc heads and beefy armor-clad green scarred bulks bristling with axes and armor. More orcs came in behind those currently being cut to pieces, no doubt sensing the depression in the landscape and trying it as a route to sneak up on the enemy lines. Instead they got a nasty surprise from Mercer squeezing the trigger on the squad automatic weapon and Soprano directing fire.

Sergeant Kang nearby engaged something that looked like a cross between a small dog and a lizard. Bipedal. Humanoid, sorta. Carrying a small spear and a dagger that could have been the tooth from a megalodon shark. I'd see one in a museum once. The dog-lizard thing landed down in the sandy bottom of the gully and Sergeant Kang, who'd been watching the lip of the gully in his sector, saw it spring down and land near the SAW gunner and Private Soprano. Kang pivoted on his belly and double-tapped the thing with two rounds that sent it sprawling off in the dirt. When it landed, he shot it again and yelled at me. "Watch your sector!"

My sector, facing our lines, was a dizzying array of outgoing fire streaking through the shadowy green trees and bright crystals of stars revealed by my night vision. It was a lot to process. Especially the tracer ricochets that seemed to want nothing more to do with the battle and disappeared off into the universe.

I heard Jasper and the other Rangers open up from the flanks, but I watched our exit and made sure we didn't get cut off when the time came to move. The rounds were moving so fast and close above our heads it felt like you could just stand up and they'd tear your head off and keep going off into this strange world of stars and night forever. I pushed myself deeper into the sandy bottom and waited for the order to move. Hoping it would come soon.

Three minutes of fighting like this, taking random spurts of enemy who seemed too overwhelmed by the fire from our lines to realize there were targets among them in the dry streambed, and then Mercer cried out, "Loading!"

The Rangers moved into a new posture to accommodate the reload. I thought it would be a process and I knew it would have been for me. I was ordered to shift fire to Kang's sector while Kang covered forward. I could see Soprano assisting. It was easier than I thought it would be. At the same time Mercer got a new belt fed into the ammo tray and that was when the first of the enemy cavalry came thundering down the gully.

These weren't orcs.

They were human-shaped riders dressed in shrouds and armor. Like ghost riders. Hoods over their heads, they rode lean, bony, and gray or even dark horses. The first one came down the gully at a full gallop, following the streambed up from the south and riding close to the gaunt horse's neck as the rider tried to avoid fire. He appeared around the bend farther down the dry streambed and Mercer had just pushed the ammo tray closed when the rider saw us and simply charged as if to ride us down, waving a long sword that shimmered in the night.

Mercer pulled the trigger release and started firing.

Rounds smashed into the weird horse and rider, but even though the beast screamed like something straight from a nightmare, it kept on coming straight at us. Sergeant Kang was engaging an ogre, a big mean one with a massive bow that was larger than anything I'd ever seen. The ogre, smashing his way through the trees above, had apparently leaned down over the gully to check and see what was going on down in here. The thing was easily nine feet tall, and it moved fast, its powerful muscles pulling the giant arrow it had nocked and ready to go back into firing position. It wore nothing but a tasseled kilt and high leather boots caked with mud and debris. A giant sword that was little more than a chunk of beaten pig iron hung from its belt.

Sergeant Kang squeezed a whole mag across the ogre's bare chest. The thing didn't seem like it much minded. It turned and fired its bow, sending an arrow right at Mercer, who swore and began to grunt hoarsely, attempting to control the sudden pain.

In the dark light of night vision, I watched the straight and true green beam of my targeting laser land on the looming brawny ogre's brow as it drew another massive black arrow into its bow. I'd kept my MK18 on semi because I didn't want to freak out and burn through more mags on full auto. I squeezed fast, but not so fast I couldn't keep the laser right on the ogre's upper torso.

Again it was the blur of combat, and while certain elements were hyper-real, I was also cognizant of two things at the same time. One, the arrow that had struck Mercer, which was about four feet long, had gone straight through his thigh and pinned him to the ground. I could see that in the foreground as I fired at the ogre, not needing to look through the sight but instead letting the IR beam settle each time I pulled the trigger. Allowing the targeting laser do all the work of finding where the rounds needed to go.

Meanwhile the rider and nightmare bony horse were still bearing down on the SAW gunner and Private Soprano. Mercer Rangered through the pain and kept firing, hitting the screaming horse and the dark rider trying to hide behind its rearing fear-taut neck.

At the same time, I was firing at the ogre as it nocked and pulled back its second arrow. One of my rounds must've climbed from upper center mass because the thing's jaw suddenly exploded, spraying bone fragments and iridescent gore in night vision. The monstrosity dropped its bow and threw both of its mallet-like paws up to its face as it fell forward into the gully and broke its neck.

Yeah. I heard it. It was loud and clear. Like the dry snap of a big dead branch in a quiet forest on a lonely winter's afternoon despite the battle all around us. Just like that.

When I looked back, I saw that Mercer had brought down the first gaunt horse and shrouded rider of rags and bones. This must've been the enemy cavalry's scout, or their version of the point man, because more riders were appearing around the bend in the gully to the south, down along the enemy's line.

The riders surged and Sergeant Kang mashed the firing device clacker for the Claymore. As if to say, I see your doomsday riders and raise you one M18A1 Claymore mine. The explosion devastated the sickly horses and riders, sending steel balls tearing through horse flesh, gaunt riders, and forest.

That was when we got the order to pull back. The line was shifting fire and the snipers had us acquired. And if that sounded like we were suddenly on Easy Street, the captain made it clear to Jasper that we weren't.

"CO says the gully's filled with tangos ahead of our position. Gotta clear it the whole way back, guys. Snipers supporting." After this, Jasper got us organized and moving.

What happened next was three hundred meters of pure nightmare.

With more riders still coming up the gully and Soprano now acting as the SAW gunner while Sergeant Kang went to carry the wounded Mercer, we gave up our defensive position in the wash and headed out the back door.

Soprano was firing short bursts into the riders as Kang and I dragged the wounded man after Jasper, who'd taken point. Sergeant Kang had managed to get an emergency tourniquet around Mercer's leg above the wound; the arrow had been cut at both ends and left in. To his credit, Mercer didn't pass out or scream bloody murder when they quick-applied a tourniquet and some clotting agent. He did promise someone he was going to kill them slowly someday.

It was a tight squeeze into the next section of the gully and we barely got Mercer through it. Something rubbed the wounded area and he arched his neck and back and it was all I could do to hold on to him until he went limp and finally passed out, his face and arms covered in cold sweat.

Kang shouted over his back, "Private Soprano! We're leaving! C'mon!"

More fire from the small gunner. A long burst and then an almost comical, "Eh, Sergeant! Hole up... I'm-a comin'." He spoke like some awful actor doing his version of bad Italian-American.

We were holding the unconscious Mercer up against the side of the gully and Kang was telling the gunner to "Fall back, man" when the dark-eyed and smiling Soprano squeezed past us like it was just another day on the subway and not actually raining flaming arrows all around us while trying to thread the needle of making it through a combat front with both sides throwing everything they had at each other.

Then near at hand, some sort of ballistae had been moved up to fire on the hill. Sniper Hill to the north. We could hear their high and ominous twangs as the grunting and howling crews worked to fire and reload and then fire again at the Rangers on the hill.

"*Scusa*," murmured Soprano almost politely as he pushed past us while we held up the wounded man and he kept the SAW upright. "Hey *Sergente*... this-a count for Ranger School, right?" He laughed as he passed by. "'Cause-a I was due to go and all, *Sergente*, before we got to this-ah... how to say... this... crazy place..."

Mercer groaned and went paler.

Sergeant Kang replied in short, clipped tones. "Not now, Soprano. Save the accent and go forward. Sergeant Jasper needs you with him."

I could hear Jasper and the other Rangers engaging up there, but I couldn't see what was going on. Then the little gunner was off with the machine gun that seemed two sizes too big for him.

Kang slapped Mercer across the face, and not gently.

"C'mon, Ranger! Don't go into the light!"

But Mercer either didn't care or simply wondered too much what that light was all about anyway.

"Let go of him," Sergeant Kang ordered me, and I didn't. But I did say something really stupid as suddenly ahead of us in the dark gully we heard Soprano open up hard on something that screamed like a horror movie version of a tentacled beast that lived in a pond. It was titanic and ear-splitting as Soprano hosed it with the SAW.

I said to Sergeant Kang, *"We ain't leavin' him!"*

Which was a stupid thing to say to a Ranger.

I didn't see the look Sergeant Kang, who was Korean, and yes I spoke that one too, gave me. I'm sure it was pure wither. As in, if looks could kill I'd be cooling in some morgue on the wrong side of town.

"Rangers don't leave anyone behind," Kang muttered as the unconscious gunner fell toward him while he bent and in one smooth motion, so perfect it seemed choregraphed, he hoisted the limp Mercer up and into a fireman's carry over one shoulder.

Then...

"Stay with me," he grunted, hefting his rifle up.

# CHAPTER TWENTY

THREE hundred meters of pure nightmare still lay directly ahead. It was enough keeping the orcs and shadow riders off our backs. They kept pushing from the rear and it was only Kang firing and falling back, with me covering as he carried the still-unconscious Mercer, that kept them from riding us down right there in the gully. I was doing what Kang directed me to do, providing cover and making sure our way forward was clear as we maintained visual with the rest of Sergeant Jasper's team fighting forward. The team leader and the other two Rangers were killing their way through pockets of orcs who'd made it this far and were staging for their next rush into Phase Line Charlie. The last thing they expected to see was Rangers sweeping up the gully and engaging as they came, shooting the orcs down.

Jasper had already declared "Mag out" indicating he was down to his last magazine. Chatter over the team comm erupted about redistributing. And that was when I came up on Soprano who was busy getting in the last reload he carried for the SAW. He kneeled in the darkness of a part of the gully wash filled with the twisted and maimed bodies of dead orc warriors. Their faces were frozen in wicked snarls, even in death.

Sergeant Kang came up behind us, turning and firing short bursts to keep the pursuit back and then hustling forward to the next cover. Arrows suddenly rained down into the wash. These, at least, weren't on fire. But it indicated that the enemy was talking between its various elements and someone had decided to group-select and target us with indirect ranged fire. Like this was some kind of computer wargame simulation. That was the only way my mind could understand how they managed to fire at us down inside the twisting gully. For the most part, the incoming arrow fire fell across the sand and fallen logs that had washed down in here during storms of the not-so-distant past. The arrows made different sounds when they struck. At first they hit the sandy bottom with soft, almost whispery hushes as they suddenly appeared in the streambed. Then they hit logs with loud *CHUNKs*. By then we'd covered under the logs as best we could, and Sergeant Kang threw Mercer down on the sand and lay on top of him to protect the wounded Ranger.

One of the arrows managed to slam into Soprano's knee plate and shattered with a loud crack. The comical Italian gunner exclaimed, "Hey… lookee that, *mi amico*." *Amico* means friend. Yeah. I speak Italian too. Actually, I think I already mentioned that. "I tooka arrow righta in the knee. Like in that game. Now I can retire and be a town *guarda*!"

*Guarda* means guard. Obviously. Other than that, I had no idea what he was talking about.

The arrow fire ceased and moments later a dozen heavily armed orcs surged from the south along the dry streambed, pushing forward fast and lobbing spears at us. I was the lightest armed and the first out from under cover. Soprano was still duck-walking from under the fallen log we'd been covering under and Kang was just getting to his knees and putting in a new mag for his rifle when the orcs swarmed, running fast up the wash, axes out and screaming bloody murder.

I fired at the leader, pulling the trigger on the MK18 as fast as I could squeeze off rounds. Then I was out and there were still more coming straight at us. I reversed the rifle and slammed it into the helmeted head of the first one to reach us because there was no time to get a new magazine in. I thrust the butt of the MK18 forward and fast just like Drill Sergeant Ward had taught us all back in Basic Training and caught that one right between the eyes and along the bridge of his wide flared black nostrils. It rang his bell for sure, but he wasn't down.

Another of the roaring orcs battle-cried and swung a notched sword at me. It was short and small like the kind ancient Roman centurions used. A gladius. The gladius hit my front plate and bounced off, but the blow knocked the wind out of me, and I stumbled backward, letting my rifle go and thinking only of getting out my sidearm once I could breathe again.

I was on my butt when I had my M18 out and I just started pulling the trigger on that one as it closed to finish me off with a stab. At that point I had no idea how badly I'd been hit. Whether the sword had slashed through my armor and into me... I had no idea. I didn't feel any pain, but maybe, some other part of my mind was saying, maybe I was in shock and an artery had been cut deep. It was probably serious, but I was just thinking it was best not to die right this second.

Maybe someone could help me if I survived this fight.

I continued to fire, emptying the magazine at the orcs pushing forward. There were three now and I couldn't tell if I was hitting anyone because my eyes were watering and like I said I was having trouble breathing. My M18 had a targeting laser, but I hadn't activated it. It was the sergeant major's and I remember thinking as the last round left the weapon and the slide locked back that I was supposed to "clean" Volman. Retire. R&R. And that I hadn't done that yet. Now I was going to get hacked and chopped up into little pieces by monsters from some fantasy game turned nightmare.

Of all the ends my mother had ever foreseen for me, which was her way of loving me despite her patrician up-bringing, she probably hadn't seen this one. Life is crazy and unexpected like that. It moves fast, as some like to say. And apparently death wasn't any different.

Then Soprano opened up and I watched as right before my eyes, belt-fed 5.56 in adult-sized doses slammed into the misshapen heads, exploding brains and sending bone matter all against the sides of the gully. All of it really up close and luridly graphic in the moonlight. His work belonged in a museum with the other Italian masters, I thought as I processed all the destruction. And then I realized, *Oh, this is how they think.* Rangers. Violence is also an art. To them.

I recovered my rifle and breathing in gasps as I fumbled for a new mag when Sergeant Kang, with Mercer back over his shoulder and still holding his rifle, hauled me to my feet.

"Load your sidearm, PFC," he grunted at me, and started off up the gully once more.

Soprano was still hosing the orcs farther back down the gully with the SAW, keeping them back as we pushed forward once more.

Then the sniper fire from the hill got re-tasked to assist our flight and crossing back into Phase Charlie. Some new creatures that looked like small dragon-dog humanoids came *yip yip yipping* in at us, waving their curved little daggers and shouting something unintelligible that sounded like "*Breeeeeyaaark!*"

The rounds coming from *Mjölnir* up on the hill just vaporized these things as they struck.

I followed Kang around the next bend in the streambed and we found the rest of Sergeant Jasper's team linked up with the main body and letting us through the line. And just as Soprano ran through and behind the improvised fighting position the Rangers here were fighting from, carrying the empty squad automatic weapon and running like a track star, the flanks redirected their fire on the gully and closed off that route with extreme outgoing violence for our pursuers. The mortar team even obliged with a few rounds of white phosphorus just to make sure they caught fire. I had to flip my NVGs up real quick once those things came.

We'd made it to Phase Line Charlie. Barely.

Chief Rapp was there and apprised on Mercer's condition. He'd brought PFC Kennedy. Even though Charlie was on the verge of collapsing, and we were pulling back to the hill itself, Chief Rapp started a transfusion on Mercer right there using PFC Kennedy as a universal blood donor. The *Ranger O-Low Titer Protocol* was something we'd all been briefed on and trained in during RASP. It had a high rate of success in preventing battlefield deaths. Identified universal blood donors such as Kennedy carried a "Universal" kit that could assist the medics in making a critical blood transfusion in minutes right there on the battlefield.

Chief Rapp was a stud of course. Special Forces guys are not just competent at what they do, they're gifted. First he got some tranexamic acid in the wounded man while Kennedy got the kid ready. Seconds later Mercer was being carried rearward and transfused at the same time.

That was it for his fight. At least for now. For the rest of us...

If we thought that was the main attack... if we thought that had been the best they could throw at us... we were wrong. Turtled on Sniper Hill at the northern end of the island with every fighting Ranger and their weapon facing outward toward the enemy, we were now in a fight for our lives. The enemy released everything they had, and it was clear from the get-go that they were going to wipe us out tonight or die trying.

That was when the captain ordered us into gas masks and detonated the body bags full of chlorine gas as we retreated up the hill.

# CHAPTER TWENTY-ONE

THE wounded were organized at the first line of defenses on Sniper Hill. The more seriously wounded were carried up to the next casualty collection point halfway up and protected by a large rock that jutted out the side of the steep slope. Past the rock lay the trenches that had been dug up to the top of Sniper Hill, passing various improvised defensive positions.

The defense of the hill was made easier because there were only two accessible trails upward: the western route and the eastern route. The hill was too steep to ascend safely without using either of these routes. But then again, at least some of these creatures out to kill us had wings.

The Rangers, mainly the sniper and mortar teams, had fortified these trails as best they could for the majority of the enemy, not given to fly. Holding the giant rock about a quarter way up was left to a rifle squad, while both heavy weapons sections pulled back to the trenches on either side of the hill.

Below, the orcs and other monsters were boiling up from the ruins of the defenses at Phase Line Charlie, clearly unsure if we had pulled back. The snipers targeted the heavier elements like the trolls and ogres and either put them down or wounded them badly. Occasional boulders were flung up into the dark night to land on the side of the hill and go rolling back down. Little damage was done, but it was clear the orcs staging down in the woods and gully at the bottom of the hill were going to have to deal with those rolling rocks.

In gas masks we watched the battle suddenly grind to a halt as the enemy dealt with the invisible chlorine gas. With night vision we could see them struggle, and we ceased fire just to conserve ammo and let the gas deal with as many as it could. Ten minutes later there were a lot of dead down there. But as suddenly as the chemical death came, a windstorm arrived out of nowhere and drove the lingering gas off to the west. It wasn't a natural wind, like some night breeze that comes up unexpectedly with the night. This felt hot and dry like a desert wind. And it smelled of sulfur. You could feel its sting in your eyes even through the filters of your mask.

I checked my watch. It was just after 2100 and I was with Kurtz's weapons section. No one had assigned me to any position and the sergeant major hadn't appeared, so I'd just followed Tanner and the rest of the section up along the eastern trail to the first defensive position. Above us were a few more defensive chokepoints and then the top of Sniper Hill and the mortar teams. We were running out of hill, and the word was… ammunition too. The first sergeant came by and made sure we all had some, redistributing what little we had, making sure everyone had at least three mags. I tried to spread mine out between Tanner and another Ranger, but the first sergeant insisted I keep that much.

We got the "all clear" over the net and doffed the gas masks. Some complained about itchy skin and said if we'd gone to full MOPP we'd be fine. Others reminded those guys that MOPP 4 was a hassle.

At that point we were still running NVGs there in the fighting positions. To the naked eye we must have looked like the orcs below in the gray-green darkness, pushing past each other, handing out supplies, and in my case trying to dig in deeper. Kurtz had put me to work with an entrenching tool to expand our fighting position beyond the access chokepoint.

A few minutes later Specialist Rico opened up with the two-forty on a group of orcs below who were trying for the rock the rifle team was holding while the last of the wounded were moved upslope. Rounds from the heavy machine gun smacked into the gaggle of orcs attempting to push forward. The blazing burst tore them to pieces and left their lifeless bodies all over the approach to the rock. Then Kurtz yelled at me to get back to work while he attached a new belt to feed the team's two-forty. There weren't a lot of 7.62 belts left and soon the command came down from Captain Knife Hand to conserve and only engage if they pushed the trenches directly.

Word was we had five more KIAs on Phase Line Charlie. I didn't hear any names I knew.

I was digging dirt and tossing it outside the trench for all I was worth when the fireballs from below started slamming into the hill all around. The first one I didn't see at all. I only heard Brumm swear and shout "RPG!"

Except it wasn't a rocket-propelled grenade typical of the launcher system every band of *hajis* in the world seemed to have on hand to take out light-skinned fighting vehicles, helicopters, and defensive fighting positions. This… this was just a big ball of fire. I saw it streak overhead and slam into some trees farther up the hill. The explosion was terrific and in an instant the trees were consumed in an expanding cloud of flame that mushroomed out over the slope and pushed a gusty blast of hot air down across us. It didn't smell like gasoline or explosives. It smelled like brimstone and burnt charcoal. An ancient and earthy smell that felt as old as time itself.

Another fireball slammed into the western side of the hill, just missing the heavy weapons section over there.

"Pull the two-forty down!" shouted Kurtz, and Rico made to move the ammunition belts he'd linked. "They know where we're at and they're targeting. Switch over to cover the trench."

In seconds the two of them, Sergeant Kurtz and Specialist Rico, had the medium machine gun repositioned toward the chokepoint that gave access to the trench from below. Meanwhile Brumm and his SAW took the position where the two-forty had been and scanned downslope. The Rangers below were being dislodged from the jutting rock. Orcs in armor and ogres with big double-bladed axes were swarming the lower position.

An arrow slammed into the dirt berm where the two-forty had been. It planted there and quivered and I could see that the feathers were oily and dark. Like a raven's.

Exposed, Brumm began to dump fire from the SAW below the jutting rock to drive off further waves of attackers and allow the Rangers down there to pull back into the trench and get upslope to the fighting positions. Tanner threw himself down into the dirt at the lip of the position and started engaging while Kurtz pulled the M320 from its holster and got it into action, hitting the enemy with launched grenades.

Two minutes later the survivors in the rifle squad came through our position and moved farther upslope to man new defensive positions. The enemy was now using so many fireballs that night vision was washing out with streaks of blazing incoming intense light and also the fires that had started along the slope around us. I had no idea where they were coming from or what was producing them. The air was thick with drifting gray smoke and the flames were creating gusty drafts of hot air all along the face of the hill.

Brumm had just come down from the firing position to load his last drum for the 249 when Tanner noticed the stoic gunner had been struck by an enemy arrow. Out of Brumm's shoulder stood a black arrow fletched with crow feathers. The wood was gray, and the point disappeared inside his fatigues.

"Brumm... think yer hit, man," remarked Tanner as though he were commenting on nothing more than the weather.

Brumm grunted and muttered, "Ain't nothin'."

Kurtz was up from next to the two-forty and shining a red light into Brumm's wound. He shouted at me to take the assistant gunner's spot next to Rico. I lay down in the dirt and got close to Rico, slinging my rifle over my shoulder.

"Nah," whispered Rico as he made small checks on his gun while keeping an eye on the narrow opening not fifteen meters away that led into our trench. "Keep your rifle down next to you on the ground so you can get it up and into action if I need to clear a malfunction." I did as I was told, and he showed me exactly how to keep the linked ammo aligned with the feed tray so the weapon could continue to operate smoothly while working.

"They're comin' up now!" shouted Tanner, who'd taken the initial fighting position the two-forty had been placed at and was taking random shots as opportunities provided themselves.

This was now our OP, our observation position, and it allowed us to see what the enemies below were doing. They could either try for the trench, or try to come up steep open ground, exposed to fire. Tanner was standing, and he'd step up to the lip of the trench there, take a shot at someone and scan the situation. Invariably a couple of black fletched arrows would come whistling up at him and he'd drop back down onto the floor of the fighting position and give us a quick situation report.

That had just happened before he said, "They're comin' up now!"

"Here they come," hissed Rico in the same instant and then added a few Spanish words that indicated exactly what he thought of them. Something about milk and feces and their mothers. I'd heard those phrases before, but I'd never understood their usage. I guess it was a cultural thing.

But it was clear Rico was looking forward to their impending meeting with his "Novia." The M240 machine gun he was assigned to wield.

I was thinking about those words because even in their vulgarity they were comforting to me. Just breaking them down and hearing their ethnic pronunciations in my head felt safe to me. Comforting. Because right now, what would happen in the next few minutes, this was going to be the opposite of that.

The orcs came first, throwing themselves through the narrow opening. Their wide, almost frog-like mouths bristled with rotten fangs and drooling thick saliva. They had shorter legs and more barreled chests than the orcs we'd faced in the gully. Their tattered leather armor was emblazoned with a rusty red fist holding a dagger.

I saw the bloody fist as clear as day even without NVGs, which I'd removed once the fireballs and fires got too intense and started to blow out the night vision. The firelight was throwing itself right against that section of the trench, and everything that stepped into it was illuminated as though taking center stage in some bad off-Broadway play.

Whether Rico noticed the bloody fist on their armor or not, I didn't know. And he didn't care. All I knew was he opened fire with a short burst, found his range was good, and then started to carefully and methodically murder them. This was a machine gunner's dream. Nowhere for the green things to go except through the chokepoint set up in the hill's defenses. The weapon barked and then spat forth a long burst that raked the incoming orcs with sudden explosive impacts that caused sprays of blood, bone, and gore to paint the walls of the trench down there.

They croaked and barked, and that was as unholy a thing as I'd ever heard. One threw an axe as he died, and it slammed into the side of the pit above our heads. He twisted away as Rico hit him, as though he might just run off, and then the specialist hit him with a new burst, sending a couple of rounds through that one's spine. The thing collapsed and lay in a heap.

More came to take its place.

And more died in the face of the relentless two-forty at close range.

I could hear Kurtz shouting for Tanner to engage certain targets along the slope and close at hand. It was clear the orcs were now trying to hit us from both the trench and the slope. Above the thunk and thunder of the two-forty I could hear the ringing fire of the MK18s as I let linked ammo feed through my gloves, keeping the river of it as smooth as possible and flowing into the death machine. I made neat piles of the brass linkage below and to the right of the machine gun. Every dozen or so bursts I would take my right hand and push the piles down and spread them out so they didn't get so tall as to interfere with the ejection and potentially cause a malfunction. The trench was too close and too tight for it to do anything but bounce all over the place and occasionally land somewhere it shouldn't. Like down your shirt, fire-poker hot.

A second later lights of all colors swarmed the trench and began to shift about. Like some kind of technicolor dancing light show from the 1960s. I thought I was having a stroke until I realized everyone else saw them too.

More orcs tried for the opening again and Rico burned through another two feet of belted 7.62 ammo, tearing them apart as they came. I checked the ammo cans and found we were running low. Kurtz had already made sure there was another belt linked and ready to go, and when the time came Rico made it happen and I watched so I could do it in the future.

I had my MK18 up and was firing from the prone. One orc tried to poke his head into the trench, and I fired at him, missing with the first shot and hitting with the second. It scrambled back into the darkness, and the chaos and distraction of the dancing lights gave it enough time to get away from me.

When the next surge came, Rico opened fire, but one of them tossed some kind of clay container filled with oil at us. A flaming rag was corked in one end. The toss fell across the side of the trench in front of us and sent burning oil speeding everywhere across the thick dirt.

I was up on my knees as quick as possible, grabbing the entrenching tool I'd left sticking out of the dirt nearby. I shoveled dirt on the flames and batted at them to put them out.

In the same moment Kurtz got hit by a rock. It knocked him back into the trench and across my legs. When I turned away from the portion of the access trench we were covering with the two-forty to look at him, he glared at me with bug eyes watering and a red face working in anger and rage. He hissed something, but the wind had been completely knocked out of him by the thrown stone.

"Tanner!" shouted Rico between bursts of fire. "Gonna need to help Talker with the barrel change." I looked over to see the barrel of our two-forty glowing slightly red and smoking in the cool night air. Even I knew that wasn't good.

The orcs were pushing forward, snarling and croaking as they came over their dead in front of us, literally pulling themselves into the face of our fire. Upslope, another fireball hit one of the fighting positions and I could hear men shouting over there. Someone was on fire.

There was nothing you could have told me at that moment that would have made me believe anything other than we were about to get overrun and hacked into a thousand pieces. They were pushing our flank with everything they had. The ones in front of us carried scimitars with wide rusty blades. And I kid you not, lightning, an actual lightning bolt, walloped our fighting position, its thundercrack sound shattering the protection our headsets and FAST helmets provided.

Tanner was bent over me, all three of us squeezing into a trench meant for one person, handling the barrel change when the first orc to reach us swung something that wasn't an axe. Later, when talking with PFC Kennedy and recounting the whole battle from our perspective, he'd tell me the weapon had most likely been a flanged mace and it usually did "one-dee-six damage."

I had no idea what that meant.

I only knew that the wide-mouthed bellow-roaring orc who'd suddenly appeared out of the smoke and ruined bodies along the trench had slammed down a weapon right on Specialist Rico's helmet. More were coming in.

There was a hollow *thunk* and I was sure Rico's bell had just been rung by the orc with the heavy mace. The blow was so hard it drove the Ranger's face right down onto the two-forty and shattered his nose.

Kurtz came in over the top, gasping out commands we couldn't hear and firing at the orcs now filling the trench to get us. Kurtz had his version of the famous World War One trench gun out, slam-firing into the snarling faces of the orcs.

Later I'd find out almost every Ranger had brought a personal weapon along for the ride. They'd known this was a one-way trip into the future and they'd all wanted some backup for close encounters of the weird kind. For Kurtz that would be a matte-black short-barreled shotgun with a Raptor Grip like something out of a Mad Max movie. The Mossberg Shockwave. It carried six shotgun shells and it went off in fast, loud, concussive *boom*s above the roar of the surrounding battle. Five shells cleared the assault as Sergeant Kurtz pushed forward, working hard and slam-firing the weapon as fast as possible. In just a few brutal seconds the utterly surprised orc assault was checked, and Kurtz fired the last round, one-handed, into an orc war chief trying to crawl away from the mess in the trench. Then the sergeant was falling back and thumbing in more shells as a new cohort came to try their luck against us.

Tanner grabbed Rico and heaved him off the gun while bellowing at me to open fire on the next bunch.

I'd fired a two-forty once. In RASP.

And again, I'd imagined on that one range day long ago that I'd never actually have to fire one again because all linguists do is talk to the indigs and find out what the insurgents are up to. So here I was, not doing anything like I'd planned.

Plan, meet life. Sorry, plan. You just got rolled.

Suddenly I was more alive than I'd ever been in my entire life. I've done a few things in my short time on the face of the planet. Jump school was crazy fun. Sure. Sidra Paradises was crazy fun, and dangerous, and that somehow made the weekend we spent together in Paris one of the top ten things I knew I'd think about when I was old and ready to shove off someday. One time I drove a Porsche and hit a hundred and eight-six miles an hour. That was pretty cool. That was with Sidra also. All the crazy times were with her. She laughed like a lunatic as we raced through the fog and rain and pretended there was never going to be a tomorrow to live for. That "now" she was always talking about was everything then.

I've done those things.

They were exciting... in another life.

But there has never been anything in what I consider a too-short life as of the writing of this account, that even compared with full cyclic rate of fire on an M240. Full rock-and-roll on.

There. Is. Nothing. Like. It.

This was the unreality of the situation. Looking back it was real enough, but not the mundane reality of remembering that time you took out the trash or saw that majestic view. Those things you remember with your brain. This moment is remembered on a cellular level, an ancient level. There were so many dead orc bodies, spent, broken, and twisted in my narrow and close field of fire that without anyone telling me I just kept pouring fire into the rest of the orcs pushing through that opening.

As has been noted, I have a lead foot and a lead trigger finger.

And yeah. I was screaming at them. And Tanner was dying laughing and telling me to "kill the whole tribe, Talker," and of all the things that will ever happen to me for the rest of what remains, that moment was the most Ranger moment I ever hope to have.

There was nothing like it.

When death was so close and coming straight at you and you just smiled back at it and kept pulling the trigger on a blazing murder machine.

There is no normal after that moment. There's no going back.

Later I talked to Sergeant Thor about it. About "normal" being gone. And this was his reply.

"There is a normal after that, Talker. But it's the new normal. Normal is relative, as in, what's normal to the spider is pure terror to the fly. Be the predator, always, Talker. Always. That's normal for a Ranger now."

In short order the belt was burned short and Kurtz, still clutching his wicked trench gun, had to come up and croak at me to, "Cease fire, Talker! Ain't no more."

I think he'd been hit in the throat by the thrown stone. His eyes were still watering and red and he was opening and closing his mouth like he was trying to suck air and not getting much in return. The look in his eyes was pure murder and as I lowered the weapon and surveyed the trench full of ruined monsters, I came back to myself. I tried to hand the big machine gun to Tanner, but he just backed away, holding the ammo belt and box. He'd followed me up. Laughing as I fired and couldn't stop.

This is madness.

Kurtz took the two-forty away, gently, almost reverently, and then he looked me in the eyes, nodding once. The look of murder gone.

"Good to go," he croaked. "Killer."

This madness.

This is fun.

# CHAPTER TWENTY-TWO

I was sent back to the top of the hill to get more 7.62. The sergeant major was running the ammo redistribution and there wasn't much left to go around. It was midnight. Just after. Zero and change. The wounded lay inside an inner ring of defenses on the narrow hilltop. The snipers were forward along the top of the hill and firing at distant targets down there among the ruined trees and blasted and burning landscape now that the chlorine gas had dissipated. The orc horde and other monsters were coming up for us again. I turned and flipped back to my NVGs to see how much I could see down there. With my mind on the state of our ammo I almost wished for a second I hadn't looked.

The entire island was swarming with orcs and other strange and misshapen creatures. The strangest were a group of what even I recognized as *centaurs*. Half man, half horse. Firing longbows from the river. The arrows they fired came up at us individually as the horse-men rode back and forth along the shallows, covering behind large rocks and fallen logs. It was the enemy's version of designated marksmen. Good shooters. And their arrows detonated in explosive gaseous balls of green fire. Most of their shots came down around the mortar pits, where one of the indirect fire teams was being seen to by Chief Rapp. He was treating them for exposure to chemical agents of some sort and trying to flush their eyes and open their air passages. But some arrows missed the hill and landed harmlessly off down in the river on the other side.

Of course all the other unearthly creatures were still down there too. The orcs were swarming like busy ants and moving forward with trolls and ogres and lumbering giants like the ones we'd taken out the other night. There was no uniformity. Every creature was distinctly weird and different with scars and gear that indicated stories well beyond these three nights of battle. I saw a giant with two heads. It dragged a massive ironbound war club the size of an SUV. And this next wave of giants was mostly using large shields, though really they looked more like the sides of houses that had been ripped away and set to block anything coming at their carriers. The trolls and ogres covered behind trees and hurled large boulders up at us whenever they could, but all the while they were getting closer and closer, taking more of the hill as we pulled back nearer to the top. The ascent would be no problem for the giants and other behemoths. But it would be for us.

A new worry developed. Things this strong really wouldn't have any problem carrying away the Forge. We needed to put them all down before that could happen.

One of the Rangers in the fighting positions used a Carl Gustaf and sent it into a giant just reaching the big rock at the bottom of the hill. The round used was an HEDP. High explosive dual purpose. It punched straight through the giant and exploded in a ball of fire, showering flaming guts all over the orcs supporting its attack. At the same time, a bright line of tracer fire from the heavy weapons section on the western side raked a menacing troll who'd been lobbing stones like rockets up at us. Someone fired an 81mm round over there and tore off the troll's leg, the round exploding in the dirt behind it and probably decimating another twenty orcs and those dragon-dog things moving forward under the support of two mobile ballistae pounding the lower positions along the hill. The two-forty on that side of the battle ripped into the downed troll again, tearing it to shreds, and the monster nightmare twitched and flopped around like a python made of tree trunks, trying to cover itself with its flailing claws as rounds landed all across its dark bulk.

"That was the last one!" shouted the first sergeant to the sergeant major. Meaning we were out of Carl Gustaf munitions. And that was bad news because I could count at least ten to fifteen giants down there and coming forward at us among the ruined trees.

Lightning lanced out from somewhere back near the C-17 and slammed into the two-forty position on the western side of the hill. The gun fell ominously silent and I could hear the chatter of wounded needing help over the comm.

"Get these cans back down to Sergeant Kurtz, Talker," said the sergeant major who then yelled at PFC Kennedy to come and take two more and follow me back to what was now the forwardmost fighting position on our eastern flank.

"Oh, and Talker…" boomed the sergeant major over the din of the battle that was all around and everywhere along the tiny hill. "Your ruck and gear are over there." He pointed where. He'd brought my gear up from the plane. "Take 'em because we might need to *di di mao* at any moment."

I didn't speak Vietnamese, but the term was common enough in the Army. It meant *Get Out of Dodge. Beat feet. Run for your life.*

That was the situation.

I set the drums of 7.62 down and got my ruck on. The staff we'd taken off the high-value-target sorcerer was still tied to it with 550 cord.

Drums in each hand, PFC Kennedy followed me back down the trench that led to Sergeant Kurtz's weapons team. We were halfway there, lugging as much ammunition as we could carry, when the entire cacophony and light show of the battle was instantly overwhelmed by a sudden snap of violent electricity down below on the island proper. Out in the field where our plane had set down. Purple light flared and illuminated the low-hanging clouds, washing over the enemy and all of us on the hill. Like a sudden old-time camera flash, but all in electric purple.

There was a moment where—this is going to be hard to describe but I'll do it the best I can—there was this moment where it felt like everything that was near, was suddenly very far away. And at the same time everything far away, was suddenly near. I could, and I found out later that we all heard the same thing, but I could hear something echoing and portentous, similar to a warehouse door, one of those big industrial doors you might hear in a shipping facility, rolling open like a freight train suddenly appearing out of nowhere at an unguarded crossing in the night on a lonely country road. Or maybe that was how my mind interpreted what exactly I was hearing. Some... door... opening... out there in the universe. The sound of heavy chains suddenly rolling out. Except the sound was both ethereal and more present than the actual battle and all its clamor being fought around us. The chains were like the sound of an anchor being let down into the darkest depths of an ocean that didn't have a bottom. Or a bottom you were better off not thinking about if you didn't want to go absolutely insane.

It was both a sensation and a sick feeling. And at the same time... I knew it was really none of those things. But that was how my mind made sense of it. The light. The noise of the door. The rolling chains. The sense that a door was opening here, and in some other faraway place. An anchor being dropped, and the near becoming far, and the far suddenly becoming near. As though the foreground and the horizon had suddenly changed places in the universe. Like that was actually a thing that was possible here in weird Fantasmo World where monsters tried to kill you and sorcerers could become invisible. And horrors from the outer dark could look like people you knew.

I remembered the ring. The ring that had turned me invisible right in front of the sergeant major. If things got bad... it was the ultimate *di di mao. Get out of Dodge. The last bus to Escapistan.*

Except the ticket for that bus was a ticket for one. And in the same moment I had the thought, I was ashamed that I'd had it at all. Because it was the opposite of what Sergeant Kang had done back down there in the gully when things got real bleak and Mercer was hit.

*"Rangers don't leave anyone behind."*

The ring was a ticket for one.

That sudden purple flash, like the light from a nuclear weapon blasting through each and every one of us on that battlefield...

... It was in that flash that I saw everything, all the outcomes, heard all the noises, and realized I'd never use that ring to get myself out of trouble as long as I was here with the Rangers. If I was gonna Ranger... I'd Ranger all the way to death alongside them.

I saw that.

I saw everything.

Every heaving orc. Every angry giant. Every evil troll. Every raging ogre. The little dog dragon things that were constant harriers. The wicked centaurs firing their poison arrows. The shadow riders in black, with probably nothing more than bones beneath those ragged shrouds and shadowy hoods. A creature down there that was like a small misshapen human. Large nose, needle-sharp teeth. It and those of its kind carried small swords and poison spears.

There were bipedal giant frogs the size of men that had been down in the river the whole time. Under the water and waiting along the bottoms in the deep places. They were still down there, staring up at us from just below the surface of the dark water, and I could feel their intense hunger and their desire to take us down to those deep dark places beneath the black waters like crocodiles do when their prey is between their jaws. To hide us and wait until our bodies have bloated and rotted. Then the feasting would be good. The frog-things were chanting dark bubbly sayings that seemed to hang in the sound of the rolling chains I heard dropping down into the deep wells of the universe's forgotten places. Places we were never meant to go. Places no one was ever meant to see.

There was a snake man down there in the trees. Just a giant snake with a human torso and arms and a flat, broad-bladed scimitar that seemed like something out of

*1001 Arabian Nights*. He had golden arm bracelets that were items of great protection. A flicking tongue that darted between fangs dripping with deadly poison. He was directing the troops all around him. Sappers. Hunching homunculi that looked like crosses between misshapen dwarfs and something far more demonic. Something from those deep dark wells in the universe no one was ever supposed to find.

There were other strange sorcerers down there. Workers of dark magics from all across this ruin of a world everyone had forgotten long ago. They chanted and muttered mutant languages and phrases not meant for human ears down among the charred trees. Firing their fireballs and lightnings up at us when they could. Arrows of acid and flame. Glamours of dancing lights and invisible blankets of hypnotic sleep. Their unseen servants questing and reporting. Back and forth during much of the battle. No two alike. None of them looking like that first sorcerer in the Chinese peasant's hat hiding out in the copse on the other side of the river.

It was a photographer's flash and it captured everything in my mind's eye. And for just a second, I could hear all of their thoughts. Each and every one. And if it had continued for more than a second…

If it had gone on one moment longer…

… I would have gone stark raving mad.

It was a chorus of a thousand languages I'd never speak. Except there was nothing choral about it. It was chaos and madness and discordant destruction. It was five thousand or more self-serving psychotics working together for a common evil if only because they were more afraid of something far greater than themselves. Something that promised them fates far worse than death.

Something worse than *King Triton*.

There was a center to that snapshot blast of magic flash. That purple explosion of light and universe that appeared from inside the C-17.

And then that imaginary anchor chain I'd heard reeling in... it drew away from there. Those warehouse doors slammed ominously shut. And the purple light was sucked from the dark atmosphere over the battle.

We'd all heard it. All seen it. Some probably never processed it. Others did, and didn't know what to make of it. What to do with it.

The dark and chaos of the battle resumed like it couldn't even remember it had been interrupted just seconds before, and I heard all their murder thoughts fading from my mind. Fading to be replaced by the sonic booms of *Mjölnir* smashing giants' skulls one massive fifty-caliber round at a time. Sergeant Kurtz shouting to pull back to the next trench as the bellowing ogres assaulted and swarmed in at his team, firing massive arrows from their huge great bows and thundering their insane roars as if blasting sonic booms of promised murder right into the faces of those Rangers hellbent on killing them with everything they could get their hands on. Someone shouting, "Eat this!" and tossing a grenade right into their midst.

It was Tanner.

I heard their promises disappear in the sudden explosion of the grenade. I heard the rest of their vast horde assuring us death now that the true work was done. Now that the pleasantries had been gotten out of the way. They were released from some dire and dark blood oath that had bound them to this attack. They were free to come and murder us all to death now.

That was their reward for their service to the thing that controlled the purple light and worked the great magics at its core.

We were their prize.

This was the real battle now.

And it was on.

# CHAPTER TWENTY-THREE

KURTZ and his section had pulled back to the next defensive position. The last one we were to hold before falling back to the final positions atop the hill. The two-forty was silent when we got there with the resupply. The team was engaging the orcs in the ascending trench with secondaries. On the slope outside the trench, Brumm was holding them back with the chattering squad automatic weapon, but he was dangerously low on ammo and made sure his squad leader knew all about it. For the stoic gunner this was a downright Shakespearean monologue straight out of *Henry V*.

"Gonna be down to cussin' and bad intentions in about thirty rounds or so, Sar'nt."

Then the specialist unloaded with a fury, draining the SAW and making good on his prophecy as he swore violently. We, PFC Kennedy and I, were setting down the ammo cans for the two-forty when it happened. Obviously the SAW gunner was trying to hit something important, as he'd burned the last of his ammo to do so.

Brumm shrugged off the SAW sling and jumped back into the trench as a fusillade of crow-feathered arrows slammed into the hill all around in reply. Kurtz and Tanner were busy holding the trench from small alcoves they'd carved into the sides. Taking turns popping invaders as the raging orcs tried to take the next ten meters of the trench we were barely holding on to.

Another sudden rain of arrows whistled in and slammed into the dirt along the side of the hill above our heads. Their archers were getting closer and improving their aim.

And then the head of a giant appeared above the lip of the trench. It was huge and bald with one leering eye that burned pure hate, boosting on malice like some junkie looking for a fix. There were small, bloody wounds in its forehead and cheeks. Or rather the savage impact wounds from Brumm's two-four-nine *seemed* small across the cratered moon of its massive ugly giant face. A huge hand the size of a dumpster came up into view, clawing at the side of the trench the Rangers were fighting from. The giant was pulling himself up the hill, using our trench as a handhold, or trying to; mostly he ended up just pulling a huge section of scarred earth away, tearing a massive gap in the slit the Rangers had dug out.

Brumm pulled a grenade and tossed it into the gap, while at the same time reaching for his M18 and trying to cover along the side of what was left of the trench leading to the top.

"Frag out!" he shouted as Kennedy and I threw ourselves down over the drums of ammunition. Maybe because we knew they needed to be protected from blast damage. Or maybe just because they were there. Rico, who'd regained consciousness, flopped over and covered with his arms.

The grenade detonated right under the crawling, climbing giant. The thing bellowed like a howling demon in the night, its roar echoing off into the forest and distant hills. Brumm's M67 pill was the apparent cure for a giant when prescribed from only a few meters. If definitely didn't make its night any better.

"Were you gonna tell us about the giant?" Sergeant Kurtz shouted at the gunner.

Brumm just looked murderous as he prepared to pop out and empty his mag point-blank on the giant's ugly face.

White star-shells arced out across the hilltop, throwing the looming gargantuan into shadow as it arched its back from the explosion that had just showered its neck and chest with hot explosive fragments. Then the giant was fully revealed as the illumination shells shifted out over the wild battle along the lower slopes. It towered above us like some colossus from a lost age. Roaring anger in the falling starlight.

Beyond the MK18s and a few grenades, there wasn't much left to fight it with.

And it was pissed.

"Talker... we're gonna need a bigger frag."

Kennedy was right next to me. We were on our knees, and Kurtz was swearing and dragging a can of 7.62 ammo toward the two-forty. Hoping to get it loaded and up before the giant smashed both of its meat locker fists down on the cluster of us.

"Talker," said Kennedy in the half light of the falling white star-shell. The giant was standing up now, rising like some massive edifice suddenly being erected before our eyes. It was almost impossible to comprehend the sight of it in that moment.

How many times had death been close tonight? I'd lost count. Prior to this mission I'd calculated there would be two, maybe three times at best when the highly valuable linguist I intended to serve as would be in actual real might-get-killed danger. That kind of duty was for studs like the Rangers. My job was to say "We come in peace" in three different Arabic dialects. But now I'd used up my entire allotment of might-get-killeds all in one night and then some, and even those near-death experiences paled in comparison to the moment facing me now, as the giant who'd survived Brumm's competent attention with the SAW, and then a direct up-close-and-personal grenade det, rose above us, raising its titanic fists even higher into a night colored by red war, to pulp the tiny little Rangers it found trying to hold it off in that torn-apart section of the trench we'd been fighting from.

We were stupid and insignificant compared to this gargantuan nightmare.

And I kept thinking… *We're gonna die now.*

And then there was PFC Kennedy. Who was thinking something else.

"Talker… can I see that staff on your ruck?"

The giant bellowed like some war elephant from an elder age.

The staff was still attached to my ruck. The HVT sorcerer's staff with the carved head of a malevolent dragon. The one we'd taken off the high-value target.

The giant prepared to crush us all.

I nodded dumbly at Kennedy, who already had a flick knife out. he cut the paracord and took hold of the sorcerer's staff in one motion. Some flare must've gone off out over the battle, or another explosion, because down there in the dark of the trench I could see PFC Kennedy staring at the staff through his coke-bottle RPGs. That's what we call Army-issue eyewear. Rape protection glasses—RPGs. Or birth control glasses. BCGs. Because no girl's ever gonna find those things attractive enough to attack you when you're running your game at the off-post EM club.

In the light coming off the battle, I watched him study the gnarled staff. Maybe my fear of imminent death by crushing made everything startlingly clear, but it wasn't until that moment that I noticed that PFC Kennedy was half-Asian. Later I'd find out his mom was Korean. His dad some American guy who'd become a judge. He was the very image of geek. Bony and tallish. Angular face. Dreamy eyes made freakishly large by the RPGs. Pale Asian skin and light freckles the gringo half of his parentage had contributed to the union. And he played games about imaginary worlds with strange-shaped little dice, assuming characters that were every bit as real to the players as real people were real, in real life.

Role-playing games.

Another kind of RPG.

He stood suddenly with the twisted dragon-headed staff in both hands. On the floor of the pit, shooting from a crouch, Brumm blazed away with the M18 and a mouthful of dip, determined to, if nothing else, annoy the giant as much as possible before it killed him. He was the opposite of the overwhelming fear I was currently experiencing. I'll admit that. My network was down. I was "in the black." But Brumm and Kurtz were pure hate, hating the giant right into its big ugly face even if we were all about to get smashed.

Kennedy's voice rang out, cracking because he wasn't the type to use it much at that volume. You could tell he was quiet and nerdy. Probably opinionated enough to have learned it was best to keep his mouth shut. One had to wonder how he'd ended up in the Rangers. But now, like some Shakespearean actor playing a role in a bad B-movie about a wizard and a bunch of kids trying to kill a dragon menacing the local town, he shouted right up into the face of the giant towering above us all.

"I am Malendron! Emerald Mage of Xathia!"

That was where his voice cracked, and some dark part of me found that funny enough to take note of, despite the fact that the giant's lone eye was glaring down at us with every intention of crushing us to death in the next instant. I could see the monster had been wounded in a dozen places, yet it didn't seem to mind. It was bleeding out rivers of blood from all those wounds, and its insanely malevolent mind couldn't have cared less.

If I had to guess what it was thinking at that moment, I'd translate it as something along the lines of, "*Hulk Smash!*"

Then I saw the living fire, just like little fireflies at first, crawling up from the bottom of the sorcerer's staff that Kennedy the Magnificent, or whatever he'd just called himself, was holding up in the face of our immense destructor. In the blink of an eye the fireflies coalesced into a rope of living flame, and then all at once the rope became a huge whip that lashed out at the giant.

It wasn't fire now. It was white-hot plasma. And as it hit the giant it exploded, blowing him clear off the side of the hill and out into the darkness of the night like he was a gnat that had just been swatted. Not just knocking him back, but literally flinging him away like in those action movies when the villain gets blown off the skyscraper and flies outward, hands flailing in slow motion as death becomes both imperative and imminent in descent. All so we can get to the hero's tagline.

*Talk about a big fall.*

But something wittier than that. Something that a team of overpaid Hollywood screenwriters might come up with between martini lunches and doe-eyed starlets.

I knew the giant fell, because after about three long seconds of hang time something huge struck the earth below the hill and went off like a MOAB. A big one. A Mother of All Bombs.

At the same moment a wave of orcs—these were carrying small skirmisher bows—raced forward to exploit the breach, firing their arrows and drawing their next one as they moved surefootedly through the darkness all around us. Even while the ground was still shaking.

Kurtz was just getting the two-forty up and ready to go. Brumm was putting a mag into his empty M18. Tanner was holding the trench because they were still pushing from there, and me... well, I just sat there with my mouth open because that giant being blown off the hill by PFC Kennedy's trick was pretty amazing. Way better than anything I'd seen in every year's must-see CGI abomination.

I mean... c'mon. A giant just got roasted and then blown off the side of a hill in the middle of a firefight.

That was pretty cool.

Then the orc skirmishers were at the lip of the ruined trench and shooting, moving forward, and just as the arrows started to fall into the exposed section of the trench, PFC Kennedy pulled his next trick.

Exactly how did he know how to do any of this? I had no idea. But he pointed the dragon's head right into the swarm of oncoming savage orcs, and it literally became a flamethrower worthy of any military technology. Black and white footage of Marines clearing caves on some island in the Pacific during World War II flashed in my brain as a burning jet of flame splashed out over the cruel orc faces. They were hunched over their bows and moving forward as a cohesive unit, and in the next second they were all on fire and done for. Roasted right down to their bones. Their flesh just... melted.

It was one of the most horrible things I'd ever seen.

Some orcs at the back tried to run. A couple fired their arrows but the crawling flames cooked those too. Anyone closer than that never stood a chance.

Even Sergeant Kurtz stood there in amazement watching PFC Kennedy—the Ranger batt's dogsbody and perpetually-under-threat-of-Article-15 or RFS, Released For Standards, low man on the totem pole—wipe out no less than thirty orcs and a giant in mere seconds.

PFC Kennedy. He was cackling with delight as he unleashed the power of the ancient staff. You know, just like power-mad villains do in movies when they finally get the MacGuffin and decided to use it for evil, not good.

Totally consumed with their own awesomeness.

In the next instant he shot about five massive fireballs down into the attacking forces along the hill. Bigger than anything that had been used on us. We couldn't see what happened, but the explosions were terrific. Then, all of a sudden, he just turned around with a strange look on his face like he was gonna say something interesting and collapsed. Fell over without even trying to protect himself from hitting the packed dirt floor of the trench. The way guys fainted in formation during change-of-command ceremonies that seemed like they'd never end. The dragon staff went one way, and Kennedy the other.

I caught the staff.

There were more orcs and goblins coming for the ruined section of the trench now. Rocks and arrows rained down on us and Brumm was up with his M18, covering at the side and firing.

It was clear we could no longer hold this part of the defense. Kennedy had only bought us some time.

"Fall back!" shouted Sergeant Kurtz.

We were about to be overrun.

# CHAPTER TWENTY-FOUR

THE enemy's last push wasn't so much a push as a final go-for-broke surge. There was only one direction we could go now. Only one direction we could be pushed toward. And that was down the back of the very steep hill and into the deep end of the river.

With wounded and civilians, that wasn't going to happen.

Things were not looking good. For all the forces of evil we'd waxed, it fell like the only thing that had come of it was giving up ground. That felt like losing. Honestly, at that point I was convinced we'd *lost*. Past tense. But not the Rangers. To them, it was like they had the enemy right where they wanted them. Everything had been done to lure the enemy into this final, perfect trap where the Rangers could shoot targets in every direction.

It was some time after 0300. I knew that because 0255 was the last read I saw on my watch before it stopped working. That was a while ago. Our smartphones were dying, too. We'd been charging them at the Forge, which contained a small internal powerplant, but they were starting to run dry. Same story with the ammo. We'd been ordered to use semi-auto fire only, due to low ammunition reserves, and we were down to the last redistribution. Some guys had started picking up enemy weapons. Gnarly axes.

Jagged spears. Rusty, blood-covered swords. All weapons with some kind of reach. And of course, the tomahawks the Rangers carried were ready as well, as our defense constricted and constricted around the hilltop everyone called Sniper Hill, and I thought of as Ranger Alamo.

I'm an optimist. Really.

The last push came, and it was nothing but a brawl. I went to the top of the hill twice, first dragging the lifeless Kennedy who wasn't dead but seemed to be for all intents and purposes, then assisting the dazed Specialist Rico. So I was already there at the peak when Kurtz's section, or what remained of them, came back up for the final defense. The two-forty was tossed aside. It was bone dry and there was no ammo to be had for it. Off to my left I could see the sniper teams, shooter and spotter, continuing to fire down into the surging masses of orcs, trolls, goblins, and other unknowable things making their way up the face of the hill to come and get us. The monsters were getting crafty about staying low, using cover, and even slithering through the piles of their own dead to get close enough to attack. They had figured out that our "boom sticks," as they most likely called them, needed to be avoided. And all the while their drums and horns were calling out to one another, indicating they were timing and coordinating their last big assault.

The air was loaded with tension. You could feel it.

And why shouldn't they come for us now? They'd taken the worst we had to offer and their numbers seemed no less motivated for it.

These were things, monsters, a kind of people in their own way, that had probably lived and breathed desperate survival from moment one of their horrible existences. They weren't like us. There was no civilization, no hospitals, no police and emergency services to protect them when they were young and not warriors. They were probably more like Spartans who'd been neglected and maltreated from birth in order to select for better warriors.

They knew nothing but survival and conflict.

Which is to say, they were more used to walking the razor's edge between life and death than we were.

But that didn't matter to the Rangers. Not in the least. To the Rangers, it didn't even matter that we were down to our last mags with no support and no wire to fall back behind. No place to hunker down or even retreat to. No air cav to make gun runs. This was it. This was last stand at Ranger Alamo time, and yet the men around me had no doubt that they were going to *make 'em pay for it.*

Kurtz kept saying that as he organized his defense on our wing of the hill. "Make 'em pay, dammit! Make 'em pay."

The snipers were the only ones not low on rounds. They kept up fire with methodical intensity. Working the enemy for the targets they'd prioritized for death. The big ones. The "tanks" of the enemy. The trolls and ogres. The war leaders. I saw Sergeant Thor, and his face never came away from the stock of the magnificent *Mjölnir*. Every time I heard the massive boom of the anti-material rifle, debris suddenly pushed away by the explosive power, he was shifting for his next target. Listening to the spotter working the range finder. Acquire and fire. Barely a few breaths as they killed another. And another. And another...

And for all that killing, it didn't seem to make a damn bit of difference in the size of the dark horde coming up the slopes for us.

The sergeant major appeared, checked me over, and moved on without saying a word for a long moment. I figured he had nothing to say and then, "Find a weapon, Talker. One of theirs. Gonna need it, son."

Then he was moving on down the line, checking his troops. The mortar teams were out of rounds and moving forward to the line, sharing out their mags to guys who were dry.

I knew things were bad when Chief Rapp showed up, jocked up and ready to go with all his high-speed SF gear and weapons. He'd definitely switched over from Life-Saver to Death-Dealer.

We were on the left flank, or eastern edge of the hill. The heavy weapons section was taking the access trench that gave out onto the forward slope. And Chief Rapp just walked up to us, casual like he's just stopping in to say hello, big white teeth smiling in contrast to his Mississippi-mud dark skin. Like everything was gonna be great soon as we got this done.

"Guess I'll fight with you boys," the special operator said to Sergeant Kurtz.

Kurtz nodded and asked the chief what his team could do to improve the defense.

The chief lowered his rifle, letting it hang by the sling with the butt resting on his chest, and suggested positions we should take up to mutually support each other in what looked like a last-stand situation. He had us roughly in a circle at that side of the hill. We dragged containers and clamshells into heaps for some cover.

"This our circle, boys. Circle of trust," said the chief, his basso profundo voice rich and sonorous in the middle of the night cold. "Rule number one... no one violates the circle of trust."

I could see what he was doing. As long as we held this circle along our flank, the enemy couldn't flank the snipers or reach the wounded at the center of the defenses. If the circle broke, then the enemy could sweep the hilltop, rolling up each section one by one.

Captain Knife Hand and the XO came along shortly. The enemy was busy firing flaming bolts from the ballistae they couldn't get up the hill. The massive flaming spears streaked through the air but overshot the hill. It was impressive, but of no tactical value.

The captain saw Chief Rapp's layout, nodded, and moved off quickly to check the rest of the sections. He trusted the SF advisor with a Ranger captain's most valuable asset: his troops. Nothing else needed to be said. Nothing else could be improved on in the highly trained SF tactical advisor's plan to hold the line here along the eastern edge of the defenses.

Twenty minutes later, and the night was only promising to get darker. The moon was gone, and it was nothing but pitch black when the horde of monsters came screaming up the last of the hill and made their final push. This was a charge. Pure and simple. No flaming arrows. No war drums or *Uroo Uroo* horns. They came up silent and determined, holding in the roars until the last as they scrambled over the dead, going for broke one last time. They'd pushed us this far; just a little bit more and there'd be nothing left to push. You could see that was their plan.

Plan, meet Rangers.

I was covering behind a stack of clamshells that seemed flimsy at best. To the inner rear of the circle of trust.

Meaning I was close to the wounded. I had no idea what to expect, which was probably for the best. I just kept watching my sector.

Others along the line were already shooting when I saw the humanoid frog creatures coming up the slope from behind us. I called out targets and started to engage at the one-hundred-meter mark, semi-auto and putting rounds into the bullfrog shamans with spears. I'd decided they were shamans, dark holy priests, because there was something in them that evoked the German word for shaman. *Schmane*. They wore ragged loincloths and necklaces made of teeth—a popular fashion statement out here—and they wobbled as they flopped up through the weeds down there at the base of the hill.

I spent a mag killing them until they weren't coming up anymore. As I scanned the darkness down below, I heard overwhelming fire start up behind me. The orcs were coming out of the trenches below the base of the hill, boiling out like a chemical reaction from some bizarre science experiment. Don't try this at home, kids. You'll never get rid of the stains and you won't like what the orcs do to the carpets.

Brumm had someone else's MK18, probably off one of the more badly wounded. He was busy engaging the orcs, squeezing hard and fast to keep them from getting out of the trench. Pointing the weapon and selecting new targets like he was going for expert on a range full of pop-ups. Never mind these pop-ups were going to flay you alive if they got close enough.

It was incredible: as fast as you put one down, two more crawled forward, and if you targeted those two, seven more were squeezing out to lob hand axes and spears. I felt one barely miss my bucket and cleared an angle to fire and shoot at an orc getting ready to throw another. A fast-moving goblin that managed to do what six of its comrades hadn't been able to do—get close—leapt out of the line of fire Kurtz was pouring into his sector, curved dagger out, and flung itself at the Ranger sergeant. It jabbed him with the dagger, but it was hard to tell if it stuck deep.

Bad mistake for the goblin.

Kurtz dropped his rifle—it was single-point slung so it just dangled—and throttled the thing with one hand. Then he jammed the tanto knife he kept on his plate carrier right into its brain. It went limp like a puppet, and Kurtz tossed it aside like it was nothing and he had no more time for it as he brought his rifle back into play and shot three more in rapid succession. The rounds left smoke trails that ended in goblin and orc chests.

Chief Rapp had a whole front to himself. Basically, the section of the hill that linked up with Kurtz's sector and then attached to the snipers who now looked to be shooting at targets close at hand. Just beneath the lip of the hill where it was steepest, and the horde couldn't assault directly.

The chief worked his rifle easily for such a big man. His marksmanship was incredible. Things he shot stayed dead. The orcs had pushed over the lip of the hill, coming up an almost vertical section of the slope, and thrust heavy iron shields out in front of them to protect their foothold against our line. The first few to do this died as the chief nailed them in the head at ten meters. But, as was the enemy's way, they had numbers, so if they lost a few dozen just to take a few more meters, no problem for them. Or so it seemed. Foothold was everything to them. They had bodies to burn.

Eventually one orc, covering behind a shield up, monkeyed into place with another to lock big iron shields and form a defensive line. The shields were heavy enough to deflect rounds. I would have rolled a grenade at them, and was on the verge of doing so, but the chief just waited for an opening, his focus riveted on the sight picture at the end of the barrel of his rifle as it danced and shifted left to right like he was playing a game with them, getting them to drop their guard, and then he fired. Total focus, never mind the gunfire, rocks, and arrows. Blowing off a head or putting a round into a peeking eye was the entire world for the giant Special Forces operator.

The shield wall collapsed as the chief showed them how their plan wouldn't work. But the orcs didn't care. They just pushed more forward to stab and cut. Rangers were going hand-to-hand now. Slashing tomahawks against vicious little short swords. Sweeping enemy hand weapons aside and going full savage as they planted their axes in skulls and chests. The enemy kept coming. This was their big moment and they were going for it. As though they knew Chief Rapp and the rest of us couldn't have too much more of our "boom magic" left. Maybe that's what their own chiefs and shamans were telling them in the dark chants I could sometimes hear between the bouts of our gunfire and the punctuations of explosions as the last of the grenades were used.

A troll hit the right flank, and I saw someone, a Ranger, lifted up and bitten in half. Then two other Rangers swinging tactical tomahawks leaped onto it and started wailing away like jackhammers, flailing their agile axes down into the thing where they'd grabbed on to it. A second later the troll went over onto its back, and all of them went rolling off down into the darkness at the bottom of the hill, crashing and crushing through the orc horde coming up.

I saw the sergeant major blazing away near the wounded. Firing his M18 near point-blank into an ogre and three orcs who'd somehow gotten in between the snipers and the right flank. He gave no ground. First round he put through the ogre's brain, gore and matter exploding out the back of the misshapen lump. Then he continued to put rounds into it as it swung a giant two-handed sword even as it fell and almost hit another Ranger.

There was a bright flash, a flashbang of some sort, and I couldn't see anything for a few desperate seconds.

I shielded my eyes and scanned my sector. A group of orcs were trying to come up the way the frog shaman men had. I checked the sergeant major, but he was gone and the three orcs who'd supported the dead ogre with the big sword who'd come at the wounded were dead now.

Chief Rapp was next to me and tossing grenades down at the orcs. One two and three. The orcs down at the bottom of the hill near the ruined corpses of the frogmen just stood there as the explosives went off. They were torn to shreds.

"Stay in this, Talker," Chief Rapp said calmly. "Almost through it. I can tell." Then he was back and shooting down more orcs scrambling over the edge of the hill.

Knives and arrows showered the Rangers and the chief, and some stuck. Whether in the armor or the flesh was unclear. The enemy moved fast, like a cross between a spider and a monkey. And none of that mattered to the SF operator at the front of the line. He continued to shoot until his magazine ran dry, and then he had another one out. His movements seemed so slow, so slow and so calm like he wasn't bothered in the least. Almost too slow, like they'd get him before he could be ready to fire again. But that was all just an optical illusion. His slowness made him smooth. And the smooth made him a kind of incredible fast.

Unlike me, who was still having to think every time I needed a new magazine. By the way...

Last one.

I knew what to say even though it didn't matter. It just felt like admitting defeat at that moment.

But I said it anyway.

"Mag out!"

I swapped the empty for the last loaded magazine I had and targeted more orcs with my MK18 rifle. They were coming out of the trench and trying to move behind us. I kept shooting them as fast as they could boil.

Then something happened. And the something that happened was this... though I didn't know it at the time. I can only write about it now having digested it. Dissected it. Thought about it in the quiet since. Lived through it to tell no one in this account no one will ever read.

I was mad as hell because I was down to my last loaded magazine. And proud of that fact at the same time.

*Mag out!*

Black on ammo. I'd used up every round issued to me to kill the enemy. I was down to the last of what I had been entrusted with. And there was something in that... some pride that meant something I couldn't quite explain, knowing I was down to my last. Knowing I was making my last stand right here with everyone else. That no one had cut and run. That I had not. And the anger was really that I wouldn't have any more rounds to kill any more enemies with. Which is a good kind of anger. I made every round in that mag count. I made them pay.

Then I found a small sword. It was a dirty, dented, banged-up thing. Notched and scratched. The hilt oily and smelly. It had to have come from the discount Rent-A-Center clearance aisle of used swords. Remaindered at half price two-for-a-penny just-steal-these we-don't-care swords that one could find on that hill at somewhere after three o'clock in the morning. Long night. Somewhere between never and dawn.

It was mine.

Now that the last of my ammunition was used up, I would use this, and I would go on killing them for the obvious little that remained of me. I would teach them, as I had with all my rounds, the error of ever meeting me out in the dark.

*Be meaner than it, Talker.*

Roger, Sergeant Major.

I'd never felt anything like that before. I was a long way from the known… and fine with that.

I imagine that's what warriors, real warriors, Rangers, carry with them every day. That's what makes them Rangers. I felt it for a moment as we were being surrounded, shot down by clusters of arrows, and overrun on that hilltop.

The arrow fire had not stopped. Several Rangers had black arrows sticking out over their carriers, thighs, rucks, themselves.

I had killed this far. I could kill a little more.

I was heaving with rage when the dark rider came up the hill, his horse rearing and fear-struck as it rode down the orcs in the trench just to get at Chief Rapp. The grave-shroud cloak and rags that had covered it were thrown aside. Black armor, well-made and dusty, lay underneath. It was a skeleton. Skeletal. It wasn't human. It had a death's head, a skull for a head. It came out of the trench, the horse crying madly, hood thrown back and swinging a great silver sword at us. And there were more, more of the dark riders riding straight up the hill and vaulting the lip as the Rangers mowed down the last of the orcs, the last push with the ammo they still possessed.

The riders screamed, and the scream was an ethereal howl and a hiss all at once. One rider swept his sword at a Ranger and practically cut him in half.

Slick as a snake, Sergeant Thor turned with *Mjölnir* and rapid-fired the .50 caliber Barrett anti-materiel right into the rider bearing down on another Ranger engaging a swarm of orcs with the last of his ammo. Every shot from *Mjölnir* hit, leaving giant smoking holes and tearing off armor fragments and finally knocking the skeleton in armor off the horse. The horse was hit and died screaming.

Thor advanced, drawing a bead on the skeletal warrior who was not dead, or at least was no deader than it had been to begin with. The thing swept aside its tattered cloak and flung its tremendous silver blade out in a wide arc, cutting wide to keep any harassment away as it gained its black boots and got ready to fight.

Thor fired one shot at the skeleton's skull, and it exploded in a dusty *puff*. The thing was down.

I had my cheap sword in my hand. Behind me, Kurtz had a tomahawk and his M18 out. Brumm was behind him, and they were rushing the trench, shooting the orcs and slashing at them.

The enemy turned, and finally, finally began to flee.

It was over.

We'd driven them off the hill.

To the east the sky was getting light, and I could hear great beasts trampling off through the night, smashing trees and tearing them down as they fled for the river and the dark shadows of the wilderness beyond. Seeking caves and dark places they thought we would not go down into.

We'd won.

For now.

# CHAPTER TWENTY-FIVE

WE sat in the quiet of early morning as the last of the night shadows faded in the rising of the sun. Dawn was breaking, and there was mist down there on the river flowing around the little island. Ranger Alamo. The light was golden, turning the trees out across the river lighter shades of pastoral greens, evoking spring instead of the dark ominous foreboding late-winter tangles they'd been in our desperate days before.

The topic of what season it actually was, and if seasons meant anything anymore here ten thousand years in the future, had been hotly debated by everyone during brief breaks in the endless tasks to prepare for each night's onslaught. We'd left Fifty-One in late August. The weather had been sweltering everywhere across the globe, and a lot of the reports of inexplicable random acts of violence and mass hysteria had been chalked up to a crazy heat wave sweeping the world in those end-of-days times. Lighting everything on fire both literally and figuratively. Like the world had a fever. Like it was fighting off something bad. And losing.

It was a lot to take in. And you really had no idea what to believe. There were even reported rumors of sudden outbreaks of mass blindness. Things were crazy, and the world seemed intent on embracing the madness.

Anyway, back before we left, it had been a late, hot, sweltering end-of-summer simmer that made you wish for the cool of fall. Maybe even the first blush of winter. Since we'd arrived, the place seemed to be in late winter. Ten thousand years or so in the future, everyone was still complaining about the weather, about the relentless chill in the air. There was no place to get warm. Even the grounded C-17 was constantly cold. It didn't snow and there was never any frost in the morning, but it was cold with a chill that never departed, and when an early-morning breeze or something in the late afternoon came up, it took the warm right out of you and froze you down to the bone. Like a forgotten porterhouse steak left in the freezer too long.

But now, here atop Sniper Hill, sitting in the first light of a new morning and surrounded by piles of dead monsters that hadn't smelled too good when they'd been alive, it felt like some sea change had just taken place. Like the seasons, or even the micro-seasons, had just flipped the next page on the calendar in the night while we fought to the death. Careless of our struggles. It was shaping up to be one of those beautiful days. You could tell from the very start of it.

Things were different now.

The situation had changed for us.

Or maybe it hadn't. That was still to be determined. But it felt like it. If only because we could count ourselves among the living few, and not the many dead littering the top of the hill, its sides, and the island and river below. Everywhere you looked.

NCOs were going around getting the ACE reports, and none of them were going to be "blue sky" coded. There were casualties, ammo was down to practically nothing, and lots of equipment was either missing or damaged. So about as far from a blue sky as it gets. Info was being disseminated. Twelve more KIAs. That's how many we'd lost last night after Phase Line Charlie collapsed.

I tried to remember how many of those I saw first hand. The Ranger bitten in half. The guys who went rolling down with the troll—they had to be gone, right?

The attempt to recall quickly felt heavy. A burden. I let it go by reciting Macbeth's Tomorrow and tomorrow and tomorrow soliloquy in one language after another. Out, out brief candle.

Everyone was flat smoked. Even the relentlessly preparing Rangers just sat there for a few minutes as the day turned from pre-dawn to dawn. Still holding their weapons and staring at the dead like they could murder them all over again. Some of the more callow souls dug into their MREs. But no weapon maintenance, clearing of bodies, or improving of positions was conducted for those first few minutes of dawn.

You just looked around to see who was still alive. Glad you saw the faces you did. Sad when you didn't.

The Rangers had fought for their lives, and now they were done, if only for a moment. Even the NCOs sensed this, moving about their endless business with less general chastisement than usual. Quietly busy and even encouraging at points. The Rangers had earned a few minutes' peace, and the NCOs made sure they had it. They just needed to ignore the fact that the brief respite took place on the top of a corpse-covered hill.

This was nothing new for some of them. You could see the ones that didn't seem to mind it. If anything, it made them happier. And hungry for the tasteless MREs they'd been issued before the battle. Some finished theirs and asked their buddies whether they were going to finish their own. As if to say hunger didn't care. Hunger was hunger.

And you never knew what was coming next.

Soon word got around that Sergeant Jasper had been the Ranger the troll had bitten in half in the middle of the last fight. Later we'd find out Kang and Soprano were still alive. They were the two who'd jumped the troll with tactical tomahawks and then gone rolling off down the hill with the huge beast. So I'd been wrong about seeing those men die.

Soprano had been knocked out and lay unnoticed in a pile of dead orcs. Kang had E-and-E'd, *escape and evasion*, downslope and gone on a killing spree behind enemy lines, cutting throats in the dark where he could find them. When they found him, he was covered in blood and eating an MRE he'd found on another dead Ranger. He didn't talk for a few hours, but came around by nightfall. Not that he was wordy in the first place. None of them are. The Rangers, that is.

Me, even I was a little quiet. My throat was dry, and I couldn't remember the last time I'd drunk any water. I needed coffee. I needed coffee badly.

I mixed cold water and instant coffee in my canteen and sat there drinking what I told myself was a cold-brew. It tasted like chlorine. I told myself that was the roaster's choice. Mind over matter.

You don't mind. It don't matter.

Everyone agreed Sergeant Kang had straight-up Rangered. Hardcore. The sergeant major got Kang sorted and hydrated and then muttered down to the buck sergeant,

"Don't try so hard, Sergeant Kang. You'll make us all look bad." And then he was off to another task.

I saw Kang nod to himself as the command sergeant major walked away. Then he smiled a little as he began to eat another MRE, inspecting the various packets within. Seeing and not really seeing. You could tell that. But even then, he was coming back around. All it took was the approval of a senior NCO he wanted to be like more than anything in the world, and he would come back for his brother Rangers and try to forget what he'd seen down there alone in the dark.

I understood leadership a little better then. I watched the whole interaction while I was helping out with the wounded.

The birds came out just before sunrise, but they were cautious about sending forth their songs for a few minutes. Then the first, tentative trill came, and not long after life was in full force out among the trees.

We sat there, waiting for another attack, and when it didn't come, they got us up and moving, and that's when the informal body-tossing contest began. Work would take our minds off the horrors we'd just lived through. Or at least, that's what I suspected.

The Rangers were tossing dead orcs off the hill, letting them roll downslope toward the river. Points were awarded based on how close the tossed body made it to the river's edge.

In a matter of minutes there were rules for the game of *Toss the Dead Orc*, and soon there were two-man teams and—of course—betting. What else were you supposed to do?

I had about two hours with the wounded, helping Chief Rapp and the Baroness and a few of the other Rangers who'd been specially trained to serve as secondary medics. Like I said, this all happened while the hill was being cleared. No one had any idea what we were gonna do next. Even the NCOs expected to get the "hold until relieved" order. It was clear that despite low ammo to no ammo, they were preparing to hold the hill again for another night. Regardless of current events.

Captain Knife Hand led a patrol down to recover the dead, find the missing and wounded, and recon the C-17.

Spoiler. The Forge was gone.

I didn't need the still-unconscious PFC Kennedy to tell me that that strange purple light show halfway through the battle before the final assault had had something to do with that. Teleportation magic or something else that once was considered ridiculous. Like they, the big whoever behind this attack, used the "magic" this world made real to basically hijack our Forge and get it out of here. Chief McCluskey? King Triton? I remembered that sickening feeling of the near becoming close, and the close telescoping far away as it all went down. The sound of an anchor in the universe dropping and then being reeled back into some unknown space we were never meant to see. Or know of.

Whatever that had been, however my brain had interpreted those signals, that had to have had something to do with the hijack of the Forge during the battle.

Later, the snipers spotted her first.

Those of us helping the wounded and clearing corpses noticed a commotion. The snipers—not Thor, he was cleaning weapons—spotted a target down there on the river. A rider on a dappled gray horse. Standing at the water's edge on the far side of the river.

"Hope she don't step on a mine," muttered Tanner as he heaved one of those dragon-dog-men off the side of the hill. "'Cause that'd be real bad for her."

Her. Yeah. Now that I studied the figure it had the shape of a girl. Rangers had good eyes and of course they made the distinction. I had to concentrate to get those details. But they'd spotted her and identified her as a "her." Then again, the snipers had the best optics in the world. They were probably studying every inch of her up close through their scopes.

I couldn't get too involved. I was busy holding up an IV for one of the Rangers because that was the help Chief Rapp needed. Professional IV holder-uppers.

But then the call came in to the first sergeant who was running the hilltop to send me down with Tanner. Someone else would have to do my super-important job of IV holding because now… I was gonna do some languages. Stand back everyone. Linguist comin' through.

More than a few of the Rangers gave me the old stink eye because I was getting to go down and interact with a female. That she might be a dangerous witch-vampire-succubus didn't seem to bother them. Each and every one of them was convinced he could run some kind of game on her and was probably getting his best lines together. Ten thousand years in the future was beginning to remind some of the Rangers that there were other things to be missed besides unlimited coffee and dip.

Heads up. What if there were just orc women here in the fantastical future?

It wouldn't have stopped them. Fact.

Still, I drew the long straw. So, lucky me. A few witty interactions with the cute co-pilot had me feeling pretty confident about my future if I survived getting hacked to pieces. As long as Sergeant Thor stayed glued to his scope I was probably going to win any competitions to see who was going to recolonize this world.

We grabbed our gear, me and Tanner, him along for the ride because I was now considered valuable and in need of protection. It wouldn't do to have one of the dead orcs out there playing possum on the field suddenly come to life and stab the only guy who knew how to speak a bunch of different languages.

As we left the hill I spotted Volman doing nothing but sitting there helpless among the wounded. Deep State wasn't hurt. He was wrapped in a poncho someone had given him and just sat there staring off into space like some earthquake survivor. Content to let the work of his survival be handled by others.

I was reminded that the sergeant major expected me to do something about him. And not just *something*. Y'know… actually kill him. I had hoped the sun would rise on an orc sword stuck into his carcass and that little problem having been solved for me. No such luck, as the sun instead rose on his pathetic form wrapped in a poncho liner within the casualty collection point.

I may seem to be understating the gravity of this. But I'd been through some training that made me understand why the action expected of me was a necessary one with respect to the ongoing mission. I'm not saying I was hip about it. I'm just saying I understood the rationale. Still, I hadn't done it yet. So there was that to consider. That moment of truth.

Not far down from the top of the hill I could see the rider and her horse. They'd crossed through the shallows of the river and managed not to get blown up by any left-over mines or high ex that hadn't been detonated during the three nights of battle. The girl was now along the shore near Kurtz's weapons section's original defensive positions. Talking with Captain Knife Hand, the sergeant major, and the pilot. A Ranger security team had set up a perimeter around the meeting.

But before we get to that I need to take a moment to describe the battlefield as it looked that morning after three nights of fighting. Coming down the hill and crossing the island.

I don't know—as in... I don't know why I'm doing this. This account. Who is this really for? What? Am I gonna sell my war memoirs on the other side of this? To whom? There are, as far as we know, no publishing houses left ten thousand years in the future. And even if, let's just say, we go back in time to the present we left. Disregard that apparently the world was doomed at that moment and what we're seeing now is the bitter harvest of that long-ago plague that ruined the whole mess. Disregard all that and say the world got another twenty to a hundred years for me to live out the remainder of my life in relative non-monster normalcy. Who in the world would believe the things I've written down are actual memories, and not just the insane ravings of some dork science fiction writer?

Going back in time isn't even remotely possible. That QST gate thingy... that ain't here. And during the brief in the big hangar at Fifty-One they specifically made it clear that time travel was a one-way deal. You can only skip forward. Not back. Apparently, Bob Dylan was right about something.

So what? I take a cart and mule from distant human settlement to distant human settlement, loaded down with codexes of my writing painfully copied by hand to see who might be interested?

"Do any of you fine people know how to read? No? Ah! Well, these also make excellent fire-starters."

For real. Who'd ever buy it? Who'd ever even read it?

The answer is: uh... no one.

And no one is going to believe this.

So... why am I doing this? Why am I writing all this down?

The only answer I can come up with is that someone has to do it. Someone needs to put it all down in an account. A record. The facts. Warts and all. And so... I nominate me and the Mont Blanc pen my mother gave me as a sarcastic, and yet very expensive, gift saying that I was wasting my life joining the Army.

Well—who's laughing now, Mom? I'm still alive ten thousand years later, and I'm probably the world's greatest writer by default, seeing as I am probably the world's only writer.

Game, set, and match, Mom.

Even that's not the real reason for writing it all down. That's just me trying to get it all out. Everything I was feeling after three days of life-and-death struggling.

No, the real reason is that if Chief Petty Officer McCluskey was to be believed about anything he told us, then everything going on needs to be written down.

I'm betting that... yes, he told us a lot of lies. But in order to make them believable, he told us some truths to wash it all down with. Pro liars will tell you that's the best way to do it. To lie. A little truth helps the lie go down.

So, parsing everything SEAL McCluskey tried to download on us... I'd say the part about technology breaking down was probably pretty accurate. Why? Because he didn't have any. No firearms. No smartphone. No watch.

Further, the monsters who'd attacked us for three days now had attacked in some sort of orderly fashion indicating civilization and culture. Tribal. Kingdoms. Warlords. They were organized. But they had nothing more than rude Iron Age technology. The most sophisticated crafted technology we saw employed against us was a ballista. A giant crossbow invented by the Romans, I think, used for siege operations. Or some other Hellenic civilization thought it up and the Romans took it. That was how they did things. If I could Google stuff I'd find out. But Google's about ten thousand years out of date now.

So that's another reason for this account... to preserve the knowledge acquired. I don't know what I'll do when I run out of room in this fancy journal I brought in my pack when all the other Rangers were smuggling favorite weapons and backup ammo in theirs. I'll scavenge. Make paper, or maybe the Forge could have made paper, I'm sure that it could've. But of course, it's gone now in a big giant mind-bending purple flash off to who knows wherever.

So... yeah.

Finally, I'm writing this all down to mark the dead. I've written their names down in the front of this journal. That's important. If anything, I'm doing it for the Rangers. I'll tell what they did, what the ancient Greeks called *Deeds*, and I'll remember them after death. That's the least I can do.

If it weren't for the dead I wouldn't be here. None of us would.

That's why I'm doing it. This. This accounting of the facts. Warts and all. This is why I'm here.

And so... the battlefield. On the morning after, as I climbed down the hill to meet with our mysterious guest.

Here's what I saw.

Descending the hill, we had to leave the trench on the western face of the slope. It was so clogged with dead and rotting orcs, along with other strange creatures, torn to pieces by our savage machine-gun fire, that it wasn't even passable. The stench, even in the breeze, was overwhelming. We pulled our shemaghs up and continued carefully downslope.

Below, I could see the mostly burned carcass of the one-eyed giant that PFC Kennedy, as *Merlin the Magnificent* or whatever he'd called himself, had blown off the hill with the dead sorcerer's dragon-head staff. Most of the rib cage and guts had burned up. The head was thrown back and leering skyward with its milky eye rolled up in its head. The fact that the skull hadn't burned and that it was still a human in face, in the loosest sense of the word, made the horror show somehow much worse.

I muttered to myself as we passed various tableaus of butchery such as the half-burned giant that this was the worst thing I'd ever seen.

And then about ten steps later I'd see something much worse and say the same thing.

We made the bottom of the hill and stayed out of the gully. There were lots of bodies, or parts of bodies, down there, and again we weren't completely convinced everyone was good and dead. Plus the flies seemed thicker down in the dry streambed. Maybe because the air was cold and moldy in there. We followed a sandy trail passing crater shells where mortars had rained down steel death on the attacking orcs, goblins, and other misshapen monsters that tried to stage their assault on the hill.

Several had been blown into the trees and gored by bare limbs up there. That was pretty disgusting. Like the wide-eyed and ravaged corpses were just bad art-school installation pieces done by psychotic art majors who'd lost their post-postmodern minds. Trees that had been struck by mortar fire had fallen on other orcs and crushed them. Mostly. We passed a large log one of the Ranger teams had fought from when falling back. There was expended brass all over the sand there. Orcs as close as five meters had gunshot wounds. Farther on we passed a troll that had been holed and gutted with a Carl Gustaf. 84mm round right to the stomach.

That smell was a special kind of rotten.

"Brumm got this one too," muttered Tanner. He spit a stream of dip juice all over the black and hairy misshapen body of the ruined troll. It was huge. As wide as three men, shoulder-to-shoulder, almost. And it stank to high heaven. It was wearing colossal boots that were covered in muck and slime. A massive club made from the twisted trunk of some dark-wooded tree lay a short way off. Its features were almost comical if you didn't look at the death rictus snarl and its yellowing and broken teeth gritted in pain as it had died badly out here among the trees in the night. It had wart-ridden flesh folds over its eyes, making them deep-set. The nose was long and shaped like a potato gone bad. Its skin was black like the skin of a gorilla. And it was covered in boils that oozed even after death.

"That's sick," said Tanner as one of the boils popped softly in the morning silence and then oozed out its greenish-yellow load into the sand to mix with the congealed blood and dried gore.

The flies loved this.

I was just glad the horrible thing was dead. I was glad Brumm had such an affinity with the Carl Gustaf. I'd hate to meet one of these things out here in the dark, alone.

We passed more lines and waves of dead orcs that had been shot down as they advanced on the Ranger defenses. The thing I noticed about these was that they fell into types. As though they'd been organized into fighting units. Seeing them come for you at the end of your sights, looking for all intents and purposes like the pure nightmare monsters they were, green skin, claws, fangs, and roaring some ancient tribal battle cry, it was easy to just classify them all as monsters. But here in the morning light, you could see how the Rangers, as they fell back toward the hill, had killed groups of them with either sudden overwhelming firepower or from ambush. Or landed targeted mortar strikes amid their bubbling massings. And they'd gotten groups. Groups of roughly similar types working together.

We passed skirmishers with short bows. Caught advancing through a small clearing by an ambush of Ranger automatic fire. We came upon the expended brass first, out in the woods and high grass. Dribbled everywhere. Tanner noting it and play-by-playing the whole fight as he saw it all go down.

"These guys engaged from here. So... over there should be more brass if they ran the ambush right."

Tanner probably could have been an NCO, and tabbed, if he didn't have two ex-wives and three DUIs. He made that clear whenever possible.

We checked Tanner's hypothesis. They did run the ambush right. There was more brass over there. And the dead orcs lay there stinking in the morning heat to prove it.

Then we checked the skirmishers. Shot down in the clearing. Bloating bellies, shattered bone. Pools of congealed blood and brain matter in the sands. Blood spray painting the high grass that barely moved down here in the still stench of the corpse-filled island morning.

The flies were really going to work.

Later we found infantry. Or what we decided to call *orc heavy infantry*. These were large orcs with armor kits that consisted of iron skullcaps and scaled chest armor that looked poorly put together. Big heavy shields. Forged axes, instead of bone or rock wrapped around clubs, and spears. Swords they hadn't drawn.

Grenades had ruined these. And then more gunfire.

Finally, when we came out along the river's edge, I saw the security perimeter of Rangers being run by a fire team sergeant. The rest on one knee and facing outward. And at the center, Captain Knife Hand, the command sergeant major, and the pilot.

The sergeant major saw us and waved us over. Then I remembered again I was supposed to have retired Volman. The guy currently sitting like dead weight among the wounded and planning some new way to make life more difficult than it already was for everybody.

"She don't speak English, Talker," said the command sergeant major once Captain Knife Hand, the pilot, and him had me in their midst to explain the situation. "We need you to go talk to her and find out what she wants. Captain here is going to listen along, and if you can translate, he'll instruct you how to respond. Copy, PFC?"

"Copy, Sergeant Major." But there was a problem. "I don't even know if I understand what she speaks, Sergeant Major. So…"

"Just do your best," said the captain, who looked like he had a minor case of indigestion rather than the full-blown nausea the rest of us had. The smell down here, by the river, where the enemy corpses, including the giant Brumm had killed on the first night, had been soaking and rotting in the water… it was like a bag of diarrhea down here. Not to put too fine a point on it. But like I said, this is an account of what actually happened, and that means warts and all.

It smelled really bad and the flies were so thick I was dreading having to lower my shemagh so she could see me speak. That was standard translator protocol. Make sure they can see your lips moving. Better for communication with people who already had a language barrier between you and them. In combat, language barriers led to misunderstandings. And misunderstandings led to people getting killed.

So cut down on the misunderstandings and make communication as clear as possible.

I'd have to speak while not ingesting flies, and did I mention the entire river smelled like a bag of diarrhea after a Taco Tuesday in which the consumers had voted Taco Bell the best Mexican food in the entire world?

I did mention that. I know.

It bears repeating.

I really need to make that point and I think I have. Even now… I can honestly still smell it as of this writing and we're nowhere near that river now. It was bad. Real bad.

I walked out to the edge of the river with Captain Knife Hand to talk to the first person who hadn't tried to murder us or stab us in the back since getting here. I wasn't saying she wouldn't later. I'll confess, it was nice having the captain with me. I was pretty sure he could kill her even if she was a *were*-vampire-succubus.

Later, when PFC Kennedy came around, he explained that that was a thing. A possibility. Were-vampire-succubus. Who knew?

Her dappled gray horse was off grazing on some non-bloody grass nearby. A rarity given the state of the field. She stood with her hands down and clasped in front of her. A completely non-threatening posture. She was cloaked, and as we got close I could see that the cloak, which was green like the forest around us, covered armor I nearly overlooked. It was a dull, almost translucent silver, made of some kind of fine chain mesh. She wore high leather boots that appeared well-made and supple. For a moment I hoped—just... hoped—that everything McCluskey told us was a lie, and that there were indeed human civilizations here in the fantastical and barbaric future... and that there would be coffee.

I'm selfish that way.

Then she reached up and pulled back her hood, and we met our first elf.

# CHAPTER TWENTY-SIX

I won't bore you with all the details of how I found out we had a language in common. Actually two languages. Korean and *hochdeutsche*. High German. There was some trial and error—and listening first to another unknown language she spoke before I got a trail on something vaguely familiar—that finally registered a hit for me. I sighed when she spoke that first language and cursed myself for not learning the made-up Tolkien language the nerdiest among my scholarly peers loved to make fun of others for not speaking, because she sounded a lot like that. But other than a few words and phrases I couldn't seem to remember at the time, I didn't speak Tolkien, or whatever they'd called it.

And listen, I was tired.

I'd barely caught any sleep during the last three days of trying not to get killed by an orc horde, doing the command sergeant major's dark bidding, well, thinking about doing it, and moving behind enemy lines, digging trenches, and generally running for my life. Plus there was Kurtz, and that dude wore you down just being in his presence. Not by anything he said, because he didn't say much, or anything he did, though he was always doing something. Very Ranger-Rangering NCO. He wore you down because he was Kurtz and he hated the world and you by extension because you were in it. The weight of his hatred was like an extra sixty pounds in your ruck. You could handle it... but over time it wore you out. And you began to question why it was even in there. And you hated it.

Very tiring. Very tired. I was very tired.

My mind was working at half capacity, at best, and I still hadn't eaten my morning's cruddy MRE when the call to get moving down the hill came. Not that I was hungry then. You had to be pretty stone cold to eat anything on the island of diarrhea meets bag of death this place had become. There were Rangers doing just that right now. But I suspected it was all just another unofficial Ranger pissing contest to see who could be more gruesomely hardcore than anyone else. They got some secret thrill out of that. Right now, I'd snort a line of instant coffee if I could. But that was as hardcore as I was willing to go.

The point I'm laboring to make here, is that I wasn't exactly at my best.

After passing all that carnage on the way down the hill, the shattered and torn-apart orcs and the gutted troll oozing pustulant boils, I felt exactly the same way I'd once felt after a night in Vegas in which a friend said we wouldn't need a hotel room. We'd just "pick up chicks" who had one.

We didn't.

And I slept in a booth at an all-you-can-eat buffet until they kicked me out at eight a.m. when they set up the make-your-own-waffle station. Tossed me outside and blinking into the harsh Vegas daylight feeling like I was nothing more than a walking husk that city and every horrible person in it had sucked the life from. That was exactly how I felt walking toward the meeting with the elf girl in armor who'd come inside our metaphorical wire on a dappled gray horse.

I wasn't in top form. To say the least.

But the moment she lowered the hood of her forest-green cloak, I had a new problem I needed to deal with.

She was flat-out gorgeous.

For an elf. Then again, she was the only elf I'd ever met, and so maybe all of them were like this. If so... the fantastical future wasn't looking all bad. Nail down that coffee hookup and I might get by.

Perfect heart-shaped face. Stunning silver eyes. Yup. Silver, translucent eyes. Otherworldly. Pale, flawless skin. And yeah, long pointy ears that twitched at sounds in the forest—and even that was kind of cute and sexy. It appealed to a freaky side of me that I didn't even know existed until now. She had straight black hair, so black it was almost blue. Full lips.

Female. Me like.

Now I was hungry, undercaffeinated, tired, scared to death, having the time of my life, and... probably in some form of love. Plus lust, obviously. I was probably as close to feeling Ranger now as I ever would be.

And it was time to work at talking.

Listen. Speaking languages can be pretty hectic. Not *working a two-forty to the level of load, fire, engage, reduce malfunction, reload, literally see the remaining moments of your life manifested in the length of the ammunition belt left on a machine gun in the face of an overwhelming enemy attack on the score of something last seen during the Korean War and its special form of hell, the human wave attack* hectic, but tough all the same in its own way. You gotta play heads-up ball. Otherwise miscommunications lead to misunderstandings which usually lead to death. For someone.

Still, no environment I'd ever done translation in had these particular parameters. Tired, cranky, in lust, and… need. As in need coffee. Badly.

Plus, ten thousand years in the future.

Okay. So cut me a break. I couldn't speak instantaneous Tolkien on demand. Plus, nothing I'd ever learned in all those ivy-covered institutions ever indicated I'd actually need to. If you'd have forced me to bet on what fictional language might serve me best in the future, I'd have said Klingon. And I've have been wrong.

So as I babbled through some languages I knew, trying out common phrases, it was *Anyong haseyo* she responded to first. Reacted to, in other words. Not *Do you speak Korean,* which I'd already tried. She responded to the formal greeting non-Korean speakers would use with Korean speakers.

And when I asked her if she spoke Korean, she had no idea what "Korean" was. That didn't register for her.

But starting from there we got some basic communication going, and that's when the German started to appear in her speech patterns. She referred to it as *Grau Sprache. Gloomy* or *Gray Speech.*

But it was when we flipped back to the Korean that she didn't even call Korean that she stopped the whole conversation dead, throwing up her hands in clear confusion. And frustration. I'll admit that was kinda earnestly sexy. Again, even on dead body island, I was deeply in love with her already.

I'll just interject this here now that I have time to think about it as I write it all down. Think about why I fell so instantly for her. Because right there, at that moment speaking next to a fetid-corpse-swollen river and after three days of otherworldly monsters trying to kill all of us, she was the opposite of everything around us.

I could tell that from the start.

She was kind. Innocent. Pure, even. There was something untouched by all this evil lying dead all about her that made her stand out in stark contrast. She was *good*. It... radiated out from her and filled the air all around. Like some new-age hippie-dippy vibe. And maybe, beyond that self-serving coffee addiction I was nursing, maybe I was afraid, had been afraid all along, that along with all the other things missing ten thousand years in the future, that missing right along with everything else was that there was no good left in the world anymore.

So it makes sense, as I think about it now, that amid all that future shock and fear that I was going to live the rest of my life in a coffee-less, good-less hell, and those are not the same -*lesses*, despite their substantial overlap, that I would respond as I did when I found standing in front of me a real live... hot maiden fantasy chick. Like one from an epic about knights and unicorns and maidens who are pure and strong and good of heart. Arthurian long-form epic poem stuff. With eye candy to boot. That didn't hurt.

And the fantasy chick was real. And hot. Real hot. And I was being useful! I was speaking languages! Victory me.

As if to say, *Look everyone... I'm officially not useless. I'm talking to the hot babe.*

I looked back up at the suckers on the hill pointing their rifles down at me and watching through their optics. Then I smiled so they knew that I knew they knew. That she was hot, and I was talking to her first.

I turned back to her and stared at her earnest, heart-shaped face. And somehow that made me want to cry a little. Because it meant that good wasn't dead just yet. It was still alive even if she was the last flame carrying it around here in this crazy messed-up future.

I felt it best not to weep in front of her, as we had just met. And also Captain Knife Hand, who was following the whole conversation like a man waiting for two DMV workers to greenlight his paperwork so he could get on with his day, even though he didn't understand a word of it, probably would've karate-chopped my carotid artery if he saw me start to cry. If just out of general embarrassment for the entire unit.

So I didn't.

Later, the captain told me he'd picked up a little Korean when he was an infantry platoon leader on the DMZ. But he assured me what he knew was completely inappropriate for first-contact situations.

There she was, in her forest-green cloak that did little to hide her shapely though well-armored charms. Her earnest and cutely confused face. She even stamped one boot in frustration, bringing the whole conversation to a halt.

"How," she began haltingly. Our versions of Korean were little more than distant cousins of one another, but they were still more closely related than our versions of German. So I muddled through. I'm pro like that. "How..." she continued, "is... you speak... Shadow Cant?"

I clarified that I didn't understand what was meant by *Shadow Cant*. She ran through a few of the phrases we had just spoken in Korean, though again the word for the Korean language meant nothing to her. *Hanguk-eo*.

"Do you mean *Hanguk-eo* is... *Shadow Cant*?"

She thought about this for a moment, biting her lip and raising one alabaster hand to her forehead to brush away a bothersome fly. Hey, another neat thing I noticed about her. Around her, the smell was gone. It was like it refused to come near her. Or rather, her presence drove it away. Only that one fly managed a kamikaze run to make it next to her. It got sluggish and slow and barely missed getting hit by her hand as she brushed it away. I suspect it was glad to get away from her and fly off toward all the ruined juicy bodies bloating in the river.

Back near the others, the sergeant major and the perimeter security fire team, the flies were swarming, and the Rangers were in constant motion batting them away.

Then she nodded, and I'm translating here. "Yes. Most sacred language of... Shadow Elves. Never... ever... spoken outside the... most sacred gatherings... and hunts."

She stared at me hard, like she was willing me to be just a myth of morning mist and vapor rising off the nearby river. Like I was not to be believed if her world-view were to continue as it had.

"How... do you... know this... Shadow Cant?" she asked in frustration.

# CHAPTER TWENTY-SEVEN

IT was at that moment Deep State Volman decided to show up and start shouting at our new friend and possible ally. The hot elf girl. To be honest... it wasn't a real good look for us.

He immediately identified her as a "friendly," probably because we weren't shooting at her, and instead of attempting to ascertain not just how, but also why she'd threaded the gauntlet of enemy orcs hiding out there beyond the river's edge and waiting for another night to attack, he decided to co-opt her for his little power struggle. The one he was waging all alone, internally, against everyone else in the detachment.

"Excuse me," said Volman, with all the statecraft and ceremony of a New York City subway operator as he pushed past the Ranger perimeter security team who'd tried to stop him. The command sergeant major gave a tired nod to let him pass un-throat-punched. He came tramping through the tall grass toward our hopefully new friend. Intent on ruining that as quickly as possible.

He was shouting questions and orders in every direction at everyone in an attempt to seem "in charge." His sudden attack was stunning and divisive, and truth be told, I could see it caught the captain and the command sergeant major off guard for a moment. Or at least they seemed unsure how to proceed when the bureaucratic chaos ensued.

I was pretty clear on how the command sergeant major *wanted* to proceed.

Retirement. Cleaned. Dead. Which I was supposed to have done by now. Bad look for me.

"Who is she?" shouted Volman as he came close to her. "Who is she exactly, gentlemen?"

It was clear he didn't think any of us were actually gentlemen. Including the captain and the pilot who were officially supposed to be.

And then...

"Ma'am. Ma'am. Ma'am," he barked at her. His voice was like an annoying dog late in the night. "I'm with the US government, and I'm the ranking diplomatic authority here." Emphasis on the personal pronouns. "Disregard these men. They work for me. Can you tell me where your superiors are so I can open diplomatic relations?"

To the captain he shouted at almost the same moment, "I'm in charge here now, Captain." All of this with an intense hostility we would have found useful on the line last night at Oh-Dark Murder when the hordes were trying to overrun us all and slit our throats.

To me, as he got close, he jabbed his finger and barked, "You. You do languages, Private First Class. Start translating exactly what I say. Verbatim. Right now, or I will have charges preferred against you and you'll be shot immediately for treason. Try me, PFC! Just try me and see."

The command sergeant major gave me a look, and honestly, I wasn't all that sure what it meant. It was a combination of *Don't do it* and *You're on your own now.*

The captain looked like he was ready to throat-punch Deep State Guy. Repeatedly. Not a muscle moved on old Knife Hand, but you could tell his whole body was coiled with rage ready to be unleashed violently. And that he didn't need to visualize how it would be done. How he would crush Deep State's larynx with one rapid-fire punch fired like a jackhammer. And then continue to do it just for fun or because he had some issues he needed to work out. Because that was just automatic for him. Other people dying at his hands was something he had no trouble visualizing. He just needed to decide that beast mode was socially or conditionally acceptable with regard to the mission, and then it would happen.

It had been a long three days for all of us.

"Tell her this..." continued Deep State Volman, failing to notice the exchange of murder-looks currently surrounding and regarding him. He was truly the most clueless person I'd ever met. It was obvious he'd sensed that his moment to take control was right about now. That there was a new element involved and in play, and he needed to be in complete charge, and this was it. If he could bring external pressures to bear against the captain, then maybe things might start to go the way he wanted them to go. Which, as far as he was concerned, was the only way they could possibly go. There was no room for any other decisions than his. We were not to be trusted at all.

Only his elite brilliance could manage this current crisis, and now was the moment to start crisis-managing.

Typical government.

"Tell her I am the duly appointed representative of the president of the United States of America," Volman said, his voice strident and barking in the fly-buzzing silence. "And that... tell her... that we need to open diplomatic relations with her people immediately. Does she have people? Tell her she and her people are to deal only with me, directly, from now on! Is that clear, PFC?"

He'd passed some kind of edge of sanity. His voice was ragged and hoarse as he practically shouted at me what he wanted translated. There was spittle. He was heaving with rage and sweating, and I could tell the events of the last three days, and most likely last night specifically, had severely messed with his head. Fried a wire. He was afraid. He was all alone. And he was desperate to be in control.

He was also surrounded by Rangers. People who, had their energies not been channeled positively, relatively speaking, would have been problems back on the block for law enforcement and government authorities. Not the kind of people you'd want for enemies.

That should have been Deep State Volman's biggest concern, but the clueless idiot he was, he wasn't concerned at all. Didn't even think about the highly trained killers surrounding him.

Imagine being that dumb.

He was going to be in charge from now on even if it meant all of us getting killed. That was clear.

I could see the sergeant major and the captain watching me. Seeing what I would do. Reading my mind as best they could because I seemed to be a critical part of the interaction. Then I saw the sergeant major give me a slight nod. And I thought I knew what that meant. Or at least... I hoped I did. And now it was time to see if my guess was right.

"This is our village madman," I said in Korean to the hot elf girl. Then I turned and bowed reverently toward

Idiot Volman. Indicating to her, hopefully, that he was who I was referring to as the "village madman." Volman stopped heaving and swelled with sudden pride at having been acknowledged as an obviously important person. A look of naked superiority crossed his face as he basked in my faux adulation. He had finally won. In his mind. Even though he had no idea what I was saying because he didn't speak Korean.

I turned back to her and continued "translating."

"Where we come from, we consider these sad unfortunates... worthy of our care and respect. They often rant incoherently like this when not defecating on themselves, or trying stare at the sun until they go blind. I deeply apologize for this interruption, Miss. If you will bear with us, he will shortly find some ridiculous invisible goat to chase around, claiming it will give him a magic horn full of beans. It is his way. He is simple and has always been so."

She looked at me with slight amazement. Just a touch. And then she turned and bowed to Deep State Volman, joining the pantomime.

I'll confess the slight amazement she cast my way was pretty sexy.

Volman didn't stop her, and he only barely told me to stop her. "Tell her not to do that," he said without conviction, feigning irritation. "We are a democracy. We don't do bowing. Though you should probably thank her for coming to rescue us."

I nodded to Volman that I would indeed translate all this. Faithfully.

Then I turned to the elf and said, "Everyone calls me Talker. I speak for my people when they don't understand languages we encounter. What is your name? He asks if you've seen his magical goat. There is no magical goat. He's an idiot who falls into deep holes and doesn't have the sense to climb out. Pity him. We do."

She stared at me for a long moment. Then spoke. "I am called… Last of Autumn… among my people. Tell him… I haven't seen any… goat. I would know a… magical goat… if I saw one."

I turned to Volman.

"She agrees to negotiations with you. Her people are not with the enemies that have attacked us over the last three nights. I have no idea what her intentions are."

Deep State Volman thought about this for a moment. Then barked, "Ask her if there is someplace nearby, a city, a, uh, a refugee camp, or some 'civilized' place where we can get behind some walls and find safety until I can open formal negotiations. Tell her the Rangers are out of ammunition and no longer combat-effective. We have wounded and we need food and safety immediately. Tell her our situation is extremely dire."

Then he grabbed my shoulder, and his hand was like an iron claw.

"You'd better be telling her this verbatim, Private, because I'll find out."

Excuse me. I'm a PFC. A private first class, buddy. See that rocker? They don't just give those away to anybody.

"Got it," I replied. "A-firmative."

*A-firmative* is the unofficial, and still official, way to indicate how much you really don't like someone of a higher rank right to their face. Either over comms or in person. That's because you can't get in trouble for saying it, but everyone knows exactly what it means by the way it's said.

He shot me a look of that pure contempt he constantly distilled. If I had been a cockroach, he wouldn't have hesitated to stomp me flat and brush me off with the side of his adventure-guy Timberlands.

I turned back to Autumn. Last of Autumn.

"He's having one of his bad days. He claims the goat he is seeking grants magic wishes and that when he finds it, he will wish for all the cheese there ever was… and also, to fly like a bird so he can touch the moon. He was dropped on his head as a small child."

I smiled, hoping Deep State Volman didn't see the slight jerk of my head and bare widening of my eyes to indicate that everything coming out of his mouth was silly nonsense and needed to be treated as such by her.

Did facial expressions in non-humans such as elves approximate our own? I had no idea. But she seemed to go along with it for the moment.

"We…" I pointed at everyone else except Volman, and he didn't catch that. "We're wondering what… you're doing here. We are very pleased to meet you." I continued acting as though I were communicating what I'd been instructed to say by the Deep State guy. "As you can see, we have fought a great battle here. We have no idea why these…" I pointed at the maimed corpses of the orcs floating in the river and shot to pieces along the banks, "have attacked us."

I nodded to Volman to indicate I'd finished a faithful and verbatim translation of his words. Which I hadn't in the least.

Autumn, Last of Autumn, looked around and began to speak.

"My people are in hiding from... same foes who have... come against you. I do not know who you are. You are strange... and not from any of the lands... known to us. That is... plain to see. But... we are... foes of the Black Prince... any that are foemen to him may... possibly... becoming allies to us? I have to ascertain your... intentions."

She didn't say "ascertain." Or "foemen." Not those particular words anyway. Remember, she was speaking not-Korean. Pidgin Shadow Cant. And translation isn't just a matter of swapping out words. You have to capture nuance, connotation. Even style. It's as much art as it is science. Not to oversell it.

But this is the gist of what she said, as best I can represent it.

I turned back to Volman.

"She says we're in trouble, sir. She and her people are enemies of the... orcs."

Volman made a face.

"First of all... Private. 'Orc' isn't an official term. I've designated it a racial slur and I'd prefer to refer to them as 'insurgents' until we properly identify their culture. Slang and slurs start us off on the wrong foot with a people who may one day be our ally despite your captain's best efforts to make them our present enemies."

"Her words."

Volman looked directly at Autumn and started talking loudly like she was both deaf and stupid. I used this opportunity to wink at the sergeant major and the captain. Letting them know I wasn't translating for Volman. Or at least that's what I wanted them to understand via a single quick wink. I was pretty sure the captain had never been winked at by a PFC and that if he ever had been, that PFC was now buried in a shallow grave out in the woods.

Even now, as I write this, I feel ashamed of the wink. However, there is no hand and arm signal in the Ranger handbook that conveys "Don't worry, I'm not actually translating this lunatic."

Maybe in the updated version there will be.

"I need to meet with your 'head person' immediately," said Volman as loudly and as stridently as possible. Like he was now ordering her around too. "Can you take me to her or him—I'm deeply sorry if I don't understand your pronouns—so I can request assistance for my people."

He was making hand signs. Two fingers "walking" back and forth to indicate movement. His fingers up around his head like a crown to indicate someone in charge, including himself. When he said "my people," he swept one arm out to indicate both the corpses and soldiers under "his command." He did this with all the warmth of a used car salesman at one of those shady lots just off base of every military installation. The places we're forbidden to go and where everyone spends their re-enlistment bonus on a new (used) Camaro for four more years of going to exciting places and killing interesting people with your best friends.

I "translated" this again.

"What's our situation?" I asked her, and didn't wait for an answer. "I'm pretty sure my leaders would like to work with your people. But... I don't know if we can survive another attack."

"They will come... tonight again," she said, looking seriously around at the dead orcs. Then: "I offer you... the fellowship of my people and a place around our... cookfires. Our hidden home is... day's march... if we move through the night. Yes. Your... situation... here is most... dire. They will be back tonight with even more warriors. The tribes of the Nether Sorcerer, who is... ally to the Black Prince... are many and... unending. They will never stop. My people have greatly... suffered. In the deserts of the east they say they," she pointed at the orcs once again, "are as numerous as the sands of the sea. They will lay you waste... in time... if you do not... escape this place. Now."

I turned back to Volman.

"She says we must leave soon to reach her people and that they will give us friendship and protection. She says the or—" I caught myself, but not quickly enough. "The insurgents will be back again to hit us even harder. Tonight, most likely."

"Good," said Volman, slapping both hands together like he'd just closed a deal on someone's soul. Or a new (used) Camaro. "Tell her I'll be ready to leave within the hour. I just need to get my stuff from the top of the hill."

Then he turned to the captain.

"I order you to wait here and hold this position until I can negotiate with these people and arrange for our further relations. Then I'll return."

Back to me.

"You're with me, Private."

Without waiting for an answer from the Ranger captain, he was off and stomping through the woods again, pushing past the Ranger security cordon who got the wave from the command sergeant major to just let the man go. Un-throat-punched.

I turned to the elf named Last of Autumn.

"He says he's seen that magic goat just now and that he will go and capture it for you. He thanks you for helping him on his quest and considers you a princess. If you will excuse me, for a moment, I need to take him somewhere before he soils himself. I'll be back in a few minutes. You'll be safe with my friends here. I think we will very much want your assistance. And friendship, Autumn."

She made a face I read easily. A blush. The color in her cheeks was amazing to see. It made her come alive, more alive than she had been before. She was embarrassed. Like I'd used the *familiar* instead of the *proper* version of her name. *Autumn* instead of *Last of Autumn*. That was an easy linguist spot.

"I mean... Last of Autumn."

She nodded formally and then bowed her head.

I was following Volman back off to the hill. Tanner made to go with me, but I waved him off, shrugging my shoulders like I had no idea what was up. But I knew what was up. I knew more than anybody what was about to be up. Except maybe the command sergeant major.

Tanner stayed and watched me go.

"It's time, son," muttered the command sergeant major as I passed.

# CHAPTER TWENTY-EIGHT

IT wasn't like I had the clearest set of instructions. And I could see how it could all go real wrong if I'd read the room incorrectly. I told myself this as I followed after Volman, who was moving fast now, tramping through the underbrush and stumbling over ruined corpses all while breathing heavily. Talking a mile a minute about what we were going to do next. What we were going to accomplish now that things were going his way finally. We were going to go off with a stranger on nothing more than the hope they were a friend, so Volman could "take control of the situation," as he saw it. He had big plans about an embassy. He was already babbling on and on about it.

He was mad, of course.

He was delusional.

He'd snapped. That much was also clear.

And that made him dangerous to us. To the mission. To our survival. More dangerous than he'd been when the sergeant major had first told me to *retire* him. It was one thing to try and mingle among the Rangers and foment dissent. He had some points. Everyone's re-enlistment was up. Technically, by about ten thousand years. Given enough time he would have found the troublemakers and made things difficult for everyone. Especially considering it looked like hanging together was the only way we were going to get through this alive.

Whatever *this* was.

As we walked back toward the hill, Volman was telling me I was no longer in the Army and that I was being deputized as an official State Department employee and that I was now to report to him and him only. I was a GS-4 now. He gave me a promotion and told me I owed him. Big-time. He sounded half mad. If not full mad.

He pushed past the brush and into the trees, never minding the ruined corpses of the orcs, trolls, giants, and other misshapen beasts I'd yet to encounter. It was like walking through a morgue that decided to turn into a funhouse run by cheap carnies with a very sick sense of humor.

It was a whole new kind of morning after.

He was about fifteen feet in front of me. I'd slung my rifle, quietly drawn the sergeant major's pistol, and was screwing in the silencer when he suddenly turned around, wild-eyed, and flopped down on a ruined log that had mostly splintered. It had taken a direct hit from a mortar round sometime the night before. We'd come to a small clearing that had been shelled when things were looking desperate.

Things were still desperate.

There was a severed arm lying in the sand, but he didn't seem to notice it. It wasn't human. Huge, brawny, green. Spiked leather gauntlet that looked pristine apart from the blood and gore.

And I'm standing there with a silenced pistol, staring at Volman. My intentions were obvious.

Or at least I mean... they would be to me if I suddenly turned around, paranoid and stressed out, and saw a guy with a silenced sidearm following me. I would have realized I was about to get hit. Assassinated. Killed. Retired. Cleaned. Pretty obvious. But of course... that's the kind of hit man I am. I make sure to play all my cards before pulling the trigger. Like standing there right in front of your target with a loaded silenced weapon and pretty clear intentions about what's going to happen next. Like the pros don't.

So there I am, red-handed.

And he chooses not to see the reality of his situation.

He just sat down on the log and had his iPhone out in an instant. Lost in its world of endless screens. He was typing into it furiously, both index fingers working as he stabbed angrily at the keys.

We were about a quarter mile away from everyone. From the team down near the river. From everyone on the hill. The flies were thick and swarming and the new heat in this day, a thing that hadn't been there since we'd arrived, was hot and getting hotter. Volman wiped sweat from his brow while making, if his muttering was any indication, a checklist for diplomatic relations with Autumn's people.

"Did she say what her name was?" he asked sharply, not waiting for the answer before he asked another question, still not looking up from his screen. "Did she say what her people were called? We need to start co-opting them to our agenda if we're going to get embedded here. That's a big priority!"

I shot him.

He'd seen me with the pistol, so when he looked up at me again, I expected that his mind would put two and two together. As in, *Hey, that guy with the silenced pistol just shot me. I didn't think he'd do that. But, well, he did.*

But that wasn't the look.

The look was pure surprise. This hadn't been part of any plan his fevered mind had conceived. This wasn't an option as far as he was concerned.

Well, it was.

I hadn't shot him in the head. Didn't want to take the chance of missing even at close range. My hand, the one holding the sergeant major's sidearm, had been shaking the whole time. I didn't trust me. And if I sound calm now in this warts-and-all account, a cool assassin, I wasn't at the time. Trust me. My mouth was dry and I felt halfway between passing out and throwing up... just before I shot him.

If there was any coolness, chalk it up to fatigue. I was just empty enough to do this right now.

So I pointed the weapon at his chest, center mass, and fired as he planned to conquer the world at everyone else's expense.

At first I thought I missed, because the round didn't knock him over or back, like in the movies. Or like the pop-ups at the range. He just sat there. And then I could see blood spreading across his L.L.Bean adventure shirt and I watched as he looked up at me, mouth working like he wanted to scream, and didn't. Couldn't.

The iPhone dropped onto the sand.

And I knew this was the right thing. To do. I decided right there that I wasn't going to do any of this I-feel-bad-about-the-bad-things-I've-done bull.

I filed this under *necessary right now maybe not feel bad ever.*

And I reminded myself how close things had gotten last night. And that I could be one of the dead. And that a bunch of Rangers had fought together and were alive this morning and playing body toss with their enemies and that had to count for something in the big scheme of things.

Volman was on his knees, mouth still opening and closing silently, when I fired twice more. My hand was steadier now. First shot was left-of-center upper chest. Where the heart and the major arteries are.

*John* had called that the Pump and Pipes.

It was always the best choice.

I think Volman was dead when I fired the next shot a few seconds later. He was on the ground. Face thankfully pushed into the sand. I put the last shot in the back of his skull and called it done.

Then I turned and went back to the river's edge where the sergeant major and the captain were waiting. Where Autumn was.

But that wasn't her name. I'd just started calling her that in my head. And that had caused her to react in a…

*Last of Autumn.*

That was what she'd said she was called by her people. Like they were… I don't know… like they were Indians who'd once roamed the American plains. Noble and savage at the same time.

*Stands with a Buffalo* and *Raging Bull.* Like they were something special, and nomads, all at once. People we should have tried to better understand. And maybe they should have done the same with us. That would have gone a long way with both sides.

I didn't look back at Volman. But I knew. He was the opposite of her. And what I'd done was necessary.

# CHAPTER TWENTY-NINE

I told you. Warts and all.

# CHAPTER THIRTY

ON my way back to the river's edge, I took the gully back near Sergeant Kurtz's old position, if only just to avoid the circuses of flies that were hot and close in the day's rising heat up where most of the dead bodies were clustered. That's when I came upon the forgotten and forlorn Jabba. Our prisoner. The one I'd interrogated for the sergeant major.

The little goblin was just sitting there in the gully, dejected. All by himself. He hadn't managed to get free from the zip ties and chains he'd been left in, and none of his comrades had bothered to help during the assault last night when they'd owned most of the island. Or maybe they never even saw him here in the dark. Our prisoner.

He saw me coming along the gully and watched me warily, cowering against the massive piece of deadwood in the bare rock-covered dry streambed. I could see he'd tried every which way to get himself loose. But all to no avail.

I approached cautiously.

"How come your tribe never came to get you?"

I said this first in Arabic and tried it again in Turkic. I think he understood it both ways by the twitch of his floppy ears, one of which had been nicked in some long-ago battle. The look in his beady eyes was one of mistrust. They were big and brown, and the former malevolence was all gone now. They were almost melancholy in a way. Reflective. Resigned. As though awaiting some fate and merely supposing I was here to pronounce it. Like a dog three days too long at the pound.

The grim realization of all our fates setting in. That was it. There was something almost human about seeing that in the little monster's face.

"No fit'tah fight-fight anymore. Slave now. Sugburahshazz say... say Jabba slave now to Sugburahshazz and Howling Rock Clan. Sug say... he come back after killah-all and mark me with hot dagger. Then Jabba no more war. Jabba serve Sugburahshazz. Jabba live until big pot boiling needs eats. Then..."

His claws went wide. As if to say, *That's all she wrote, folks.*

I looked at him for a long moment and tried not to think about what I'd just done because what I'd just done was done for all the right reasons, and none of them were moral. But still, it was one of those things that had to be done. And so... I'd done it.

I'd live with it. Fine.

"I don't think... Sugbur..."

"Sugburahshazz," finished the little thing. "Sugburahshazz clan war chief. Biggie gobbie kind. Bigger than Nomashahazz the Crooked Nose. Big. Big. Bigga allee."

He almost seemed proud of this. That there were big "gobbie kind" even if it was not him who was big. It gave him a momentary comfort, and I felt sorry for him. Because I don't think those others he'd named probably ever thought of him with anything like pride. Just a guess. But I was betting it was a good one.

"I don't think he's coming back, Jabba."

I looked off toward the hill. Remembered all the dead enemies we'd passed on the way down to the river. Even here, standing in the dry gully, I could smell the waves of monsters that had been cut down out there, shot through, exploded, had rained mortars upon, and otherwise been done to death by every means the desperate Rangers could think up. And then some.

Sugburahshazz and the rest of the clan were probably being used for Ranger Body Toss. If they'd made it that far.

"No coming back?" asked Jabba quietly.

I shook my head. "Don't think so."

"You leave Jabba die?"

I shook my head again.

He closed his eyes and then... exposed his neck. It was obvious that in his culture I was supposed to slit it now. Or, given the fangs of the orcs and needle-sharp teeth of the tinier goblins, they probably just tore open a jugular. That would be their preferred method of execution.

"Tell ya what, Jabba..."

He opened one big watery eye and stared at me. The neck was still bare and taut. His football-shaped head and ears tilting away from me.

"I'll let you live," I offered.

Jabba blinked both his eyes and shot his head around, sniffing the air. Ears twitching. Tongue tasting.

It was at that moment I had a thought. *He's kinda like a pet dog.* I was just going to leave him and let him work out how to get free, but then I thought... maybe one act of mercy might wash away what I'd just done. What I was trying to ignore and what was circling around in the back of my mind.

And I also thought, if he's like a dog... then maybe... just maybe... I could train him. Plus, he was a source of intel. In his own way he knew a lot more than we did about this strange new world surrounding us. He knew something about the players and enemy locations. And who knew? Enemies of "gobbies" might just be friends to Rangers.

"You make Jabba slave?" the little thing asked forlornly.

"No," I said. "You wear the chain until I trust you. You carry gear. You help Rangers and you behave, and I'll feed you and keep you safe from everyone. Deal?"

Jabba nodded his goofy head up and down vigorously. Then stopped as a new thought occurred to him. A new thought that caused a glimmer of mischievousness to cross his comic features. You could see the advantage he had in his mind swimming across his expressive face. You could see that what he was thinking was very important to him.

"Will Jabba have more... moon god potion? To help Ran-jers?" he whispered as though talking about something most sacred.

Every muscle in his body strained forward expectantly. As if to telegraph, *Will this be the outcome?*

"Yeah," I said. "There's some left. You do good... and you tell me everything I want to know... no lies. And there'll be some moon god potion for Jabba."

"Yeah, yeah, yeah," panted Jabba, suddenly breathless. "Jabba do anything. Anything warrior want done. Steal, kill, stab with green poison. Jabba do all tricks for soldier man. Moon god potion now for Jabba Jabba?"

I shook my head.

He'd used his own name twice, and I wondered what that meant. I was learning about goblins now. And I'd get an up-close-and-personal master class about them from this one. That had to have some value for the command team.

"No. None of those things, Jabba. Just carry and behave. No steal... or kill... or poison. No tricks. Just information. Help Rangers. And then a Coke... er, I mean... a moon god potion."

# CHAPTER THIRTY-ONE

LEAVING the eager little goblin, I made my way back to the river's edge. When I came out of the thick brush along the bank, the Ranger fire team was still watching outward in a rough perimeter circle using cover to maintain security. The captain was talking with other company elements using his comm equipment. I had a feeling a warning order was in the air. In other words, the captain was getting everyone ready for our next mission. Whether that was gonna be stay and fight with the little we had left, or run for it, I had no idea.

The sergeant major was examining Autumn's horse. The elf stood pensively nearby, watching and waiting, to see what we would do next. Clearly, she was uneasy about the current situation. I approached the command sergeant major and spoke quietly to him.

"It's done, Sergeant Major."

He looked up at me from rubbing his hands along the horse's sides, and for a moment I was unsure if he knew what I meant. That Deep State Volman was *retired*. Cleaned. Dead. He continued whispering to the dappled gray horse and telling it not to be afraid. Clearly, he knew horses.

"What's done?" he said absently after a moment, studying the flanks of the beast. Still whispering to it. Telling it that it was a beautiful horse. And there was nothing to fear. The horse's ears flicked in the heat, and I felt that the horse didn't quite believe the sergeant major, but it endured the good vibes patiently, if not stoically. Because it wanted to. Certainly, it could smell all the death in the air.

I leaned in close.

"Deep State, Sergeant Major. *Retired.*"

My heart caught in my throat as I suddenly wondered if I'd made some completely horrific mistake and offed a dude because I read the room wrong. What if I'd overreacted and misread things? Badly. Gone too far, way too far, and taken matters into my own hands? What if I was actually some kind of sociopath incapable of reading other people and I'd...

... well, solved a problem the way sociopaths tended to solve problems.

What if I was the monster?

"All right, Talker," said the sergeant major over the horse. My breathing began to return to normal. "That's what needed to happen," the senior-most NCO continued, murmuring so low no one else could hear. "Ya good?" he asked after a second, looking me straight in the eye and searching to see what he might find there. Remorse, guilt, sociopathy?

I nodded and stepped back. The brief nod of his head told me he understood it might be a little bit of everything. Which was probably normal and meant I probably wasn't a sociopath.

A moment later Captain Knife Hand came over, having finished his communication with the element on the hill. His fabled knife hand was out and punctuating sentences. Reinforcing orders.

"PFC," he said at me. "I need you to get with her." He shot his knife hand over toward Autumn. Last of Autumn. Needed to remember that. Didn't want to commit some grave societal *faux pas*, an embarrassing or tactless act or remark in a social situation, that turned every elf in this crazy world against us just because I'd disrespected the first ambassador, as it were, to meet us. In French, *faux pas* literally meant *false step*. Who knew what political mess we'd walked into and how things might go all hillbilly Hatfields and McCoys in a second if we didn't get everything just right? Except with snarling brute orcs gone murderous and clearly well-armed and armored elves who at least possessed some sort of cavalry skills.

These are the things a linguist thinks about when he finds himself smack dab in the middle of competing cultures. And when I say *thinks*, I really mean *fears*.

Making things worse than they already are.

"Can do, sir," I said to the captain, and I went to Autumn to get things moving again now that Volman was no longer an issue. Correction… Last of Autumn. I managed to at least get that right as I started the conversation with her once more.

Long story short: she could help us. She could get us inside her people's perimeter, and it was what she wanted to do. But if we were going to do it, we needed to do it quick-like. Daylight was burning, and the "dark forces"—her words—owned the night. She used the Korean word for *dark* and the German word for *forces*.

*Eoduun Kräfte.*

The bright spot was she knew ways the orcs wouldn't follow us through the "night seasons."

I went back to the captain and reported her offer. And then stood there and got to listen in on what the sergeant major and the captain were discussing. The sergeant major resumed breaking down our situation.

"As I was saying, sir," he began, "this position is now untenable. The situation is not blue sky—ACE reports have us down to fifty percent of combat load for each Ranger still able to fight effectively. We have three Carls salvaged from the aircraft. We're outta demo, and the mortar teams are bone dry. They're now riflemen for all intents and purposes, sir. That's the situation. We couldn't hold this place anywhere close to last night. First assault and we'll be dry on ammo. Then it's axes and swords, sir. I say we make bramble rafts, get into the river, and execute aquatic escape and evasion. It's what Rangers do best, and it'll put some distance between us and the enemy. Which would be a good thing come nightfall, sir."

The captain said nothing. Head down, he listened and studied the dirt beneath his boots. Like he had an invisible sand table down there that showed him exactly everything the command sergeant major was describing. The unvarnished, and desperate, truth of our dire situation. And that everything on that map he was seeing confirmed everything he was being told.

Things didn't look good.

"Captain," continued the sergeant major. "These boys are pros. Shooters. Warriors. Solid Ranger skills. Half of 'em are tabbed but all of 'em live the scroll and that's what counts. But they are not ready to fight effectively, and I mean hand-to-hand like a fighting force something out of the ancient Greeks and Romans. Like the forces we're facing. We do that and try to apply shooter skills, and we're gonna have one very brief, very one-sided, fight with the enemy. Frankly, sir… it's my opinion we *di di mao* the field and find someplace to hunker until we get our minds around current events and run a game plan of some sort. Personally, I'm for finding that snot-nosed SEAL and slitting his throat before we take our Forge back with extreme violence. But… I might have personal feelings on that subject, sir."

The captain thought about this for a second, then nodded. "I agree with your assessment, Sergeant Major. Problem is we have no idea where this… girl…" he indicated Last of Autumn, "is taking us. She says…"

He looked over at me.

"PFC, did she say we were twenty-four hours' march from her friendlies?"

I confirmed she had indicated such.

"That's twenty-four hours of movement through hostile territory, Sergeant Major, with no idea of the effective fighting capability of these friendlies we'll be linking up with. There's no good call I can see here. Correct me if I'm wrong, Sergeant Major. On the other hand, if we take the river, we'll be exposed and moving into the unknown— and, it appears, away from friendlies."

Neither man said anything.

And then I did something stupid. I spoke up.

"Sir. Command Sergeant Major. I know I shouldn't speak, but—"

"PFC," said Captain Knife Hand, stopping me before I could go further. "I'm aware of your skills, and considering right now you're the only one who can communicate with a possible ally, I think I'd take any pertinent assessment you've got to assist me in making a decision that will affect all our outcomes. Because although this position might be difficult to hold, at least we're holding it right now. We head out there, and we're fighting and evading at the same time. In the dark, I might add. Carrying everything we can that's left in stores from the plane. And our wounded. That is not a good combat posture. Especially with no clear destination in mind. No recon. No intel. Nothing."

He looked at me. And the look said I better have something valuable to say, because he was inclined to stay here on the island and keep killing the enemy until we changed their minds about bothering us further.

"Go ahead, PFC."

I swallowed and felt my throat turn dry desert dust just as I started to speak, because nothing coveys hardened professional soldier like your voice cracking in front of a Ranger captain. Then I realized I couldn't remember the last time I'd drunk any water. Honestly... I needed coffee. I would have killed for coffee.

Then I thought of Volman lying dead under the orcs I'd left him under.

And it wasn't as funny as it used to be. The *killing for coffee* part.

Still, I really would kill right then for a fresh-brewed pour-over in some hipster coffee shop. At the very least kill an orc. I could absolutely go for that.

"Sir," I said, "she seems honest. And like... I don't know... good, too, if that counts for anything. Like she just came here to try and help us out. I can tell she, and her people, probably need help too. I wouldn't be surprised if they're in the same situation as us. True, I have no idea what her people's capabilities are, but... look at her. The horse is healthy and in good shape. She's got forged armor, which indicates some level of technology and culture above that of our attackers. And she says her people have places the orcs don't go. Right now... that sounds like that's where we need to be, sir."

And then I shut my mouth and backed up a step, indicating I had no more stupid to further contribute to the conversation and that I was deeply sorry for interrupting, especially if the sergeant major was about to White Line Drill me to death for the grievous and unforgivable infraction of speaking during a command team meeting.

"Talker's right, sir," muttered the sergeant major, folding his long arms contemplatively after a moment. Then he looked at the dappled gray the elf had brought with her. "I know a good horse when I see one, sir. That's a good horse. Well treated and well cared for. Horse is real uneasy about all this. Meaning it don't like all those dead things we just slaughtered. Or what it smells in the wind across the river. And another thing... look at her."

We all did.

"Flies don't go near her, Captain," continued the command sergeant major. "There's something about her. I don't know what it is... but she's our only ally right now, sir. And like I said, now that we've lost the Forge, we're down to what we got. Which might get us through most of one firefight. Add that the men are four days sleep deprived and operating on one MRE a day and we are indeed reaching a critical-lack-of-performance moment. We get someplace safe, maybe we can make a plan to go take the Forge back from that SEAL, sir. But right now... we ain't capable of much beyond dying in place real brave-like. That's the facts as I see 'em, sir."

The captain lowered his head and stepped away from the conversation, staring at that invisible sand table beneath his feet once more. Walking through the real sand and bloodstained grass down toward the burbling river a few steps away as if there might be some easy answer over there. There wasn't, and we all knew it. And I think everyone was glad not to be him. Not to have to make the decision that would most likely get us all killed. I was.

For a long moment the captain just stared at the passage of water. In a few hours it would be noon. And later it would be dark.

Then they would come for us.

Again.

We had enough ammunition for *most of a firefight*, according to the sergeant major.

I, for one, found that rather sobering.

We'd either face it here… or maybe we'd dodge it out there. You could tell that was what Captain Knife Hand was thinking right at that moment. You could tell that for a leader there was no easy choice here for him to make, no choice at all that didn't involve putting his men in danger again. More people were getting killed one way or the other. Maybe even all of us like some lost Roman legion that went a little too far out into the barbarian unknown and never came back. Beyond the familiar, missing forever. Forever. That could be us. And he was seeing every ambush we'd face out there and knowing once we'd surrendered the island there'd be no rear to fall back to. Out there we'd be surrounded until we got somewhere safe. If such a place even existed.

But then again… weren't we surrounded here too?

He turned and put his combat helmet on.

"Sergeant Major. Get us ready to withdraw from the island. We'll organize patrols and conduct a forced march by stealth with flank security patrols to watch the clock on all sides. Scouts will recon by stealth."

Then he looked at me.

"PFC…" He stared hard at me for a long moment, like he was putting together ten plans all at once in his head. Then…

"Talker. Get her to describe our route and try to make a map. We'll need it out there tonight."

# CHAPTER THIRTY-TWO

WE left the mostly green-carcass-covered island in the middle of the river at early evening nautical twilight. The scouts' leader, Sergeant Hardt, told me that was the perfect time for a "stalk and walk" because it's the time when it's most difficult to see and it still plays with night vision a bit.

The Rangers spent the day collecting and organizing as many of the salvageable supplies as could be found among the ruins of the C-17, then getting the wounded ready for transport, some rest, and gear prep for the night march. We were "going ranging," as I would learn later in the op order briefing. It would be close to twenty-four hours on the move, deep inside enemy territory, with no rest.

Everything not needed for an immediate fight was going in our rucks. If I had thought I knew how to get my gear quiet and ready, my last two hours on the island found me inadequate in this area. Sergeant Thor fixed my major malfunctions and had me doing burpees in full rattle once he'd rigged it, just to show me how quiet you could get and still do active stuff like creep around and knife people in the back. The cheat is you used a lot of hundred mile an hour tape and made sure the carrier fit snug, but not too tight. You also shed a lot of useless gear that looked cool and did nothing.

We'd move quick and silent, using the Rules of Ranging as they applied to movement with respect to recon. We were focusing on speed of movement. We needed to get to the objective as fast as possible, but at the same time it was important, due to the condition of our fighting force and current state of ammunition, that we move no closer to the enemy than we had to. Normally we'd have scouts in front, behind, and on the flanks. "The clock," as it was called. But there weren't enough scouts tonight. One scout team far forward was all we had.

The most crucial component for the entire force was stealth. That meant camo, noise, and light discipline was total, or as total as could be attained. The NCOs advised us not to use any more Vicks VapoRub to relieve the dead body smell and to instead rub grass and leaves in our noses to get that smell of death out of our olfactory senses once we crossed over the river. Hopefully we'd still be able to smell the enemy, as they tended to stink real bad.

Conversely, we needed to cover our own smell—which meant rolling in leaves and getting as woodsy as possible. Our issue Crye assault uniforms, covered in blood and gore, were discarded. The enemy seemed to have a pretty good sense of smell, so no chances were taken. It occurred to me that I needed to get with Jabba on this and see what he was capable of, sense-wise.

I'd spent most of the day getting better at speaking with Last of Autumn and developing a sand table map for the route to our three en route rally points and final destination, a place she called "Hidden Cave." In the afternoon, the captain, the sergeant major, and the platoon leaders and platoon sergeants came down to the riverside for the op order. Last of Autumn and I walked them through the route she had given me and gave the markings we would land-nav by. Then we stepped back and the captain broke down how we were going to do this.

Movement would be conducted by patrol in single file. Teams would assemble into ten-man squads moving within sight of each other. Spacing would be twenty meters between teams and fifty between platoons. Line of sight could be broken as long as comm was maintained. Communication between all elements during the move would be key.

Everyone except the scouts, who would be three hundred meters forward, and the rear security team, the same to the rear, would be carrying overstuffed rucks and extra gear. Everything we could possibly take. Antibiotics and clamshells stuffed with all essential medical gear. More ammo. Explosives. Everything. The teams were pack mules, and engagement was to be avoided at all costs in favor of movement as fast, and as stealthily, as possible. Things were not to pop off. Avoid contact with the enemy at all times. If things went sideways, we'd find ourselves in a fight we might not be able to disengage from.

There would be three en route rally points to reach our final objective, and the captain and the sergeant major would be leapfrogging each other to reach those points with security teams ahead of the main body to ensure the rallies were safe and in locations that were off the beaten track and secure. Night vision was mostly dead. Battery power was reaching critical shortage levels. The radios were still operational, but communication via visual marking signals left by the lead elements was incorporated into the PACE plan. Primary, Alternate, Contingency, and Emergency. We would use the radios until they stopped working, then would switch to visual hand and arm signals, and after that it would be visual markings on the ground or in the trees. Finally, if nothing else, the sound of weapons fire would let everyone know that our mission for the movement had failed, and that contact with the enemy had been made. That was when the worst-case scenario went into effect. The element in contact was to stay in contact and hopefully allow all other teams to bypass the enemy and escape en route to the final objective. If they survived, they could E&E on their own, but they were to make sure that the entire element did not get decisively engaged. Someone had to make it.

The captain would be supervising the disengagement and withdrawal from the island as the command sergeant major led the main force to the first rally point at the top of a high pass through the hills to our north. If the enemy located and pursued us away from the island, the captain, who had what remained of the high ex, and a fire team acting as rear security, would attempt to buy the rest of us time to get upslope to the pass and disappear to the other side.

But, and Captain Knife Hand was clear about this, "This is a withdrawal. We are going to fade and avoid engagement. We're going ghost."

Next the sergeant major took over and established the signal and communication for the route and organized the order of march. I was surprised to find out I would be with the scouts for the sole purpose of assisting in communication with the elf, who would be showing us the route and acting as our indigenous guide.

We were already up the first hill leading toward the ridgeline we'd cross that night when I looked back in the last light of the end of the day and saw the rising black smoke of the funeral pyre the Rangers had made for their dead before finally withdrawing from the island they'd fought so hard for. That had been the last item in the op order. The Viking Farewell. The fallen had served the 75th Ranger Regiment and fought well. Now they were going out on their shields. They would not be forgotten, and their names are written down in my journal under a phrase from the Ranger Creed I learned during my short time in RASP: "I will never leave a fallen comrade to fall into the hands of the enemy." That had to be adhered to, or else the sergeant major risked these Rangers starting to fall apart. The creed was all we had now, especially with the dwindling supplies of ammunition, demo, chewing tobacco, and, oh yeah, coffee. Something had to hold this force together, and that's exactly what the Ranger C is for. Exactly why it's recited as a mantra during any and all events and situations where it's appropriate—and it's always appropriate, for one reason or another. So much so that a lot of the Rangers had portions of it tattooed on their bodies, scribbled into the margins of their Bibles, or etched into pieces of their equipment. The command sergeant major, as he started the fire and intoned those words in his West Texas gravel, was using it right for exactly the purpose it was intended for.

They would not be forgotten.

I watched the thin column of smoke and saw the rear security team cross the river in the last light of the warm day. Spring was here. And summer would soon come.

I wondered if we would be here to see it.

# CHAPTER THIRTY-THREE

THE Ranger company scout section left before anyone else. That was the job of the scouts. Go out and scout. Find first what we'd be running into so we could kill it or evade it. Their job was to make the unknown known before it became a problem. And of course, everything surrounding us currently was unknown.

The route Last of Autumn had laid out for us was fairly simple, and if it worked it would get us clear of the enemy and on our way to her people pretty quickly. The first section of the march was the hardest part. That was for two reasons. Reason one being the enemy would have its best chance to locate and destroy us during those early hours of the march in the night as we'd be closer to our last known position. Reason two was because the overland route was all uphill. We were carrying wounded and every piece of equipment not nailed down was on our backs. Who knew what we'd need once we got where we were going? So we were taking as much as we could carry and fight with. And then some.

We crossed over the river along the western bank and then made a short trek through a body-littered forest the enemy had been operating in. Most of these corpses had been killed on night two by indirect fire. We started up a series of hills that lined this edge of the river valley and used the ridgeline to cross toward a steep canyon farther to the north. There would be, according to Last of Autumn, a thin trail up that narrow canyon that the Shadow Elves, Last of Autumn's people, used on occasion but hadn't in some time. The bottom of that trail was Phase Line Fox, and the en route rally point was designated Domino. We'd reach it by midnight if we didn't hit any snags.

Phase Line Eagle was on top of the pass the canyon led up along. Beyond the top of the pass was "Old Witch Pool," as it was called in Last of Autumn's language. A small stream that started there would eventually turn into a river downslope leading toward some ruins out on the plain below. The ruins, or what she called "The Philosopher King's Palace," were Objective Rally Point Match to the east along the river. After that we would depart the river and enter the Upper Charwood Forest, where we'd find the Shadow Elves' Hidden Cave somewhere within.

Basically, it was north to the hills, east to the canyon, north again along a small river, then east into a forest they called the Upper Charwood.

She made it clear everything was dangerous until we reached the Charwood. I relayed that to the sergeant major. He made a face that indicated this was obvious but didn't bother to comment other than being mature enough to say, "Good to know."

Yeah, I said to myself as I got my ruck ready, obviously everything was dangerous. What was I thinking?

She showed us stars we could navigate by, and soon the teams were starting out in the deepening gloom, staggered to follow one another.

I'd been placed with the scout team and our elven guide. The Ranger scout team consisted of five Rangers and Sergeant Thor, who'd been added as sniper support for his training and experience as a pro Swamp Fox. There was one hangup. While working on the sand table for the route march with Autumn, I remembered Jabba and went off to retrieve him. When I came back trailing a goblin at the end of a length of 550 cord and a chain around his neck, the elf had a ninja sword out in a flash, and she was more than ready to use it to slice and dice the little thing in about two cuts. Funny, none of us had noticed her weapons before. And now here it was out and menacing all of us as I approached with the chained-up little Jabba, who was freaking out in the face of what he perceived as a mortal enemy. Last of Autumn. Jabba scrambled behind me for cover and protection as she shouted something in Tolkien Elven I can only guess meant something close to *"Die, Goblin Scum."*

She seemed quite angry. And yes, she was sexy like that, too. Her face was pure dark storm cloud rage, and I was pretty sure being on the receiving end of that would not be a pleasant experience. A few minutes later the sergeant major was involved and asking me what the hell I was doing.

"This is our prisoner," I told him. "The one I interrogated, Sergeant Major. I'm bringing him with us."

The sergeant major gave me a look that suggested he was baffled, or perturbed, or both, at why the enemy thing was still alive after the pertinent information had been extracted and the creature's usefulness expended. But since we were in polite and open company it was clear we couldn't be as straightforward as we had been on the subject of now-deceased Deep State Volman.

Side note. No one had missed Volman so far.

It all eventually got straightened out once I explained the goblin was disposed to work with us and might provide valuable intel later on throughout the mission. But Last of Autumn would have nothing to do with Jabba, and her whole bearing changed permanently after the incident, even though I kept explaining that the Jabba was a *joein*, or prisoner in Korean. German too. *Häftling*.

Her seething hatred for him had changed her delicately placid and beautiful features into those of fiery avenging angel in the space of a moment. An avenging angel I would be none too happy about meeting if I were on the wrong side of the equation and at the tip of her shiny ninja sword of razor-sharp death.

The sword. Interesting. She was quick with it. Not McCluskey fast, but it was still pretty ninja. The weapon wasn't like any of those the Rangers had picked up to use when ammo got down to nonexistent. What she was pointing at Jabba was something more like a fabled blade. Something straight out of an epic tale about serpents and Vikings. But at the same time, something a deadly Ronin might use to murder a thousand samurai on an endless quest for revenge. It was beautiful and definitely well-made. A fine thing. Not like, but in the same category of fineness as, McCluskey's black blade had been. *Coldfire,* the SEAL had called it.

At that moment I wanted to ask her if she knew of this King Triton, but… now didn't seem like a good time, what with her waving around a very dangerous weapon she was intent on drawing gobbie blood with.

She kept hissing at the goblin and calling it a "*Diener der Finsternis!*" in Grau Sprache.

*Servant of Darkness.*

Jabba earnestly shook his head like he was trying to tell some cops back on the block that he was just hanging out with those other guys the *po-po* were looking for. He was innocence defined and guilty as hell.

Jabba was even jabbering the equivalent of "*It's cool*" in Turkic.

It was all kind of funny. Until she took someone's eye out with the blade, and then it was liable to get out of hand. And then it would be even funnier years later. To the survivors that is.

Like I said, it all got straightened out, and Tanner was called in to take charge of the prisoner. I ordered Jabba to obey everything Tanner said, and I gave Tanner a few phrases in Turkic to order the little goblin around.

By nightfall the goblin was overloaded with two huge duffels and carrying the weapons section's extra gear as we departed the river island. No mean feat. They were feeding him scraps from their MREs like he was a dog, and truth be told the little goblin didn't seem to mind much. Brumm had even taught him to jump up and down and roll over. They left the goblin on the 550 cord leash with a chain around his neck, but he was gonna earn his keep along the way. Those swollen duffels were heavy. Oh, and plus, he was carrying a 7.62 drum in each gangly claw. He was impossibly, and comically, overloaded, and yet like I said, he didn't seem to mind. In fact he was grinning ridiculously. I think someone had let him try some Rip It they'd smuggled along for the ride. Once he was fueled up on a near-lethal dose of caffeine and vitamin B12 the little goblin seemed almost happy to be with us, proving once again that Rip It was mission-critical.

Private Soprano had been reassigned from Jasper's fire team, which had been cannibalized to fill other squads who'd taken casualties. Soprano was now the AG for Specialist Rico.

"Get a load of this guy," laughed the new assistant gunner. Gone was his comical Italian parody, replaced by a deep Bronx *patois* that gave away his hometown sure as command sergeant major's drawl.

The exaggerated accent, likely a knee slapper among his friends back in the shadows of Yankee Stadium, made a comeback. "Looka da little monkey man!" Jabba was only slightly smaller than Soprano. "He's-a too funny to kill. Hey... monkey, you bite and I'll splitta your skull, *sì, capisce?*"

Now, heading into the night and up through a dark forest climbing toward the foothills, the scouts moved, sweeping ahead of Last of Autumn and myself at the center of their patrol wedge. We followed the scouts pointing out their initial course track. She was interfacing with "Hard," or as he was officially known, Sergeant Hardt. Hard and Kurtz were cut from the same cloth. Completely competent. Zero personality. Strong opinions on everyone weaker than themselves. Spoiler: everyone was weaker. Both tabbed, and I'd bet my whole instant coffee stash they had their tabs tattooed to boot.

All I got from the Ranger scout leader when I reported with Autumn was "Try not to make much noise and make sure she understands me and I understand her, or there are going to be problems for you, PFC."

During the patrol brief, Thor stepped in and told Hardt I was "good to go," and that dialed Hard back a bit. Slightly. A little. But you could tell he was wired tight and didn't want any mistakes out of me that might jam up his section's *chi*.

In Mandarin, chi literally means "air" or "breath." Figuratively it refers to the vital energy in all living things. Spelled *qi* in the Pinyin romanization. *Chi* or *ch'i* in the Wade-Giles transcription.

This is me contributing.

In any case, *I* didn't want to jam up anyone's chi. Armed dudes operating out in the unknown dark, surrounded by the enemy, needed as much energy flow as possible. Especially with me out here with them. Jammed chi probably meant all of us getting hacked and stabbed to death by something mythical and angry. I was intent on avoiding this fate until I had at least one last decent cup of coffee somewhere. I had reached the "Not Particular" phase of this little adventure. As in, if we had run into the worst gas station in the world with coffee that had been brewed sometime last week... I would have hit it and been exceedingly grateful.

We started out at evening nautical twilight, like I think I said, and just before we did, Last of Autumn whispered a few Tolkien words in her dappled-gray horse's ears, and after that the horse followed the patrol wedge, but so far back it was almost out of sight. Every so often I'd look back with the barely working NVGs and see the horse standing near a thicket, almost invisible, still following us like a good boy. I wasn't even sure if the horse was a boy. But he, or she, was a pro at stealth.

Once we were underway, the comm was up and the following teams started out on our back trail. The scouts under Sergeant Hardt knew what they were doing. They were constantly back and forth, up and down terrain high points and checking visibility along the route. Our rucks were impossibly overloaded, but as scouts we weren't loaded down as heavily as the rest of the company. That allowed us to move faster and quieter. And the scouts were definitely quiet. But they were also carrying weapons and gear, and when the air was still enough and there was no background noise like rushing water or wind through the trees, you could just barely hear their muffled hustling movements as they went softly from tree to tree in two-man teams. Covering and watching. Whispering into their throat mics.

But Autumn—Last of Autumn—I was forcing myself to use her proper name given the discomfort and embarrassment my familiarizing of it had caused her—Last of Autumn moved without a sound. None. She made the quiet scouts sound like elephants trampling through dead grass. And she was wearing armor to boot. That silvery fine mesh tunic beneath her forest-green cloak. There were times when I moved forward, following Sergeant Hardt's form in the gray-green glow of our precious night vision—the scouts carried rechargeable and solar chargers, but there was still a shortage—when I couldn't hear her at all and I had to look back to see if we'd somehow left her behind. Instead I would find she'd moved ahead of me without me even noticing her. She could move incredibly fast. And her cloak... at times in the night vision it was like some type of active camouflage system that adjusted to the viewer's conditions to blend her into the background and make her near invisible. You had to look hard to find her. At one halt, while Sergeant Hardt and the point man were checking the top of a hill and the gully below we were about to descend into, I took off my NVGs to let my eyes acclimatize to human night vision, and I tried to find her where I'd just seen her with electronic-assisted night vision.

Nothing.

She was flat-out invisible in the dark night under the stars in the shadows along the silent hills.

And then she was right next to me and whispering in Shadow Cant.

"Tell... Sergeant Hardt... circle. Close... to me."

She was carrying a dark ashwood bow and a quiver full of silver-feathered arrows she'd taken off her horse from the bare equipment she'd packed.

"Defensive?" I wanted to clarify what she needed so I could relay to Hard, who was forward and coming back now, alerting us we'd be ready to move shortly. Sergeant Thor was near the top of the hill on overwatch with his rifle.

"To... to..." She was searching for the right word and not finding it. "To... inform. No... to illuminate your... fellowship."

Ah. She wanted to tell us something. Explain something. But even as I connected with Sergeant Hardt I thought to myself that she could just tell me and then I could relay to everyone. Maybe she didn't understand the concept of our radio communication.

I relayed, and Hardt came in to link up with her. Shrinking the scouts into a tight patrol circle and getting close. A moment later they were all there with Sergeant Thor, hunching his way down through the bracken and dead tall grass along the side of the hill. Rifle upright and squatting down next to Hardt, me, and Autumn.

I nodded to her that we were all here and she could proceed with what she needed to tell us.

And then I translated what she told us. Short version: She'd figured out that our "magic" for seeing in the dark wasn't that good. According to her. Also, she could tell by our whispers that we were communicating in what she called some kind of magic "shadow speech" all our own. Like hers, but different. Apparently, there were correlations in this world. Not radio. But something. She understood we were communicating.

Then she said, "Can... make better with... I can." She stopped and found the right words she needed. "Hunters' Fellowship."

She asked us to take off our night vision and if she might proceed with what she called, "make better."

Sergeant Hardt sighed audibly, clearly annoyed by the superstitious indig jibber-jabber he would now be forced to endure. He knew she was a VIP and that Captain Knife Hand had given her some level of authority. So, best to play along.

She was kneeling as we flipped up our NVGs to show we were complying.

"Okay, Talker... what next?" spat Hardt bitterly with no small amount of impatience. "Clock's burning and we need to stay ahead of the follow-on teams."

"They're ready," I told Autumn. "Make better now."

I had no idea what *make better* meant and I was pretty sure my elf-pidgin-patois sounded stupid to the Rangers. And... also I had a feeling it was all about to get very weird.

She closed her eyes and I could see her full lips mumbling something in the moonlight under the stars. Did I mention she was exotically beautiful like nothing and no one I had ever seen before? Not in a while, at least, right? She just whispered for a long moment, swaying in a circle, and then raised up her hands, which... started to glow a soft blue.

Yup.

Magic stuff.

The Rangers watched in amazemed disbelief as she opened her clenched fists and little ghostly blue fireflies fled from her palms and began to circle around all of us, raining down...

I could feel Sergeant Hardt dying inside as he was forced to have...

Fairy dust.

Rain down on him.

Never have I seen someone look so utterly miserable. To him this was a violation of noise and light discipline of the highest order. Under normal, non-magical circumstances, something like this would be punishable by having the rest of the scout team beat me into unconsciousness.

I mean... what else do you want me to call it? It was Tinkerbell-type fairy dust. It was crazy. And hauntingly beautiful at the same time. Of all the things I'd lived to see in my very short life, which probably wasn't going to last much longer, it was one of the coolest things that had ever happened to me. That was the real magic. The wonder of it. It was like gossamer moonlight made real, and it was something special. Something we never would have experienced when the world wasn't ruined. Something wonderful found in the ashes of all that was lost to us. Ghostly blue fairy dust that floated over and around all of us. Bippity boppity boo.

And the crescent moon resting in the inky sky suddenly spiked its luminary output to that of straight-up noon on the brightest day of the year.

We. Could. See. Like. Never. Before.

Everything.

As clear as day and far better than our regular unassisted or even assisted eyes ever could.

I've never done psychotropic drugs or any other hallucinogenic, but I'm willing to bet the experience was similar. Our eyes were pinned wide open and relaxed at the same time. When I looked at Hardt and Thor, their pupils were huge. As in *yuuuuge*. Everyone was staring about in amazement. Every detail, texture, surface... all of it was revealed in layers we'd never thought possible. Our gray-green night vision was now replaced by something the US Army and DARPA would've classified as sixth-generation night vision in white phosphorescence.

The kind of boot-strapped alien tech only Delta got to use, if you believed the crazier conspiracy theories.

But way trippier.

I looked downslope past the horse and was stunned to find my vision telescoping way down toward the river, which was completely out of sight with normal vision. I found myself looking at the faces of the Rangers coming up from the river and felt as though I could reach out and touch them.

Great distances could suddenly be focused up close and personal.

It took a moment to figure it all out. A real freak-out, fall-off-the-edge-of-the-universe moment when none of it felt comfortable. But then it settled down, and a supreme sense of calm came out of nowhere and washed over us. I'd been sweating all through the hump up the hill and then freezing cold as the sweat dried and we waited for Hard and the point man to recon our next movement. It was gonna be like that all night. Now? Now I felt warm. Comfortable. Blissed out. But still completely aware of every sound for miles around us. My brain was processing it all like I was one with the Force or something. That Matrix moment where he suddenly *knows kung fu.*

Pretty cool, huh?

Then everyone in the scout team could hear everyone else's thoughts.

# CHAPTER THIRTY-FOUR

YEAH. It was pretty freaky at first to hear everyone in the scout team's thoughts. But quickly we got it sorted and then it was kind of cool after that. It wasn't like hearing each other's *exact* thoughts. But you could tell whose gear was rubbing them raw or who needed to piss. Sergeant Hardt found out about his nickname and was none too pleased with that. He also found out who hated him. Which was pretty much everyone. Big surprise. He replied with, "I hate all of you twice as much as what you think you call hate."

The promise of severe retribution at a later date was unspoken, but understood. Thankfully I was just a guest in the scout section. Hopefully I would avoid the doom of white line drills whenever we got the next break from running for our lives and shooting everything.

Hardt did hear me snort. It just escaped as I marveled at the Kurtz levels of contempt he was able to muster. So even if I did escape retribution, I was pretty sure Sergeant Kurtz would be informed and asked to PT me appropriately and extensively once we didn't need to fight, or run, for our lives again. But that was all down the road. We might all get killed before that. So I had that going for me.

Once we got it all settled on how to communicate with our new Elven Mind Meld Last of Autumn whammied us with, we got back underway with our new incredible night-vision toy. The elf called it "Moon Vision."

Hearing each other's thoughts quickly demonstrated its tactical benefit in that you received a weird sort of background noise of the senses of anyone you were communicating with via thoughts. In other words, you could see in your mind's eye, while still using your new regular awesome vision, exactly what the other person you were thinking at was seeing. And hearing. And of course thinking. For scouts working with subvocal throat mikes, this was awesome.

And it came in handy pretty quickly.

During their route recon, Sergeant Hardt and the point spotted a patrol of orcs who'd been following the crevices between the hills. They'd come up the gully we were just about to make a linear crossing of. We had company, and we all saw it ourselves as we watched a kind of fantastic replay of Sergeant Hardt's memory. There were eight orcs filing along the gully, trying to get ahead of us and cut us off with an ambush. Skirmisher types. Leather armor, horns, hunting bows. Small daggers. They ran like a pack of wolves, loping after unseen prey. There was something tribal and primal about them, and it was both fascinating and disturbing to watch. At least it was for me. Instantly every other Ranger's thoughts, via Elven Mind Meld, centered on killing them. Badly.

These orcs were even uglier in the awesomeness of Moon Vision. There was a tall stand of willowy trees down there in the gully between the two foothills, and the orcs had gone into its dark clutch and hadn't come out. So most likely they were still down there waiting for some escaping squad to come wandering through their ambush.

"Captain says not to engage," Sergeant Hardt spoke in our minds, quickly getting the hang of the Elven Mind Meld's mental communication features. "But as I see it, we have to cross on to the next section of the ridgeline over there."

I translated for Autumn. She didn't need it. Somehow the Hunters' Fellowship Mind Meld thing made it clear to her the parameters of our mission and what Hardt was trying to express. It seemed to transcend language for the time being. In return her thoughts came back as pictures, not so much as words. Kinda makes me wonder why she didn't just start with this back at the camp instead of us fumbling to find some common language. Maybe the Moon Vision only comes *after* they decide you're all right.

At any rate, I could see her thoughts now. Unfortunately, they didn't involve me in any romantically thrilling way. In short, she was up for killing the orcs with her bow.

We saw the picture of her firing the weapon. Putting arrows right through the throats of the awful orcs as she advanced downslope and stormed their ambush from the flank. Then, in her version of how she wanted us to conduct the assault, she identified a specific caution for us. The skirmisher-hunter types we'd seen in Hardt's communication of events, each of them carried a crude ram's horn on their belts. Through pictures she clearly indicated that if we attacked, it was crucial we hit them all at once as a group before they could sound their horns to alert nearby enemy units.

Her mind made it clear this was a real possibility. The orcs had crossed onto the island and found their prey gone. Now this dark force was fanning out in every direction, trying to hunt us down and destroy us. First one to find us would sound the alert. Then the rest would swarm en masse from every direction of the compass toward it and we'd be caught out in the open with no defenses to get behind. In her mind I saw the wide sweep of the whole river valley with the island at the center, with something akin to sonic pulses overlaid to indicate the alerting horns calling to one another. I saw a version of the sand table we'd been working on, but of a type only in her mind. Her fantasy version laid out like some ancient general's maps on a campaign table. Something from the age of Roman legions and Alexander the Great. With all kinds of symbols and runes that indicated different types of enemy units to her.

Orc Heavy Infantry.

Scout Infantry.

Goblin Army.

Orc Archers.

Trolls and giants forming a kind of heavy artillery force that also had the capability to transform to assaulters.

The symbiosis she had created with her mind and ours translated these things for us to understand. And there were other things she was trying to tell us that our minds could not comprehend. Not as a whole. But I sensed there were other wizards, witches, and dark sorcerers in play for the other side. Brought in to annihilate us once we were pinned.

They were all to our west on the other side of the river, hunting in the dark under the thin moonlight. Crazy, huh?

If any one enemy unit alerted the rest of the hunting horde, then those *Uroo Uroo* pulses would erupt all along the twisting river valley in the night. They would triangulate and eliminate us quickly.

"Okay, so if we're gonna do this," I heard Hardt say, as if in a trance, "then we're gonna have to do this silent and violent. Because if I read you right, Last of Autumn, there's no way around this group down there hiding in the trees in the gully."

We heard her message in our minds a second later. It was a message without words, but somehow it was still her voice, and it was crystal calm and clear in our heads.

"True."

# CHAPTER THIRTY-FIVE

IN the night under the stars, the wedge of Rangers moved low and slow through the tall dead grass on the far side of the hill. A breeze had picked up, and thankfully it was coming across the ridge, shifting the tall grass gently and turning the hills into liquid silver by moonlight. The orc ambush was upwind.

Five scouts were running suppressed MK18s, and the elf was at the tip of their spear, leading them forward to the hit. Sergeant Hardt was tracking right behind her and off to her left, running the team with hand signals despite the Elven Mind Meld. Some habits die hard. But Autumn's mind magic was also doing its thing and identifying target positions as they got close enough to penetrate the canopy of trees down there in the gully where the ambush was set up.

Every member of the Ranger detachment had been issued high-speed gear and suppressors for their rifles, because who knew what the world was going to be like two to five in the future according to original mission parameters? If they'd known it was gonna be ten thousand years ahead, they might've issued us high-tensile carbon-edged tactical axes and crossbows. But everyone was surprised by that. Including the people whose job it was to not be. The mission planners. They live in a world of dreams and terrors and if they're right less than forty-five percent of the time they're hailed as brilliant tacticians, never mind the body count.

If you tried that math at Starbucks you'd be fired after your first shift as a barista.

Great. And now I'm thinking about coffee.

Anyway. I'd remained on the hill in the overwatch position with Sergeant Thor, who'd brought his MK11 sniper rifle set up for close engagement. We'd try to hit any squirters from the overwatch that survived the impending raid by the scout team with murder in their hearts and minds. Me acting as spotter, Thor engaging.

I got the details of how it all went down from one of the scouts later on during a halt for Sergeant Hardt to comm with the captain and deliver a sitrep on the takedown.

The scouts had just made it into the thicket when she began firing her bow.

There were eight orcs in there, all in ambush positions watching the animal trail that ran along the gully and right through the small clump of trees that nestled between the two hills. The tangos hadn't been watching the hillsides and had planned only to jump anyone coming down the trail. They were completely surprised when they got hit from the side.

"Went down like this," the scout told me. "She had the targets all marked out in our minds with that crazy Moon Watch or whatevs. It was clear the ones we were each supposed to hit because it was like the moon was shining down real special on our assigned targets. Like the way a game hints you about who to talk to. And..." he continued incredulously, "we knew, Talker. We could like sense it, bro, that we each had a priority target to do. Five of us, eight of them.

"We're going in, and I'm wonderin' who's gonna pick up the slack on the remaining three. I mean, I can tell they're someone's assigned targets, I just can't tell who gonna do the splatter. Anyway, we're just violating our way in real quiet-like when she lets her first arrow go, and as fast as that one's away, she already got another one out of her quiver with barely a sound. That one whistles off just as fast to catch the other. She nails two, and Hard gives the go-ahead for us to engage. Five seconds and they're all dead just like that. Each of us got one and she got three. I shit you not, that was the best shooting I ever done, and I qual'd expert last time at the range. You think she moon-juiced our accuracy or something, Talk? One even had an arrow stickin' straight out of its eye. That was sick as in sick is slick, Talker-man."

Cool story, bro. Notice how many times he used my nickname and the variants he applied to it? I feel like some biologist living in the Congo who's gained the trust of the killer gorillas. The hit was expert but, really I'm more excited about the familiar use of my nickname. Honestly, it's the small victories that make life worth living.

In the silence after the hit, Sergeant Thor and I followed Last of Autumn's horse down into the thicket while we waited for Sergeant Hardt to give the commander an update. The scouts got a chance to rest and see to their gear. That's when Corporal Delgado told me how it all went down. Ten minutes later we were on the move again and humping toward the next set of hills along the ridgeline.

Back at the island, the rear security element observed and reported the enemy hitting again, in what seemed larger numbers than the night before. Of course the horde quickly figured out we weren't there and scattered in large and small elements in every direction, trying to pick up our trail, or us. Three teams had already had close calls.

Ours came next.

We were climbing up the last hill with a panoramic view of the moonlit valley running off into the east and the west behind us. Still under the effects of Moon Vision, we could see everything. And again, our eyes could do that focusing trick. From up here the dead grass swaying along the high hills looked like the waves of a silver sea in deep swell. Down below we could see the Ranger teams in their individual groups struggling along the same route we'd come up. All around our people we could see the enemies' hunters moving this way and that trying to get a location on us.

So far, so good. But the margin for error was slim to none.

And then just below us and ahead we saw the centaurs with a troop of goat men— half goat on the bottom, half man up top but with ram's horns growing from greasy, dark curls of hair. These were running in two columns behind the centaurs.

We hunkered just below the top of the ridge. The scouts had been taking dead grass and adding it into their gear, so when we sank down it wasn't full ghillie suit invisibility, but good enough at this distance and time of night. This new scouting element of centaurs and goat men hadn't spotted us, but we'd gotten a solid look at them with our spooky Moon Vision. Up close and personal whether they liked it or not.

The centaurs wore shining armor over their torsos. Hammered scales of pretty decent make. Much better than that of the orc ground infantry. Across the armor's chest was embossed the head of a figure I didn't need to be a player of PFC Kennedy's games to recognize. Anyone who'd taken the most introductory of Ancient Greek history or mythology classes could've spotted the head of a Medusa from way off. She wasn't ugly as depicted on old coins and statues—she had a nice face as near as you could tell from an image stamped into a central plate on their armor—but the snakes left no doubt who she was. They were like living tentacles writhing across the chest plates. The plate itself looked like it was made of some ghostly white marble, and in the night with our powerfully enhanced vision, it was like looking at something from a netherworld.

The centaurs were cruel-faced and haughty, sneering and calling out to one another as they galloped ahead. They led the small scouting troop of goat men from the front, carrying spears and bows and ranging across their path. As though they were attempting to pick up our tracks. These were hunters. And they were getting close to finding us. If we hadn't gotten held up hitting the orcs, and we were that much further ahead, they would have.

An image, like a movie, came straight into our minds from Last of Autumn. How the centaurs fought. We saw in our minds images of these same half men, half horses riding in fast among a series of half-sunken ruins in some kind of swamp forest. Cracked marble columns and broken statues of elves in great and fantastic armor, often riding beautiful horses that seemed lifelike and powerful even though they were made of carved stone. Kings and warlords from some long-ago age overgrown with vines and standing among ancient piles of ruin being claimed by a forest turning to swamp. The spray and foam of the brackish moss-laden water churned up around the centaurs' hooves as they came through the water, shooting down elves, living ones just like Last of Autumn. Only these were males in light breast-plates with heavier swords than the one she carried. The ninja sword. These were acting as defenders, and the centaurs came in fast like they were raiding a settlement.

They shot down the male elves and it wasn't much of a fair fight. There were three centaurs to every elven warrior. The elves fought valiantly, sometimes with as many as five or six shafts sticking out of their chests as they bellowed war cries and swung mighty swords. But in the end, they went down under the overwhelming numbers, and moments later the cruel half-horse, half-man centaurs were carrying off small elven children, leaving slaughtered elven women in the muck water and bloody grass near the broken ruins.

You could feel Last of Autumn's fiery hatred erupt in the brief vision. And I could tell it had been there all along like it was part of her DNA. But there was something that told me the rest of the scouts seeing this didn't get that bit. I can't explain it other than to say I just knew it. Like everyone was watching the circus and I'd spotted the child in the shadows picking pockets or playing with matches under the bleachers. Something small, dark, and hurt. Something that burned with a fire whose name was Revenge. And that was as dangerous as a wild animal. Probably even more so than anything we'd faced here so far.

My mind told me I needed to remember that and not forget it. It was… an important detail about her. But *detail* didn't seem like the right word.

Then she was talking to me in Shadow Cant. Using words, speaking directly. She'd moved through the dead grass almost silently to come and kneel beside me as all of us studied the centaur hunting party making their way up to the ridgeline.

"These are bad. Very... dangerous. Raiders for the Black Prince out of the... Crow's March. Servants of Sultria. I have to lead them away now... or they will find."

That was the other part. They were climbing the ridgeline on a near parallel track to ours. We could see them working their way up a finger coming down off the heights. The troop of goat men who followed looked even more malevolent than the centaurs at the head of their troop. More of a brutal pirate vibe than the fine sneering cavalier nature of the horse-men. Their grotesque faces were pure lechery. Hairy with devil-goaty faces. They wore golden hoops in their ears and carried short cutlasses along with an assortment of daggers and small cutting weapons. They hooted and barked as they walked beneath the moonlight. It was clear they were out looking for trouble tonight.

Who among their side wasn't?

Sergeant Hardt quickly assessed the situation tactically, and Autumn concurred with his take. If they found us, they'd harry us with the mounted centaurs, staying off and shooting their bows at us while the little goat men came in fast to get close and start cutting us up.

Yeah, we might be able to hold them off. They might not survive contact with our "boom sticks," and that would put more than a few down here in a battle along the side of the hill. But they weren't just going to try to fight us unit to unit. They were going to sound those *Uroo Uroo* horns. Or some variant thereof. In no time every one of theirs, the whole horde out there looking for us, would be heading straight for the route that the rest of the Rangers were using to escape to the canyon that led up and out of this haunted valley. We could get bogged down real fast, and that wouldn't be good.

"Direct engagement is a no-go," said Sergeant Hardt.

Problem was if we sat and let them take the high ground, they might get up there and just stay in our way. Or they might spot the other teams moving up through the hills and start rallying their forces to deny them an escape route while maintaining the high ground. Somehow they had to be dealt with and quick. Other than opening fire up here along the ridge line and drawing attention, it didn't seem that there were a lot of options.

Last of Autumn flashed her solution in our minds a moment later. Already her dappled gray horse was coming up from the shadows of the draw he'd been waiting in.

"I need to... get them away... from you. Back down into the valley. They... will chase, thinking we... my people... are coming to help now. They... not want that outcome."

I relayed this to Sergeant Hardt. Her plan to lead them away on a wild goose chase. Give the scouts an opportunity to secure the ridge. At least with the high ground secured, if it did turn into another full-scale engagement, then our company held a better position to fight from. The rest of the teams could come and anchor there, and we could make what would undoubtedly be our last stand. If we had to.

Then I added something on the fly. Something she hadn't requested and I hadn't considered until I just blurted it out. "I need to go with her, Sar'nt. She'll need to stay in communication with the rest of the detachment, and I'm the only one that can communicate if she hasn't used her trick." Referring to the Moon Vision thing. "If that doesn't work on everyone else in the other teams."

Hardt studied me for a long moment and then checked in with the brooding Sergeant Thor who was studying the centaurs down there. Planning how many he could shoot down and how fast he could do it for the Thor high score. A small night breeze came up and shifted the dead grass around us in long waves once again. We could smell the ripe stench of the goat men.

Last of Autumn shook her head when she figured out I intended to go with her on her attempt to draw fire.

"If they see you... your kind... know we have made... alliance. Know your people are moving... this direction. They move all their terrible host here... stop you now. If just me... scout... they may not even... sound alarm. They may want me for themselves. Saying nothing... to the rest."

Silence.

The dappled gray horse had come up and the centaurs and goat men hadn't spotted us yet. But it was only a matter of time before that changed if they continued heading upslope. We'd be as clear as daylight in a few minutes. You could smell the sour vinegar of bad wine on the goat men's breathy gasping as they climbed harder, humping packs as large as our own. Cackling and bleating mournfully like goats do. Whether this ability to smell was due to the effects of what Autumn had given us with the Moon Vision, or they just stunk that bad, I didn't know. Maybe they were huge gutter drunks. They seemed the type if anyone in dark fantasyland was.

"She's right, Talker," said Sergeant Hardt. "You stay with us. Seems like she can handle herself."

Except that was counter to everything Ranger. You always needed a buddy. Someone on your wing, or your six.

I'd already remembered the ring. In fact, I'd been thinking about it along the march and how to apply it. Tactically. I'd almost volunteered to use it when we'd encountered the orc ambush down in the gully. But to what effect? I'd sneak in among them and start killing bloodthirsty orcs all by myself? Yet once that sorcerer had directly attacked us, the ring hadn't worked too well for him. If it had, we wouldn't right now have his stuff. Would we? So there was that to consider. I'd kill one or two, and then it's just me and the rest to figure it all out. Never great odds even with an MK18 carbine and all the ill will you could bear against someone and all their buddies.

Truth was, there were a few times I could have used the ring by now. Like with Volman, maybe. Or up on Sniper Hill. Though I'm not convinced it would have helped in either case. And honestly, the thought hadn't crossed my mind when the opportunity presented itself. You'd think that if you had in your pocket a magic ring that could make you invisible, it would be on your mind constantly. When you've got a magic hammer, everything looks like a magic nail. Right? But it doesn't. It isn't. And you don't. Or, anyway, in my case I didn't. In my defense, I had a few things going on.

Now, however…

"Okay, guys… hang on," I said.

I slipped the ring out of my cargo pocket and put it on. And I must've turned invisible because Sergeant Hardt swore and muttered, "Where'd Talker go?"

"I'm right here."

I slipped the ring off.

"We took this off an HVT," I said. "Turns me invisible. Stuff like this works now. Here, Sar'nt."

I saw Last of Autumn looking at me warily. I sensed the moment for me to get my way and go with her wherever she was going. The ring had conveyed some kind of temporary authority over the Rangers. Not by the magic that came with it, but rather the simple magic of pulling a neat trick and getting a few seconds of awe in which to pull a con and get your way for better or for worse.

Linguists use this trick often. Mastery of languages other people don't speak can let you get away with some really shady stuff.

Just for fun, of course.

"So... I'll go with her," I said. "We lose 'em and come right back. You continue on mission, Sar'nt Hardt. Roger?"

All he could do was mumble a "Roger," because I'd just turned invisible. And that was a pretty neat trick when you thought about it.

# CHAPTER THIRTY-SIX

THE centaurs were just heading up the final few meters of the ridge when they spotted Last of Autumn but not me riding away hard and fast. They saw Last of Autumn on her horse, the dappled gray, racing away under the moonlight, heading back down into the dark forest along the river valley. They missed that I was behind her, invisible and hanging on for dear life.

I'd ridden a horse once.

One time.

Now we were going at perilously breakneck speed down the side of what I considered a very dangerous hill on an unsafe grade. As in, if the galloping horse hit one rabbit hole it would be our necks that were broken.

I would have told her to slow down, but... weak.

So I just held on and tried not to fall off. In the dark and the wind, I cranked my head around to see the centaurs rearing up, as if to get a better look at Autumn, their fleeing prey, and then turning around in flurries of dirt to race back down the hill after her. The goat men had already turned and were loping with bandy-legged strides, braying into the air, and making for us as fast as they could.

You could tell that each faction within the enemy hunting force wanted to be the first to get the elf, but not just that—each creature wanted to beat even their own kind to reach her before anyone else as she galloped madly away downslope, heading back into the dark forest below.

The first arrows flew, and none were aimed too well. The centaurs had those powerful ranged marksmen re-curved bows. The kind of bows Mongolian horse-mounted archers had once used to ruin half the known world. But in this case, quality didn't lead to accuracy. Though, given the vision Autumn had shown us, I wasn't counting on them missing again. The horny goat men, on the other hand, whirled crude slings about their heads as they bounded and leapt down the hill, then let small deadly stones fly at us with fairly good accuracy.

One whistled just past my invisible face as we raced away.

Our plan worked. The hunting force that would have run smack dab into the Ranger scouts at the top of the ridge was now tearing off in pursuit of this prized prey. And bonus: they weren't signaling other enemy elements with their *Uroo Uroo* horns.

They wanted her for themselves.

Coupled with the memory she had shown us in Moon Vision, that sent cold shivers down my spine.

They were what I thought evil should look like.

Two minutes later we were heading into the thick stands of trees that signaled the outer edges of the woods along the slopes that led down to the twisting river. No doubt Sergeant Hardt was updating command with our plan. If no one engaged, the best the Rangers could hope for was that the enemy continued its outward fragmenta-tion in every direction, losing the ability to bring forces to bear against our main body before we reached the climb up the narrow canyon to Phase Line Domino. If by midnight we reached the rally at Fox, the bottom of the canyon, and started our ascent, then to me, that was a win for us. The enemy would have to follow Rangers up a dangerous pass. Rangers would make that very difficult for them. Whereas right now, crossing the night under the fading crescent moon along the open and rising foothills, any elements caught out in the open, with wounded and overloaded on equipment, faced a pretty tough fight. Surrounded of course.

No Ranger likes to fight that kind of battle.

But there would be hell to pay whatever the outcome. The enemy would pay dearly whether they liked it or not. Caught, the Rangers would go honey badger in a heartbeat. There would be much regret on the part of the enemy even if they did manage to pick and win that fight.

We had a head start, Last of Autumn and I on horseback, but it was clear the centaurs were faster. After all, they were horses without riders. They came forward quickly, getting ahead of the goat men who were kicking, punching and tripping one another to try and get to us first, lustily baying like goats do.

Now arrows were falling into the trees around us and soon our forward motion was slowed as Last of Autumn and her horse wove through the dense forest and down onto a trail that ran deeper into the late-night woods. It was an old trail that hadn't seemed used in a long time. Shadows loomed up at us—giant trees that reminded me too much of the glowering trolls we'd faced the night before. Deadfall and dead growth had fallen across the track, and rains had collapsed the way in places. I wondered who had made this path. And then I looked up and toward our left at the edge of the forest. Some of the centaurs had taken intercept routes, and they were gaining on us by using the open ground outside the forest to get ahead of our escape.

And of course, my weight and what gear I hadn't left with the scouts was added to Last of Autumn's horse's burden. Still the big beast thundered ahead into the gloom of the forest, heaving to get ahead of our desperate pursuers.

The first centaur, a big mean brute with an almost prissy face, roared down through the trees of the upper forest, spear out and no bow in hand. He made an incredible and fantastic leap over a fallen log up there above the trail and came flying down onto the path ahead of us. But his momentum carried him farther downslope, and when I looked back, he was scrambling around like a fallen horse trying to get up, get his hooves under him, and get back along our trail as fast as he could.

An arrow from out of nowhere whistled past my ear and off into the wind and the night as we raced further into the dark.

A massive tree lay across the old ruined trail ahead, and Autumn drove her horse off and into the forest to get around it. We slowed and followed a draw off the trail that led deeper down toward the bottom of the river valley.

"Great," I said above the wind and thunder of hooves beating out a staccato tempo. "We've lost 'em. What next?"

She said nothing for a long moment and then she reined in the horse and we literally started sliding down an impossibly steep slope covered by dead leaves. Steeper than anything I'd ever thought it was possible for a horse to go down. Much less in the dark. Chased by horse-man-beasts. With spears and bad intentions.

Everything was dust and moonlight and we slammed into not just a outstretched branches. I held on to her and my weapon at the same time. If it came to a fight, I'd need it.

We made the bottom of the slope and she slid off the horse and said, "Come with me now!"

The meaning was clear. We were going to try and lose them on foot while the horse used his unburdened speed to get away in another direction.

She had her bow out and an arrow nocked. She patted the dappled gray, murmured Tolkien words I couldn't understand, and sent him disappearing into the night gloom of the forest like some undersea monster swimming off into the shadowy depths never to be seen again.

We were running through the trees, and I could hear myself. Hear my battle rattle even though I'd gotten it quieter than I'd ever thought possible to work with the scouts. But compared to me she made no sound at all. At least I was invisible. Still had the ring on. But I knew she could hear me, and she kept telling me to follow her this way or that. Or to watch this branch, or this step. It was clear she knew where she was going.

I didn't.

"Where are we going?" I gasped as my cardio started to get under control.

"To a place where we can ambush them," she replied inside my head.

Then she shouted back at me in Shadow Cant Korean. Suddenly. A warning.

*"Watch out!"*

Another centaur came from out of nowhere in the darkness all around us. I was so busy following her, I was only dimly aware of the four-legged thunder of his sudden onslaught through the forest press. He came out of the woods to our right and she turned and fired her bow on the fly. Twice. Fast. One arrow after the other. Both silver-feathered shafts slammed into the muscled gut of the horse-man, just below the plates of the centaur's torso armor. The thing tumbled, its front legs going out from under it as it crashed headfirst into a tree.

I'm pretty sure I heard its skull break when it hit.

"Come now," whispered Autumn in my head. "So close. We don't want to be caught out here."

Further off I could hear more pursuers. And the sounds of the braying goat men racing bandy-legged down through the deadfall into the area she was leading us through. In my mind I could see their lecherous leers and toothy smiles, horns down and about no good business as they fought to be the first to find us.

Then what?

I don't think I wanted to know.

I made up my mind they wouldn't get her.

Mess with her, and get the full blur. The blur being how many rounds I could mag dump on them. I promised them that and got ready to engage these jerks. I was definitely strapped, and they were about to get clapped.

Autumn had slowed to a jog and now we were leaping down a twisty set of carved steppingstones. They were covered in dead, red leaves and looked to have been so for some time. My Moon Vision saw all this whereas my regular eyes could not. And I doubt the Army's latest night vision would have seen a thing. There wasn't enough light here for them to do their job.

The steppingstones twisted down the side of the hill, and in a few minutes I could hear the distant river. The question was... would we run into any other enemies besides the ones chasing us out here tonight? If we did, things would get messy and out of hand real fast.

A hustle of goat men spotted us and came leaping down along the top of the trail. Calling out like crying goats come to feed. She turned and fired at one, putting the arrow straight through the beer-bellied thing's gut.

I sighted and squeezed off a suppressed burst on another. He went rolling down through the dead leaves on the hill.

All around us I could see them moving. They'd fanned out into a hunting semicircle. My fire hadn't slowed them in the least. If anything, it drove them on to get to us even faster and close this end of the noose on us.

On her, anyway. They couldn't see me. Perhaps I was lucky they didn't react to the sound of my boom stick by sending up a smoke signal of the *Uroo Uroo* variety. *Boom-stickers here. Come get some.* But I doubt they knew what suppressed fire sounded like and expect they were confused to hear that sound coming from, as far as they could see, an elf.

And they wanted her for themselves.

Bad.

She grabbed my hand even though I was invisible and pulled me off through a high wall of shrubs we'd been heading straight toward. Like someone had once grown the giant wild hedge here and long ago they'd left it to its own will. And though it had grown wild and tangled, the hedge had never given up that memory of the wall it had once been trained to be.

She could see me regardless of the ring. I slipped it off of my finger and back into my cargo pocket, sealing the flap to make sure the ring stayed in there good and tight.

She sliced through thick tendrils as we pushed through the hedge. Razor-sharp ninja sword out and in one hand. Hacking up and down to clear a path forward and through the tangle of twisting branches and cutting leaves. Her breath coming in delicate little heaves. The bow in her other hand. Whistling stones flew into the wall of shrubs all about us, the goat men hooting and calling to one another as they sensed their prey run to ground.

And then we forced our way through to the other side and came face to face with a dazzling ancient ruin bathed in the bare moonlight from above.

True, the Moon Vision no doubt played the primary role in making its white marble a thing of beauty. Even so, it was unlike anything I'd ever beheld in my life before this moment. It was like a building, or a tower, that had collapsed, and its fragments had become the ruins of a king's crown. There could be no doubt the place was ancient, hinting at past glories of some epic age we'd never know.

"What is this..." I mumbled stupidly as I followed her into it. In awe of its mystery and dark splendor. Forgetting the stabby little goat men scrabbling about through the underbrush behind us. "It's incredible," I added. Helpfully.

In my comm I was getting traffic from the sergeant major. It was coming in distorted and broken. But he was definitely trying to get ahold of me. And that probably meant it was important.

"This..." she began breathlessly, striding forward fast to get inside the circle of bone-white moonlit stone that formed the broken crown of the fantastic once-ago tower that had fallen in on itself in the distant past. I hustled after her, MK18 up and scanning the access points through the hedge. Waiting for little goat men to drop through. "This is the Temple of… Hidden King. Elves who once lived… worshipped here… by the river's edge."

We walked through the remains of a fabulous collapsed arch. Like something out of an ornate cathedral. It was covered in scrawled runes worked delicately over the stone. Faint and beyond anything I would have ever thought possible without some kind of advanced industrial carving or etching machine. And I didn't even know if such a thing existed in our times. I mean, did people back in our time, even then, could they do this level of fantastic detail stuff by hand?

I'd seen these kinds of markings before. I didn't know it at the time, but later as I thought about it, I figured it out. Now I can tell you it was Tolkien Elvish. From long ago. The made-up language my more obsessive linguistics colleagues had hobbied in. And yet here were walls and walls of chiseled tablets of text in this ancient and made-up language like it was a real thing. The real medium of informational exchange in some vast culture that had once ruled these lands. Not a hobby from a fusty old book. Inside the circumference of the primeval temple, almost all of what remained of the old walls was covered in rows upon rows of the script. It was everywhere and it was endless.

And meaningless to me.

But not meaningless.

Some forever-language-learning background app in my mind came to the conclusion I would have to figure this language out if I was to uncover the secrets of this world.

I might have sighed out loud. But truth be told… I like challenges. I love the puzzle of languages. So it wasn't as bad as I was making it out to be. I was just tired, and there, hunted in the middle of the night by goat men, there was no end I could see that wasn't real bad for all of us.

"Come with me," she said once more. Then almost as fast as Chief McCluskey had moved with the sword in Chief Rapp's hands, taking it away and placing the razor-sharp edge against the special operator's neck that day back in the C-17, she stuck her sword in the bare dirt where a missing flagstone had long ago been pulled up, and almost at the same time she pulled and fired an arrow in one fluid motion at a goat man assassin who'd crept in through the hedge and whom I had not seen.

The shot whistled away and spitted him through the throat. The goat man started gagging and spouting blood. It died seconds later, blood seeping out through its dirty fingers and black nails, the whites of its eyes rolling up into its horny skull.

It wasn't a pretty sight.

I was scanning every sector, following the sights on my MK18 which interfaced beautifully with Moon Vision in ways no one had probably ever imagined. Using NVGs and sights was horrible. At best. You had to be a nerd-level shooter to enjoy that particular experience. But with Moon Vision and its strange telescoping awareness, it was like my eyes *became* the sights. Our senses had definitely been augmented.

I could hear the hooves of the goat men scuffing about beyond the wall of shrubs. They whispered like demons in horror movies do when they're driving someone mad without being seen. It was half hiss and half malevolent giggle.

"Down here," Autumn whispered at me.

I turned and saw she was at the lip of a central well. A giant hole. A giant gaping hole, in which ancient and cracked marble steps led down into dark depths.

"What's down there?" I asked.

She turned back, her face beautiful and frightened at the same time in the dark. I could see every detail of her, and she was fascinating. Her eyes endless silver starry universes you could stare into and maybe get lost in forever. But she was frightened, and that had me concerned. Maybe this hadn't been such a great plan after all. Maybe she knew that.

The Rangers were now free to make it to the first en route rally point, and as far as that was concerned… good to go. We'd done it. We'd drawn the enemy off. Or at least we'd bought our side a little more time to get a little closer to escaping this haunted river valley. And right now, the way things looked, every step closer to the objective was a win. One step at a time. One foot in front of the other until you got somewhere. Straight out of the Drill Sergeant Ward playbook.

*Good enough*, I told myself, and asked her what was down there in the well beneath the ruined temple. It was clear we were going down. Fine. Let's do this. It might as well be this.

"A demon," she said up at me.

And then we started down into the darkness.

# CHAPTER THIRTY-SEVEN

THE ruined old place we found ourselves descending into was like some fantastical temple from out of the mists of forgotten legends and long-ago myths. Something amazing an angered titan had come and smashed into the deep places of the earth to teach mortals their place. A place you'd only see in that summer's mega blockbuster about worlds just like those the Rangers now found themselves in. It was too overwhelming and awe-inspiring to be taken in. Every shadowy corridor and luminescent light shaft exposed a statue that hinted at lost stories I would never know, things that would remain mysteries for the next ten thousand years to come and the next ten thousand years that would follow. It was like finding and reading the last paragraph in a great book that was otherwise gone forever. You only got part of the story. And even just that much was epic.

It brought to me the oddest sensation because I knew this feeling…

It was like a marvelous abandoned mall that had once been the place to be, twenty years or so ago. And a lifetime. A place where girls were met after school on a Friday night to catch that year's blockbuster at the now-silent movie theater near the forever-dark arcade that would never *whir* and *beep* again. Where one could once pick up a fresh "lid" from one of the seven different stores that sold sports memorabilia—the glories of our grand past. Check out the food court and try to see all the stories, lives, loves, and dramas that had once played out among the leaf-covered tiles and overturned chairs dirty with long-ago rainwater from a roof that had caved in. Now the stores are darkened and hidden behind shuttered gates that will never rise again.

This was us. Weep, Ozymandias.

Imaginary worlds must have brave heroes. Our memories of those long-lost malls of our youth must've said as much ten thousand years ago as this was saying to me now. Like some demand that it must be if we are to face the winter of old age. The realities of the way things have gone, and how they are now.

Perhaps I'm overselling what I saw down there. Getting a little purple with my prose. I'm a new writer. Maybe even the only writer left in the world we ended up in. So... forgive me. I'm still figuring it all out. How to tell a story. Malls were before my time, really. But I'd seen the pictures. Watched the retro movies full of actors my age but targeted at my parent's generation. And I saw the way they impacted my mother to the point that I felt it. I knew what she was feeling. When I think back about what was below the ruin of that temple Last of Autumn led me deep into... it was like that. Those memories of memories I would never know. It made me feel how you feel sometimes when you catch the vaguest harmony of a song you once knew, but know there's more you can't remember. A song you loved. But haven't heard for a long time.

The well of the temple might have once been some kind of open subterranean garden, sunken below the main level, and open to what must have been a great latticework dome of carved stone. Now that dome had fallen in, collapsed across delicate ancient white marble floors dirty and grown over with moss and giant feathery ferns. Strange necrotic purple mushrooms grew and pulsed down there in the depths, giving off a faint and definitely unholy sinister light. There was a feeling of diabolical intelligence down there. Something that was as malevolent as it was mindless. Dark-purposed and mindless at once. And hungry. Very hungry.

"You said this was where elves worshipped? But not your people?" I whispered as we threaded down cut marble steps past ruined statues of beautiful women, seemingly elves by their ears, holding torches, books, wheat. All of it carved in stone. All of it ruined by time, marred by damage.

She was focusing hard down into the darkness. Fighting to find our way forward through the maze of destruction. Even the special abilities the Moon Vision conferred seemed to struggle down here against that overwhelming dark and malevolence that radiated from somewhere far below. As though whatever was waiting unseen in the darkness down there didn't want to be revealed.

Not just yet.

She stopped like a cat intent on hunting a bird, then looked back at me over her shoulder and shook her head, putting one delicate finger over her lips. Sword out, she continued down.

The goat men and centaurs above us could still be heard, circling the ruin and challenging one another to go in after us. We could hear the stamp of their hooves and their madly whispered plans. They were sure they had us cornered, if the dark glee in their voices was to be believed. I had no idea what language they spoke, but I was catching hints of German. Or what Last of Autumn called *Grau Sprache*. Gray speech.

She'd cursed Jabba in it. Did that mean it was the language of the enemy? I filed that away as intel in case I ever made it back to the Rangers. I'd need to develop that and find out what it meant. What it implied. But honestly... at that moment, descending into the well of darkness below the ruin of the broken old moonlit temple above, I wasn't convinced I'd be getting out of here alive.

Especially if there was a demon down below.

Was there? Could there even be demons? Had there ever been?

Yes, answered a voice inside of me and I knew it was true.

We made it down to a main floor below the temple, and I could see that it was not as totally dark and utterly mysterious as it had first seemed. Bright shafts of startlingly blue moonlight shot down into the gloom from the sections where the roof had caved in high above, once again making everything beautiful in that post-apocalyptic mall meltdown sort of way.

I wondered about this whole world and all of its stories I would never know. I wanted to know them all. Maybe that was why I was here. To know the stories of these places. To write them down. Or at least one of them. *Our* story. So that whatever became of the Rangers wouldn't be like this forgotten and sunken ruin lost out here in the forest forever. Mysteries no one would ever know again. I would do my best not to let that happen. For as long as I could hang with the Rangers, I'd mark it all down in the permanent record. The deeds. The heroes. The myths and the legends. And try, in some small way, to defy the relentless destruction of time.

A thought occurred to me at that time. That I was being arrogant. That I was assuming that because I didn't know, no one else did. That Last of Autumn, who knew of this place and knew to come to this place, couldn't know its stories. I resolved to lament less and learn more.

There was a thick, almost throbbing silence down here in the gloomy darkness below the shattered upper levels.

She led me along a passage whispering, "The gotaur are excellent trackers. They'll follow. This way." Using basic linguistics, it was pretty easy to figure out who the gotaur were. The goat men. But what about the centaurs? Surely the half man, half horses couldn't try to come down here.

As if on cue I heard the *clop clop clopping* of one of them at the top of the ruined stairs. To them, the elf was a prize worth folly.

I followed, and soon we were threading our way along a narrow passage that, had I not been *plus-one*d by the Moon Vision, would have had me stumbling blindly and probably sending me off into a bottomless pit.

Yeah. There were pits down there, and no bottom was visible from along the ledges. It was that kind of place.

"What about that demon?" I whispered. The silence pulsed and breathed like a living thing.

She said nothing.

Soon we came out into an underground cavern that was kind of like a pit in its own way. A small waterfall fell from ground level high above, cascaded down the side of the ruined shaft, and disappeared down into the darkness way below. There was no splash. No sound of any pool down there in the deep dark. At least, not that I could hear from the ledge we found ourselves inching along.

The moonlight reflected off the falling water, providing more illumination here, and that was good because the ledge around the side of the shaft was much too narrow to be navigated comfortably in the dark. Or comfortably in the light, for that matter. I wondered if the centaurs would manage it. I could hear the hooves above making their way down through the upper levels.

We were moving toward a fissure in the wall along the side of the shaft on the far side. Well below where we were. The ledge was on a slight grade, corkscrewing downward. And the closer we got to that fissure, the more we worked our way around the shaft, the stronger was the foul stench. Which was strong enough to begin with. There was something about that fissure that didn't feel right. That crack in the wall felt like an infection in the very being of this place. Even with the ruin of the temple and the caves below, the fissure itself was a separate thing from all of it. Separate and far worse. I knew that. I felt it. Something rotten and festering was in there, and its cold malevolence was inside my mind.

*The demon.*

She'd said that. Last of Autumn. In my mind.

She pointed and whispered the word once more. Aloud this time. Pointing toward the fissure. The doom crack.

"*Demon.*"

My plan, if anyone was asking, would have been to do the exact opposite of what we were currently doing. Which was continuing on around the ledge straight down toward the spot where the fissure in the wall waited.

No one was asking.

I flipped the selector switch on the MK18 to *kill*. Opting for full auto instead of semi, considering ammunition reserves and loaded magazines, or "kill sticks" as the Rangers called them, weren't exactly surplus. Still, I intended to be hard to kill.

*Be meaner than it*, the sergeant major had said.

We were creeping, me making as little sound as I could, Autumn making none, closing on the ragged fissure in the cave wall. Then she stopped.

She turned to the raw rock wall and whispered something. I barely caught it in the throbbing malevolent silence. It was a Tolkien word, and I had no idea what it meant. But what happened next was pretty cool all the same.

"*Málo.*" That was the word. She whispered it softly. So quietly that I barely heard. As though she didn't want to wake someone—or something—up. And then just barely, the cave wall slid inward from two sides of a silvery seam that hadn't been there a second ago. There was a darkness beyond the gap in the wall and she looked back at me once, happiness and relief crossing her earnest features, and then we slipped through the crack in the wall.

A second later, as the centaurs and the gotaurs came down into the cave well, the hidden door closed behind us.

# CHAPTER THIRTY-EIGHT

WE found ourselves inside an alcove. Something the size of an office storage room. But a secret storage room behind the real live actual secret door we'd just gone through. Something straight out of a murder mystery set in a haunted house, or a fantasy story about lost and hidden kingdoms long forgotten beneath the earth. Or a pirate novel, for there were pirate treasure chests inside the room, along with a wide wooden plank of a table piled with strange vials and bottles of colored liquids all of which glowed iridescently.

A sudden, peculiar thought popped into my mind. Perhaps one of these contained coffee. I hoped, really. I joked and said so in that way where you're really not joking.

She had no idea what I was talking about and I had to fight off a brief bout of ennui when I realized there might perhaps be no more coffee left in the world. I resolved right then and there to find some, grow it, harvest it, and brew it myself.

I had no idea how to do that.

But... I could learn.

The secret door, when I turned around to look back at it, looked like a door from this side. A silver door. Whereas on the other side it had looked like part of the rock wall we'd been crawling along. It was crossed with a silvery tracing of lines that shimmered magically in the darkness, showing runes I didn't understand and the image of a crescent moon beneath a snow-capped mountain.

"What is this place?" I whispered in the closeness of the room.

She sat on a stool and stared up at the ceiling as she fumbled in her cloak and brought out something wrapped in fragrant-smelling leaves. Cakes. She handed me one and then began to eat her own almost ravenously. She must have had a high metabolism—that would explain her speed and her apparent need for calories. She ate, chewing fast, still staring upward as though she could see the centaurs and gotaurs coming down the ledge above. Her long ears twitched delicately once or twice at some noise I could not detect, and I realized she was using her ears, and their most likely fantastic ability to hear, to triangulate the current position of our enemies.

It was pretty clear to me what she'd done. She'd led them along right down to the fissure that was much more than a mere crack in the cave wall. It felt like something far worse. Like a doorway you didn't want to go behind, and might not be able to leave once you did.

And then she'd ducked us into a secret room right outside her trap.

That was clever. Ranger clever.

Outside and above I heard the muffled *clop clop clop* of centaur hooves. The hissing giggles of the hunting goat men. The gotaurs, she'd called them. They were close to the door, but the silence between us and them was like an invisible thing that could be felt and not seen. Like stuffy white noise inside a pair of headphones. I had to assume it was magic of some sort. Some feature in the door. But

I was more amazed they, the centaurs especially, but the gotaurs too, were coming down, hooves and all, along that narrow ledge. And then, as if an answer must be provided for my disbelief that they would attempt such a thing... one of them fell off the ledge out there. A centaur. It went neighing off, whinnying in terror as it fell for what seemed forever into the deep dark depths below.

She seemed to read my mind.

"No," she said softly as the centaurs and gotaur began to cry to one another. Some no doubt advocating that they turn back now. Others enraged and braying in their unknown language. "They cannot hear us in here."

And after a few moments they started down again out there along the sides of the well. They were resolute in their intent to do evil. They would have what they'd come for, no matter the cost.

The first centaur passed just outside the well-hidden secret door and continued on along the cavern ledge toward the crack in the wall.

"This place was the... a holy place..." she said. "To the Dragon Elves that were first... after the Great Ruin. They built the temple above and... delved the sanctums and catacombs below. Vast and extensive. They did things... things... that should not be done. Not... known."

Something rattled out there in the main shaft. Rattled like a diamondback out in the lonely desert scrub when you're walking all alone and suddenly realize you're in someone else's home. Time to be careful. Warning. Danger. Warning you to get away from it or face the consequences of bite and poison as you lie there dying. I knew that sound. I'd hiked and camped a lot in the Southwest with my dad when I was young. This sound sounded a lot like that rattlesnake warning inside my head. But also... not. Somehow different. Somehow wrong. The rattle started off almost slow, and seductive. Like a Middle Eastern musical prelude to a keening desert dirge. Only for a few seconds. And then it was loose and wild like sudden electricity live in the air all around us. And the sound of the rattling was lost in an otherworldly hiss and moan that sounded wrong on every level you can imagine. Cold water splashed across my spine as invisible long-legged spiders ran up into my brain. That's how I heard it. But I also knew... and this is where it gets weird... I knew where the seams in the universe began to show. I could hear what it sounded like to the centaurs and the goat men.

Suddenly I had the worst, or weirdest, headache I'd ever had. Just for an instant. Only a flash. Then it was gone. It was like my mind, and my brain, were on fire for just that second. That wasn't the worst part. The sudden fever... that was normal, or what I realized was now normal. My mind always burning with thoughts and ideas and dreams just like every human mind out there. Fever was normal human thought. And then suddenly when that moan and rattle came from the dark fissure... I knew for a fact it was from the dark fissure... when it moaned, when it wailed... it wailed for the longing of a void it called the *Outer Dark*. Oblivion. Destruction. Home.

Out there now, as the fever of normal thought returned and the call of oblivion faded from my mind, I could hear the sounds of tentacles and the neighing screams of the centaurs as they were snared, entangled, and then strangled... and finally dragged toward the hungry thing inside the fissure. The ancient oblivion thing. The thing of evil. The demon.

The thing that had nothing to do with any of this.

The gotaurs tried to flee, but the whipping tentacles came for them too, erupting from the fissure and snaking out into the void of the cavern, questing for souls, anything, to consume to abate the pain that was the thing in the crack's nostalgia for oblivion. *The Outer Dark*.

My sudden worst-ever weird headache was gone and all I had left was a memory of losing my place in the universe at the height of it. I was sure in that horrible half moment between existences that the thing in the fissure had a thousand lidless eyes. And each and every one had looked straight at me in the brief moment before the slaughter. The feeding. The frenzy. The memories of beautiful nothingness. Its eyes, every last one of them, were so very ancient and so very old. They had seen other horrors beyond the imaginings of sane and rational minds. Other worlds ruined. Other endless voids known.

"Are you okay?" she asked as I came back to myself in a cold sweat.

Yeah. Now I was back in the small secret room alongside the ledge in the well and the sounds of the rattles and whips were fading from the universe. As if withdrawing from reality. The centaurs and the gotaurs made no sounds. And I knew they never would again.

Autumn seemed worried as I sat there bathed in my own streaming cold sweat. All I knew was I was pretty sure I never wanted to have that kind of headache again. Or hear... hear the rattles and the... the sound of endless nothingness.

No. Not me. Never again. No thanks.

"T-tell me." I was stuttering when I tried to speak. I just wanted her to talk now. Like I knew her voice was an anchor in a universe I'd suddenly realized wasn't as empty as I might have imagined it to be in times previous. And right now, I needed her voice, that comforting anchor, in order not to slip off into some void between the cracks where real monsters like the thing in the fissure lie in dark and unfound places, dreaming dreams of endless destructions.

"Tell me what was that w-w-word…"

She looked at me and I could feel myself sliding toward a ledge with nothing beyond. A vast nothingness you could never get yourself out of. And no place to grab on to.

"Th-th-the one w-with… door!" I spat out finally. And then she began to talk, and the more she did so in her soft voice with all its depths and comforts, the more it brought me back from that edge at forever. And slowly, I began to feel better. "Oh-oh-open."

A brief look of confusion crossed her beautiful features for a moment. And then she understood what I'd asked. The meaning of a word I'd heard. My own kind of anchor. The game of languages.

"*Málo*," she said. "It is… High Speech… for *friend*."

"I-i-s that the l-l-language… of the Dragon El-el-elves?"

She nodded.

I nodded back, forcing myself into the very act of communication like it was a handhold I might grab to arrest my slide off the universe along that Forever Edge where the thing in the fissure lay waiting.

*High Speech*, I thought, and felt my mind find where it was supposed to be, and not where it had wanted to go. Toward that edge, and all the oblivions beyond. The edge along the well of the universe.

The point of no return.

The Tolkien language from our past. That game of linguistics scholars. Here, it was called High Speech. Okay. Good. I could work with that, I told my chattering, shaking self.

"G-g-g-good."

"When we reach my people..." she began, and she uncorked one of the small vials that had been on the wide table in the room. It was filled with a vibrant emerald liquid. Small wisps of fragrant rosemary came from its unsealed top. Glowing green in the soft and silent darkness between us. Only the silver tracery of magic in the door provided any kind of light by which to see. I sensed that the thing in the crack stifled the effects of Moon Vision. Like its darkness was a drowning thing that smothered everything that got near it. "You must only speak in *Grau Sprache* or High Speech. Never Shadow Cant. Never... with... my... people."

I asked her why.

"No. It is... never done. Not... outside must know of... it. Otherwise there will be... much death."

I told her I understood. And that she would need to start teaching me phrases I could use in High Speech. She looked unsure for a moment, but, like the realist I would find her to be, some kind of irony in a world that seemed so fantastic, she taught me my first words of High Speech. Elven. *Yes* and *no*.

Yes: *lá*.

No: *alá*.

Easy. We were off and learning and my fear-struck mind, which had felt like it was coming unraveled in ways I'd never even imagined, was coming back to where it needed to be. Playing the games and puzzle-riddles of languages. To me, worlds had fallen apart before. And language, languages, the study of them, had always been my safe harbor for as long as I could remember. A shelter against uncertainty and chaos.

I took a deep breath and whispered, "*Málo.*"

She nodded at me. *Friend.* Her beautiful silver eyes shining brightly. Brighter than I'd ever noticed. She blinked once... and it was like I knew her even more now. *Friend. Málo.* It was a powerful word here. To her... it meant something more. Like a drink of water to a dying person crossing a desert all alone for a very long time. Seeking an oasis by rumors alone.

Friend.

A drink of water from that real oasis.

Yes.

*Lá.*

Like a gamble that had somehow paid off despite the odds. That was the look in her eyes too.

"What happened to the Dragon Elves?" I asked in the silence. She shook her head sadly and offered me the vial of iridescent emerald liquid. It smelled good. Like rosemary and mint.

"Drink." She said it first in Shadow Cant Korean, then in High Speech Tolkien.

I did. Instantly I felt warm, and good. Refreshed and not tired. Yeah, it wasn't coffee. But it was good. And where I had felt tired and ragged and cold from the endless events of recent days, now I felt empty of all the garbage of those same days and nights. In fact, I felt like I'd just gotten a great night's rest and a solid workout the morning after.

I felt calm and relaxed, and my coffee addict's mind wanted to always feel this way. Always.

She watched me as my mind processed the wave of good vibes.

"Dragon Elves are…" I looked up toward the ruin above this secret room. The fallen temple and the rotten cavern beneath it. The ruins hinting at former glories long-ago passed. "They are gone now?"

She nodded again. Sadly.

"Was this their home?"

She smiled wanly and looked around, taking in a deep breath that seemed to indicate either peace or the acceptance of some burden she had carried for all her days. I couldn't tell which.

"No," she said, and she began to open the ancient brass-bound pirate chests on the floor, removing small and curious items, including more potions. She called the emerald vial a potion. What an amazing thing. Like I said, it wasn't coffee, but it would do until I started my own farm.

"Fallen… Tarragon… was their home. But… not… no… anymore."

I stood and realized my MK18 was still ready to engage. I switched it back to *safe*. Checked it once over. Checked my gear. It was clear we'd be leaving soon.

"No," she continued as she worked. "The dragon… S'sruth the Cruel… destroyed all Dragon Elves. Drove them out. Hunted them. Piled their… hoard and now… now he sleeps beneath the ruins… the Eternal Palace… of the First of Elves… guarding his ill-gotten… take."

She hissed these words out. The story of them was a complete change in personality for her. She seemed so angry and cold as she finished her business with the pirate chests.

"Were the Shadow Elves…" I didn't know what to say. *Friends to the Dragon Elves? Happy that another tribe had died by dragon?*

I didn't know.

Oh, and believe me, the fact that there were dragons in this world was not lost on me. I'm still thinking about it as of this writing. But it's almost too much to consider right now what with everything about to happen as I put all this down. Does she mean a dragon like what people used to call large lizards like the Komodo a dragon? Or does she mean a real-life Arthurian *slay the dragon* dragon? I forget which knight had that bit of particular business. But it wasn't just Arthurian tales. Dragons abounded in the mythology of many ancient cultures. I'd noticed them when studying languages and root origins. They appeared so many times it passed mere coincidence, and on long late-night walks home from the library in the dark between the streetlights it made one wonder what the repeated occurrence of them was all about.

At least as far as languages were concerned. The game of puzzles.

Had there really been dragons from before the modern age we'd come forward from? And in the wake of the collapse after the pandemic we'd fled, had they returned once again to rule and torment the world? To *take,* as Autumn had said. Using Korean, the forbidden language of the Shadow Cant. *Gajda. Take.* That was pretty mind-blowing. The dragon had taken what was theirs. The Dragon Elves. And what was that bit she'd mentioned about the Dragon Elves being the first after 'the Ruin'? And *knowing things they weren't supposed to know.*

As a scholar I found it all pretty fascinating. Endless questions were already appearing in my hard drive.

As a soldier carrying an MK18 with less than a basic combat load… it was also a little scary.

She turned toward me, satisfied she had gathered everything she needed from the two bound chests in the hidden little secret room next to…

…forget that part. It hurt my mind to think about it even then. Even now.

"Shadow Elves are wanderers," she said after a moment. "Wandering." Not halting as she found the right words. Like she'd been thinking about them and how to explain what was needed to answer my questions as she'd worked at the chests. Or even whether to tell me. "Cast out long ago. We have journeyed here, to reclaim from the dragon what is rightfully ours."

And then, with a cold look in her eyes, she turned to face me in the bare silver light thrown from the magic secret door in the wall.

"And we will."

# CHAPTER THIRTY-NINE

WE exited the broken and beautiful ruins. It was close to midnight as far as I could tell. Maybe another hour or so to go. The scouts should be getting close to the first objective rally point at Phase Line Fox. The bottom of the steep canyon the Rangers needed to go up and over the ridge of to escape this valley.

Last of Autumn knew the way, and we came out of the forest along the river. The comm came to life with the orders from the captain to keep moving forward. A small enemy force had located one of the teams responsible for some of the more heavily wounded, and were trying to hit them with ranged arrow fire from out in the dark. Reports indicated it looked like orcs. A light force, but soon there would be more. Circling out in the dark below one of the hilltops and trying to come in for the kill. The Rangers were setting up a hasty defense to give the wounded time enough to keep moving forward.

Problem was the enemy appeared to have called in a troll and an assault force of heavier orcs to pin down the teams. However exactly they did that. Drums and *Urooo Uroo* horns? Magic?

Captain Knife Hand and the rear security team were coming in to hit the enemy from the flank and hopefully give the team hauling the wounded time to get to the clear and closer to RP One and some sniper support from higher up along the ridge.

I explained the situation to Last of Autumn as we mounted her horse and rode off along the edges of the night-quiet forest. With a mere whistle, high and melodically mournful like some lonely and always questioning night bird, Autumn had summoned the giant gray dapple from out of the shadowy thickets. Once she understood the tactical situation facing the Rangers as they humped for the pass, she indicated she might know how to help.

We passed along darkened shadowy halls of trees and through quiet copses of ancient hulking leafy brutes long left alone to grow and erupt into the canopy of the primeval forest along the sides of the valley floor. There were traces of other ruins, and I had to wonder how much we were missing as we made our way back toward the line of march. It would seem these Dragon Elves had once been the primary population in the region. Now all that remained of them were the mysterious broken fragments of what they had once been. Unknown greatness lost to the years and overrun by the wild.

It was like going to Rome and seeing the Colosseum. Or even the pyramids. But then again, I mused to myself, if we'd been gone ten thousand years—which, according to the pilot's celestial navigation software, was indeed roughly the correct length of time—then these ruins could be older than anything we'd thought was "old" way back in what we'd considered the present ten thousand years ago. That day at Area 51 measured the pyramids as much younger than the amount of time we'd been gone. If these Dragon Elves were considered the first after the Ruin, then these fragments of temples and palaces and who-knew-what might go back to as far as the years just after we departed the scene via the QST gate. And if so... how? What happened after we left? What happened during what the history of the Shadow Elves called the Great Ruin?

By orders of magnitude that was pretty mind-blowing to consider if you let yourself think about it for a moment. That the Colosseum and the pyramids were young compared to these elven ruins if adjusted for the starting points of historical observation.

We were out of the forest now. We'd had to lie low and avoid an enemy patrol of creatures that looked like tall humanoid dogs. They carried spears and staffs. In the clarity of Moon Vision I could see their snouts snarling and tasting the night mist for a scent. At one point they began to bark fiercely at one another and spread out as though looking for something.

For us, no doubt.

Last of Autumn, cool as anything, just sat there on her horse, and slowly, with controlled movements of her knees, took us quietly beyond their search cordon. She seemed used to this kind of stuff. And I had to wonder... was she some kind of scout? Or an assassin?

*I* wasn't much of a scout. But I was officially an assassin now.

So we had that much in common.

Soon we were back in the hills along the valley's side, nearing the steep canyon up to the ridge. The firefight ahead, higher up the slopes, was plain as day even without Moon Vision. Or I assume it would have been. But of course, Moon Vision made it all so much easier. We lay in the shadow of a hill, studying the battle above. I explained the disposition of our troops to her and what we were trying to accomplish and why that was important. When I told her we were trying to rescue the wounded she nodded and simply said, "Of course you must."

And that was a better thing to have in common with one another than being assassins. Respect for the wounded. Unlike the goblins who'd left their dead, dying, and captured behind, Jabba and all the dead on Bag of Diarrhea Island, her people knew the value of leaving no one behind. That was endemic to the Ranger lifestyle. No one got left behind. You were going home alive, or on your shield. But you'd make it. Like it had been coded into their granite stone hard drive with a jackhammer.

What we were watching now was a running firefight taking place. Rangers in the security team holding the ridge, the wounded being led down toward a stream running through a gully between two hills. If they could follow the streambed and work their way out of the firefight, then they had a straight shot up to RP One.

Besides the rear security fire team being led by Captain Knife Hand, there was no one else coming to assist the Rangers trying to give the wounded cover to get clear. But that had been a command choice. The sergeant major was busy moving everyone else on to the ORP at Phase Line Fox, the entrance to the canyon. It was tight enough there that if the Rangers needed to fight a Spartan Hot Gates–style defense, they could do that there better than anyone else. If they hung back and ended up fighting a battle on a hill, ad hoc and pell-mell, the whole company would soon be engaged and surrounded on open ground.

As we watched, the rear security team came in, moving fast to establish a base of fire and nail the enemy archers trying to lob black-feathered arrows down into the gully and at the Rangers holding the hilltop. We could hear the sudden whistling of the massed arrow strikes incoming on pinned-down Rangers.

Because the Rangers had no night vision now—the captain had told me the batteries were dead or dying—and no Moon Vision, as that had been given to the scouts only, they had no idea where the troll and heavy orc force was coming in from. But we, Last of Autumn and I, *we* could see the enemy assaulters staging to storm the hill. The troll, a giant compared to the rest we'd seen so far, but lean like a walking snake, was literally slithering forward on its belly to get close enough for a real surprise. The orcs hunkering around it, all in heavy armor with horned helmets and double-bladed battle axes, kept low as well as they moved forward in wedges as they closed for the final push.

These were trained. And trained well.

There were now three Rangers on the hill and they were firing on semi, taking shots where they could, but in a few moments they'd be facing a force four times their size. A short rush, even under fire, and the troll and the heavy orcs would be all over them swinging axes and butchering their way to break the line.

I alerted the captain that we'd spotted the new assault force and he came back with "Negative on visual."

I could see the problem. The finger of the hill they were firing on was protecting the enemy assault force from being spotted. The quick reaction force under the command of the captain had set up on a hill farther downslope to provide fire support and hopefully draw the enemy away from the wounded being humped up the next hill. Truthfully, the troll and the orcs could have gone straight up the gully and run right into the rear of the wounded team.

Someone used a grenade on a cluster of archers. It detonated and shut down that attacking force for the moment.

But that enemy assault force was going to wipe out the three Rangers on the hill in the next few seconds, and there was nothing anyone could do about it.

The captain advised they were going to abandon the support position and assault directly into the enemy force. That would be bad. The Rangers would surprise the enemy from the flank, but because of the finger of the hill, they'd need to be right in it with the enemy before they could engage with direct fire. This would negate the combat multiplier firearms provided over hand-to-hand weapons; with as fast as the troll alone moved, hand-to-hand would start immediately. Plus, if they used a Carl G right there, on the fly and in the dark with no night vision, at a minimum it meant a wasted shot. At the max it would explode close enough to be a real problem for the Rangers assaulting through.

"Tell them… to stay," said Last of Autumn, her voice breathy and urgent.

She slipped off the horse. Then nodded at me to shift forward and take the reins.

"You must ride him now." And then she held out her hand for me to pull her back up to ride behind me. I had no idea what she was doing, and I also had no idea how to "drive" a horse. Is *drive* even the right word?

But I'll tell you one thing. As I hauled her up, we both felt wild electricity slip between us. The electric feeling of first touch when two people might, just might have a thing for each other. It was alive, and there was something new about it. That new relationship feel when you're both just excited and the thing that's between you is just yours and yours alone. No one else knows about it yet and the two of you barely do because you've only just discovered it. Like a secret. A good secret you want to keep and shout to the world at the same time. A secret neither of us could even admit to because we were in the middle of a firefight and all. Y'know how that is?

"Tell your... king," she said in my ear as we rode forward. "Tell him... stay where he is. I'll deal with the... dark host."

Ha. She thought Captain Knife Hand was our king. Well, on second thought, he kinda was. And *dark host*? That sounded more ominous than I would have liked as we rode straight at them.

I radioed the captain.

"Warlord, this is Niner Alpha Niner..."

My call sign is stupid.

"Indig says she can take the troll," I continued. "Requesting you hold position and stand by. We're coming in from the south."

Her call sign—"Indig"—was pretty lame too. But still.

Oh yeah, and I'd just told a Ranger captain how to fight a battle. Pretty cool. We'll see. That's what I was thinking when she kicked the flanks of the dappled gray and began to speak in my mind.

"I'm going to kill the troll, Talker. But you must control Mist. He's a good horse. But he can be stubborn when he wants his way. And his way is to fight. Always."

I realized Mist was the name of her horse. I also realized this was the first time she'd addressed me by what she assumed was my real name. Formalities were breaking down. Walls were collapsing. It wasn't coffee... but it was something that made me feel real good too.

"He will listen to you. But once I kill the troll, I may fall asleep. Can you protect me while—"

"Yes!" I shouted at her above the thunder of Mist's hooves as we pounded down the slope of the hill. Heading straight into the rear of the hopefully unsuspecting enemy forces of orcs and giant troll getting ready to wipe out our Rangers. Never mind the firefight going on across all three hills. "You can trust me, Autumn."

And then... I felt her squeeze me tight with her arm. With one hand. The other was summoning a glowing ball of living white-hot plasma.

It felt like hope distilled. The squeeze. Not the ball of fire getting larger by the second. That was just cool on all kinds of levels.

Yeah. That happened. And I'd be lying if I didn't tell you it made me feel more alive than that time I'd gone near two hundred miles an hour on the autobahn at two a.m. with a dangerously beautiful girl who had a death wish I'd find out about soon enough.

I at least had the presence of mind to remember from RASP that asking the supporting forces to "shift fire" as we rode right into the enemies' midst might prevent us from getting shot. The fact that our front line was marked by a screaming horse with two riders, one of whom was holding a glowing ball of fire, helped them in discerning who not specifically to shoot at.

The Rangers on the hill shifted fire, and Captain Knife Hand stopped the fire team he was with as we came in hard on the troll assault force's six. Mist tearing up wet turf as pounding hooves beat out a staccato charge beneath us.

The orcs had no idea we were on them until we rode in close and she hurled that ball of plasma right at the troll who was rising to his clawed feet for the final rush into the Ranger line. In an instant, the glowing ball of white-hot fire became a huge heaving Romulan space torpedo of searing plasma and slammed into the looming, lean, weird troll with the lurching long arms and dangling claws. As the fireball went in, it illuminated the whole enemy force along the ground in a sudden sparkling streaking light show. Every twisted and mean face was turned toward its surprise hot streak.

And as the powerful plasma-fireball-Romulan-torpedo exploded against the troll's torso, I felt Autumn's arm, the one grasping me, go limp. She was sliding off the speeding horse and I heard her in my mind screaming, "Talker!" She'd fall and probably break her slender neck. Meanwhile I was busy gawking and watching an entire enemy force get immolated in less than half a second by the fireball she'd just lobbed at them.

I barely held on to her before she fell, as Mist tore away from the sudden firestorm enveloping orcs and a burning troll. Awkwardly. But I did manage to hang on to her.

We rode past flaming orcs running in every direction away from the giant troll who'd just exploded, also in every direction. And I screamed the most Ranger thing I could think of at what remained of them.

"Surprise, losers!"

# CHAPTER FORTY

WITHIN the hour, the first ORP was secured at the bottom of the canyon and teams were coming in to rest, redistribute, and head out again toward the next phase line up at the top of the canyon. The captain took charge, and the command sergeant major, along with the scouts, led the way up toward Black Witch Pool.

It was clear the enemy was on to us, our location and direction of march. Other than trying a few sorties against our rear at the entrance to the canyon, they didn't do much to hit us directly as we got ready to jump. They knew where we were going, and they'd try to cut us off using another route once we reached the other side of the ridge.

Last of Autumn had recovered from her fainting spell and was hungrily munching another one of her leaf-wrapped cakes. I asked her if the orcs could actually intercept us on the other side. She seemed distracted for a moment, but as she ate more she came back into the tactical situation we were facing.

"They can," she said. "But if we move fast... they may not be able to."

We were forward, reunited with the scouts and the sergeant major, working our way up through a tight crevice in the canyon climb. Ahead of us, in the silver moonlight, we could see ancient stairs carved into the living rock spiraling higher along the face of the cliff. They climbed up through the ragged gash in the small mountain that was really just a large hill and then upward and onto the top of the ridge high above.

The going was getting tough, and slow. Rock-hewn steps climbing up the face of the wall were near vertical. We stopped when one of the scouts almost walked off a cut ledge and out into open air. Sergeant Hardt barely got a hand on the fatigued Ranger before he went over and down past everyone else below.

The exhaustion was getting real. Even for Rangers. Three days of fighting. A night march. And now mountain climbing. All of it on a thin promise that there might be some defense we could get behind most of a day's march ahead.

If you thought about that at all, your motivation took a dump. So you didn't. You just kept picking 'em up, and putting 'em down. Boots, that is.

Sergeant Hardt passed me, checking everyone, moving fast, and working dip. Seeming tireless and endless in his ability to go all the way. He saw the look in my eyes as I bent over under the heavy load I'd assumed for the climb. Saw me doing the terrible no-win math.

"Don't think about it, Talker."

That was all he said. No snappy motivational phrase. No insult. Just a simple command *not to think*. So I didn't. And it worked.

An hour later the captain called a halt and told us to clear our minds. It was going on two o'clock in the morning and we were dragging, legs smoked. Every step was like doing squats with close to two hundred pounds of gear on your back. Mistakes were bound to happen at this rate and under these conditions. Problem was... we couldn't afford even one. We were broke with no survival credit to spare.

We got a brief rest, all the Rangers with their backs to the wall, eased against the cold rock, on a comparatively wide ledge in the midst of the cliff climb. Some took the opportunity to piss off of the ledge. Others just dropped and changed socks.

I think one guy even fell asleep.

Then...

"Last of the Rip It!" one of the Ranger scouts called out as he popped the top on a can of the stuff and guzzled the coveted energy drink. Others were doing the same. Those who didn't have, got a pull. Mouths were packed with fresh wintergreen dip, or instant coffee in my case, and once more we began the arduous climb upward.

"Ain't nothin' but a thang," noted one of the Ranger scouts. "Embrace it. Wanna be hard, gotta live hard."

Others could be heard saying similar things. We didn't have the strength to laugh. But it was funny, nonetheless. Here's one I remember between two Rangers.

*"Right... Once this is over, I'll quit tomorrow."*

*"You said that like three days in a row."*

*"Well, when I wake up... it's today. I can't quit today. Only tomorrow."*

*"Something is clearly wrong with me that this makes sense."*

Soon the climb was as steep as it would get and to look back was to court vertigo, and invite a bad fall. We were nearing the top of the ascent. So of course that's when a sudden swarm of evil birds screeched out of the night and were everywhere and all around us. Like something out of a movie about killer birds who ravage unsuspecting towns. I think that movie was called *The Birds*.

Thankfully, no one fell. Rangers are pretty solid on mountaineering. Me, I was frightened to death, so I took my time with everything because I've found the laws of physics to be inviolable and completely unforgiving. On the plus side, fear cured my fatigue.

But like I said, swarms of black birds, ravens someone said later, came shooting up out of the night and trying to knock us off the cut stairs as we climbed up that last bit. Like they purposely didn't want us to make it to the top. They fluttered all about us, hammered at our gear, flapped in our eyes like mad things, all while shrieking angrily at us. And then they were gone just as fast as they'd appeared. For one long moment the narrow canyon had been filed with a sonic sea of chaos that was their mad calling back and forth to one another. Warning us back from something worse? Or promising us something far more horrible? It was hard to tell which in the moment. The experience had seemed like madness personified and you could almost hear them crying out something as they tried to knock us back down to the rocks below with their frenetic feathery treachery. Some warning. Some promise. Some threat.

*"You are not wanted here."*

All of it over and over again and again from a thousand birds all crying the same thing all at once, but never in any kind of chorus. Every rebuke angry and hectoring. It was psychosis personified and I just pulled into myself, bent down, kept my place on the stairs, and tried not to fall off to my death on the rocks far below.

Other Rangers swiped at them and fought them off. Because of course, that's what Rangers would do to everything. A few even got ahold of one or two and pulverized them into the cliff face, which was a pretty solid hand and arm signal for the level of annoyance and frustration the ravens brought with them.

There's a whole phase in Ranger School where they just play with deadly snakes. Why? In case the enemy invents some sort of deadly snake-shooting catapult or something? When they told me that part, about just handing deadly snakes back and forth to one another, I could hear myself thinking *Yeah, that's a pass on Ranger School.*

Except there was that other part of me that likes learning things and getting certificates of achievement. That part is straight junkie. That part would handle snakes if there's an achievement involved.

I blame the Read-a-Thon program from my elementary school days.

Almost as soon as the terror birds had come, they were gone. And the canyon once more descended into ominous silence. The ledges filled for just a moment with awestruck Rangers, the wounded and the overburdened, staring at the empty night all around.

Then, as one, they began to climb again.

This was just Tuesday for them. Never mind all that supernatural otherworldly horror. It was Tuesday for Rangers.

We finished the climb and came out on a high slope that led up into a twisted old vineyard of ancient vines long dead. Short stunted trees stood with the dead grapevines organized in curving rows, twisted and gnarled by the wind. They reminded me of olive trees, but I wasn't sure about that in the dark. The grapevines were like the wine vineyards I had been to in my travels before the Army. During winter. Except dead and twisty. Trimmed and pruned to look like the horns of demon skulls. This place was that kind of place. It had that feeling. Timeless endless death. It was always dead dry winter up here. There's no life or love in it. You could feel that almost from the get-go.

From the top of the ledge, using our powerful Moon Vision, the scouts could see the forces of the enemy in the valley below swarming off toward other hills and passes along our flanks. It was clear they had some idea where we were. And some plan to get ahead and cut us off. They were fast, busy large misshapen masses that seemed... dark... like a virus spreading across the land.

And then...

"Look at that."

One of the scouts spotted it. Following the direction he was pointing, we saw it too.

It was another giant. Big, huge. As in Godzilla huge. It was the most unreal thing to ever see in your life and even as you watched it, you kept saying, *Well that's not real.*

Except it was.

Far off and coming slowly toward us across the land like some myth of an elder age when titans strode the earth, stepping over mountains and crossing oceans, this giant was headed down along the mountain range. It had to be the size of a small skyscraper. And here, trying to force ourselves up each step of the pass, we could hear the dull artillery strikes of its massive feet going off against the ground as it came on. It was still miles off. Moving slow. But given time it would arrive. That was easy to see. And easier to believe.

It had a big lumpy face and a hawkish nose. A long beard. It was dressed in robes, and the most prominent feature we could make out was its iron crown. Like the crown of some ancient king.

"I think it's carrying a sword too," said someone with better eyes than most. But that detail could not be confirmed. The order went to the rear to see if PFC Kennedy was up to identifying our new enemy and how we might possibly deal with such a thing with only three Carl Gustaf rounds left. And an 84mm HEDP round didn't look like it was going to do much to a thing that size anyway. Except maybe get its attention so it could come over and stomp you flat with no further thoughts on the subject.

The Rangers voiced their concerns in impolite speech. Basically, the consensus was, "What're we gonna do about that?" Followed quickly by, "I volunteer to kill that thing if it means I can get a four-day pass. One solid headshot with the Carl G might do it, Sergeant Major."

Last of Autumn caught the drift. She'd come back from the dead after a vitamin boost and IV rehydration courtesy of Chief Rapp. She tugged on my sleeve and said, "There's nothing we... can do to fight... Cloodmoor the Terrible. No one can stand against him. But if we reach the Philosopher's Palace then... all will be well. He cannot pass the old river there. It is... law."

I relayed this to Sergeant Hardt, who told the captain, and soon we were on the move again. Hustling faster under our packs and burdens with new resolve now. Heading deeper into the dead and rolling vineyard. The distant artillery strikes of the giant's steps slowly getting louder and louder. The ground shaking a little more with each one.

Our only option was effectively to run.

A badly maintained witch's shack would be coming next at the end of an old track through the dead vineyards.

The moon's light wouldn't last much longer, and I wondered what would become of the Moon Vision then. Was it permanent, or did it fade after time? There was no pausing to ask and find out. Last of Autumn urged us to move forward quickly. When I asked her what dangers lay ahead that we should be aware of before we met them, she just told me, "The danger here… is already aware of your… presence. Move fast… little of time left… to us." And then softly in the silence at the center of the scouts as they moved forward, weapons sweeping their sectors, she added, "It… is waiting for us, Talker."

The night was unusually warm now. And there was something wrong about that. We were higher up in elevation, and it had already been cold with a wet chill down in the river valley. Now, it felt like a summer night up here. We were sweating through our gear as we moved through the ruins of the ancient vineyard. The terrain was low and rolling, and we followed a badly used track through the dead and twisted vines, their withered heads looking like the horns of comic book demons planted in the dry dirt, as I've already mentioned. They were unnerving. A few minutes later we spotted the dilapidated shack Autumn had warned us of. Sergeant Hardt called a halt and the captain came forward to assess the situation.

As far as I could see, we could easily head off through the dead vines and circumvent the dilapidated falling-down shack altogether. Autumn had let us know this was the chokepoint in our route. That we'd need to stop and "deal with the old witch woman," she'd said. *Manyeo yeoja.* Her words. The Shadow Cant I couldn't use once we reached her people.

Sergeant Thor, who was scanning the hills and the shack through his rifle, noted something unusual.

"Hey, this Moon Vision don't work on the hut?" he rumbled in the darkness of our patrol circle.

"Affirmative on that, Sar'nt," said the scouts' designated marksman.

For some reason, the shack remained a source of dark shadows inside the bright world of Moon Vision. I tried to iris in and study the place, but they were right. The shadows that surrounded the derelict place kept it in a kind of permanent gloom. Thick. Like black velvet, those dark shadows absorbed the light of the moon and gave nothing back for comfort. You could see from here it was just an old rundown dwelling long forgotten and falling into slow ruin. A collapsing front porch and one lone candle burning somewhere inside upstairs in what had to be a single room at the top of the house. A high room, loft, or attic. But the light was greasy and thin. And it was the opposite of the comfort that often came from such simple primitive lighting. Then, as I peered close…

"Got a target," murmured Thor. "Old woman. Rocking chair. Porch. East end. She's looking right at me."

I squinted my eyes and studied the porch from our position on the trail leading past the shack. And just barely, just barely… you could see an old, old woman in a rocking chair. Shifting slowly back and forth to the accompaniment of a creak you could hear now. It was well past midnight and heading on toward three in the morning. This was definitely creepy. I asked myself, how did I know she was old? Features and details weren't clear from this distance and especially with the gloom. Age wasn't apparent. But something in the way she rocked slightly back and forth in the creaking chair made you think... no... *know*... she was old. Older than anyone you'd ever met. You just knew that in some place in your mind you didn't go to often.

Then the light of a cigar came up to her ruined face, and smoke like vaporous ghosts wraithed out into the night all around her. Sensuously. A small late-hour breeze, the last of the night, the hour would turn toward morning soon, and on that breeze you could smell the raw scent of the stub of the cigar she smoked in the dark. It smelled foul and stagnant.

Then you felt the earth shift slightly. The dead leaves of the grapevines shook all around us. That massive giant was closing, and the ground strikes were like a ticking horrible doomsday clock made by unseen forces. Maybe a few hours now before he overtook us. What had Last of Autumn called him? *Cloodmoor*?

The Terrible.

What kind of name was that?

Whatever. That thing bearing down on us made sitting here in the vines and sweating feel like a giant waste of time. You felt stuck and knew there was some other place you should be real soon and it wasn't here. Staying was a good way to get yourself stomped flat, eventually. Sooner rather than later.

"What does our indig say we need to do?" asked the commander, coming up to kneel beside the scout section leader. We were huddling in a deep furrow of dead, dry dirt, and you could feel your own nerves and anxiety like a palpable thing beating out of control inside your chest and radiating out into your arms and fingers. A jittery thing let loose inside you that could be touched and handled and screamed when you tried to tell it to just relax.

Again, these were Rangers. They'd just fought one of the biggest battles the US military had faced since the Korean War. And now we were all freaking out over an old woman rocking in a chair and smoking a cigar well after midnight. She made even the toughest uneasy. But I had no doubt they were going to confront her and smoke her even if they all got turned into toads doing so.

It was weird.

I translated for Autumn and gave the captain her response.

"She says we need to go forward and parley with the old woman in order to pass. She'll offer us three choices. We have to choose one to pass her land and reach the pool on the other side of the ridge. Otherwise she indicates the old witch could give us a real bad time. Sir."

One of the Rangers hissed, "Seriously, man. That's jacked up. Let's just have Sar'nt Thor do her at range!"

The captain studied the situation. He activated his NVGs hoping for some juice still left in the batteries. By the wan green light around his eyes I could see he was getting some night vision. But whatever he saw was the equivalent of what we were getting with Moon Vision.

"Get PFC Kennedy up here," muttered Captain Knife Hand.

File that under things I never thought I'd hear. Two weeks ago the Ranger company had been hell-bent on driving Kennedy out of its hallowed ranks for some arcane reason probably no one who wasn't a Ranger would understand. Every unit has that one soldier who spends their time in the barrel. The guy who's on everyone's list. He's always on extra duty. And sometimes it's for good reason. Too many off-post incidents. Too many counseling statements. Not hardcore enough. Now here we were, here's the Ranger captain, literally the best of the best as far as combat infantry officers are concerned. Sober and murderous. And he's calling for a PFC who probably dropped out of college because he wanted to see if he could *Call of Duty* for real when he wasn't reading books or playing games about wizards and elves. He was literally the soldier that sergeants like Kurtz and Hardt hated the most with the pumps that kept them alive where their bitter black hearts should have been.

I laughed to myself and I knew I was afraid because the laughter felt good. And wild. Like some kind of defiance against the noose closing about our necks that was the impending giant about to stomp us all flat. And then I wondered two things. Was this the old woman that Sims, who everyone now just called "Old Man" because of his gray hair and worn features, was this the one he'd seen? The one that had used the Spanish word *gilipollas* and turned him into an old man with nothing more than a curse and a pointed finger.

Incidentally, Old Man had survived the battle on the island and his buddy hadn't. Crazy. Now everyone called him Old Man and he made it clear, cantankerously so, that he didn't like it one bit and kept angrily reminding everyone he was actually just twenty-three years old. Technically. But his angry protests came off as crabby and the equivalent of "Stay off my lawn," which just made the other Rangers laugh at him even more because they're merciless and cruel that way. And because it was funny also.

Old Man even had a ruck hump now. Something reserved for NCOs thirty-five and older who'd spent their best years humping in line units and now hobbled into the PX for cases of beer and cheap novels to distract their minds from the constant pain they lived with.

And it was Sims, Old Man, who brought Kennedy forward to the scouts after the commander called for him. Old Man was carrying both of their rifles, and Kennedy had hold of the dragon-headed sorcerer's staff with both pale hands. That had been a command decision. That Kennedy work the mysterious staff as a weapon now. But he was not to use it unless ordered to do so. Clearly it was dangerous. And Kennedy was the only one who could make it work. Then again, no one had else had tried to. So who knew.

"Hey Old Man," said Thor when Sims led PFC Kennedy up to the scouts planted in the dry dirt of the dead vineyard. Clearly Kennedy was still operating at half speed after passing out from the last time he'd used the staff.

"Shut up," hissed Old Man, who was only a specialist himself. But because he looked old, he got away with it now like he was some twenty-year man. Sergeant Thor snorted and let it go. It was clear Old Man's new rank would now be something between NCO and warrant officer. Because his hair had gone gray, he now got to be crabby and cantankerous to everyone if only because he seemed like everyone's grandpa.

"Sir," said Kennedy, sitting down cross-legged with the powerful staff across his knees. The captain ignored this.

"PFC," said the captain, starting this conversation off like it was an actual normal military conversation. Target objectives. Sit-report. Normal military stuff. "We're facing a witch, PFC. What can you tell us about this... this type of enemy?"

Clearly the captain had embraced.

Then again, what other choice did he have? He was the ultimate realist.

"Ummmm..." began Kennedy, and I was sure every NCO there would suddenly kill him for daring to address an officer with the equivalent of a non-syllabic grunt. But then one of the giant's footsteps struck the ground and shook more dead leaves off dead vines and the sense of mission and priorities were clearly explained without the use of words. Or corrective punishment. Cloodmoor was getting closer and I was betting for sure it knew exactly where it was headed. Straight for us. Then stompy-stomp time.

"That's probably a storm giant," said PFC Kennedy, casting his watery eyes off toward the dark horizon. The moon was going down and storm clouds were moving in from the east. Interesting. "But to your point, sir..." His words were slow like he had all the time in the world. Like he knew he was now incredibly valuable to the people who had hated him to death just a few short days ago. That he had them right where he wanted them all.

Go figure. Life comes at ya fast.

"Let's see..." continued the PFC. "Early Dungeons & Dragons, what they called Advanced back then... and which in *my* opinion..." But then he must have seen some murder look cross the captain's permanent look of sour indigestion, as he cut short his lecture on the history of games you play with pens and paper and oddly shaped dice. "Right... powers," he said. "They, witches that is, sir, they could... curse you, summon devils. That would be pretty bad right now. Wouldn't want to deal with one of those. Cause wounds. Turn you into stuff. Hypnotize you... you know... like make you fall in love... with someone." He cleared his throat awkwardly. The word *love* seemed to make him uncomfortable. Like there were probably pics of sexy anime witches on his phone.

He recovered once the scout leader prompted him with another question.

"Are they like…" asked Sergeant Hardt, who seemed like he wanted to pound PFC Kennedy right between the RPGs worse than the captain. "Good or bad, PFC?"

"Well," began Kennedy, adjusting his issue glasses, unaware of how close he'd just come to death by Hardt. "Good and bad are relative in D&D, Sar'nt. And it's evil. Not bad, Sar'nt. At least it was in the older editions. But I think the term you're looking for, Sar'nt Hardt… is lawful or chaotic. If I remember, they're supposed to be lawful. But again, I have no idea if what we're facing here is based on a game I play. There's just a lot of stuff that seems very… similar. If that's what you're asking me. So let's say—"

Captain Knife Hand held up a knife hand to stop the conversation right there.

PFC Kennedy stopped instantly. Which was probably a good thing for him if he wanted to go on living. Kennedy might have been some kind of wizard, but Captain Knife Hand was still the commanding officer of a Ranger company. And he'd probably forgotten how many more people he'd killed with his hands than everyone else had killed with rifles, explosives, and even called-in airstrikes.

"If we have to fight her… is she gonna use magic, PFC?"

"She turned me into a…" Sims barked out suddenly like some angry customer at an Applebee's who'd gotten a bad order of Onion Ring Dippers or whatever they served there. His indignant interruption clearly righteous. For an old guy.

But he didn't finish. Didn't say "old man." At the last minute he probably saw the trap he'd set for himself. The nickname that had already stuck, and would stick even harder if he uttered the words. Even once.

Everyone ignored him anyway. That was part of his amazing new Old Man Powers. The CO didn't even see him and didn't have Sergeant Hardt pull out Sims's liver and show it to him.

*Wow*, I thought to myself as an aside, *if Sims would just embrace his... Old Man-ness... he could get away with murder around the Rangers.* It would be like winning the Medal of Honor and staying in. Everyone had to salute you forever.

"Do I have that right, PFC?" continued the captain. "She'll try to attack us using some kind of magic, if negotiations go badly?"

In the ensuing silence, the strike of the closing storm giant's massive footfalls, hitting the earth somewhere out there in the dark, punctuated the moment. Crushing a lot of who knew what. Like it was practicing for us.

Kennedy nodded an affirmative.

"Yeah. I mean... yes, sir. That's her thing. The witch monster class... that is. She'll do that. But my guess is she'll want something from us to let us pass if I understand the situation right."

The captain thought about this for a brief second. You could tell, even he was feeling the time crunch. We needed to get moving to avoid getting crushed from the rear and flanked from the sides on the other side of this.

"Can you fight her?" asked the captain to PFC Kennedy. Then gave the worst look of indigestion I'd ever seen cross his face. Like he couldn't believe he was actually acknowledging what he'd just said. He nodded toward the powerful staff on Kennedy's crossed legs. Have I noted the rest of us were on one knee in standard Ranger? "Can you fight her with that?" he said, indicating the arcane staff.

Then Kennedy said the most Ranger of things that was probably ever going to come out of his mouth. He took a deep unsteady breath and looked Captain Knife Hand right in the eyes.

"I feel like someone walloped me with about two hundred pounds of flu, sir. But yeah, she gives us a problem, I'll light her and smoke her like a pack o' Kools. If that's what you want, sir."

Captain Knife Hand gave his version of a quick smile. It was unnatural and almost sick-looking. But it was clear he was impressed with his PFC's motivation. It was Ranger all the way.

"Solid copy, PFC," he said finally. "All right, let's go forward and parley with the old woman. See what she wants. If not... then we burn the witch."

# CHAPTER FORTY-ONE

OUR approach to the shack at the back of the vineyards was steady and clear. We weren't trying to sneak up on her after Last of Autumn's warning that she was aware of our presence via supernatural means. *Supernatural means* was starting to get factored into a lot of decision-making trees. The Rangers were quick to adapt so they might overcome.

Captain Knife Hand's security team lead the way with a patrol wedge. Last of Autumn and PFC Kennedy were following, with me along for the ride in case the witch spoke any currently dead languages that weren't so dead after all.

So far, my pre-enlistment intention to not be at the tip of every spear was proving to be a false hope. But every soldier will tell you their recruiter lied about something. Usually it's Hawaii as your first-pick duty station. Everyone falls for that one.

Meanwhile ground strikes of the closing giant thundered and rumbled in the distance like an unrelenting countdown timer that was imminently more real than any end-of-the-world movie prop had ever aspired to be.

We needed to get a move on real fast.

As we approached, it became clear that the shack, a sprawling affair with what from the outside could well have been one lone two-story room covering the spread of the place, was... oddly constructed. Angles didn't make sense. Visually speaking. Except when you concentrated on them, then they kinda did even though the image of them left a sick feeling in the pit of your stomach. The roof above the perilously leaning second story was definitely witch-flavored. Sloped like a witch's hat and badly constructed and even more poorly maintained. A lone off-kilter cross-hatched window leered down at us from up there. Within that strange room the greasy light of an unseen candle burned alone.

We got a better look at her now. Just a small shadowy figure, gently drifting back and forth in a rocking chair deep within the shadows of the dark porch. The roof there sagged and bent, looking like it would collapse down on her given the slightest breath from the breeze coming up through the dead vineyards. Later I'd wonder if the shack was trying to protect her.

And that was when I was sent out to parley. The security team stopped, weapons ready and facing outward into the dead vineyard. The lone ember of the witch's cigar burning off and on inside the shadows of the porch as she drew and released smoke ghosts in the night.

This whole thing felt sweaty and wrong.

The Rangers had better optics and were most likely running the last juice out of their night-vision peepers. Me, if I was going to attempt to communicate with an unfriendly indig then I figured it was best not to sport the alien-looking NVG optics. I could have used the Moon Vision right about then, but as I said that particular trick Last of Autumn had downloaded on us wasn't working so well here. Just like, though I only realized it now, just like it had faded down in the gloomy cavern below the ruined temple. Near…

… that thing in the fissure that had pulled the centaurs and the goat men into its endless oblivion embrace. Luring them with some distant song I'd barely been able to hear in my mind. And never wanted to hear again.

The *demon*, Last of Autumn had called it.

Don't think about it, Talker.

"See what she speaks, PFC," ordered Captain Knife Hand in the wind and the dark of the front yard between the shack and the rasping vineyards being pushed along in hushed broom strokes by the strengthening breeze coming up.

The wind was picking up now.

*Weeeeee.*

I crossed the hard-packed dirt of the yard and got as close as I dared to the overhang of the shadowy porch. I peered within the gloom, trying to get a better look at her.

Did I mention the giant was getting closer? The strikes were going off down in the valley below with constant regularity.

"Hurry," muttered one of the Rangers angrily as I passed beyond their defensive formation to go out alone and talk to a witch.

I'd been thinking about what to try first on her of the eight languages I knew well. Which language might get us talking? Quickly. Time was obviously of the essence and if I didn't stick the landing pretty fast we were gonna waste valuable get-out-of-Dodge time to avoid getting stomped flat by the impossibly huge giant coming down the valley and giving the impression more and more by the second that he was indeed coming straight for us.

So, I'd been thinking…

When Old Man showed up. Or just Sims as he'd been known before some strange old lady effectively cursed him to become suddenly old in the middle of a fight. I thought back to his encounter during the second night of the battle on the island. When the witch had appeared at the forward fighting position and turned him into Old Man. She'd used Spanish. A very specific dialect. So I'd start there. Maybe all witches were part of some group, like a union or guild or professional networking association, and they spoke the same language?

And wouldn't you know it? I got a hit right off the bat. Spanish worked.

"Excuse me," I began. "But we need to pass through your land and we were told we needed to get permission. From you. *Doña.*" That was basically the gist of my opening volley. To the point and polite. I thought about calling her *señorita*. Sometimes older women in Spanish like it when you flirt a little. But she was a witch and all, so, I could see anything I did going horribly wrong and ending up with me getting turned into a toad, or this world's toad equivalent.

I could also see the command sergeant major being disappointed with me and making me the new PFC Kennedy. Digging latrine trenches with tiny toad arms would be hard. And embarrassing. But I'm vain that way. So best to be cautiously respectful and see where that got all of us.

I started with my opening line and was rewarded for a few seconds with nothing more than the lonely creak of her rocking chair shifting back and forth against the warped boards of the rotting porch. She just rocked there, the lone cigar dancing in the dark, as she listened to the hovering silence between us.

If Central Casting needed a witch, they should get this woman's number. She had the act down pat. So far.

But she didn't keep me waiting for long. Maybe she was concerned about the impending giant too, on some base level.

"That big boy gonna be here soon, soldier from the other side o' time," she began in a very colloquial Spanish dialect. Her voice both croaky and whiny.

So that was… news. She was at least aware, if not concerned, about the impending giant. But, full stop. In her hillbilly Spanish, as I've tried to transcribe and flavor for this written record no one will probably ever read, what was with the *soldier from the other side o' time* stuff?

There was something to dig into there. Later of course. There wasn't time now. Not with Cloodmoor of the No Doubt Massive Feet due on stage for his grand entrance. I told the captain we had a conversation going, thinking he was still behind the security team in the center of the wedge. He wasn't. He was right behind me. No visible weapon. Or at least no weapon if you didn't count the knife hand. Both hands were probably knife hands. So, two knife hands counting for two weapons. But he was right there. Almost as silent as Last of Autumn, he'd come forward with me to support the parley.

Which, now that she'd spoken to me in the creepy grandma witch hillbilly Spanish, felt good. Having him there. I swear, the air had actually gotten chillier as she began to speak. Her voice was a rusty old croak. Like a hinge that needed an entire can of WD-40 to get the squeak out of. A child talking in an imaginary friend voice that wasn't cute. Or a clown you just wanted to punch in the face for reasons you couldn't quite articulate. The witch's voice was all those things, and old and papery too.

Captain Knife Hand nodded to me message received, continuing to watch her like some tiger in the dark. I like the occasional poem and it was at that moment I remembered a line from an old one I'd read once.

*Tyger Tyger, burning bright,*
*In the forests of the night;*
*What immortal hand or eye,*
*Could frame thy fearful symmetry?*

That was by Blake. And I would think of it every time I saw the captain after that night with the old witch. It was then, right there, in front of her falling-down shack, that I realized he was more than just a soldier. Leader of one the deadliest fighting forces in the world. The Rangers. He was an animal. A wild animal. And you took your life in your hands if you met him in the dark night.

I don't pity the witch.

But she had no idea what she was dealing with. Or she didn't understand what her foreknowledge of us being *soldiers from the other side of time* actually meant. But even if she did... she had no idea how far the captain was willing to go to see his men through. I don't think anyone did. But her...

She. Had. No. Idea. Who. She. Was. Dealing. With. Period.

"Elf girl say she can lead ya through my patch no questions asked and all," crooned the old woman. "No prizes. No pretties for Sarita. No homage to a wielder o' my incredible powers."

That's how the witch began. Whining about petty grievances and intimating threats of doom released. Indicating we'd gotten off on the wrong foot from the first step with someone of her apparently respected stature. To me it just seemed like negotiation. Like some local yokel who's got you right where he wants you because he's the only guy in Possum Trot Falls who sells tires in the nowhere town you just happened to get a flat in.

That's all.

But she continued on with her list of slights and veiled threats.

"She and her kind… purty little elf girl… they know my price well enough. Ah got three. Three you can choose if ya ken, soldiers from t'other side o' time."

She paused to take a long draw on the stub of her smelly cigar. It glowed hellishly in the gloom under the hanging porch. Illuminating some of her crooked and haggard features by its brimstone coal.

"And you… will ye choose? Or…" She pointed the glowing end of the cigar at each of us. "Or ye want ta pass on none 't'all and tell yer women ye lived and didn't cross ol' Sarita."

I translated back to the captain.

A long moment of silence passed as he stood there, motionless in the dark, parsing what she'd offered. Then he simply muttered, "Ask her what she wants, PFC."

At that moment I was pretty sure that whatever she named, sacrifice a goat, clean the Augean stables, whatever, Captain Knife Hand was gonna do it just to get us past this. And if, as of this reading, you're wondering why we sat there and dealt with the old witch instead of just lighting up her homestead and moving on... well, two reasons.

Reason One was we were low on ammo and heading into the unknown. Pretty sure we'd be forced to fight again at some point. There would be no parley if we got surrounded on open ground by the hunting forces trying to cut us off ahead on the other side of the windswept ridge we were trying to cross. So if we had a chance, an opportunity to talk our way through something, then it was probably at least a good idea to try. Save some rounds at the minimum.

Reason Number Two was a little bit harder to articulate at the time. But now, on the other side of what was about to happen, I understand it better. So I can at least give it a try. There was something dangerous about the old woman. Either it was the way Last of Autumn had treated her with an almost dangerous respect, or just the whole scene there in the lopsided shack among the dead vineyards going on close to the witching hour of three a.m. Oh three hundred. Between midnight and dawn. Halfway between Heaven and Hell. The feeling of loose power live and in the gloom... it was there and you could almost reach out and touch it. We all sensed it. Sensed this was something to measure twice because you'd only get one cut to try and get to the other side where you might get to go on living for a few more hours until you had to burn the last of your ammo on orcs or werewolves in some dead end.

It's just... some of us were planning a different response, a different cut altogether, than what the captain was capable of in order to save his men. Us. Me. I was still in *talk it out* mode.

But there are some people, things, that can't be reasoned with. She knew she had us in a tight spot.

"Ask her what she wants," growled the captain in the dark, eyes shining like two pieces of coal on blue fire. Like a tiger out in the night and hunting. Like he was in a trance. Calm and meditative. Before the storm. The kind prizefighters go into before a big bout. Stone Cold Killer serenity.

I did as I was told and asked the witch what she wanted.

"Ah got three... Talker."

*Talker*. She knows my name. My nickname.

That's completely crazy. But I soldier on 'cause I'm pro that way.

"Three's what I always got and none of them are easy," she continues. *Ol' Sarita*, she called herself. "But all are true. You and yours do one and you can walk on by no harm come to ye and yours. Never mind now big boy a-comin'. Ah 'spect ah'll be dealin' with him directly in time 'fore long."

She mumbled and laughed to herself when I told her to go ahead and tell us what our options were.

"Well..." she said after a long draw on the stubby foul cigar. "Ah'll take the services of yo' best killah for a year. He'll be slave to me and ah'll send him into the east to deliver a message to the Witch Queens o' Caspia. But really, know this, soldier 'fore the ruin, I'm a-sendin' him to kill one o' them beauties for an old wrong done ta me. Sheeah the Silent, she must die I say true. He may not return, the one ya give for the quest, but if he do... he'll have no mem'ry o' the time he spent under my sway. And ta end a year ah'll return him to ye and you'll be free o' ta debt an passage cross't my ol' vineyard. The old hut won't never hurt your trespass none."

Okay, I thought to myself. There's a lot to unpack there. But I got to translating and tried to block out the fact that the giant out across the valley was indeed getting closer. Dead leaves in the twisted vines dropped in clusters now with each thunderous ground strike.

And also the part about *the hut won't never hurt*. That struck me as odd. And it bothered me. But I didn't say anything.

"Okay. I've told my captain," I told her. "What's our next choice?"

She coughed a wet phlegmy *glop* and spat off into the darkness, inhaling once again from her ghastly-smelling cigar when she'd finished clearing the ragged trench that was her throat.

"Out back and down ta pool is a ol' pond. Tell you somethin' true... It's deep, Talker. Deeper than anyone ever know. Way down ta the roots there's an underground cavern down there, and a race that ain't never been a-discovered. Got themselves a king right-like. Around his neck he wears ta old black pearl that was lost to me long year'n ago. More powerful than that ring you got hidden where no one can see, Soldier Boy. It's a Pearl of Annihilation from the Ol' Ones o' Tarragon-y all gone now. You and your men swim down inta there and wipe 'em all out and bring me back ta black pearl... why then you can pass and keep all ta gold that's down there and ye and your'n manage ta find. The old elves used t' come here a-long 'fore the hut made its home here. Before the time o' Elmyra who was my mother inta the Darkest Arts which is my fearful powers. She rode the hut then. But 'fore all that, that old deep dark pond was a lucky place to the firsts. Elves o' Tarragon came here ta make their wishy-wishes and some went down ta there and found they an ol' cavern and stayed like hermits going blind. Become a new race that breathes waters like the Kro-Ma-Taugh frog-mans o' ta southern waste swamps. They worship a dark and angry god they-uns do, you be sure. Won't be easy, even for ye and your'n killahs… Talker. But ye make the slaughter down there in the lightless depths and ye can pass on. Hut will have it so."

I translated.

Again I noticed her speaking of the *hut* as a kind of living thing that had some say in this transaction. There was something about that that tickled a memory of a myth I'd heard once back in my scholarly other life. But the giant's steps, louder by the second, were distracting me from total recall of all the useless knowledge I'd ever accumulated.

I finished her insane offer for us to swim down into a dark pool and kill our way through some aquatic race with home ground advantage. So far, sending Sergeant Thor off to be a zombie killer of some sort sounded like the most rational of options. And even that sounded seriously crazy.

I doubted Captain Knife Hand would go…

The captain keyed his radio mic and spoke. "Sergeant Major. Get moving down the road and to the other side of the ridge. We don't make it out of this… keep moving. Get the wounded clear now. We'll link on Rally Three. Warlord out."

The witch cooed like a pigeon at this in the silence that followed.

"Ahhhh… well well well… ah see yo cap'n's made his choice then… Talker. Foolish o' him ta want t' fight it out with the likes o' me. But my vines hath needed a good drink o' fresh warm blood for some time ere the ages o' Sut... and they'll have it tonight I 'spect."

All around us the sound of dry crackles and sharp snaps began to rise and echo out of the dead vineyard. Vines, the horns of planted demons, twisted and moved forward, reaching out for us, slithering in, sealing us off from the trail that led back to the main road that would take us over the ridge.

The witch was cackling. Of course.

The captain shouted from the yard like he was directing fire on an enemy heavy machine gun nest. "Talker, tell her we pass, or she dies in the next thirty seconds."

Captain Knife Hand wasn't interested in playing any of her occult games.

But the witch was right back like this was some poker game, calling the captain's bluff from the darkness of the porch with her ancient-screen-door whine.

She cackled with delight and pointed a crooked finger at one of the Rangers. A green ray shot forth and knocked that Ranger to the ground.

"Ah'll turn ya all into creatures o' the darkest darkness and ye'll serve me well before I send ya off to the Black Prince..." she screamed with delight.

Then the captain popped the safety pin on the M14 thermite grenade he'd brought and concealed, stepped forward, and tossed it right through the open door of the ancient shack. Her... *hut*. Thermite kind of explodes, but not really. What it does do, is burn real hot for a long time. An old wooden shack like that was going to go up in seconds.

The witch screamed suddenly like a stuck pig and a banshee. She was out of her rocking chair and running for the black void of the door that led back into the *hut*. Where the captain had tossed the thermite.

At the same time the captain pulled his sidearm gunfighter fast and started putting rounds into her as she ran. She never reached the void door and instead collapsed in a pile of old gray rags near the threshold and on the warped boards of the porch, moaning softly as the flames began to rise within the… twisting hut?

Inside the shack, the flames from the intense and unrelenting fire of the detonated thermite grenade spread quickly. Greedily licking up the wooden slats and catching old curtains with strange symbols sewn into them. As the entire place began to heave and convulse.

She was moaning on the porch. Over and over saying the same words.

"Ma' hut. Ma' poor hut. Ma' beautiful hut."

We pulled back, the Rangers hacking at the flanking vines as PFC Kennedy invoked the dragon staff and blasted a flaming path through the main tendrils and clusters leading back to the road through the vineyards. By the time we'd cut our way back to the teams hauling the wounded element along the road over the ridge and down the other side, the hut was fully engulfed in leaping flames.

And it was twisting. Writhing. Writhing like it was in agony from the flames consuming it. *Writhing in pain* I believe are the right words. The *hut* was. An inanimate object… suffering.

File that under things you thought you'd never see. A building tormented like a living thing on fire and engulfed in spreading flames.

We were over the ridge and we could hear the witch screaming from back there in the burning ruins. Her shrieks and moans floating over the smoldering vineyards. Inside my head I could hear her whispering in that cold cruel croak she'd spoken to me with. *"Ye have no idea what yer man just burnt up, Talker. There were worlds in there. Worlds inside ma' hut."*

And then, heading down through the dark trees on the other side of the ridge, getting ahead of the walking giant and finding the beginning of the stream that would take us down to the edge of Charwood Forest, her voice stopped and all I heard was the echo of it fading across the last of the night.

"You've no idea. Talker. There were other worlds in there."

*Worlds inside the hut.*

# CHAPTER FORTY-TWO

BY the time we got down the hill and onto the other side of the ridge, the Rangers were in full flight but in no way disorganized. Rangers know how to move farther, faster, harder than any other soldier. It's hard-coded in during the selection process. The vineyards and the shack behind us were on fire and the dying screams of the witch were fading with the last of the night. Orcs had been spotted trying to cut us off from the east. The giant's feet thundered. NCOs were pushing everyone hard to keep moving as fast as they could.

Even the wounded.

I heard Kurtz barking, "Keep your people tight and line of sight. No one gets left, Brumm!"

Chatter on the comm was coming in from the captain, who was putting a new plan into action. We were stopping beyond the pond where the stream began to turn into a tributary that fed a larger waterway to the north at the entrance to the Charwood. We were going to make bramble rafts to get the wounded downriver faster. The water was pretty swift up here, but it would put some distance between us and the enemy. Mainly the giant.

Some of the heavier supplies were being floated via strapped rucks and watertight bags filled with air. The security team and scouts were being sent forward at the double to stay ahead of the floating main element.

I was busy working to get a bramble raft assembled and help the wounded "onto" it, which just meant they'd be hanging on to it as it floated downstream. Ambulatory wounded who could manage were using their rucks as flotation devices and lashing them together. Like I said, the current was swift and who knew if it got dangerous. But we didn't have any other choice, and the Rangers were pros at water obstacles and navigation.

Dawn wasn't far off now and the unseen giant howled relentlessly as it climbed up out of the valley on the other side of the ridge. The scouts had also spotted fast-moving swarms of orcs coming down out of passes nearby. Autumn told me something new had our scent; she could sense their presence coming for us now but whatever these newcomers were called, I didn't get a sense of what they were. If we didn't move, we'd be in a fight with whatever they were very soon and there was no reason to think it would be an easy one.

Autumn stared off upslope as though in a trance. "They're in the vineyards now." She told me the smoke had confused them for the moment, but once they got through it and found the river... they'd be on us.

I relayed all that to the sergeant major, and he just told me to take one of the wounded Rangers, Sergeant McGuire, and get into the river. It would be my job to hold on to him. I used some 550 and a carabiner to make sure he stayed really close.

After that I saw Last of Autumn mounting her horse and riding off ahead to assist the scouts who were clearing the sides of the river as the first orcs began to get ahead of us.

It was like a noose was slipping about our neck again.

I went into the cold current, assisting the Ranger named McGuire who'd been hit by a ballista bolt during the final night of the battle on the hill. His plate carrier had absorbed the brunt of the blow, but it had broken every rib in his chest, and he was having trouble just breathing. Somehow, don't ask me how, he'd kept walking for most of the exfil. But now it was time for him to float, and it was my job to keep him breathing with his head above the surface. Chief Rapp organized the float and paired us up with a team of Rangers. The Special Forces medic told me to watch for bloody sputum as a sign of a possible tension pneumothorax. As in air filling the lungs and pushing on the heart, strangling the patient. So we had that going for us. We got him entangled in the bramble raft and pushed us off into the current with four other Rangers.

Behind us, just over the ridgeline with dawn in the east, the giant howled forlornly.

This was going to be really close.

The water was cold and fast and the looming rocks looked pretty dangerous to me. They were blue and gray and jagged in the first soft light of the new day. The current was dark and cold and there were whirlpools beneath the surface that sucked at your boots, and you knew if your boots got caught on a rock or an underground branch and you got stuck, you'd get pulled out of the raft and left behind. Regardless of what the Rangers thought or said, if you got sucked down you were staying down.

I knew things were getting serious when we hit the first set of rapids and our bramble raft went out of control and slammed into a large rock so hard it felt like it was going to disintegrate with all of us hanging on. The Rangers held it together, but we were clearly out of control. I held on to the hissing and gasping McGuire, just trying to keep his head above the rushing water.

As we came out of that first set of rapids, arrows began to whistle from the dark woods all around. In the moments of foam and fury along the rapids the sun had risen and while the air was still cold and we were soaked to the bone, the day was promising to be golden.

It would be nice if we lived to see much of it.

One of the Rangers blazed away with his sidearm at a misshapen orc who'd come down to the bank to throw a barbed spear at us.

Then one of the Rangers took an arrow right through his arm and another Ranger pushed himself up on the out-of-control raft and grabbed the wounded man before he slipped away and under the water. There had been no time to make our weapons watertight for river crossing. Someone on another raft opened fire on the shadowy trees the dark-feathered arrows were screaming out of. Whether anything hit or not was hard to say as we were being swiftly carried off down the river and knocked into rocks and drowned all at the same time. I was sure I was losing gear. There were firefights going off in the woods all around us and we had no comm. So who knew what was going on? The scouts were obviously engaging the outliers, who had to be as tired as we were. They'd had to travel a much longer distance to even attempt to cut us off here.

*But what about magic?* I asked myself.

I didn't know the answer.

In time the river slowed to a crawl and we caught sight of Autumn and the scouts near a bend in the river along a small sandy beach. They were signaling us to disembark there as the rear security teams pulled out of the river course under heavy arrow fire. The Rangers on my raft pulled hard for the beach, and to my credit I'd kept McGuire alive even though he looked half-drowned and like he wanted to die right there. He tried to stand on the sand, but his legs gave out. He stayed conscious. The man was tough. He coughed and then said it felt worse than when, "I got shot over in the Sandbox." We gave him a moment to catch his breath as he knelt there silently fighting back tears and spitting up blood. Other rafts floated onto the beach.

One of the Rangers got down to examine Sergeant McGuire and asked, "You got the tat, Sar'nt?"

"What tat?" I asked, completely in the dark. The Ranger worked fast but decided against the next step. We were losing time. We needed to move.

"Some guys get a tat between the fourth and fifth rib that says *Puncture Here*," said the Ranger as he got up and got ready to move. "If it gets bad he'll start to strangle, and you'll need to do a needle D. Ever do one?"

Needle decompression.

I had not.

The Rangers had established a perimeter and were holding the orcs off with ranged fire. Some arrows managed to get close and land in the dirt and the sand along the shore with sudden soft hisses. Occasionally one hit driftwood with a loud *thunk*.

I took a moment to scan our immediate surroundings as the Rangers and their NCOs organized for the next phase of the move. The small stream was a bad hold and we were about to be encircled. It was time to get out of the noose before it closed around our necks. We were between the ridge and the forest in open field. The river curved off toward the east and the rising sun, a tributary that fed the main body of the waterway that ran through that area off to the north. Above the river course was a large prairie of grass and wildflowers of every color.

And to our rear was the impossible sight that suddenly demanded everyone's attention. The giant.

By morning's light the massive Cloodmoor had surmounted the ridge. *Cloodmoor the Terrible*, she'd called him. Autumn. Last of Autumn. The elf girl who'd gotten us out of a jam and managed to get us this far. Everyone, mouths open, watched for a full thirty seconds as the impossible Cloodmoor scanned the morning landscape and spotted us far below. Then with a howl he picked up a huge boulder and just flung it at us. The thing must've weighed tons and all we could do was watch as the rock-turned-meteor headed straight at us, arcing through the new morning mist and sky.

So. Cloodmoor had no problem with hurling multi-ton rocks.

Luckily the giant's game was weak. He shot an airball. The boulder went over the river and off into the grassy prairie beyond. To our north. We turned to watch it fly overhead and off into the waving grass, amazed it hadn't crushed us.

It was in that direction that we were given our first glimpse of the Philosopher's Palace. Where the main river passed near the beginning of what had to be Charwood Forest as described by Last of Autumn. Beyond the river over there rose the fantastic white marble ruins of an ancient fortress whose walls had long ago been smashed down and wrecked. Huge blocks of white stone lay in the river and the long grass and in the trees. More of that same cathedral architecture I'd witnessed on my adventure with Autumn inside the temple was in evidence where the main body of the ruins waited. High broken towers, fractured fantastic columns, and the skeletons of grand cathedrals or perhaps even observatories where shattered crystalline shards of glass still twinkled high up in the first morning light.

"Hurry…" said Last of Autumn next to me and in my ear. "Tell your king… you must make it there. Soon. You will be… safe. Your scouts… they know now. You will be safe… once on the other side of the river Ashwyne."

Cloodmoor was moving fast along the ridge, pulling up and tossing badly hurled stones as he came at us. Sending rockets through the air between us. The distance to the far ruins was well over a mile. Maybe two. We'd never—

A rock the size of a car came down in the stream near the beach and sent up a plume of spray like a building imploding. One of the last Ranger rafts coming in barely escaped getting hit.

NCOs already had the scouts' orders and knew the destination of our next phase line. The ruins. We'd run for it. If we weren't safe there, we could at least use the river crossing to make our last stand. There would be no fighting along the way. No counterattacks. Just defending ourselves in order to keep moving as fast as we could to reach the next river.

It was a race now. An all-out race for our lives.

"C'mon," said Sergeant Kurtz bitterly as he pulled his section away from the water's edge. Running wasn't his thing and it showed. He was looking right at me and he didn't stop after he'd ordered me to move. He knew I'd follow. There was no other way to get out of this. But you could tell he didn't like it one bit. Not at all. You could tell Sergeant Kurtz would rather have stayed and fought Cloodmoor the Whatever with the last of any ammo anyone would give him. Kurtz was a fight to the death no matter what kind of guy.

As though he knew the world, whatever world he found himself in, hated him. And he hated it right back in its face without blinking. But orders were orders and it was time to run.

I watched the tired and soaking-wet Rangers hunch under their burdens of weapons and supplies and overloaded rucks—Jabba too, looking like he could just die from exhaustion—as they started off across the tall soft grass beyond our beach. Other Ranger teams were already moving out as best they could. The captain and the rear security team were waiting until everyone that was coming out of the river had done so.

"Ain't nothin' but the Mog Mile, Talker." It was Brumm. Still humping the 249. I was holding up McGuire who looked like he could barely stand, much less run a mile.

The Mogadishu Mile.

The legendary story of a group of Rangers who ran through hell, small-arms fire and RPGs and overwhelming hostiles, to escape an operation gone extremely bad. They do it every year back at Fort Benning. To commemorate the heroism displayed that day. The Rangering done. Except without the gunfire and death.

*The Mog Mile.* After this it would be the Cloodmoor Mile. But that wasn't a sure thing at this point.

"He make it?" asked Specialist Brumm of McGuire. Then he bent down in the dying sergeant's face. "You make it, Sar'nt? Almost there."

All McGuire could do was look up, gasp, and then... nod that he could make it.

"We'll make it, Sar'nt," said Brumm. "Take his other arm, Talker. I'll take this side. We'll help him along."

We were off, doing as best we could to make it while boulders rained down from the sky like incoming artillery strikes and orc pursuers racing out of the ether green of tall grass, the Rangers shooting the vicious killers down before they could pick off our wounded.

# CHAPTER FORTY-THREE

THE captain was leading a withdrawal across the prairie, a withdrawal that was turning into a running firefight through tall grass and across smaller muddy tributaries that cut through the wetlands in that area. Depressions in the landscape and other obstacles allowed the Rangers to stay low and keep moving as the orc horde tried to pin us down and cut teams of Rangers off.

There is no lying about this part. The going got extremely tough. Moving with the beat-up Sergeant McGuire, Specialist Brumm and I were the slowest. Teams that could outright carry the unconscious half-dead were faster than us, but due to the nature of Sergeant McGuire's crushed chest, we had to be very careful with him. It was best to just let him move under his own power with our assistance as I checked to make sure he wasn't strangling on his own blood.

We passed clusters of Rangers burning ammo on the orcs swarming to get close. Arrows rained down into the mud and tall grass as outgoing rounds zipped off into the brush in adamant reply. Neither side could mind the incoming boulder artillery delivered via the giant Cloodmoor now coming down the face of the far ridge we'd surmounted last night. Howling in rage at us and no doubt promising to stomp us flat. *Uroo Uroo* horns blared out the coming kill.

We passed Captain Knife Hand's team and were down to our last hundred yards to reach the river Ashwyne when a boulder round came in danger close, hit nearby, and literally threw us into stagnant water as the earth buckled and shifted in the aftershock.

Someone in another team got crushed. The boulder the giant had thrown rolled off and away and dirt and mud came flying down all over us.

"C'mon," gasped Sergeant McGuire as we tried to get him onto his feet. "We... can... do..."

He hacked once, violently, and groaned as he made it to his boots. "... it."

Then I got eyes on the new threat Last of Autumn had warned was coming. The biggest wolf I'd ever seen in my life, and two of his friends, came bounding in from another direction, across the boulder-crushed grass and churned mud. Coming from a direction not guarded by the captain's fire team we'd just passed.

"Head's up, Talker!" shouted Specialist Brumm as he shifted his 249 up and away from his body with one arm to engage the wolves with a spray of fire while still holding on to McGuire with the other. The slavering wolves with burning red eyes came in hard and fast, and gunfire in adult-sized doses ruined one, but the other two leapt onto us, snarling and biting. It was like getting hit by a flying chainsaw. I had no idea what happened in the second after that as I tried to hold on to the wounded man and protect myself at the same time. And even that was too much to keep track of.

The one that hit me must have been moving at something approximating runaway freight train speed. It knocked me and the wounded sergeant back into the grass and mud, pinning me and snarling and yeah, there was literally feral wolf drool dripping down in long ropy strings across my face. The thing snapped and went for my throat immediately, and I was reduced to trying to squirm away from it, pushing with both arms as it latched on to my plate carrier with its jaws and dragged me powerfully from side to side. My body felt like it was in the grip of a powerful fang tornado. Like the wolf knew it had to peel away the protective outer layers of my armor to get to what it wanted to get to real bad and was intent on having.

My blood. My throat.

I smashed it in the snout with my FAST helmet and my eyes closed at the same time.

And then I had... a completely rational thought.

My hands were free if I let go of this snapping terror.

My rifle was slung across my torso on which the snarling, snapping wolf was currently pinning me with all its weight. So there was no way I was getting it up and into play.

I had about ten seconds before it released my carrier and just went for my now very exposed throat.

But my hands were free. If I wanted them to be.

I grabbed the sergeant major's sidearm, glad I'd kept a round in the chamber, shucked it from its holster, and thrust it forward into the wolf's black hair along its taut underbelly. I squeezed the magazine dry over the next few seconds, sending hot rounds tearing through the creature's abdomen and intestines. Bullets came out around its spine, messy bloody sprays of bone and matter erupting in the morning mist.

It howled mournfully like something that had been horribly and badly wounded, which it had, and yet it refused to stop pinning me as I fired dry, the slide locking to the rear. I could feel its warm blood pumping out all over my gear as it looked up into the sky, snarled once more at the rising sun, almost angrily like it was a promise or a curse, and then died panting out its last.

I pushed the heavy carcass off me and scrambled for Sergeant McGuire, checking to see that Brumm had ruined the other wolf with his 249, which he had, though not before the big wolf had done some vicious work with its claws across Brumm's face and eyes. The Ranger was so bloody I couldn't tell if he'd lost an eye or had merely had the flesh torn from his face.

He grabbed the 249 which had somehow been dropped in the struggle, sling and all, and had it back around his torso a second later.

"C'mon!" he shouted in Kurtz's NCO bark regardless of the horror show that was his face now. "Time to move, Talker!"

McGuire had either died or passed out from both of us getting rocked by the incoming wolf. He was no longer capable of self-movement. I bent down to check his pulse, my ears buzzing and the heat of the morning making me swoon for a second. The heartbeat was there, but it was distant.

Another boulder round rocketed across the hazy morning sky above and slammed into the river we needed to cross.

"We gotta move now, Talker!" shouted Brumm. "Captain's pulling back to the river."

Before I joined, I'd gotten in shape. I knew the Army, and the Rangers, everything I was asking for, was going to be physically challenging. Especially to someone who had spent most of his life in academia. But people kept telling me *Nah, you'll just be a linguist. Nothing to worry about. You'll sit in a little box listening in on transmissions and translating in an office somewhere. Nothing physical required.* And then there was the dream of picking locks for *John* and the Company. Remember all that. But I knew what I wanted, and just like languages, I'd found it was best to be prepared for the worst. Like when you spoke to a native and they came at you rapid-fire with all kinds of slang and colloquialisms that weren't covered in the lesson books about Doña Hernandez going to *la biblioteca* on her *bicicleta*.

So I'd trained. That last year as I finished up my doctorate, I got into triathlons. Amateur ones, of course. But I did 'em and I felt like dying and I did 'em anyway. The good news was once I showed up for enlistment I had no problems in Basic, Airborne, or RASP. That's not to say it wasn't hard. The drill sergeants and instructors, when they really wanted to… they could smoke you. They could find your wall. Indeed, they really could. I cannot emphasize that point enough. It was like they could smell your weakness and the one place you didn't want to go. And that's where they went. You could only White Line Drill for so long. Or sit against a wall in an imaginary chair for hours on end as your thighs and quads turned to living fire. Or run past the battalion headquarters around the airfield once more for the second time in a row.

In other words… they could find your wall, and throw you straight into it. All you did was bounce off and pray the torture would end sooner rather than later.

I grabbed the lifeless Sergeant McGuire just like I'd been taught in the first aid lifesaving course back in Basic

Training. I hauled him up, bent low, and had him over my shoulder. Then air squat up and hope you don't slip a disc. *Oh please,* I thought as I grunted and strained to get my feet under me with the full bulk of Sergeant McGuire resting atop my shoulder, *please don't let me slip a disc now. There's probably not been a chiropractor around for ten thousand years.*

Believe me, I was as surprised as Brumm was when I had the Ranger Sergeant up and over my shoulder. Guy was six-two and probably two-twenty of solid muscle. Add his gear and I didn't even want to think about the weight.

But truth be told… I felt like a stud at having got this far. So maybe I could do this.

"Let's move," grunted Specialist Brumm, and he took off through the tall grass leaving the bloodstains and dead wolves behind.

I took one step and knew instantly I was never gonna make it twenty feet much less another hundred yards.

Then I took another step and maybe I wasn't *not* gonna make it. Whatever that means.

I envisioned one football field. That was as far as I needed to go. That's all. Just do that.

Three steps and I was just falling forward to keep moving, balancing the massive Ranger on my shoulder as I stomped through the mud and tall grass following after the specialist. Ahead, Brumm was firing into the brush at our left at targets I couldn't see and didn't have the reserve energy to look at. Screaming at me to move as he covered us. Hot brass caught my arms as I passed him working the 249. Cutting down grass and dark misshapen figures that had tried to murder us with spears from which claws and oily crow feathers dangled.

A huge rock whistled in and hit the tall grass off to our right. The earth shook. *Uroo Uroo* horns rang out so close I swore there had to be tribes of vicious killer orcs everywhere in the grass all around us. We had to be surrounded. But I just kept moving forward. Putting one leg in front of the other in order to keep moving for that end zone beyond the river.

My legs were burning and I felt like I didn't have much left in me. In fact, honestly, I was sure I didn't. There was a wall coming and I wasn't getting over this one. No way, no how. Three nights of fighting. A night and a day on the run. The thing in the fissure. No real coffee. Maybe one MRE. I was done when we reached the river, I promised myself. Just done when and if we got there. Just staggering along with most likely a dead man on my back was all that was left of me. Then I remembered Kang carrying Mercer through the gully during an entire firefight just to reach the line of safety. Ruck and rifle to boot. Fighting and leading all the way.

I felt guilty that I'd declared how far I was willing to go, and go no further. That wasn't Kang. And it wasn't Ranger. But I was outta gas.

"Better man..." I gasped to the prosecuting attorney inside my head. And didn't have the strength to finish saying that Sergeant Kang was a better man than I'd ever thought I might be back when I was doing all those trainings and triathlons, trying to beat all my own best times like it meant something. Everything I'd done, all of it, to be ready for this day when I wasn't enough.

I wasn't proud of admitting I wasn't enough and was just realizing that now. I'd had it. I was just done when we reached the river.

Rangers were streaming across it as we emerged from the tules along the bank. Some turning to fire at orcs, huge ones, that came racing into the water, savage battle axes upraised and ready to crash down on anyone's skull. Outgoing rounds ripped into these beasts and they died thrashing and face-down in the water as another boulder artillery round streaked in and sent up a giant water plume.

"C'mon, Talk!" shouted Brumm at me, still burning the last of his ammo in short bursts as we cleared the muddy bank. He was right next to me and I knew he wasn't giving up. He'd go as long as he could, as long as needed, or he'd die killing something to get there.

If I thought the grass and wet mud of the wetlands was tough to slog through, then I had another thing coming from the river we needed to cross with the dead weight of Sergeant McGuire on my back. It was like wading through glue. I barely got my feet under me and almost lost McGuire as I went under the dark water. But Brumm had me, steadied me, and dumped the last of his ammo on a cluster of orcs with scimitars and oily rags over their fangs. Brumm pulled me forward across the muddy water and I just tried to keep my legs under me and my boots out of the sucking mud and Sergeant McGuire on my back. *Keep carrying the sergeant*, I told myself. *Just do that and then you can quit.*

Then I just decided I wasn't going to give up. No big revelation. No idea that I could even keep going much further. But I just wasn't gonna. Not today.

Maybe tomorrow I'd quit.

But not today.

Today I was just gonna do my job until everything went black.

The far bank was just ahead and it felt like we'd never make it. But I knew I would and there would probably be some new thing after that to deal with. I looked up, sweat or blood streaming down into my eyes and stinging them. There was an old man, tall and bent, or kind of crooked-looking at the same time, robes and a tall gnarled staff, striding down toward the bank from the ruins of the Philosopher's Palace. Last of Autumn was dismounted and firing arrows back across the river as she moved ahead of this tall, striking figure. If I had to guess someone was a wizard straight out a cheesy movie, or something like in the games PFC Kennedy plays, then I would have said this guy was it. He had Central Casting Wizard down pat.

I felt one boot catch in the mud under the water and I yanked my body forward, twisting around to get more leverage as I looked back and caught sight of the bank we'd just left.

The orcs owned it. Arrows flew. Axes were hurled. Wolves bounded out into the water. The Rangers were about to get overrun right there.

We were never gonna make it.

I saw Captain Knife Hand slash a vicious brute of an orc with a combat knife, cutting the thing across the throat as it tried to drive its own dagger right into the captain's chest. The thing died and twisted away from our commander. Then Knife Hand had his MK18 carbine up in an efficient, almost machine-like manner as he engaged two more orcs coming after him with spears. He was all business despite current events as he sent smoking rounds at ten meters into both of his attackers. It was clear he wouldn't surrender the river until everyone was out.

And neither would I.

I was sure that was true of all of us.

Then I saw the orc coming for us. Moving fast. Almost unseen by everyone. Including Brumm, who was crawling up the bank, pulling me and McGuire out of the water. He didn't see the fast-moving predator coming straight for us.

The orc would get us. Sure as the sun would shine tomorrow, whether we were there to see it or not.

"*Stop!*" shouted the old man on the bank above, raising his old gnarled staff into the air. Though I knew he said it in another language not English. Some dialect that was a cross between Scandinavian and Germanic. His voice was like a thunderclap and it made a shock wave race out across the water of the river, knocking orcs down and back into the tall grass. They gnashed their fangs and shook their dirty claws at the old man as they were thrown off the far bank.

Rangers were on me, taking McGuire off my back as I crawled through the mud, Specialist Brumm helping me to my feet. Others were shooting at the orcs as they began to retreat back into the prairie and the river tributaries. I stood, my legs shaking, breathing heavily as I fumbled in my ruck, hands shaking for, you guessed it, one of my instant coffee packets. I had time. I had a break. Who knew what was coming next? Something horrible probably. This place, the Ruin they called it, this was a truly terrible place. One star. Would not recommend.

What we'd have to run for our lives from next was anyone's guess.

And there were no coffee shops and I was tired.

Yeah, I knew there was a giant still crossing through the fleeing army of orcs streaming back across the tall grass and muddy little rivers out there along the prairie we'd just escaped with our lives from. No doubt stomping many of his own side flat. The giant even held one massive rock up and back over his shoulder like he was going to drill it right down on us in the next few seconds. It looked big enough to crush every Ranger there beside the river.

"*Stop!*" shouted the old, bent, and crooked man in robes as he raised his gnarled staff into the air high over his floppy conical wizard's hat. This word boomed across the terrain, growing with a ferocity an incoming storm. "You know the agreements of old, Cloodmoor Kinslayer! You know that to cross this sacred river is to invite the wakenings of the Eld. To make null the agreements that prevent the final End War."

All of this in Germanic. I only distantly realized I was hearing it in this language. I was so intent on mixing the grounds in the last of my warm canteen water I couldn't care less. I got it mixed, hands shaking violently. I downed it, feeling it spill sloppily to the sides of my mouth, closing my eyes to block out the sight of the towering giant who was no doubt not going to listen to this wizard from Central Casting. I turned, eyes still closed to face the morning sun. Coffee and morning sunshine. Is there anything better? Anything more human? I think not. So I just enjoyed it like a normal civilized person not covered in blood and wolf guts. Like someone who'd just gotten out of bed after a good night's rest and needed to start the day doing meaningful and creative work. Learning languages. Not someone standing under the shadow of a looming giant who was going to hurl the boulder it was holding like this year's favorite to win the Cy Young award on opening day. Right down on everyone. Showing smoke to start the season off right.

Opening day ten thousand years ago and a good cup of coffee. That's where I was. Not bad. I pretended I had all of that, and more. So much more. So much that was gone now and maybe missing forever. But right now, in my mind... I had it all. And it was still mine.

There would be no chin music when that giant threw his shot. We were gonna get beaned, and good. And that would be the end of us. All of us. We'd fought all that fight, come all this way, only to get beaned and stomped by the inevitable giant.

So why not.

I closed my eyes and drank warm canteen instant coffee and listened to the old man prattle on with his archaic and dire wizardly warnings in a dead language in the face of our looming destruction. Nah, it wasn't a cold brew or a pour-over. Or even a nice plain cup of coffee from a Dunkin' Donuts. But it was mine. And it was morning. And the sun was on my face.

It was the opposite of the last week.

I felt a shadow cross the sun.

And then... the giant's steps fading away. Turning back to the ridge. The old man in robes telling the giant Cloodmoor something or other to the effect of "Go back to whence ye came." All in a dead Scandinavian dialect.

The Rangers didn't cheer. They were too grim for that. But they did tell the giant what he could do with himself. The rest sat down in the mud along the riverbank. And some pulled out the MREs. Chief Rapp was working on Sergeant McGuire. McGuire would make it.

We'd made it.

Apparently, we were safe.

# CHAPTER FORTY-FOUR

IN the aftermath of anti-climax that was our almost destruction, our final last stand by the side of the river, the morning turned to early spring pastoral. Maybe it was just a trick of the seasons. A hint that we'd come at that time of the year that can't seem to make up its mind about whether it's April or May, winter or spring... or even on some really fine days, perhaps a promise of summer. A lie that everything will be as it was when we were young on that last day of the school year. Endless days and long warm nights ahead. That sounded really nice right now.

I was, bloody—some mine, most not—dirty, tired, not really hungry, wet, and cold even though I was standing in direct and very wonderful sunshine. And I was alive.

Cloodmoor the Immense was still fading out there across the landscape, disappearing over the ridge like some unbelievable nightmare that wouldn't quite leave with the morning light. The orcs and the wolves had vanished into the tall grass of the prairie like dawn's mist on the water.

Last of Autumn approached me. Her cloak muddy near the hem. Dried blood on her face. Not hers.

"Come... 'tis time to meet... Old Vandahar. He is a friend... to my people. A *Halbard*."

Then she added in *Grau Sprache* German, "A graybeard."

I looked around. Chief Rapp had McGuire stabilized and was hitting him with an IV. Someone else was on IV holder duty. The NCOs were gathering their squads, counting wounded, counting ammo... counting what was left of us. To be honest, we looked like we'd been dragged through the mud by the cat and left out on the porch for three days too long.

Birds flitted about, racing in the sunshine and seeming not to care much about battles or dead, taking no heed of blue sky reports or the fears of petty little linguists that there might not be any more real coffee left in this jacked-up world.

Birds don't care.

I finished my not-real-coffee of instant grounds and the last of my canteen water. We'd have to refill soon and the river I was looking at was filled with dead orcs and wolves. That was a problem. But probably not for long. The water was moving, pushing the corpses away with the rising sun and disappearing morning mist. And we had chlorine tabs.

I nodded to myself. I didn't know why. It was just something I could do that the dead couldn't. Not anymore. Movement instead of eternal repose. Life instead of drifting lifelessness.

"Are... you well?" Last of Autumn asked as she came close. The elf girl. Autumn. Earnestly. Staring up at me like she was the only good left in the world and she was looking for a friend. There was dried blood on her forehead. She noticed me looking at it, then reached up to wipe it away.

"It was close..." she said to herself, rubbing at the blood that wouldn't come off. "But... we made it." She paused. Then added, "Talker." And smiled.

I felt myself walk back from the edge of some cliff where I wasn't going to be all right ever again if I'd have let myself go over. I walked away from that cliff. The one I felt like I'd been standing on for four days and nights now. Wondering if I was gonna fall, or just jump.

*Are you well?* she asked. But the meaning was… are you going to be all right?

I nodded again. To her this time. Focused my eyes with the realization that they'd been unfocused and somewhere not good. Yes, I was… well. Or at least that's what I'd tell myself for as long as I could.

I gathered my gear and said, "Let's meet…" I couldn't remember the name she'd used. But I knew she'd meant the old man. The wizard from Central Casting. The guy who made a shock wave of a thunderclap with the spoken word.

She saw my struggle to remember his name. The one she'd used.

"Vandahar. He can help… sometimes," she said. Cautiously.

*Vandahar.*

In German that meant *wanderer*. Kinda. Not exactly. But her pronunciation was close enough. So maybe it was.

We crossed the grass between the river and the ruins and found the old wizard sitting on a log, smoking a long-stemmed pipe.

Of course.

I caught sight of the sergeant major and gave a shrug and nod to let him know what I was about as he organized the NCOs. The captain was moving among the wounded, assessing and encouraging, platoon leaders getting new orders. Reorganization underway. The Rangers, despite the situation, would be ready for the next fight if it went that way.

The wizard looked up, noticing us only at the last second it seemed, with baleful eyes like some ancient and tired bloodhound. There were deep lines in his cheeks and folds under his blue eyes. Arctic-blue eyes that were clear and vibrant. He seemed much older and more tired than the imposing figure of just moments before who'd driven back our enemies with only a word. Who'd faced them down at the river's edge with nothing more than an old stick of a staff.

Now he seemed like he was just an oldster sitting in a garden among the ruins. Not much concerned with anything but how the day was shaping up. And maybe some old memory he was still working out in his head.

She began in Korean. In Shadow Cant, as she'd called it.

"Noble Vandahar, I had no idea you would be here. It was good… that you happened along."

"I had to," began the old man absently, nursing his pipe. Intent on the coal within as he sat in the shade of a broken vine-covered section of wall that still stood along the outer edges of the ruins. "The old contracts don't hold as well as they once did now that the power of the Nether Lord waxes full in these last days." He looked afar and sucked on his pipe before adding, almost to himself, "Not like they used to."

The icy blue eyes snapped back to attention, resting on Last of Autumn. "These are dark times, Little Raven. What brings you out, and all alone, seeking strangers? Not much of your kind are left in the world now. Can the Old Mother spare none of her night warriors for such a fruitless task?"

She nodded, and it felt like a reverential bow. Accepting what the elder had said instead of disagreeing—if she did disagree—if just for form's sake. Some long-lost hint of the Oriental still surfacing ten thousand years later.

She waited for a moment of customary respect to indicate she'd let the old man have his say, and had heard him. Whether she agreed with him or not.

Then...

"Five nights ago, the Fae Dragons told us of the arrival of these... men... from... the sky. There is no one else left who can hunt at Hidden Cave, Old Father. And the King of Mourne no longer sallies."

She'd called the wizard *Old Father*. A term of respect. But it had felt like a jab in some way.

And who was this *King of Mourne*? Possibly an enemy of King Triton. A rival to Chief McCluskey?

"I came through the dark host by guile and stealth," continued Last of Autumn. "I found them to be men of honor, Vandahar Halbard. Brave and not like those of the Southern Cities."

*Oh ho,* I thought. *Southern Cities. Humans. Coffee?*

I know. I have a one-track mind.

"Not all those of the so-called civil places are full of cowards, Little Raven," began the old man. His voice was rich and sonorous. A born storyteller's voice. Shakespeare in the Park kind of guy, definitely. But still old and breathy. "Mighty and great warriors serve in the legions of Accadios even if their rulers are corrupt and vain indeed. And the Eastern Waystes are filled with reckless adventurers who dare dungeon-haunted ruins and even the Cracks of Time itself to pull out lost treasures and baubles, despite living amid that endless misery, bearing hardship and striving against the wakening Saur. Bravery, Little Raven… there is still some of it left in this old ruin. And now…"

He looked up at me and then fanned his pipe hand, drizzling fragrant smoke out across the Rangers who were getting ready for the next mission. Taking in the cool ruins and the almost idyllic river.

"Well! It would seem there is more of it, perhaps, now. More of bravery, that is. Do they speak… at all?" he wondered slyly. He had a comfortable familiar old nature. A cross between a grandpa and a likable con man who might take you for a beer at least and maybe a twenty at most. Someone you could trust a little, but maybe not a lot. Even though you wanted to.

"They do," I replied in Germanic.

His eyes showed mock surprise at my ability to use the language he had stopped Cloodmoor with.

Then in Shadow Cant I added, "We are warriors from…" I wasn't sure how much to give away here. Probably best not to show all the cards until the captain gave the green light. "… from far away," I finished awkwardly. "We have no idea why those…" I turned toward the prairie and the dead orcs floating away in the river. "… attacked us."

I'd used Shadow Cant, even though it was forbidden according to Last of Autumn, in hopes of showing common cause. I was getting the feeling that Gray Speech was the language of other peoples and used as a kind of common battle tongue. Maybe it was even the language of their enemies. And I didn't want to start off on the wrong foot with what was apparently a powerful new ally. Then again, who knew, maybe I was making an even bigger mistake.

It's tough being a linguist. Don't let anyone tell you different.

The old man blew smoke and seemed to think about this for a moment as he took little sips from the stem of his long pipe, staring off out over the river.

"Oh," he said softly. Almost to himself. "I think you are from *very* far away, young warrior. Very far away... indeed."

*You don't know the half of it*, I thought to myself. Then he turned as if he'd heard something I hadn't. He regarded me for another long moment, staring right through me with those endless arctic eyes. And I could see into them, and though I couldn't see what he was seeing, or what was there, I could tell those eyes had seen strange things, wonderful sights, in the frozen north. Sights no man living would ever see. These eyes had seen many of the secrets of the world. That was what I thought when I looked into Vandahar's eyes.

Maybe it was just a cheap tragedian's trick. The one card this third-rate Shakespeare in the Park actor had to play at the first and the last. Or... I thought to myself... maybe in this world now... it was true.

The old man continued to watch me as I thought these things. Then he said: "And I think there's more about you than you know just yet, young warrior. Much, much more."

He continued to study me, sucking at his pipe softly, his baleful and watery eyes regarding me as the captain and the sergeant major approached.

"Tell your king," he said, nodding to Captain Knife Hand a few steps before he reached us, "that we must move now if we are to make the cave by dark. Tell him you are safe now in this realm of the Charwood. Ol' Gren Longfingers has guaranteed it even though his kind—that being the Eld—are mostly asleep these nowadays. I understand you're tired; it's just a pleasant walk now to our resting place. There will be no more danger to your fellowship. And... there will be feasting when we arrive." He made this point grandly. "Along the way we shall discuss... matters. And see what cards we've been dealt. And how, exactly, we might play them this time."

He turned to Last of Autumn.

"I speak with her still, Little Raven," muttered the old man. "She has told me of your mission. And asked me to be along shortly to see things proper, as is my way, if not always in a timely fashion, then at the last, if not the least of moments. All is well for now, my wayward girl. But we will have to walk for the rest of the day. And it is time to be going."

# CHAPTER FORTY-FIVE

THERE happened to be an old spring flowing out of the midst of the ruins we'd finally made it to. The Philosopher's Palace. Autumn showed us where it was, and soon the NCOs had canteen and CamelBak top-offs organized. I was busy interpreting for the sergeant major and the wizard as the old man tried to answer the many practical questions about the next phase of the route and what we could expect to run into until we were "safe" in a cave somewhere.

The sergeant major seemed dubious.

Almost every answer from Vandahar was basically the same. "For now, you are safe and under the protection of the forest. And of course, I will be with you."

Once all the sergeant major's questions were answered with the same answer, I was released to refill my own canteen and get ready to move forward with the scouts who would be the first to depart.

Spacing between elements would be tight. Vigilance was being emphasized despite Vandahar's assurances.

There were only a few teams left near the fountain in the center of the ancient ruins when I got there. Tall forest giants grew up through the ruined marble and into the hazy blue sky above. The air was cool and quiet. And as I wove through the remaining walls and cracked halls of what must have once been a wide airy temple, I heard the tinkling, almost melodic notes of the fountain burbling out of an ornate well set in the floor and surrounded by a recessed amphitheater littered with statues. Carved haughty elves in full plate armor who held spears and stood at attention, many broken or cracked or fallen, but a few still in complete condition. Scroll-worked dragons curled across their impressive breastplates. They wore helms like ancient Spartans and kilts that seemed to be made of leather and metal if the carved stone was any indication.

Kurtz and his team were the last to top off from the fountain. Jabba had been left out near the gear saying "No like scary place" or something to that effect. Apparently this tranquil, almost spa-like meditative space of peace and quiet, like a real-world visual representation of an ambient music group's album cover, counted as "scary" to goblin-kind.

"You trust him?" I asked Tanner, nodding my head toward the gear and weapons. "You trust Jabba?"

Tanner, who was guzzling another canteen of water, laughed almost insanely for a second before checking himself and returning to hard Ranger. Then he burped. He actually apologized, which was uncharacteristic, and said, "Sorry, Talk. But man... this stuff tastes like the best 7 Up you've ever had, and it makes you feel like the first shot of really top-shelf tequila does, but without all the stupid that follows. Or at least I hope so, 'cause as far as I know there ain't no strippers to marry here."

He took another big drink as I bent down to the fountain set in the marble floor and stared transfixed at the clear water. Its tumble and bubble had a hypnotic quality that was fascinating to just stare at.

"Yeah," said Tanner, distantly. "We trust the little guy. He's nosy. But we got him trained. Soprano is like his new best friend."

I heard all that. But still I stared into the well trying to see the depth of it... and I could see nothing but what felt like an endlessness down in there. And to be clear, not an endlessness like the oblivion I'd felt near the thing in the crack back in the last temple I'd had the pleasure of hiding in so as not to get killed by centaurs and goat men. No. This endlessness was different. This was like an oasis that was everything. Like a vacation on that first day you arrive in paradise. When it seems like you have all the time in the world and you're nowhere near the last days when you must think about packing, getting ready, checking out, and going back to the airport to leave for reality once again.

I held my canteen under the water until it had filled. One of my fingers dipped into the well, and the water was cool but not cold. My finger, which had been cracked and dried, dirty and caked with cordite and dirt, felt... suddenly... refreshed. New. Like it had just gotten a massage and spent the day at the ladies' spa. I pulled it out and looked at it, turning it around in the warm light of the morning and the quiet ruins.

It wasn't like my finger had been washed clean, though it was that. It was more like it had been *restored*. Lines were gone, and the scar I'd gotten when I was a kid on some barbed wire I'd been hopping over... that was gone now. Strange. Maybe that scar was on the other finger? So I checked, pulling off that glove. No scar there. But dirt and baked-in cordite.

So it had to be this finger. And I was sure there had once been a scar there. I remember my mom seeing it once and *tsk*ing like she did because it was something that had happened when I was with my father. After they'd parted ways. I remember her saying, "You're no longer perfect now."

I remember being mad about that. And then, one day... I wasn't anymore.

It happened when I was sitting in a coffee shop in New York City studying Italian one rainy fall afternoon. I was there for an advanced program at NYU. Some young mother was bouncing her new baby on her knee while she waited for the baristas to make her coffee. I could tell it was maybe the first time she'd been out since the child had been born, and she'd decided to take the both of them out for a coffee. Like the two friends she hoped they'd always be. Her and her child. I remember her bouncing the baby, a chubby little boy, on her knee and saying over and over again, *"You're so perfect."*

That's how real mothers are. They see us as perfect when the rest of the world isn't going to, not long after we've stopped being new babies. I understood my mother that day. How she'd felt about me since the very beginning. That I was perfect. To her. And that, to her, for life to scar me... that was an incalculable loss. I was hers. And we'd once had that very same moment when there were no scars. When she'd dandled me on her knee. *Dandled* is an old-timey word for *bounced*.

But scars... scars were some of my best memories. Fun often came with a good scar. Ask any of the Rangers around me.

So there's that. Staring into that endless well that seemed to whisper all the good things life might offer and that's what you think about. Everything. Or at least, as much of everything as the human mind can process.

I heard someone laugh above me and turned to see Chief Rapp.

"It do have some kind of properties, don't it, PFC Talker?"

I nodded and lifted the canteen to my lips, holding it before taking a sip. Hesitating. Would there be a scar? How much does this cost? How much further from perfection this time?

"Is it safe?" I asked the SF operator as I held it there for a second.

He smiled and nodded, pulling out his own canteen.

"Safe as I can tell. I've already topped off three times. Seems to produce some endorphin boost and generally positive feelings. That's good. Nothing bad there, PFC Talker. And it's definitely loaded with some kind of alkalizing electrolytes, so that's another benefit. Just using field techniques and observation it seems vastly superior to my IVs, which is a good thing because there ain't too many of those left.

"But I'll be honest. I've had an ongoing medical condition that leaves me in a certain amount of pain every day, PFC. Picked it up somewhere we were never supposed to be, if you know what I mean. Was told I'd need to live with it for the rest of my life. And after the first canteen of this stuff… thirty-seven minutes ago…"

He'd checked his giant high-speed SF watch. All the Super Friends, as some of the Rangers like to refer to special forces when not calling them *Green Beanies*, wore one. Usually they were super-expensive. Rangers on lower enlisted pay weren't ever going to have watches like that.

Most of them were content to covetously eye Oakley tactical gloves and considered even their lower price prohibitive. Watches by elite foreign makers were orders of magnitude more expensive than Oakley gloves.

"… I can't feel that pain anymore," continued the chief. "Also, I have scar tissue from an old gunshot wound. And that, too, doesn't seem to hurt as much thirty-eight minutes after my first canteen from this water source. My muscles feel stretched and limber, though right now we should all be hobbling like we just came off a hundred-mile road march. Not dancing around like I just gave everyone vitamin B shots." The chief gave a big, wide grin. "There's something to this water, PFC. But it's safe. Drink up. Good Lord send us a gift, I ain't gonna say no. I've asked Dr. Van Strahnd to come and take some samples. Maybe we can analyze and even… who knows…" He laughed to himself and filled his canteen one more time. "Possibly even synthesize its chemical structure if we get the Forge back any time soon."

I took a sip from my canteen. It tasted sweet and clear without being sugary. I didn't get 7 Up. This was nothing like a mass-produced soft drink. It seemed like the most natural thing in the world. I felt some kind of flush happening for an instant, and that flush seemed to… *purge* something dark and unhappy from inside my mind, my guts. I burped, and I felt like I could breathe better. My lungs and nasal passages felt clear, and the air all around me tasted sweet and *dreamy*.

That's the only way I can describe it. Good vibes. *Dreamy*.

"PFC Tanner says it hits like the first taste of really top-shelf tequila," I said after I drank some more.

The chief laughed at that.

"Well… that's a bit of an overstatement. He's probably never had the really good stuff. But yes, I see the comparison. It do make you feel kinda invincible."

The Baroness, or Dr. Van Strahnd as she was officially known, came in with her ruck and case and began to take samples in vials. I left her and the chief to their work and rejoined the scouts. But I studied her for a moment from the recess of the temple-amphitheater-well of good vibes that was this place. She was one of only three civilians that had come along on this trip. One was…

… gone.

The other two had hung in right beside the Rangers and were still alive. The Forge technician and the Baroness. The Baroness was quirky and enigmatic, even bookishly sexy. And she'd made it. There was something strange about her, but I couldn't quite put my finger on it.

Minutes later, as the sun began to climb toward noon, the Rangers started out for the last leg of their march. By dusk we would reach our destination, the Hidden Cave.

Along the way there were many conversations. And what would happen next soon became clear.

# CHAPTER FORTY-SIX

REGARDLESS of what the old wizard said, Captain Knife Hand and the sergeant major weren't having any of this "Let's Take a Hippy Walk," as the command sergeant major had bluntly termed Vandahar's guidance for the next phase of the march.

It was still a combat patrol. Noise discipline and good Rangering skills would be applied and practiced at all times. Except you couldn't get the scouts, usually grim and determined even for Rangers, to shut up and stop making jokes.

"I feel Rockstar, man," said one of 'em. And then they all started regurgitating their favorite Air Force memes and laughing.

That was the first time Sergeant Hard yelled at them to "get it together." Apparently Hard was immune to Good Vibe Well Potion. I was betting Kurtz was too.

Then the scouts started whispering about surfing in Mexico next time they were on leave and that they should take some of their canteen water then so they could hit the cantinas all night long and be up by dawn to hit the waves.

This may seem stupid. But the Ranger scout section of an endless summer via thirty days of leave sounded rational and sane compared to the *If I die this is how I'd spend my Army life insurance money* conversation I'd once been forced to listen to on a long road march during Basic. That one still hurt my brain to think about. Tanner told me it was called "the SGLI Sweepstakes." SGLI is Servicemember Group Life Insurance.

I'm sure there were still waves in some place the map had once called Mexico. There had to be waves somewhere. Still, the experience the scout section was all excited about was about ten thousand years *cerrado*. Which means *closed* in Spanish. I said nothing and listened to the general good vibes they couldn't contain until Hard showed up from the op order for the march and told them to once more "get it together." And even then, they could barely stop whispering about surfing, fish tacos, and tequila.

Gandalf, or rather Vandahar the Wise or whatever, sidled up next to me as I watched the vibing Rangers get themselves fanned out and scouting. Sergeant Hardt running them with no small amount of vitriol.

"'Tis the old Well of Illathor that does cause them to behave so. Its power is deep and old in a world long gone to ruin."

We were speaking in Gray Speech. *Grau Sprache*. Germanic. But my version. Meaning Vandahar was speaking fluently in what I would call "modern German" and anyone from this time would call ancient. His vocabulary was a little on the fancy side, but otherwise he would have blended in perfectly in the Berlin or Stuttgart I had left behind.

The mysterious old man was full of surprises.

"They will feel that way until the morrow. Tell your war captain not to worry. It does not dull the edges. They are more ready for battle now than they were in the days leading to your company's battle with the Guzzim Hazadi."

I knew from Jabba that the Guzzim Hazadi were one of the tribes of orcs that had attacked us. It seemed they'd had some kind of leadership role in the opposing forces. It was time for me to start collecting more intel about this world, and walking next to the wizard should provide that. So I stayed close and followed him as he wandered behind the scouts.

I looked behind to see Last of Autumn leading her horse away from the other Ranger teams already rucking up for the last hump. I waved, but she didn't seem to see me. She seemed lost in thought. Or maybe it was fatigue. She'd been fighting and sneaking as long as we had. Now she seemed tired and content to just walk her horse while not being too concerned about enemies.

Vandahar lit his pipe, and for some time we walked in the old forest and he murmured to himself or pointed out various trees using Tolkien words to name them. This was Elven High Speech. I listened and tried to learn what I could learn. Autumn had been feeding me some of the more basic words, and while I certainly wasn't fluent yet, I was picking it up, starting to understand what I needed for rudimentary communication.

The walk was quiet for the most part. But if the Rangers were expecting a patrol through the bush, a creep up onto an enemy objective or movement to contact, what they got instead was something much closer to what the wizard had said it would be. A Hippy Walk.

A peaceful walk with nothing to fear.

And the part Vandahar didn't mention was... *with much to be amazed at.*

That was the best part of the long march through the mysterious forest.

"The Upper Charwood is an old forest. As old as the time when the stars fell and cleaved the Ruin into what it is now," mused the wizard as we walked along, passing strange stones and twisting trees that smelled of sandalwood. The scouts were out and forward. "It's truly another realm altogether. It was once called *The Green Walk,* in another language long lost to the current age of darkness. In those days the Dragon Elves ruled the west and rivaled even the growing power of the Saur in the south. But in the time since, the spreading evil of the Southern Charwood has almost enveloped the Old Green Walk, and now most who still study the ways of the great forests consider the separate parts a whole."

He stopped to examine a cluster of beautiful mushrooms that seemed made of gold and smelled like fresh laundry. He bent and scratched at them. Then sniffed.

"Not ready just yet. One more moon and they'll be fine for a good meal." He stood and sighed. Then we continued on into the emerald halls of the forest.

The wood around us grew tall, the trees reaching higher, the canopy slowly enveloping the whole world. Soon the sky was lost and it seemed like we were moving through a vast vibrant green gem of a hidden cathedral. Unfamiliar birds cried out happily, calling to one another musically as they flapped through the invisible upper reaches of trees that were even taller and stronger than the redwoods of ten thousand years ago.

An hour later we stopped at the remains of an old stone bridge that crossed over a lake laden with giant lily pads. There was no scent of death or decay here, like in swamps. Instead the air was heavy with the scent of magnolia and jasmine, and fish swam and jumped in the lake.

"Sit here for a while, lad," said the wizard. He'd found a couple of old stones carved with ancient runes, long overgrown by moss. Vandahar pulled out his pipe once more and began to make it ready. When he had it to his liking, he turned to Autumn, who still followed along behind us.

"Lead on with the scouts, girl. And make sure the Fae do not give them a hard time or pull the finer-looking ones of these... Rangers... down into one of their secret holes. We'll never find them again. They'll never give those up."

"Who are the... Fae?" I asked.

The old man worked at his pipe and muttered, "They're worse than a jealous woman when they find one they like, mind you."

"Are they friendly?" I asked, prompting a more coherent response. If there was some kind of danger here, then I needed to make sure the captain knew about it.

"Dangerous?" The old wizard guffawed as his pipe came to life. "Yes. Quite dangerous. 'Tis they who have guarded this old forest since long before the Dragon Elves. I can see you love the old languages—do you know what *Fae* means in Eld Ruin? Do you know Eld Ruin? No? It means *from*. It means they are *from* somewhere... how shall we say... other. In my long experience they are things you do not wake lightly. But they are also, to be honest, they who keep the Eld asleep, which is generally the best for all of us if you know the history of the Ruin.

"Yes," he said to himself, staring off into the emerald-green canopy as the next team of Rangers passed by, following the trail of the scouts. "Yes, that is for the best if we consider the consequences of what waking an Eld would portend. We don't need them mucking about just yet, going to war on one another. Bad enough Cloodmoor is now under the sway of the Black Prince." At this the wizards brows furrowed. "He's from those Eld days. He should know better. Though... he's the least from those Eld Days."

Vandahar's voice trailed off. He was speaking to himself more than to me, it seemed. "Why... imagine if Bothmaug the Devourer were to be set free from his prison beneath the remotest regions of the Dire Frost? Where no living man has tread? It would mean an age of war few still living could remember. It would crack the foundations once more."

I stood, feeling the need to alert the captain regarding the Fae. They sounded like something we needed to be concerned about.

"Nay, Speaker of Languages," said the old wizard, sensing my intent. "They will do ye and yours no harm today. They smell upon you the orc blood. If there is anything that unites the Fae it is their hatred of orcish kind. Your killing them has earned you passage this day. I've already talked with Marvella of Sunken Pond. She says we may pass on to the Hidden Cave, but to be quick about it. Best to heed the pond maid and be on to the cave with some haste."

The wizard went on like this. Speaking as though I should have some sense of who these people were and why they were important.

"Aye, ye are safe to pass on as long as none of yours are lured off into the deeps of this haunted place. Deeps and hidden places even I am not allowed to enter unless the circumstances are dire. Eld places from when the first kings came forth and hoarded their magical treasures in deep tombs and grottos guarded by ferocious servants of the old Eld, still powerful, even in these darkest days."

If he had meant to put my fears at ease, he should have stopped after *Aye, ye are safe to pass*. I wondered how to get on the comm and let the sergeant major know his Rangers weren't supposed to get "lured" off into the woods. Without sounding like a freak who was enjoying the Good Vibe Potion and the Hippy Walk a little too much.

"What do these... Fae... look like?" I asked after a moment. "In my world, where we are from—"

I wanted to say that I knew the word *fae*. I knew it meant *fairy*. So were we dealing with vicious Tinkerbells or what here? But the old man interrupted me with something even more stunning.

"Your world! *This* is your world, Speaker of Languages. I know where ye are from. I've studied the lost pages of the *Book of Skelos*. And I'm far older than I might look. Ye and your kind are from the Before, and ye are not the first."

Intel!

Intel that indicated there were others from the mission that had started at Area 51. I needed to develop it. Look at me... I'm doing intel.

"We know," I said. "We met one. One of ours who seems to have been here for at least twenty years."

"Aye," said the wizard. "I can guess which one you mean. A bad sort, that one. And it was the council's concern that ye could be more from the same bolt of cloth, as it were."

"King Triton?" I blurted out, and the old wizard, who seemed to have been working himself up to tell some fascinating tale probably just to hear the sound of his own voice made a face that indicated I was very rude in spoiling his ending.

"Yes. King Triton is the one." Vandahar stood with a groan. "You've deprived the storyteller of his right. An old man of his enjoyment."

"Sorry," I said. I meant it.

The wizard put away his pipe, apparently still miffed about me spoiling his story. "But… yes. Yes, that's one from the before. Before the Ruin and the time of the Titans. No good is he, and now he serves a dark master indeed."

"We knew him as Chief McCluskey. He was a SEAL. And do you mean he serves that… the Dark Prince… you mentioned earlier?"

The wizard harrumphed and we set off along the trail again, falling in behind another team of Rangers making their way. We entered into a series of forested hills beyond the quiet and fragrant pond we'd sat beside.

"Not Dark Prince, Speaker of Languages. The *Black* Prince. Lord of Vampires and ruler of all the Crow's March. But no, such is not that one's master, even though we of the Hidden Council have long suspected he mayhaps indeed be have the same curse as the nightwalkers.

"King Triton is a thrall of the Nether Sorcerer, who rules and watches from distant Umnoth. He was broken in the tower and he has only recently returned to this region of the Ruin. Tales abound that he fought in the War Against Skeletos with the shadow companies and was there when the great wall tumbled down and the city collapsed.

"His master then sent him into the west, allied to the Black Prince, with the charge of making war against Mourne. The last kingdom of the elves that lies against the edge of the world and the Lost Sea beyond."

That was a lot to keep track of. But it was intel and I was sure if I could break it down into some format the captain and the sergeant major found digestible, and not crazy, it might help us navigate the world we found ourselves in. I was making mental notes on what to clarify and what needed to be explored and expanded, but I didn't want to stop the flow of information coming from the old man. So I let the wizard continue as we walked into the sunshine of the forested hills, following an old road that twisted and turned about their rises, weaving in and out of fantastic trees that seemed to have kindly faces if you didn't look too close. I was sure it was just a trick of the light. But the more and more we passed others with the same phantom disposition, the more it became obvious that the trees *were* like living sentient things with smiling, peaceful old faces in their knotty trunks. Their eyes closed as though dreaming. Dozing in the hot sunshine filtering down through their soft leafy tops.

Then again, maybe that was just the Good Vibe Potion and the Hippy Walk.

This day was pleasant and the opposite of everything we'd experienced here so far. You know, back when an entire orc horde had been intent on wiping us all out at Ranger Alamo. This forest was dark and mysterious, but in an exciting way. And maybe there was something to that.

The wizard went on and on about enigmatic events. He hinted at old grudges this world seemed to have against itself, but in time, as the day turned toward the afternoon, he turned to me and said...

"But these are things that were going on long before ye and yours arrived here in the midst of events, Speaker. And soon your king must make a choice as to whom he will serve, and to what cause your warriors will fight for. Mind me well: there can be no middling ground here. Choose, or events will choose for you. Darkness waxes full, and the little good that is left in this world wanes indeed."

He began to walk once more but continued talking, expecting me to keep pace.

"The Shadow Elves, who have offered you safe harbor here, are guests and outcasts themselves. And truth be told, not all their kind are expecting good of you. Only that girl who braved death and fangs to see if there was some... light... that could be had in fellowship with you... only she believes. The days of the Shadow Elves are numbered more than most. It is the age of men now. The elves have been hidden since the fall of Ruined Tarragon. Never mind what they say about Mourne. 'Tis a kingdom of death with foolish notions about glory and honor. But..."

Here he sighed and stared at the ruins of a tower we could see from our vantage point along the side of a hill. Carved in stone, giants with wings held up the sides of the tower. The top was like the flared points of an iron crown. It seemed a dark and moody place and different from the other ruins and places we had passed.

"But... I must say," continued Vandahar, "their cause is just. The Shadow Elves, that is. They have come a very long way to fulfill a promise. Unfortunate for them it was a bad bargain to begin with. But they aim to see it done despite the odds and great creatures who serve the Nether Sorcerer and who are allied against them at this very hour. Though they are alone... they are not without possible allies. There are many who strive against a common enemy. Perhaps, Speaker of Languages, that is why you've come here... ye and yours... perhaps these... Rangers as you say you are... perhaps they might lead the way forward and bind to them many in a final war against a dark force like nothing the world that was, or the world that is now, has ever seen before. Perhaps the Shadow Elves are the last flame that flickers before the approaching storm. Perhaps they will show the Kingdoms of Men... the way through."

Then he turned toward Last of Autumn, who had fallen away from the scouts after safely passing the Fae and retaken her position following behind us a ways off. Head down as though praying, or tired. "She seems to think so, and though I am old, Speaker of Languages, and at the last of my time, so do I. Perhaps things turn now. And perhaps they turn for the better."

He began to walk again, mumbling "perhaps" to himself as we started back down into the forest.

# CHAPTER FORTY-SEVEN

THE afternoon was hot, and as the forest began to heat up, it came to life with strange and beautiful butterflies. Or at least that's what we thought they were at first.

But they weren't butterflies.

They were tiny humanoid figures with giant multicolored butterfly wings that ranged across the spectrums of yellow and red. They came like a sudden passionate and chaotic swarm out of the deeps of the forest, raced past the teams of tired Rangers, turned—and then were suddenly everywhere.

It was one of the most beautiful things I'd ever seen in my life, and for a long moment I stopped thinking about coffee and the lack thereof as I'd been doing as I trudged along. Then they started whispering. Whispering like a chorus singing a quiet song they could barely contain. Flitting about and dancing all around the wiped-out Rangers. Cavorting in that confused butterfly dance of a way, bobbing up and down as they flapped their oversized wings just to maintain altitude. Landing on the Rangers and their gear and weapons. Perching on the tops of rifle barrels. Whispering and tittering to one another.

Gandalf—I mean, Vandahar—was ahead of me, and when they came to him he raised his staff and began to laugh out loud. Like a crazy person. Or a wizard. Which is probably the same thing. But it was a great, good, warm bellow of a laugh, and it was comforting to hear after everything we'd been through in this strange world.

I listened to the butterfly people speaking, or singing—whatever it was—in their enigmatic whisper-language, but it was too low and chaotic for me to make out any distinct sounds or syllables.

"What are they saying?" I shouted to the wizard. If anyone would know it would be him.

He ignored me and continued to laugh at the multicolored tornado we were all now encased in. It swirled around the wizard and the tired Rangers who allowed themselves to become perches for dancing whispering butterflies. And then the Rangers were laughing too. Or chuckling at least. Utterly amazed that such delicate things existed.

"They are of... the Fae," said Autumn close to me, the beautiful butterflies dancing around her, landing in her hair and on her cloaked shoulders, whispering and then suddenly and urgently flapping off. "Fae Scouts... for the Queen of... Gossamer Throne."

I continued to marvel at the sudden thunderstorm of delicate little things. Tiny people with caps and swords, and tiny horns, and delicate little clothing, and vibrantly colored butterfly wings. And also, I continued to marvel at how beautiful she was. Last of Autumn. In this moment. I watched her smile... and then I realized it was a sad smile despite the soft afternoon sunshine. Melancholy. Happy now, if only because it was a break from some greater burden she carried and said nothing of. I wanted to take that burden from her, or go kill it. I wanted to do that so the sadness she carried would go away and never come back again.

*Uh-oh...* I told myself. *You're in...*

"They're saying... the orcs have turned back... as have the rest of the dark host. They are telling us... we are safe now. But... just for today," she almost sang.

"Is there something else coming? Something dangerous they're worried about?" I asked her.

"Why do you ask?"

"You seem sad."

She smiled and shook her head, turning once more to the little butterfly people. The Fae. Their scouts.

"No," she said after a moment of considering them. "That is their... way. All their concerns... reports... all are only ever about today. Always. They are creatures who live only... in the present moment. They don't think tomorrow and its troubles... that they will ever come. Today is everything. To them. The past is nothing. I envy them for that."

I paused, watching her. Studying her for intel. Intel I would never share with anyone. Intel I would never use to hurt or manipulate her. Intel for intel's sake. Intel because I wanted to be the scholar of her. Of Last of Autumn. No— of *Autumn*. I wanted to be the cartographer of all the places on the map... that were her.

*Yeah. I was falling.*

If I was Tanner I would've been marrying Stripper Number Three and paying twenty-five percent interest on a used Mustang.

Hadn't even thought about the cute co-pilot since...

"Is there something about the past?" I said. "Something that makes you sad?"

But before she could answer, Vandahar called out, "The queen's scouts tell us we are safe now, Rangers. A little while more and we shall reach the Hidden Cave. 'Tis a brief walk now. And then there will be much feasting and pleasant talk."

Once more the teams of Rangers, overburdened, carrying wounded, assisting the walking wounded, tired and hungry, continued on. But there was a new lightness in the day. Because sunshine and butterflies and long walks through epic emerald-green forests were a rare treat. Like a cup of coffee in the afternoon of a long day that had started way too early. This experience... it gave that same feeling.

And now I was obsessing about coffee again.

Good going, me.

But I could tell that was how the Rangers who'd trained for the suck viewed the sudden swarm of unexpected butterflies. Like some rare and surprising break that made it all worth it on some level. A magical experience that only happened for those who were faithful enough to endure, and survive, the suck. Maybe that was the unspoken reward they'd been seeking all along without ever knowing it? Maybe that was what they thought as they walked once more through the hot afternoon in the cool under the forest giants.

I traveled next to Last of Autumn for a long time. Saying nothing. Mist, the dappled gray, followed along and occasionally stopped to crop at spots of lush green grass.

"Why?" I said, breaking the silence. Just that. *Why.*

It startled her for a moment. I realized that once again she'd been in deep, almost prayerful thought. Meditation of some kind.

"I do not... understand," she said.

"Why…" I hesitated on whether to use the familiar of her name. To cross that barrier. Break that taboo. I sensed there was something that needed to be said, and maybe that was the only way to force the issue into the open warm and forest-scented air between us. Yeah, I wanted to be… *more*. With her.

"Autumn. Why did you come to help us get off that island?"

This was personal—I'd just made it so—but it was also something that involved the Rangers. Intel that was actually important. And if we were going to get out of this, then intel, in lieu of bullets, beans, and blankets, was the currency of survival.

Her mouth made a little 'o', and she looked off toward the forest. The sun was starting its fade down through the treetops. Cool shadows began to lie across the forest floor.

"You…" She hesitated. "All of you. You were… in danger. I came to… just help."

Then she bit her lip and I could tell there was more she would never allow herself to say.

"There's more, isn't there?"

She nodded reluctantly.

"Just tell me then. And I'll tell my leader. And maybe we can all find some way to help each other. Us. The Rangers, and your people."

She took a deep breath.

"My people. My people are… small in number. Nineteen are left. Most are children. And one very old… blind woman. And soon… I must go to my death."

Wait, what?

I stopped along the march. Stopped there in the forest surrounded by fantastic twisting trees that climbed up into the hot hazy afternoon. I'm sure there was a look on my face that conveyed the stunned silence I felt deep within my mind. Struck that she was facing death when she looked so young, beautiful, and alive.

She nodded.

"I must go," she added.

*Why?*

And then I asked.

"Because... a promise... broken. And now... a chance to break... a curse. A chance for life... for the young. All that's left of us."

# CHAPTER FORTY-EIGHT

TWILIGHT was coming on now and we were close. We were almost there. Almost to the end of the march. No one said so. No one wanted to believe. But you could feel it. Taste it. The forest was silent and ahead lay the massive trees and an ancient hill they surrounded. Our destination, according to Last of Autumn. The Hidden Cave.

"And that's her story, Sergeant Major. The whole truth."

The sergeant major and I were between teams and walking. Walking fast. Him normal. Me, just to keep up. The sergeant major never got tired. Or at least he never showed it. And now he had a big walking stick that seemed like it could one day be made the same as PFC Kennedy's magic dragon-headed staff.

"Say again so I can get this straight, Talker," he said. Not breaking stride. No heavy breathing. We were approaching a two-forty team. Then passing them. The sergeant major exchanged brief acknowledgments with the team leader, and then we were ahead of them in the silence of the gloaming. Ahead we could barely see what looked like lamps of green fire flickering in the dusky light beneath the forest. "She says her people came from somewhere in what used to be Asia. Have been migrating for close to five hundred years, near as you can tell, PFC. And all because they broke some promise to the old king o' this place. One that held sway over all these ruins?"

I ran through her story again. It was fantastic. It was the kind of thing that could easily not be believed. So a second breakdown of the intel was to be expected.

"As I understand it, Sergeant Major, that's correct. Apparently the 'elves'…" And yeah, I used air quotes. It still felt kinda silly talking about goblins, orcs, and elves like they were real. "Apparently the 'elves' across the Ruin—they call the whole world the *Ruin,* by the way—the elves all descended from, or at least had some kind of allegiance to this first bunch that showed up here and made their kingdom in these parts about a thousand to maybe two thousand years after we left through the QST. Everything before that's kinda murky and the Shadow Elves rely on an oral history tradition, so who knows. Anyway, there was some kind of alliance between all of the various tribes that called themselves elves. So when this kingdom, the one that was here—they called themselves the Dragon Elves in what she calls High Speech—when the Dragon Elves came under attack from an actual dragon, which had apparently come out of what they call the Wyrm Waystes, which near as I can tell is somewhere around Russia, or what used to be Russia, her people got sideways with the local ruling faction.

"The story goes that when the Dragon Elves were attacked, the Shadow Elves, their king specifically, a guy named Nori, well he chose not to come to their aid. So the last king of the Dragon Elves, a guy named Ullathor the Cursed—history also calls him the Last Dragon King—he cursed the Shadow Elves for their betrayal of a blood pact. And ever since that time the Shadow Elves have had a real run of bad luck. They lost their kingdom in the east and were driven out of the area. They became mercenaries in Central Asia and India, though of course they call those places by different names now. They even conducted a coup and established a military junta in a place called Kungaloor until they lost it at some point in the past. No idea where that's located. Sounds like Thailand or Cambodia, but don't hold me to that. They don't make maps and they don't write things down."

"To the point, PFC Talker."

"Got it, Sergeant Major. So, she says, the Shadow Elf warriors decided a long time ago that the only way to reverse their bad luck after they lost Kungaloor was to honor the oath old Nori had passed on and come to the aid of the Last Dragon King. Even if it was more than a little late for that. Seeing as that guy Ullathor the Cursed was long dead. But they felt like, then I mean, and they still feel this way now, that if they can kill the old dragon that slew Ullathor and wiped out the whole Kingdom of Tarragon, which was what the Dragon Elves called their setup, then the curse will be broken and they can have a home again. And more importantly... no more bad luck."

"*Slew?*" said the sergeant major. "Kinda fancy word you're usin' there, Talker."

"Yeah, it gets a little *Beowulf.* That was an old epic tale about serpents and swords. Early literature, Sergeant Major."

"I know what *Beowulf* is, PFC. I may be Texan, but I ain't dumb."

"Sorry, Sergeant Major. The point is... they have to slay the dragon or they're forced to wander forever. And so they've been trying to kill it for about a hundred and fifty years."

"And they can't. Apparently."

"Nope. They had a pretty good fighting force. The Shadow Elves three hundred years or so ago were like a cross between the French Foreign Legion and... well, ninjas. Peerless warriors who fought for pay and changed the course of every battle. Real *Seven Samurai* stuff."

Wisely I decided not to explain my Kurosawa reference to the senior NCO.

"That's when they decided to go on this... uh... quest, Sergeant Major. But obviously, since we're talking about this now, that doesn't go well at all. Their best warriors, pro mercenaries who've fought in every war across the near and far east, they get killed trying to take out the dragon. Wiped out, just like that. And then... it gets pretty sad. It turns into a kind of rite of passage for that tribe. Some old witch woman convinced them this was what they had to do. So now, when a warrior turns eighteen, they are forced to confront the dragon within the year, alone, or be forever disgraced. All of them have died trying. Which means no more warriors. Little less than twenty years ago, they had a small fortress to the east, but without warriors to defend it, they were dislodged by raiding centaurs from out of the Crow's March. And not just centaurs. King Triton."

"The SEAL," hissed the sergeant major.

"As near as I can tell, Sergeant Major. So now they're here, and the forest seems to have its own... let's call it politics. Apparently there's a lot going on here we're not seeing. There's a faction in the forest that's for the Shadow Elves. And there's a group that thinks the Shadow Elves are drawing the unwanted attention of enemies. Mainly this character known as the Nether Sorcerer. Most think within the year King Triton will lead a pretty big army in here and wipe out the forest and burn it to the ground. Why? Apparently he's got to clear this in order to hit the last elven kingdom. A place in the west called the Kingdom of Mourne. Ireland, I'm guessing. They, the Kingdom of Mourne, they don't want to get involved in anything. But it's shaping up that they're the main target for this Nether Sorcerer and some Dark Alliance he's got going."

"Dark Alliance," muttered the sergeant major. "Do these elves... listen to me... do these other elves get along with *our* elves?"

"Negative, Sergeant Major. They consider our elves to be the scum of the earth, or rather the *Ruin*, because of the ancient betrayal. Apparently the Kingdom of Mourne consider themselves the last true elves, and somehow the royal bloodline of the Dragon Elves still survives there. So... tribal politics, Sergeant Major."

"Just like Afghanistan and everywhere else I ever went."

"I wouldn't know, Sergeant Major. This is my first deployment."

"Well you picked a doozy to get some war stories, Talker. So—how's any of this our problem?"

I took a deep breath. Ahead the Ranger teams were entering what can only be described as a hall of stately trees. The flickering green torches were like living magic in the gloom. The air smelled sweet, and despite the dire and dark nature of the discussion we were having, there was a sense of peace here in the woods. Flowing about and enveloping everything. It felt like camping in the woods when you were a kid. The first night of a bonfire. Like something that could be reached out and touched. Like a blanket. The poncho liner everyone calls their "woobie." A made thing you felt loving hands wrapping you in because the night and world were cold and cruel. And because you were still loved.

Here was a place apart from that cold and cruel world that had tried its level best to kill us all.

"It's not, Sergeant Major. The dragon is not our problem. But the intel suggests King Triton now uses that fortress as a base of operations. The Shadow Elves' old fort they were dislodged from. And if that's the case, then that, I would guess, Sergeant Major, is most likely where we will find our Forge."

The sergeant major nodded. If ever there was a murder look in a man's eyes, it was there now. And it was gleaming.

"That's good, Talker. Captain'll want to hear that. What about the girl? Why is the dragon so important to her right now?"

"She just turned eighteen, Sergeant Major. She's the only, and possibly last, warrior in her tribe. The rest are children and an old woman. This year, before the end of fall, she has to confront the dragon to redeem the honor of her people."

# CHAPTER FORTY-NINE

WE'D made it.

Three days of fighting for our lives on that island. Dead. Wounded. No sleep. Little food. Then a night and a day of moving through hostile enemy territory with no rest and carrying everything we could on our backs while engaging enemies on the run. The giant. The witch. The last hundred yards to reach the river under boulder artillery fire and fighting off raids conducted by real-life well-organized monsters that would have easily dumped us into their cookpots and not thought twice about it.

But we'd made it despite all that.

The captain stepped forward to be greeted formally by what remained of the Shadow Elves at the entrance to the cave.

Turns out the cave wasn't a cave.

It was in fact what looked to be an ancient temple crafted in a beautifully simple style, carved into the hill itself within the massive forest that was this section of the Charwood. And while "the cave" vaguely resembled that same design of ornate and elaborate architecture of the ruins we'd passed along our journey to arrive here, it wasn't an exact match. It was like looking at the older version of those other more elaborate and elegant structures falling into ruin. This was the unsexy tried-and-true original.

Solid and dependable. And though it was occupied and shone forth with the light of fires and smell of roasting meat, you could tell it had been long abandoned in times past. And one other thing.

It was… a source.

A beginning of something.

Later, with mouthfuls of roasted venison brought down by the young hunters of the Shadow Elves, Last of Autumn recounted histories and legends saying the old temple, hidden under the rising statuesque leafy giants here deep in the Charwood, was the birthplace of the lost Dragon Elves.

"We trust these people?" asked Chief Rapp of the captain. I was with them when the command team discussed how we were gonna handle ongoing relations with our new possible allies.

The captain was about to say something. But he hesitated as though his mind was still trying to put together the words. He seemed really tired.

"If we judge 'em by the girl," offered the sergeant major, "then we can probably trust these, sir. No sign of hostility from them. No sign of the enemy since we crossed the river, and I get the feeling this… forest let's call it… don't tolerate them orc boys too much, as PFC Kennedy calls 'em. Doesn't like 'em at all. So my assessment is we're about as safe as we can be, and truth be told, there ain't much we can do about it. Even for Rangers, we've asked a lot just to get here, sir."

The captain listened and then just nodded wearily, agreeing with the assessment that we didn't have many options other than trusting those who'd showed us kindness.

The tired Rangers, those that could, stood in a rough semicircle around their captain, weapons ready. Arrayed before us on the stone portico that gave entrance to the warmly lit temple within the hill, were several young elves. Males. I guessed they ranged from the age of eight to maybe fifteen. I'm not really good at pegging the age of human children, let alone elf kids. Definitely not adults yet, in any case. They looked like Peter Pan's Lost Boys. They wore mud and white greasepaint for some kind of camouflage, but other markings adorned their olive arms and bare muscled legs. Their clothing was comprised of whatever skins they hunted, plus the feathers of unknown birds that stuck in their twisted and knotty hair.

They stared at us with sullen contempt like young boys do. Clutching bows and hunting daggers. They seemed dangerous. For kids, I mean.

For a long moment there was silence as the captain went out to stand before us at the foot of the great carved steps that led up into the almost paleolithic temple. Deep within, dark figures moved about before great fires. Hustling in preparation for whatever awaited us beyond the threshold.

The wizard cleared his throat and stepped up beside the captain, leaning on his staff, waiting, glancing about. Smiling at the murderous young boys.

The silence grew awkward. And then the oldest boy, and that's really all they were, elves nor not, just boys like all boys have ever been, never mind the long pointed ears, slender well-muscled bodies, and almond eyes—the oldest of them stepped forward and cast one long contemptuous glare over all the Rangers. As though ignorantly daring them to do their worst.

None of the Rangers did. They hadn't been given the order to kill and cause mayhem.

Satisfied in some way, the leader of the elf boy hunters sucked in a lungful of air... and then began to hoot. Like an owl. Like an angry owl hooting. He thrust his chest out, leaned his angular head back, sucked in more air... and hooted at us.

I wondered if all this was about to go horribly bad. Had already gone bad. If the Shadow Elves, or what remained of them, were suddenly xenophobic in some awful way Last of Autumn had not been. If this was about to turn into some horrible fight of what looked to be about fourteen wild boys against roughly a hundred hardened and trained killers. And me.

I sure hoped not.

Autumn... Last of Autumn... stepped forward and began to hoot as well, throwing her voice up and into the early twilight. And then, over and over in a mad chaotic attack, the rest of the boys joined in with this game of choral follow the leader. One long hoot soon evolved. One unending note. Held. Sustained. And strangely primal.

Slowly the wild boys began to harmonize, joining Autumn's note, their eyes losing their angry glares and turning to look toward the early night and the twinkling stars just visible through the tops of the forest leviathans above. And then they all joined that one note again and just held it until it slowly faded into the universe.

And the Rangers listened, mouths agape, stunned at ever having heard something so wild and primitive. So beautiful and ancient at the same time.

That was when the old woman came out. It was clear she was blind. She was led by a young girl, and she stopped at the top of the steps and began to speak.

The captain motioned me forward to translate.

She was speaking in Elven High Speech, and I caught a warning glance from Last of Autumn not to use Shadow Cant Korean. Last of Autumn helped with the translation, using Grau Sprache and filling in what I didn't catch.

Which was most of it, if I'm being honest. I'm good at picking up languages, I really am—but in my defense, this was basically still Day One of my learning Tolkien. So all in all and under the circumstances I think I was doing a pretty good job. Let the record show.

Anyway, the gist of what the old woman with the quavering voice said was that we were welcome at the sacred cookfires of the Shadow Elves because Last of Autumn had vouched for our friendship. Now we could come into the temple and eat our fill.

One of the hunter boys came forward and began to haul at the gear the Rangers were carrying. At first the Rangers didn't know what to do. But the captain allowed it and soon we were led into the vast cathedral-like space that was the ancient temple in the hill. The Hidden Cave. The birthplace, it seemed, of the lost Dragon Elves.

The ceiling was an open dome, frescoed with scenes of primitive hunters stalking their kills and mythologies that to my eyes demanded they be studied and explained. Through the opening at the dome's center we could see the night-blue sky and the stars. Three major bonfires were set in wells along the vast temple floor, and above these roasted the carcasses of wild game. Bowls of food—mostly vegetables roasted in animal fat and aromatic spices— along with carved meat and baked bread were set out on low tables.

Now Last of Autumn took charge, removing her cloak and showing the Rangers where they could eat in groups around the three bonfires. The Shadow Elves passed out food and made sure every Ranger had a rough wooden bowl filled with a little bit of everything. Then they came around with baskets of fresh-baked breads while others began to pour out a wheaty pale beer they'd somehow managed to keep cold. Call it an Elvish Hefeweizen. The Rangers fell on the food and drink, working silently to stuff their bodies with much-needed calories. When they were finished with the first bowls they were served more, and by their third course through the spartan menu many were falling over asleep amid muted conversation.

Autumn, with help from me and the boys, organized sleeping areas throughout the temple, and within the hour most of the Rangers were racking out on their rucks, barely managing to get their poncho liners over themselves. Or even their boots off.

As I finished up my final serving the incredibly delicious food, the sergeant major came and found me and ordered me to translate between the captain and the Old Mother, as she was known. It was getting dark when I approached the firepit they were gathered around inside the temple, as the other two fires and torches were lowered. Vandahar was there, as was Chief Rapp. And of course Autumn and the sergeant major. All around the room, snoring Rangers abounded.

A few of the NCOs were still moving about, taking watch. I asked the sergeant major if he was going to mount a guard and he said, "Got it handled, Talker." Not my place, not my business. But it seemed like everyone was asleep almost.

At the firepit where they were waiting for me to interpret, the captain was picking at a bowl of food he seemed little interested in. The Old Mother sat across from him. Not seeing him, but smiling nonetheless and fingering her gnarled old staff nervously.

I noticed the captain was sweating.

I figured that was due to the fire. That he was too close to its still roaring heat.

I spent the next hour explaining each other's position to the other.

Apparently the Shadow Elves were in dire straits. Zero viability as a tribe. Three girls, one old woman, and fifteen boys. Their warriors were dead, and they were effectively refugees inside a haunted forest with its own turbulent politics. War was on the horizon for much of the world beyond the edges of the Charwood. Or the Ruin, as the world was now known.

The Rangers were new to the scene. Down to critical ammunition levels, and no place to call their own.

It was Last of Autumn's take that the Eld of the forest wouldn't tolerate the newcomers much longer. The forest seemed to be a fickle and angry place. While generally good, it tended to look after its own interests most of the time, and truth was, it wasn't that crazy about the Shadow Elves' presence.

As I translated, I noticed the captain continued to wipe thin beads of sweat from the back of his head while generally looking pale and tired.

But after the last week, why wouldn't he be?

His eyes, on the other hand, those were still the eyes of that killer tiger that reminded me of the Blake poem. I'd seen what he'd done to the last old woman, witch or not, who'd tried to cross him. He'd take care of his men no matter what.

But the Old Mother wasn't like that witch at all. In fact, as far as leaders went, she wasn't much of one. She was just their mother and she was about as lost as anyone in her situation would be. She knew her tribe needed help if it was to go on being a tribe.

Her whole plan for her people was basically just to trust in their deity. An entity they referred to as *the Hidden King*.

It quickly became apparent that Last of Autumn, tactfully, was their actual leader. She just had to do it passively out of respect for her elder.

Finally, the conversation ended with the captain stating that the Rangers had a mission to accomplish before they could be of assistance to anyone. Once that was done, they, according to the captain, would help the Shadow Elves in return for their kind hospitality. The meeting ended on an indefinite and anticlimactic note as both parties broke away, leaving the wizard Vandahar to stare into the fire, brooding about the state of affairs.

It was time to sleep now, and as the captain and the sergeant major and me left the firepit—Chief Rapp had gone off to check on his wounded—the captain turned to me and said, his voice weak, a cough to clear his throat first, "Sergeant Major gave me your intel on the fortress where the SEAL may have our Forge. Develop that with our indig. I need a location and a map ASAP. See if she knows the disposition of enemy forces within the fortress. We're going to hit that location as soon as we're rested, and I need to know what we're getting into. Every detail. Got it, PFC?"

I did.

Then Captain Knife Hand said he needed some fresh air and left for the front of the temple.

The sergeant major and I stood there in the dim darkness between the red glowing firepits. Sleeping Rangers everywhere. And he told me exactly what I needed to find out from Last of Autumn regarding the mission the captain was about to plan. I listened, asked clarifying questions when I could, and then the sergeant major told me to rack out.

But before I went, I turned back to the sergeant major, who was heading for the front entrance to take watch for the rest of the night.

"All by yourself, Sergeant Major?" I asked. "All night long?"

"Yeah," he drawled. "Boys've had enough, Talker. I suspect we're pretty deep behind friendly lines as near as I can tell. Plus... don't sleep much anyway nowadays."

I offered to stay with him, but I really didn't mean it.

Thankfully, he let me go.

But there was one last thing. I'd gone ten steps when I turned around again and whispered, "The captain looks either sick, or tired, Sergeant Major."

The senior NCO stared at me through the shadows of the ancient temple as we both listened to the low snap and pop of the fragrant logs burning.

"He may be both, Talker. But don't worry, son. He's tougher than a two-dollar steak."

# CHAPTER FIFTY

OPERATION Throat Punch, as Captain Knife Hand had designated our attempt to retake the Forge, went down at dawn a little over two weeks later.

The main body of the Rangers hit the gatehouse to King Triton's fortress located on the northwestern edge of the central massif in what we'd once called France. The Auvergne, to be specific, although the topography had changed over the last ten thousand years thanks to a few major civ-killer meteor strikes.

We'd humped and riverined for close to a week and a half just to reach the objective. And by "we" I mean the Rangers cleared to participate in the assault. The Rangers wounded in the battle at Ranger Alamo remained back at Hidden Cave. If we took the fortress, which was the captain's intention, then they would be sent for once we'd secured it for ourselves.

*If* was what I was thinking. I'll be honest. Warts and all is what I promised.

We had three weapons squads, two assault platoons of three seven-man squads each, and the snipers. Close to seventy Rangers to attack *Barad Nulla*, as the crumbling old fortress was known in Elven High Speech. The *Tower of Secrets*.

Under Last of Autumn's patient tutelage I was growing and constantly trying to improve my grasp of the Tolkien mix of languages they called High Speech. My Gray Speech and Shadow Cant were improving as well, and conversation between me and Autumn was growing easier. Which was a benefit well worth working toward even if I didn't already appreciate the puzzle of languages for its own sake.

She had almost no interesting in learning English.

Once, long ago, according to Last of Autumn, the fortress had been an ancient watchtower for the Dragon Elves. They called it the Silver Eye. After the fall of the Dragon Elves it fell into long disrepair and disuse, little more than a forgotten hideout for the occasional group of bandits. But when the migrating Shadow Elves showed up in this area, they put things to rights, making a mercenary fortress out of the old place. In their waning heyday, they hired themselves out to the cities of men in the various wars along the Great Sea's northern coasts to the south. The Great Sea was what we once knew as the Med.

But the Shadow Elves kept up their insane attempt to fulfill what they had begun calling *the Prophecy*. Their mission to restore their honor by slaying the dragon beneath the ruins of Tarragon with one of their best warriors. And of course, no one ever returned from the ruins of ancient Tarragon and the lair of said dragon.

By the way, Tarragon is basically Paris as near as I can tell.

And Tarragon is just another word for dragon, incidentally. Besides being an herb.

So, back at the Hidden Cave, once the Rangers had rested and been medically cleared by Chief Rapp, weapons and ammo were counted up and teams were organized as a plan formed to assault the fortress and retake possession of the Forge.

Operation Throat Punch.

Except the fortress was near impossible to assault. The Dark Spire, as it was now known among the locals, had been built long ago on the edge of a crag overlooking a sheer fall on three sides. Its front gate was accessible only by a narrow road along that crag, and if attackers chose not to assault head-on at the front gate, they faced a near-vertical five-hundred-foot ascent up the sides of steep cliffs—only to then reach the base of the impenetrable high fortress walls. Just below the crag lay the remains of a city burned to the ground in unknown ages past.

Naturally the stronghold's defenses were all oriented toward that approaching road. These defenses consisted of two main fighting towers and a massive gatehouse along the first line of defense. The orcs who served King Triton on the towers and the gate were known for their incredible marksmanship. They wore black rags and served with an almost monastic devotion to the art of ranged warfare.

Normally, for the Rangers this would be no problem. Snipers and heavily armed assaulters with explosives could have breached the walls under supporting fire and made short work of the defenders once inside. The problem was— we were painfully low on both explosives and ammunition. Each of the supporting weapons sections had three belts of 7.62, but Last of Autumn had assured us the walls were heavy enough to withstand siege and most likely 7.62 fire.

In other words, tactically speaking, there was no way seventy Rangers, low on ammunition and explosives, were going to capture that citadel without taking heavy losses breaching the main gate, clearing the walled-off sections and overwatch towers within the fortress, all to reach the Dark Spire, or *Barad Nulla* itself, where our Forge was most likely being kept, and where Chief McCluskey, or King Triton as he probably was, located his headquarters.

And if the SEAL possessed our Forge… who knew what weapons he was producing.

Siege was not an option.

Throat Punch was a raid.

An assault to secure the objective. We had to sweep the defenses, kill everyone, and at the end of the day, own the fortress.

"And that's our specialty," said Captain Knife Hand as he walked the teams through the sand table of how our hit would go. He looked sick now. Weak, thin, and shaky like maybe he had malaria or something. According to Chief Rapp there was something going through a few of the Rangers.

"Some strain of flu," he guessed, and vowed to nuke it with as many of the retrovirals as he had on hand. "But I'm not too worried about it. Rangers are young and very healthy. The way I see it, it's simply time to update our antivirus software to the current standards of the Ruin. That's all, Talker."

As I said, we humped for a week and a half, using rivers when we could to get there fast. France—it's now called the Savage Lands by the kingdoms of men to the south along the Med—is a quiet and haunted place. Most of our days were spent on the move, hustling through vast silent wilderness and then hunkering down for nightfall when we assumed the enemy, or just monsters, were most active.

Some nights we got some horrific visuals of what this world has to offer now. But thanks to our augmented scouts section, we avoided contact and conserved ammo for the hit. We knew we'd get only one chance to take back the Perpetual Taco Machine that was our Forge, and all of us meant to do that. Getting into a fight along the way would only mean we had less ammo and resources to burn on the objective.

About that augmented scouts section. Supporting us now, in addition to Last of Autumn and the Wizard Vandahar, were the Lost Boys. And while they may have been young and little more than children within their clan, they were born trackers and hunters. Within a day's march they were teaching Hard's section how to move through this new and savage world without being seen and avoiding the most dangerous of creatures.

Like...

A hunting group of manticores that roamed a silent wooded hill far to the south along our route. Lions with leathery bat wings and almost human faces. Massive spiked tails that the Lost Boys and their leader, Carver as he would be called until his naming day on his eighteenth birthday, assure me are filled with poison that isn't deadly but will make you wish it were. You won't have to wait too long to actually be dead, though—the poison paralyzes its victim, and manticores like to eat their prey fairly quickly, chewing up the living victim who is helpless to do more than watch himself be torn apart and devoured.

Or...

A thing that hunted us until we got into the river. It was tall. Ferocious. An eight-foot-tall cross between an owl and a Grizzly. The Lost Boys warned us not to mess with it. Like that wasn't obvious. I only caught sight of it once, but it scared the hell out of me, that was for sure. It made horribly unnatural screeching noises as its deadly claws tore apart giant trees like they were mere matchsticks.

And then there were the Spidaari. Large, gray, pulpy spiders… with human torsos and heads. Yeah. They were tribal and carried crude spears. We had to pass through their forest in the daylight, as according to the Lost Boys they wouldn't come out of the swollen masses of webs that were their homes, way up high in the tops of dark and twisted trees in a wild and unkempt part of the forest, during the time the sun was up. Still, the air inside that wood felt itchy and hot, and you could swear there were spiders crawling through your hair and down along your back. Biting you and making you itch. But later when you tried to look for the bites… they were gone. Or never there in the first place.

Last of Autumn said that was the Spidaari's cursing. They chanted during the daylight, in sleeping trances within their webby lairs, cursing anyone with the ghost bites of all their children. The hatchings the Spidaari had consumed to stay alive during their dark rituals. The bites were supposed to drive you mad in time if you stayed in the wood long enough.

And then, after nightfall, the Spidaari would come down out of the treetops to collect their night's feast.

The Ruin is a dangerous world.

I was talking about the spider people to Tanner. Talking about all the ways this place was dangerous, ways we never trained for. Flying lions that poisoned you and then ate you alive. Grizzly owls. Spider people that summoned the ghosts of their dead children to make you go nuts so they could haul you up for a meal.

Tanner just spit dip and said, "Yeah, well we're worse, Talker. Way worse."

He'd been hanging around Brumm and Kurtz too much.

At dawn on the day of the hit, the two assault platoons and two weapons squads, one led by the captain, hit the main gate They had all done a twelve-hour night creep just to get in position. Recon by Hard's scouts had determined that the southeast tower had to be hit hard if the assault teams were to get close enough to the gate to rush the breach that would soon appear. That tower was filled, according to their intel, with what Last of Autumn identified as Black Hawk Orcs. Excellent archers and snipers who specialized in poison arrows that, according to the Lost Boys, could kill within seconds. Chief Rapp suspected some kind of neurotoxin was in play. He had nothing for that.

But we did have a Carl Gustaf.

Two of our three remaining rounds were used in the initial assault. The first shattered the gate into a million pieces with a direct hit from an 84mm HEDP round. The second punched a nice-sized hole midway up the face of the southeast tower, no doubt killing a few of those Black Hawk archers manning their murder holes. But the dead orcs were just a bonus. The breach was the primary intent.

Vandahar's fireball took it from there.

The wizard stood up in the middle of the battle once the 84mm round had done its work, having moved in close with the assault teams and Captain Knife Hand, and he sent a growing ball of expanding white-hot plasma right through the hole just formed in the wall of the tower. Underwhelming... at first. Then it expanded and detonated across, and through, all four levels of the squat southeastern battle tower. Roasting and choking every Black Hawk archer inside. Within seconds the entire tower was on fire and black smoke belched and bellowed out through its top and sides.

At the same moment the weapons squad with the two-forty, having taken up position on a rise that approached the gate, opened up on the gatehouse walls and the southwest tower. Any Black Hawk Orc who decided to use the parapets to get off a shot on the approaching Rangers was cut to shreds. The sergeant major led this team while the captain and Chief Rapp moved with the assault teams forward to exploit the breach in the gate.

The breach formed by the first Carl G round.

The second round was used on the southeast watchtower.

That left one final round.

The wizard threw glamours and powerful lights that danced and bobbed up against the tower walls to distract and blind the orcs who were raining down arrows from behind their firing slits, trying to target the Rangers in their assault teams who were already moving forward to breach the fortress, carrying their single-magazine MK18 carbines, SAWs, and other weapons. It was the other weapons the Rangers would use first, saving the limited ammo for the MK18s for when the hard work of room-clearing came. Led by Captain Knife Hand, who still did not look well, as morning light began to cross the features of the fortress, the Rangers led with tomahawks, fighting knives, axes, and swords taken from the last of the Shadow Elf armories as they waded into the surprised archer orcs rushing to man the defenses.

*Uroo Uroo* horns wailed out urgently. The fortress knew it was under attack now.

Dangerously exposed, engaged with the enemy in hand-to-hand combat, the Rangers took the gatehouse using the last of their grenades. The few main rooms there were cleared quickly, and the supporting heavy weapons team was called forward to set up for the next line of defenses to be assaulted.

At this point, Throat Punch called for a momentary cessation of momentum on the part of the assaulters. This was not a thing Rangers naturally wanted to do. Once they had the advantage, they wanted to buy all the territory they could as fast as possible. The system of gates and walls would be near impossible to take without more explosives and more ammunition. Consolidating on the gatehouse allowed the Rangers to set up the squad-designated marksmen for engaging the enemy defenses and keeping said enemies very concerned about what was going on at the front gate.

And here's where the one design error in *Barad Nulla* got exploited. Apparently, whoever had built the fortress thought that all defensive positions needed to be focused and strengthened forward. Not primarily. But *only*. The enemy could never come from the rear of the Dark Spire because of the sheer drop of the impressive crag.

Which meant the "towers" were really only half-built tall semicircles. Tower wall in front; completely exposed to the rear. The defenders in each tower were open to the Dark Spire behind them.

The largest of these towers, far smaller than the Dark Spire but taller than the defensive lines of half-towers forward, was, according to Last of Autumn, called the Lost Library. But the Old Mother had called it *Tumna Haudh*.

The Deep Tomb.

The old crumbling ruin of the Lost Library had been part of the fortress in better days, but according to the Old Mother, it was actually something else. Something older. Something much worse.

Now, as Captain Knife Hand organized his assault teams within the gatehouse under fire, linking up with the weapons squad and waiting for the signal to push forward to the next line, dodging incoming arrows and sudden counterattacks by the Black Hawk Orcs who were now starting to recover and get their act together, he keyed his mic and called out over the radio.

"Rogue, this is Warlord. We're established on Doorstop. Waiting on you to proceed to Living Room."

But he got nothing.

Team Rogue, which consisted of Kurtz's weapons squad and the snipers, was busy far below in *Tumna Haudh*. We were supposed to be somewhere else by now. But we were busy. Real busy, in fact.

I say *we* because I was with them. Autumn and I. Everything that happened out at the gate and the towers with the Carl Gs and the Black Hawk Orcs and the wizard fireball, that stuff I heard about later.

*While* it was happening… well, like I said, I was busy.

"Dungeon crawling," PFC Kennedy called it when we first started. Coming up through the old tombs that long preceded the construction of the *Barad Nulla*, according to the Old Mother. A dangerous dark crawl through a tomb full of traps and ghost-haunted halls where the cursed dead guarded fantastic treasures and utterly horrible demises for those stupid enough to try and plunder, much less just pass by.

But what we saw down there in the ways of treasure and horror wasn't our concern. We'd become tomb door-kickers, stacking skulls. Racing to put the snipers in position atop the Lost Library where they could shoot into the unprotected back of the defensive lines the Rangers needed to cross in order to take the Dark Spire. And to regain our Forge.

The problem was, we were late to the hit.

And we were in big trouble.

# CHAPTER FIFTY-ONE

SERGEANT Kurtz's augmented weapons squad, now designated Team Rogue, due at the Lost Library to provide sniper overwatch at just after dawn on the morning of the hit on the fortress of *Barad Nulla*... was late.

"Augmented squad" meant Kurtz and Specialist Brumm. Specialist Rico and PFC Tanner. Private Soprano attached as AG, assistant gunner. Me, official linguist and, unofficially, Kurtz's plaything. Meaning in the chain of command he was responsible for me.

I was there to interact with the indig, Last of Autumn, and also, according to the sergeant major, "Ya got that fancy invisible ring, Talker. May come in handy down there in the dark with them creepy-crawlies. May not. But I 'spect the undead can see in the dark. So, might want to be extra careful if ya go knockin' around and all. Like I said, be meaner than it, son, and that'll go a long way in any fight."

PFC Kennedy was with Rogue too, and as a source of possible intel on what the world of the Ruin might or might not look like in accordance with some old game most of us had never played, he'd increasingly gotten called into every detail of the planning for the detachment. His made-up names, strategies for imaginary monsters that might not be so imaginary now, and general *nerdstalgia*, infected everyone. It was not uncommon for some hardcore Ranger sergeant, who would have prided himself on endlessly straight-up smoking PFC Kennedy back at the batt, to ask, regarding some particular phase of mission planning he was responsible for, "What does Kennedy have to say about that?"

I actually saw the command sergeant major, normally cool and collected, go completely ballistic on one of the assault platoon NCOs who dared to voice that common refrain.

*What does Kennedy have to say about that?*

He'd become the detachment's Magic 8-Ball.

Then came the sniper section part of Kurtz's augment. Three snipers and three spotters. They'd do the dirty work on the objective. Sergeant Thor led that section. Every day since we'd been in this world, this Ruin, the sergeant had devolved more and more into his Viking warlord fantasy. Nightly pagan ceremonies complete with torches and MRE cookies were becoming an actual thing. Word had it he was asking around if anyone knew how to do tattoos. Apparently he wanted to start adding tick marks to his biceps. A sort of running kill count. Most of the Rangers had no idea how to do tats, but more than a few were willing to try. I had a pretty clear image of Sergeant Thor just cutting himself with his own karambit knife and rubbing ash into the slash. But for all that, he was still the same good-natured and friendly guy who, had he not been here, would've probably been surfing some incredibly dangerous waves down in New Zealand no one else dared to surf and picking chicks up at the local bar at night.

"When this is over, Talk," he said to me on the hump south one afternoon when it was hot and there were bees buzzing in a beautiful lavender field near a twisted old stand of wild olive trees. The day was so vibrant and beautiful it was like something out of a Van Gogh landscape. "When this is over, technically, Talk," he said all low and hushed. "We're, y'know, technically ETS'd really when you think about it."

*Expiration of Term of Service.* Yeah. About ten thousand years discharged. As in technically we'd been discharged from service about ten thousand years ago. We didn't owe the Army anything. But we did owe the detachment, the Rangers, the 75th, everything. Our lives had depended on each other back there at Ranger Alamo, and we still depended on each other. But yeah, technically *Sar'nt Thor* was right. We could do anything we wanted.

I started thinking about coffee. That's what *I* wanted. But yeah... we could—

"I was thinking I'd take off and go north."

We were walking through that field of wildflowers and lavender with the sun beating down on us and Sergeant Thor was just staring off like he could see all of it. Every crazy thing he was dreaming of. Everything he was going to go do on the other side of Throat Punch. Every epic adventure. Every Viking chick. Probably fighting a three-headed demon dog with his tomahawk and a braided beard. The Thor high score.

"I was thinking..." he continued. "Thinking I might try and head up to that Dire Frost the old guy's always going on about." Vandahar. "See if I can make it up there."

Go for the high score. Up there.

"Yeah," I said. Because there was nothing else you could say to something like that.

"You could come with, Talk. You never know... languages could come in handy up there. We could become warlords. See the things no one else has ever seen. Y'know, kings of the north and all."

We could do that. That could be an outcome—emphasis on *could*. Or we could die... oh, about a hundred different ways I could think of. Three-headed demon dog. Vampire polar bear. Other Viking warlords who wanted to stay *numero uno* in the high-stakes game of Viking Warlording, as it were. Fall into an ice crevasse where something horrible waited. The possibilities were endless.

"What about our weapons?" I asked after a moment. "They'll break down in time if the nano-plague still has teeth."

"Nah." He shook his rifle. *Mjölnir*. In old Norse that meant the *Grinder*. Or the *Crusher*. He placed it over his shoulders like it was just a weight bar and he was about to do squats. And not a powerful anti-material weapon system capable of shooting a round that would choke a horse. Letting the big rifle stretch his massive chest muscles. "We'll fight with our tomahawks. We'll find the real *Mjölnir*. Blood and steel, Talker. Blood and steel is what it's all about."

Last but apparently not least in Team Rogue was our wizard. PFC Kennedy spent much of the long walk south in the company of Vandahar, whispering and discussing many dark and mysterious things. It was clear he was learning something about what this world called *magic*, and when I tried to listen in the old wizard simply glared at me and said, "This is not for you."

His voice softened after the initial rebuke.

"You have other talents not known to you yet, one who speaks many tongues. In time, perhaps I shall show you where to go once I understand them better. But for now, we have more pressing matters." And he turned back to his tutelage of Kennedy.

When I pressed the old man later, he simply waved me off with one long and bony hand. Pipe smoke drifting in its wake.

"The Ruin changes many into what they will become. It reveals. Even now…" He looked off toward the command team nearby as we settled in for the night. The captain, the sergeant major, and Chief Rapp. They were discussing some facet of the upcoming op as we made ready to set up our night watch. "It is doing its revealing work among… some of you. Be careful. Very careful, Talker. The truth of what we all really are will come out eventually."

He was watching Captain Knife Hand, as though trying to see something that could not be easily seen. Or rather, as though he were waiting for something to appear. Our commander still looked like he had a bad case of the flu. But you wouldn't know it by the way he worked day and night. He was everywhere all the time. He rucked harder than anyone else, all up and down the line of our march. Constantly adjusting and focusing his platoon leaders and NCOs. Encouraging the Rangers in general in that calm, taciturn way, if just by his competent presence. I'd seen him late in the night, moving about the various watch points in our circle, making sure we were safe. He seemed restless. And once again I thought of Blake's poem about the tiger.

So that was Team Rogue. Kurtz's weapons squad. The snipers. Autumn. Kennedy the wizard-in-training, and me. And it was our job to surprise the enemy. Everything depended on Team Rogue showing up at the right time, with the right tools, ready to work. Or that's how the sergeant major put it.

Shooting sprees from ruined towers in mountaintop fortresses guarded by orcs and the unquiet dead was just "work" to him.

"Rogue," he'd said as we parted from the main element on that last day as we entered the mountains of what the map had once called the Auvergne in France. "All you gotta do is show up at the right time, with the right tools, ready to work. Never mind the rest."

Apparently, *rogue* was a "character class" one could play in the game of Dungeons and Dragons, though PFC Kennedy pedantically stated that in the first edition of that game they were just called *thieves*. And somewhere in the mission planning, Rogue had come to be our designation with regard to our hit on the Dark Spire, or what the elves had once called *Barad Nulla*, to reclaim our Forge.

Tanner assured me more than a few of the Rangers played Dungeons & Dragons, or had, though none had absorbed the lore quite like Kennedy. But most kept their hobby to themselves, as the more hardcore Rangers like Kurtz were liable to view games that were not sports as some kind of weakness that needed to be purged by multiple laps around the four-mile-long airfield back at batt.

As the Rangers atop the crag were hitting the main gate in standard raid-style fashion that morning, supported by a weapons squad and a wizard who could throw fireballs, Team Rogue was already twelve hours into the first phase of *their* mission.

Back Door. Sergeant Thor said this was basically a "wall shot," which was a Ranger breaching term for going through a breach in a wall, either an existing one or one made by breachers. We called it Back Door because we were hitting the fortress from a whole other direction.

We were coming at them from below.

In the two weeks of planning after reaching the Hidden Cave deep in the Charwood, Last of Autumn told us everything she and the Shadow Elves knew about the Dark Spire. We needed to take that fortress if we were going to have any chance at survival here in the Ruin. That much was clear. If the pandemic nano-plague that had wiped out the world ten thousand years ago was still active—and Chief McCluskey had indicated that it was, take that for what it was worth—but *if* it was still active, then in a matter of no time our weapons and equipment would start to fall apart. Everything right down to our fatigues. And even if the nano-plague *wasn't* still active, there was still the matter of ammunition. Either way, time was short, and we didn't have much left to lose, truth be told.

We were out of MREs, too. The elves were teaching us how to forage for local food.

The Forge could fix all that. The Forge, in the capable hands of tech Josh Penderly, who knew how to run it, and the Baroness, one of the developers of the fantastic machine, who knew the science behind it... the Forge could make us anything. Those two could have the entire Ranger detachment rearmed with brand-new equipment and full combat loads in less than a month, according to the Baroness. That was our best chance at survival in the Ruin until we figured things out.

Chief McCluskey had known that. Had known how powerful the Forge was and what a game-changer it was here ten thousand years in the future. My guess was he'd try to rule the Ruin with it once he got it up and running. He knew its value. That was why he'd burned five to ten thousand combat troops attempting to take it from us at

Ranger Alamo. He'd probably been waiting for years for one of the special ops detachments from Area 51 to show up.

But like I said, back at the temple, Last of Autumn detailed everything she knew about the fortress we were now attempting to take. And her details made it clear in short order that there was no way the Rangers, with the small amount of munitions they had, were taking the fortress via the front door. The ring of defenses the Rangers would need to thread just to reach the Dark Spire itself were too much. The odds too overwhelming. Once inside the main gate, they'd have to cross open ground between the interlocked defenses with no supporting fire or cover. Then clear that ring before hitting the next, higher level of defenses as they climbed up the last of the ancient crag toward the prize.

The Forge.

Or at least, where we hoped the Forge would be. The Dark Spire. *Barad Nulla.*

But after Old Mother's prompting, as she served me and Last of Autumn healthy bowls of her restorative vegetable stew the next day as we drew the fortress in chalk on the temple floor, the old blind woman, listening, first muttered the words "*Tumna Haudh.*"

Last of Autumn had asked some clarifying questions of her elder and been given long responses. In all the years since the Shadow Elves had been tossed from the fortress, forced to flee due to treachery, the whispers of the Deep Tomb, *Tumna Haudh*, had been frowned upon by the few remaining warriors and the rest of the tribe of once-again-wandering Shadow Elves. It was forbidden to speak of such evil. To their children it became a place of mystery and terror. The home of devils and boogeymen. *Don't eat your herbs and mushrooms, it's off to Tumna Haudh for you, little Shadow Elfling.*

Or at least that's as near as I could tell what they meant via translating between Gray Speech and Tolkien. Shadow Cant would have been easier, but of course, that was forbidden to outsiders, so we couldn't use that. This was early on, and I was still struggling with the Tolkien. Only our third day in the Hidden Cave. The Rangers, I recall, after getting a luxurious entire day's rest, were out there being PT'd to death by Chief Rapp in the woods. I'd managed to dodge some of that because I was working with Autumn, but when the first sergeant decided to Rifle PT the teams after a lunch of mixed herbs and fruits, I got caught. An hour later my arms and legs were burning.

The Army felt there were two cures for everything that ails you, Motrin and PT. And if the Army simply *felt* that, the Rangers believed it as holy writ from on high. Except they were heretics who believed endless amounts of PT cured everything. So, CrossFit people.

It was a doctrinal deviation that, as I have indicated, verged on the cult-like. Or at least that's what you thought when you were dying as you did endless mountain climbers for forty minutes and you were sure you'd never be able to walk again once the pain that would never stop, stopped.

Seriously, what doctor's office do you visit to have something looked at and the guy just starts smoking you with all the burpees in the world? Which one? Because I would not go to that doctor. That is a bad doctor.

The command team knew we needed to do this mission and they knew the Rangers needed to be ready for the one shot we were going to get in order to collectively save their lives. So there was no leave, no rest, no break, after we got to the Hidden Cave. Just that one twenty-four hours of rest after three days and a day-and-night march while being attacked the whole time. That one day of rest and then it was back to Rangering. Which meant trying to out-Ranger every other Ranger who was trying to out-Ranger every other Ranger… and so on, and so on. You get the idea.

Weapons were cleaned and re-cleaned several times over. Equipment inspections were run. And of course, medical and PT. When the Rangers got back to the temple floor inside Hidden Cave each night they were too tired to talk. They racked and did it all over again the next day. A few days later we hit the road south for the objective.

"Time's burning, Talk," said the sergeant major on the first day of the march. "We got us a rogue SEAL to dispose of."

We were back in the game.

When Autumn explained to me what she knew of the *Tumna Haudh*, and the Old Mother filled in the gaps, we had something to go to Captain Knife Hand with. As our map of the fortress began to come together in white chalk on the ancient temple floor, it was clear that the Deep Tomb was our best shot at evening the odds we'd face on the objective.

According to the captain, you needed five-to-one odds to take an enemy fortified position. We were fairly sure we didn't have that, not by a long shot. We had no idea how many enemy forces were located in and surrounding the Dark Spire, *Barad Nulla*. But we knew just how little *we* had.

The only group of Rangers who had no shortage of ammunition was the snipers. They had cases and cases to burn of their very specialized long-range engagement ammo. But using the snipers against the front door wasn't going to do much good, as the enemy had some pretty thick walls to get behind and it was clear they were getting crafty about our boom sticks. There were only so many special munitions rounds the Ranger snipers had that penetrated lighter walls, and a castle ain't mud huts and third world construction techniques. This ancient pile of rocks had weathered war, siege, and the Ruin for what seemed going back several thousand years. It was here to stay. We had to hit it where it was weak.

The front gate was made of wood. The Carl G did the work explosively there. But as soon as we did that, they'd know we were there. So we had to hit at the same time from a direction they wouldn't think we could come from. Normally, that meant Rangers jumping out of C-17s all over your rear screaming, "Surprise, losers!" Then machine-gunning down everyone you loved and laughing about it as they high-fived over your corpse. They'd probably poison your water supply and shoot up your supply lines just for bonus points.

But we couldn't do that. Our ride was rusting and falling apart back on an island that would probably get drowned in the spring rains or next winter. It wasn't gonna fly ever again. Plus, chutes were a problem.

So once we understood what the *Tumna Haudh* was, we knew what we were going to do. We'd come at them from right under their feet. We'd hit like sudden heat lighting and move like hot rolling thunder before the enemy could figure out what the game was. If we did it right, we'd have access to the remains of a tower that provided a perfect position for the snipers to go on a killing spree against the defensive positions the assaulters needed to get through. The snipers could work over the defenders from the rear of the fortress. Shooting them in the back as it were.

Why not take *everyone* through the Halls of Sleep, you ask? *Halls of Sleep*? Yeah, I'll explain that in a sec. Why not do that? Why not sneak the entire detachment in the back door and then jump out and go murdering our way to the *Barad Nulla*? Because the Halls of Sleep are really dangerous. In fact, no known person, entity, or army had ever managed to survive their passage up through the rock that was the crag. And people had tried. It was so dangerous, according to the Shadow Elves, that when Chief McCluskey took the fortress he hadn't even bothered attempting that route. It was impenetrable. Tight with traps. And dangerous in a way they didn't explain, which only made it seem more ominous and forbidding. They were fanatically superstitious about the place.

"More men," Vandahar had contributed while musing over the chalk outlines and sucking at his long-stemmed pipe while listening to us trying to coax intel out of the Old Mother. "Will mean more death down there. Much, much, more. Best to go light and slow through the Halls of Sleep beneath the fortress itself. Very dangerous indeed."

It was clear he wasn't interested in taking that route either.

"I will go with your men against the front gate. I stood at the Valka when I was young. I will stand with you now, and perhaps... perhaps we can begin to change matters going forward if we live to see the sun rise again on the day we conduct our attack. And I would offer this to you, warriors. Triton is a servant of the Dark One in the east. The Lord of Umnoth and the Pit. There is every chance he has made fellowship with the dreamers in the deep down who lie within the Halls of Sleep. And though they have no common cause, they are as evil as he is. They may warn him of the assault. If so, he will position his forces around the old tower and surround it in order to kill you all when you intend to surprise his host. Although... if he does do that... then perhaps it may be a *good* thing for our little surprise. For if it is just a small force that tries the Halls of Sleep, and if they fail, which they most likely will, then the fortress guard that goes to intercept them won't be near the gates or main defenses, and that may give those of us going in the front door, some... slight advantage."

He said all this aloud, but merely musing to himself. Not really concerned if anyone was listening. Intent on his study of the chalk map and his fragrant pipe smoke. Both equally.

"And besides," he said after another moment. "You shall have a wizard among you." He turned to PFC Kennedy. "He has the ways of Nano. The understanding of wielding. In time he may be as great as even Salazon the Mad. Or greater still if events go... our way, as it were. I shall teach him a little along the way, and perhaps we will see what he does with that. Great endings come often from small beginnings."

So on the march down toward the Auvergne in the central massif of old France, or what the peoples of the Ruin called the Savage Lands, the plan was refined and practiced. Assaulters against the main gate. Supporting fire and consolidating on the phase line. Twelve hours prior, Team Rogue would make our appearance.

We'd broken off from the main detachment three days before. Followed a small stream up through the mountains and to the base of the crag five hundred feet below the fortress. There, in the ancient rock behind a trickling waterfall, was the heavy door that gave access to the Deep Tomb. It was guarded with fanged skulls and runes, carved in the stone, which, according to Autumn, warned us of what we were about to do.

"It says…" she began haltingly. "The dead await here. And… you will never return from this place."

*Tumna Haudh.*

What was it really? This system of tombs inside the ancient rock of the crag beneath the high fortress. Because as the Old Mother had told us during the planning phase of Operation Throat Punch, it was much older than the fortress above. She, along with Vandahar, who had studied the ancient texts of a group called the "The Scholar Kings of Atlantea," who had died out about five thousand years ago when "the stars fell from the sky," related the story.

The Halls of Sleep were the ancient resting place of a sect of adventuring warlords who'd ruled locally in the ages before the Dragon Elves began their formal reign. They were once known as the *Ilner* in High Speech. Or Not-Men. The men who were not. Again, this is me fumbling through Tolkien High Speech via German. So maybe I'm getting things wrong. But, near as I could tell they were considered men who were… not.

Vandahar clarified somewhat.

"During the histories as recorded by the scribe Sustoc in the Age of Blood, they were simply ruthless men," said the old wizard, settling to his ever-present pipe and tale. "Savage raiders and pillagers who came from other lands and invaded these lands before even the Elves of Tarragon set to carve stone for that cursed city. The prefix *Il-* is negative in High Speech, thus, one they call Talker, it indicates a negative connotation. The best guess of old Sustoc was that the *Ilner* had eschewed the ways of common men.

"Men, as you may not know, were little known in this region of the world in those lost days. And when the *Ilner* arrived, they became men of power, holding sway over the primitive tribes and petty warlords of that savage time. They sought the forbidden. The dark magics of the Before, so they might have power without limit. Rumors abound in various texts, and are even hinted at in the *Book of Skelos*, or at least the fragments I have seen, that the *Ilner* craved eternal life so they might continue their conquest of the Ruin, for they were powerful indeed in those terrible days.

"And then the Elves of Tarragon-to-be came to power. A rogue warrior of the Emerald Lamp, one who would become their greatest and most notorious hero, Throm the Outcast, did battle with the *Ilner* at the Snake River and defeated their twisted and foul *saura* army. But the ancient texts indicate the *Ilner* had planned for their eventual defeat by learning the ways of the Black Sleep from none other than Sût the Undying himself, that they might rise again in another age, when Outcast Throm and his fabled spear *Tildë* had gone from the times. Alas, the Silver Spike and her dark wielder have gone the way of the *Book of Skelos*. Sad, for they are much needed in this desperate age."

He made a brief symbol to ward off some evil and returned to staring into the fire and ministering his pipe. He seemed sad and alone as he sat there.

"And *saura* means…" I prompted.

He gave me a wide-eyed look like I was the village idiot who'd just feasted on his own toe and bothered to annoy him about it. Then, "I must remember to remember how much you don't know, my boy. *Saura* in High Speech means foul, corrupt, very diabolical evil. Because of the Saur who sleep and wait no more beneath the Sands of the South, of course."

So what does all this mean for the mission? What can we expect to face down there in the Halls of Sleep?

That's what I asked the old wizard. He thought about it for a moment. A long moment.

"Evil," he whispered. "Relentless, unquiet... evil."

Okay, I thought. Rangers can do relentless *and* quiet violence. That's what they're best at. So...

So far it's a draw.

# CHAPTER FIFTY-TWO

UP the twisting boulder-laden ravine far beneath the top of the black crag, we followed silent pools of water and crossed the murmuring stream back and forth, moving tactically up toward the rumored entrance to the tomb of the *Ilner*.

Tanner was on point with his suppressed MK18. We, as opposed to the assault teams that would hit the gate in just over twelve hours, had the luxury of surplus ammunition. We would be breaching and clearing our way through a labyrinth filled with traps and enemies. So we got five mags. Each. The snipers had all the ammunition they could do. The two-forty had one and a half belts. Sergeant Kurtz followed carrying the three-twenty holstered on his gear. His Rampage shotgun stowed on his back, off his ruck. As team leader he would act as the grenadier and be responsible for any explosive breaching that might need to happen. The two gunners, Specialist Rico and Private Soprano acting as the AG, followed along carrying the beast of a light machine gun. Brumm brought up the rear of the whole team carrying the SAW on rear security. He cleared our backtrail, working dip and watching the swirling mist which had come up that evening as we made our terminal approach to the caves beneath the fortress.

The Lost Boys had said the woods and mountains were filled with orc and goblin tribes in service to King Triton. Alias, Chief McCluskey. Or at least that was our guess.

Between the lead breaching element under Kurtz at the front and Specialist Brumm in the rear, came the snipers and their spotters humping all the tools of their trade. Then Last of Autumn and myself. Kennedy was with the snipers, carrying his staff like it was one of their high-speed sniper rifles, and keeping to himself. Mumbling silent wordless phrases the wizard Vandahar had taught him. Over and over again. Practicing.

"Those like magic spells or somethin'?" Tanner asked during one of the halts on our approach to the target entrance.

Kennedy shook his head. "More like directions to keep my focus on the stuff he taught me. Apparently it can get out of hand if I don't stay on top of it."

I knew what Kennedy meant. The situation he was talking about reminded me of a common Army phrase that I first heard in Basic. Ironically, considering, that phrase is "*meet the wizard*." It describes that moment when a combination of physical and/or mental stress makes one break and get all wacky. PT'll do it, but cognitive stress does it pretty well also. "The wizard" is the person you have to meet and shake hands with, metaphorically, in order to break barriers—mental or physical. Kennedy was practicing his focus so that when it came time for him to act as a wizard, incoming and all hell breaking loose down there, he'd be ready to *meet* the wizard, too.

"How's that?" Tanner asked PFC Kennedy as everyone else sat there in the fog and rock, adjusting their gear and getting ready for the next and last move to our target.

"Like... do this and that and then you'll be able make a giant turkey dinner appear? Thanksgivin' with all the fixins? I could go for something besides elf chow, know what I mean?"

Kennedy smiled wanly.

"No," he said softly, his watery eyes distant behind his birth control glasses. "More like stuff drill sergeants used to say to you back in Basic. Y'know... motivational sayings. Keeps you focused when you're riding the lightning."

Tanner laughed. One of the snipers told him to "shut it" and reminded him they were actually on patrol. Tanner bobbed his head but gave a look that said, *You know how the snipers are.* He leaned over to me and whispered, "They're just all giddy about playing Oswald for the high score once we get up into that fortress. Don't want anything to ruin that do they, Talk?"

I guessed they didn't.

"Did the old guy actually call it that?" asked Specialist Brumm from nearby as he sat studying his M249. Brumm hated snipers. That was a known fact. He thought there was something inherently chicken about shooting people in any way other than face to face, up close and personal. Anyone who didn't want to do what needed to be done in a confined space skating across the Occam's razor of the fatal funnel the entire time was a cop-out and not worthy of his fellowship.

Brumm was lovingly cleaning bits of his weapon here and there. He wanted to be ready when it was time to go live with the two drums he had left. After that he'd probably lose all will to live. There would be no tomahawks and adventures in the great white Dire Frost for him. Getting that Forge back online and feeding his two-four-nine was the most important thing in the world. As far as he was concerned.

"'Cause that's what they used to call gettin' executed down south," he continued. "Read it in a Stephen King book. Ridin' the lightnin'. Death chair and all."

Kennedy looked up and made a face.

"Nah," he said after a moment. "He didn't say it like that. He used words you'd think a wizard would use. *Power* and *Pillars of the Earth* and *Great Deeps of Morlon*. Wherever Morlon is. Anyway, I gotta take it seriously. When I bottomed out last time it was... pretty scary. But... that *is* what it feels like when you do it. It feels like you're riding a giant lightning bolt you don't want to get off. Y'know?"

Two things.

Most of the Rangers didn't give PFC Kennedy such a hard time anymore. Except for Kurtz, of course. He would never not give PFC Kennedy a hard time. Even if Kennedy earned the Medal of Honor and became a four-star general, Kurtz would find a way to heap contempt on him. The sergeant was currently off checking the route ahead, otherwise he would have yelled at Kennedy for talking and put him in the front leaning rest position during the halt. Kurtz was that guy. The sergeant never stopped, never needed rest, and wanted nothing from anyone except for them to do their job to his impossible standards. Tanner once told me that Rangers sometimes called guys like Kurtz a "cyborg." Living human flesh over metal endoskeleton.

But regardless of the sergeant's most likely eternal contempt, Kennedy had acquired a new kind of quiet respect in the detachment. The Rangers weren't sure what to do with him, exactly, but everyone knew what he'd done to the massive giant back at the attack on Sniper Hill at Ranger Alamo. So he was being given a small measure of respect among the Rangers. The question was whether he could hang on to it or not.

And the other thing of the two things was that, as you've noted above, Vandahar could speak with Kennedy without me needing to be involved to translate back and forth. And with everyone else too. Within three days the old wizard had understood English and by the end of the week he was using it kind of fluently, if grandiloquently. He used big, high-powered, almost antique words that we'd never taught him. Or at least I had a hard time imagining which Ranger would have used words like *fulminate* or *sorcerous*. Or *pusillanimous*. *Vitriolic*. *Obfuscate*. *Vivificate*. *Sycophantic*. Where he got these words from, I honestly had no idea. The linguist in me found it utterly fascinating.

It was like the venerable wizard had absorbed our language mentally, without having to learn it word by word like some chump. Like me, actually. He tapped directly into the universal understanding of concepts within the language and just found the right word he needed in ours and then used it.

It was bizarre. But I had a feeling I'd see things far stranger in the Ruin if we survived long enough to get a look.

Hours later, we'd been moving through the last of the foggy day and our time to enter the cave at the base of the crag was just after dark. We'd have the entire night to get into position on the tower at the top of the crag high above, then check in with the captain as the main force made their attack on the front gate. We put the war paint on. The last of the cammie sticks were used on any exposed skin, and to effect a ghoulish look on our faces. Who knew, maybe these undead losers would go running in fear at the sight of us. Or accept us as distant relatives. It certainly couldn't hurt—plus, the psychological effect of putting it on under these conditions was not lost.

We were gonna do the undead like they hadn't been done the first time.

Comms were spotty. Batteries, what few had charge left, were being used. But we couldn't chance a miscommunication. So once we heard the attack, we were to take the tower from the basement below, and the snipers would go for the high score. The two-forty team would be on hand to keep the tower clear for the snipers to work.

But that was later. Now, in the misty gloom and creeping fog of the last of the day as we approached the cave, the landscape all around us was completely silent. Deathly silent.

"The mist is… good," whispered Last of Autumn, close to me. "It makes… quiet."

Kurtz shot her a look as his team came up on the last set of boulders before the sheer rock wall that rose up into the swirling fog. High above was the fortress, we knew, but it was as silent as a graveyard, and we couldn't see any of the walls or structures up there.

The quiet did nothing to make me feel better, by the way. Forget the fact we're about to violate a tomb of the supposed living dead just to pop out and surprise everyone right in the middle of a battle. Forget that. We were walking into a place that by all accounts no one had ever survived. Even the SEAL McCluskey had opted for another way to attack the fortress besides the route we were taking.

But we didn't have many options. In fact, we just had the one.

We avoided the small waterfall and worked our way behind the drizzle of water across the wet rocks. Beyond that we found the front door to the tomb, and the back door to the fortress above. All we had to do now was survive the ascent through its trap-littered passages and make it to the top in twelve hours. Hopefully under that.

Kurtz ordered us to shuck all our unnecessary gear. Or at least the assault team consisting of Kurtz, Tanner, Brumm, and Sergeant Thor. The rest of us would be carrying the extra gear and ammo in support of the breaching team. It was a good thing we had Jabba with us.

Oh yeah. I didn't mention him earlier. He'd become like more of a friendly dog than anything else. And he could carry an incredible amount of gear. Which he didn't seem to mind as long as treats found their way into his fanged mouth. I still had two Cokes left but I was saving them. Generally he'd take the candy or the cookie in any MRE, or whatever anyone else had managed to sneak along. Which really wasn't a lot for Rangers. They preferred their own weapons and dip over candy in the priority of stuff smuggled Oscar Mike. On Mission. But there always seemed to be something for him.

We'd stripped down a lot of our gear before departing the main element, but now the assaulters got even leaner. We had no NVGs. Their batteries were long dead. But Last of Autumn had assured us she would use her special Hunters' Fellowship trick. Which she did once we were inside the cave entrance that led into the tomb. We disappeared as the last of the wan daylight faded from the sky and we slithered in between large black rocks to reach the front door of the crypt. Again I watched Sergeant Kurtz suffer through having translucent blue fairy dust sparkle and rain down over him.

Even now, with every incredible thing he'd witnessed, he still did not want to be part of this fantastical world in any way, shape, or form. It was like his mind screamed and raged against believing that these impossible impossibilities were actually made real and true. He was the kind of guy who would've been happier on deployment to some third world hellhole where everyone was trying to kill him with modern weapons and a whole lot of bad intentions. That he could understand. Fairy dust and manticores... not so much. If Tanner was right, his cybernetic programming just couldn't accept it.

A moment after the ceremony ended and we could hear each other's thoughts and see things in the dark, Tanner spoke. "Fellowship up, Sar'nt. Good to go."

I saw, in that brief moment where we could read each other's thoughts, two things. Kurtz wanting to murder Tanner for crossing the stream of this unbelievable world with that of the black-and-white military he so believed in and wanted everything to be. Forever.

And what Last of Autumn was... thinking... dreaming... of.

What I saw grabbed me. Grabbed me like that first time we touched. That wild electricity that was a magic all its own far more magical than Kennedy's lightning train.

I saw what she was thinking.

Her and I. Somewhere in a small boat. Sailing into the southern waters of this world. To the cities of men. In the distance, ahead over the water we were crossing, I saw a city. Not like the kind we'd left behind. Not like New

York or LA. Paris or London. One like something out of the Middle Ages. Fortresses and squat towers. Smoke and sailing ships riding in the harbor and heading out to sea. Shining in the golden morning light of first day. I could hear the slap of the waves against the side of the old boat. The creak of the tackle. The wind was from off the quarter and the gulls were starting to come in from the port to circle our threadbare patchwork sail. I was at the tiller. I was there. And I could feel the wind, smell the salt, and hear the water all around us. Just the two of us.

Sitting forward, near the sail, Autumn wore a silvery dress and her green cloak. No armor now. No weapons. She sat watching the city we were sailing toward. The wind whipped her hair, tossing it in her face, and she reached up and brushed it away. Then she pointed at the fantastic city and turned to smile at me. A smile that was nothing but hope for all the good things life must offer. The opposite of the look in her eyes when she told me of the dragon.

It was just us there. In her dream. And… we were free.

When I opened my eyes to see the luminescent world the Hunters' Fellowship Moon Vision had revealed, lighting the inside of the dark cave in an almost night-vision starlight blue that was better than anything the US Army could ever dream up, I saw Autumn sitting on her knees in the circle we had formed. Pale hands in her lap. Eyes still closed. She was just smiling. Smiling at the thought of a dream that had nothing to do with dragons or what we were about to do.

Like that was some kind of possible future.

*I would just be Autumn then,* I heard her say in her mind. *And… it would just be us.*

# CHAPTER FIFTY-THREE

WHERE there had been darkness, now we saw everything. And what we saw was that even beyond the runes Autumn had read to us, the front door was one giant warning to just stay away. Bones littered the ground. That was the first thing you saw as Moon Vision allowed you to take in exactly where you were. Bones. White and bleached. They were everywhere. Every one of them broken, fractured, crushed to powder in some instances. Among all that, and it took time to understand what exactly you were seeing, but among all the broken and bashed-in skulls and fractured tibias and femurs, lay ancient weapons of every kind.

These too were broken and smashed. Broken and smashed weapons among broken and smashed bones of what might once have been humans... and sometimes definitely were not humans.

Swords and axes. Some rusting, others shining brightly in the luminescent blue of our Moon Vision. But nothing was whole. Everything had been destroyed at some prior date, to some extent.

"What in the ever..."

It was Brumm. His voice dry and low. I turned away from Autumn, still smiling in her dream of our escape, and followed the gunner's gaze upward as he spat out a stream of dip, splashing it across the skull of a horned and fanged humanoid that lay cracked and forgotten on the cavern floor.

Carved into the living rock above was something like a sphinx. Except its head was a grinning human skull. The carving absorbed most of the rock ceiling and looked as though it had been fashioned out of the stone up there long ago. But there was more.

Behind the skull of the looming sphinx were two crossed arrows. Massive and crossing the whole ceiling. And jutting up through the skull was a sword. The hilt reached the floor of the cave below, and in the hilt was the fractured remains of a door. The entrance to the tomb. A giant bronze door that had turned green with age and lay broken in the frame.

All of us, even the snipers to the rear, stared up at the incredible carving above our heads. We'd literally need to walk under the skull and step through an opening in the hilt of the sword to enter the tomb.

"Huh," said Kurtz.

No one said anything after that. We all waited for Kurtz to expound. He didn't. It was as silent as a graveyard in that cave and only the sound of the waterfall back at the entrance could be heard.

Silent as a grave was ironic. Because it was a tomb after all.

"What, Sar'nt?" asked Tanner.

Again, the sergeant said nothing for a long moment. Then, "Don't know," he almost whispered to himself. "But… that seems familiar somehow."

I knew what he meant. It was almost like, and maybe this was because of the Hunters' Fellowship and that momentary ability to read each other's minds, but it was almost like I could see his mind working the problem of trying to decipher the image of the skeleton sphinx looming above us. See him paging through files in his mental office, trying to find the information the image of the statue in the cavern had evoked on his hard drive.

Or maybe this was that thing Vandahar had hinted at. My talent. My revealing. Maybe my peek in his mind was that. Because I didn't feel anyone else in Kurtz's mental file room looking around for a clue. Just me. I was there.

I saw, or felt, I don't know exactly, him toss aside a 4187. Which is a form you fill out in the Army when you want to go to a specialized training school. You can fill it out for other things. But for some reason this one was about a request for specialized training. He'd picked it up for a second because it was interesting, and then mentally flipped it aside thinking it wasn't what he was looking for. I could practically see all that. Maybe this was because my supply of instant coffee was down to just three packets. Maybe rationing, the lower levels of caffeine that came from not having my usual excessive amounts as often as possible was unlocking some kind of incredible new mental powers. If so… I still choose coffee. *You* bend metal beams with your mind, Magneto. *I'll* take a solid pour-over from Costa Rica any day of the week. Nice try, Devil.

I crossed and picked up the 4187 that lay on the floor of Kurtz's mind.

Studied it.

*Applicant Requests Q-Course Selection Phase. SF.*

It almost glared up from the page into my eyes. Like it was forcing me to read it.

I still had no idea what it was about though. Why the image of a skeleton with two arrows and a sword sticking up through its jaw had anything to do with Special Forces, the Green Berets, what Chief Rapp was. But I knew this was the thing out of all the images his tired brain was trying to find, that would put it together for him. He'd just discarded it. My mind saw it was what he needed to solve the puzzle.

This place is weird.

"SF," I said to Sergeant Kurtz in the glowing darkness as he studied the fascinating structure above us.

Kurtz turned toward me. The look on his face was pure murder. Which was a good thing. Kurtz had two looks. Murder and contempt. Murder meant he was dealing with you as something important. Murder meant I'd scored a direct hit and sunk his battleship. Or in this case, connected the dots for him.

He nodded slowly as it all came together.

Then he looked back at the statue.

"This ain't totally the logo for SF. But it's... weirdly similar. I've even seen somewhere they put a skull between the arrows. Usually with a green beanie. Unofficial. But... yeah... it's kinda like the SF unit insignia."

The rest of the Rangers began to agree once they saw it. Thanks to me.

Even Kennedy piped up. "The Latin... *De Oppresso Liber*... that's missing though. But it's almost spot on if you take out the big weird skull. Maybe another detachment got here before us from Fifty-One?"

"Well," said Tanner. "Then they would have to have gone through the QST and been on scene a long time ago. They didn't make this overnight. Or even within the last two weeks. This has been here for a while."

The SEAL had said twenty years. Had others arrived before that? Centuries before?

I remembered Last of Autumn, maybe just Autumn now after the dream of the boat and the city. More specifically, I remembered her and Vandahar telling the stories of the Ruin's ancient past. The old wizard saying the *Ilner* had come onto the scene before the Dragon Elves. And as far as my knowledge of history since we'd gone through the QST was going, that would be over eight thousand years ago.

They'd sought eternal life. They'd made a deal with the Saur. Someone named Sût the Undying.

"C'mon... time to do this. Night's burning," said Kurtz. And it was.

The assault team moved up to the broken bronze door within the hilt that came down through the leering skull. The door was open, technically, but the Rangers stacked and went in just like you learn to do in the shoot house. A moment later we got the "all clear" and the rest of Team Rogue entered the tomb.

We had all of thirty seconds before the first trap sprang. Inside we saw along the walls the image of about ten or so six-armed skeletons. Maybe carved into the stone, maybe free-standing statues. They were tall. Each bony arm carried a curved sword like a scimitar. Their black eye sockets, deep-set in the stone, glared sightlessly out as their bony smiles seemed to await our next step.

That's what I saw in the seconds before they came to life. Or un-life. Or whatever.

"Creepy, Sar'nt," I heard Tanner say in the stillness of the place of the dead.

That's when the things simply stepped away from their places in the wall, all six arms apiece waving swords. The skeletons didn't wave them and dance around, circling to attack like they might in some movie. Giving the heroes the opportunity to take them one at a time. No. They rushed all of us at once. Straight at us, swinging all six swords. Sixty swords in total. It was like an unexpected flash flood of killer skeletons.

I heard Jabba *yip* and scramble away while carrying ammo drums and an impossibly overloaded ruck Soprano had set up for him.

SOP for the team was not to use the two-forty or any of the un-suppressed weapons while we made our creep toward the objective atop the Lost Library. We wanted to keep this quiet. If McCluskey heard gunfire coming out of the tombs, even five hundred feet below through solid rock, he'd know he was under attack. Then most likely the Rangers hitting the front gate would be walking into an enemy force fully expecting something to be up.

No surprise advantage for us. We had to be the epitome of *Quiet Professionals* on this one. Everyone on the team had fashioned a garrote back at the elf camp, with many being genuinely excited about their potential use during this op. Several talked about the hope of crossing a strangle off their bucket list.

Rangers. Literally your worst nightmare. One of the top reasons why if you're a third world bad guy, you'd best not piss off the United States of America.

We didn't have the ammo for anything but surprise. And just one shot to do it in.

The assault team engaged immediately with reflexive suppressed fire. Their weapons were already up in the low and ready position, and they immediately moved into aimed quick-kill shooting. Shoot house SOP. No praying and spraying. These guys hadn't only trained on breaching and clearing operations, they'd done them for the real deal in situations where everyone inside the building was filled with nothing but bad breath, worse intentions and ill-will. Plus AK-47s and suicide vests.

Wild waving, weaving, running skeletons exploded in sudden dull, dusty *smaffs* of bone as the shooters engaged in the few seconds they had before the skeletons got into "melee range."

PFC Kennedy's words.

The room was wide, maybe thirty meters, meaning the skeletons had to cover fifteen meters to the center of the room where we were. On the far wall ahead of us stood a pair of bronze doors like the first, except that these were whole whereas the first door had been fractured.

No one needed to tell the Rangers not to work standard controlled pairs in their shooting. Two to the chest and then two to the head. The skeletons had no chests. They just had bony rib cages. But they did have skulls.

I picked up a running skeleton with my sights. I was next to Autumn. She raised her hand, and in it was a small silver cross. She held it straight out at the three skeletons running right at us as I fired.

I had to slow it down and confirm my sight pictures before I broke the trigger on those shots. A moving object running and weaving slightly side to side is tough on any given day. Inside a tomb, and that running, weaving thing happens to be a skeletal warrior with six bony arms waving shiny pirate cutlasses when just seconds before you thought they were carved reliefs along the wall… that makes it a little more difficult.

Just a bit.

But Chief Rapp had next-leveled our shooting skills on the way down. Running small ranges and dry-fire exercises when he could. Giving us tips and showing us techniques that make SF some of the best shooters in the world. There are reasons why the rest of the Army refer to them as the Super Friends. One of the most important reasons is that they're pro-level shooters in extremely tense situations.

This was tense. Max pucker factor. I won't lie to you.

I pulled the trigger and watched dusty explosions smash ribs and sternum. I may have winged the thing's clavicle, bone fragments flying away in every direction, never mind the carnage all around as the Rangers unloaded on the skeletal ambush with their suppressed weapons.

Then all three skeletons Autumn had pointed her silver cross at started burning up like old paper. Catching fire at the edges and then working in from there. I remember doing something like that once when I was a kid and I was trying to make a pirate map for my yearly visit out to my dad's ranch. Had to make it look old, you know? But instead of the skeletons just burning up around the edges, they went all the way and turned to nothing but dusty gray ash.

In seconds, the skeletons were dead. Again.

One of the spotters had taken a pretty serious slash across the cheek and scalp when one of the skeletons and its six sabers got too close. Lots of blood.

"Secure the room," Kurtz growled at Brumm. "Watch to see if any more come out of the walls."

Then he was on the wounded spotter with Sergeant Thor, evaluating the injury.

"Ain't bad," Kurtz said after a few seconds. "We'll superglue it and it'll be fine."

# CHAPTER FIFTY-FOUR

THE bronze doors leading into the inner chambers of the tomb were a tough nut to crack. In the end, after much inspecting, and caution concerning traps, which we were just bluntly calling IEDs now, the decision was made to use one of the three breaching charges we'd brought along for the intrusion. Which had been all the Ranger detachment had left.

Truth was, we either took back the Forge or we were gonna have to learn to go Bronze Age in order to go Roman. And we already had, to some extent. Most of the Rangers were either now carrying found weapons or the tomahawks a few of the truly Rogers' Rangers types loved to sport. Guys like Kurtz and Thor for sure. I had a flick knife. I'd tossed that smelly old short sword after a while. It couldn't even take an edge and it was notched to hell. Probably some low totem pole gob like Jabba had carried it until the Rangers shot him to death atop Sniper Hill.

"What'll we face on the other side of the door once we breach, Kennedy?" hissed Kurtz as we got ready to storm the inner sanctums of the tomb by blasting the bronze double doors. I could feel the pain of him having to ask this of Kennedy.

Kennedy made a face at me that basically said, *How am I supposed to know?*

But our "wizard" was a lot smarter than that. He knew Kurtz was running on edge here. A ragged, dangerous, edge. Best not to provoke him.

"Well, Sar'nt," began Kennedy softly, which was his manner of speaking and probably another reason the Rangers had not found him one of their own. "This is what Dungeons & Dragons calls a dungeon, technically. But specifically... it's actually a *type* of dungeon, Sar'nt."

Kennedy, for all his power and obvious intelligence, failed to notice the murder look in Kurtz's eye.

"And what *kind* of dungeon is it, Captain Obvious?" asked Kurtz. Exasperated emphasis on *kind*.

"It's a tomb, Sar'nt," answered PFC Kennedy quickly.

Murder look intensifies.

"Yeah. We got that part. What does it *mean*, PFC, besides dead people buried down here in the dirt for a thousand years?"

"Well, technically, Sar'nt. They're not buried. They're... laid to rest, and—"

Kennedy caught the look from Kurtz that time, but he held up his hand, stopping Kurtz from either a hissed tirade or an outright unit decimation by one.

"Why that's important, Sar'nt," said Kennedy, trying to get ahead of the storm, "is... 'laid to rest' means, like these skeletons that came out of the walls, they're not in the ground. Not buried. They're in there"—here he pointed at the doors—"most likely waiting for us in some kind of undead half sleep to come in and bother them. Then they'll attack us in some way."

Kurtz heard this, nodded in understanding of the intel he was given, and probed with a further tactical question about the disposition of our enemies. "We'll be facing enemies just like these skeletons? Out in the open and ready to light it up? Or are there other types of... units... we could expect to run into down here?"

"I don't know, Sar'nt," replied Kennedy. "This world ain't exactly my game. I mean... yeah, there are similarities. And undead are surely waiting and ready to go. That's kinda their thing. The dead-sleep, let's call it, lets them do that. They're usually guarding some treasure, and we could loot that and all for useful stuff like potions or magic items. But that comes with other... problems. But yeah, there are different types of undead. Some specific to tombs. That's what you asked, Sar'nt. There're different types we could expect to run into. For sure."

"Such as...?"

Kennedy swallowed and shifted his dragon-headed staff to his other hand as we all stood there, planning our next move.

"Well, there's skeletons. Obviously. Zombies are technically undead. Wights. They're like... like undead warriors. Sunlight hurts them and I think I could do something about that with the staff. But they're not quite ghosts. There could be those too—ghosts. Banshees. Spirit types. I don't know if our weapons are even going to hurt those. Usually you've gotta have magic weapons to deal with that class of monster. Class is a type."

"Magic weapons?" asked the sergeant after a tense sigh. Did I mention his knuckles were turning white on his handguards? He hadn't put on his Mechanix gloves yet.

It's the little details that fascinate me. I know.

Kennedy nodded and looked around, almost embarrassed to be speaking aloud on such subjects. Clearly we were getting into uncomfortable territory. Gaming was something he wasn't proud of, though he obviously loved it. I understood that. In the civilian world, you might tell Kennedy to just let his freak flag fly. My experience in the military had taught me that things were different here. Competitiveness and alpha skills were encouraged. Difference was viewed with suspicion. The week of Kennedy holding forth as some kind of expert, and the authority he'd unofficially gained, seemed to vanish like mist in the presence of Kurtz's glare. But Kennedy continued because he knew it was important to our mission. And it was. There was every chance, and the chances were pretty high, that we were gonna die trying to pull this off. Remember that bit about no one ever trying the Halls of Sleep and living to tell about it?

So we needed every advantage. And intel about what we might face was all we had.

Our training time on the way down had consisted not only of dry-fire drills with Chief Rapp and glass house walkthroughs, but with monster orientation classes led by PFC Kennedy, who held court every night after the march, supported at times by Last of Autumn and Vandahar. The Ranger sergeants, to their credit, endured this nerdery and assessed the subject tactically, becoming highly inventive about the best ways to kill mythical beasts like Minotaurs and umber hulks. It was a bit harder for Hardt and Kurtz, self-appointed keepers of the flame of Ranger hardcore; during these sessions they seemed more like children stuffed into suits and sent off unwilling to Sunday school on a day perfect for fishing or skullduggery. Yet to their credit also, they too endured.

So Kennedy was going over some material we'd already covered. A refresher for the squad leader and anyone else who may not have been entirely disposed to absorb the information the first time around. Or maybe Kurtz simply wanted a second opportunity to hate both the information and the private providing it.

"A magic weapon is something like…" continued PFC Kennedy, "… like a sword of great power. King Arthur or Thundarr the Barbarian. Or—oh yeah this could be important—it could simply be made out of silver. That's good against lycanthropes but probably ghosts too. I can't remember. If we could charge up our smartphones, I have all my books on there. Oh. I guess… yeah, like my staff."

I had no idea what a Thundarr was. Conan, yeah. I'd seen the Schwarzenegger movie. It was written by Oliver Stone. I'd once taken a film appreciation class. I didn't know there were multiple famous barbarians. Like this Thundarr dude. But apparently he had a cool sword. Be on the lookout for cool swords. Good to know.

"What's a lycan-throat?" asked Thor. There was a gleam in his eye as he listened to the young PFC. Like killing something new was a thing he'd just acquired a taste for. Like collecting Pokémon. Except you killed them all in combat instead of whatever it was you did with Pokémon exactly.

Kennedy pivoted in the dark of the skeleton-bone-littered chamber. We could see each other in the gloom thanks to the Hunters' Fellowship.

"Lycan*thrope*, Sergeant. Werewolves, werebears, wererats. Those kinds of things."

"Werebears?" asked Thor. "I thought it was just wolves. Wolfman, right"

Kennedy nodded. "Werebears are possible."

The Viking sergeant muttered an almost inaudible, "Cool." Like he'd just seen the latest high-performance Ducati on the showroom floor and that was exactly where his next enlistment bonus was going.

"What else?" asked Kurtz.

Kennedy looked up at the tomb's ceiling and sucked in a deep breath. "Uh… ghasts. There could be those. They're like ghouls that smell like death real bad. Ghouls, of course, are sorta… dead people that were really bad in life. People who got hanged. Cursed, you could say. And they just hang around and feed on corpses."

"Sounds fun," noted Tanner. No one laughed.

"Mummies and vampires of course," continued Kennedy.

I hadn't told anyone McCluskey had revealed himself to be the latter. The command team felt like they'd lose credibility by disseminating that the SEAL had said he was, and so it had remained knowledge available only to a select few. I could see Captain Knife Hand's reasoning. Rangers, even though they were Rangers, tough as nails and twice as hard as iron, were already dealing with a lot of freaky stuff. They didn't need bloodsucking SEALs added to the mix.

I thought that was a bad call. In my opinion from having observed and lived among them, telling them that they were going to get to waste a SEAL gone vampire would've been like handing out free Rip Its and dip.

Their day would have just gotten a lot better.

Either way, now was the time for full disclosure. Like I said… we needed everything if we were going to get out of this alive. If McCluskey was undead, then most likely he'd have some kind of alliance, affinity, call it whatever you want, with what we might be facing ahead down here.

Chances were he could possibly communicate with them in some form. So I told them what I knew about Chief McCluskey, the Man in Black who'd come across the river on day two of the battle back at Ranger Alamo. I told them he had indicated he was some kind of vampire and that this transformation had happened at some point in his twenty years in the Ruin, if his story was to be believed. It was already common knowledge among the Rangers that the stranger, this Man in Black and probable King Triton, was a SEAL from one of the detachments back at Area 51. Only the he's-also-a-vampire part was news to them.

Minor detail.

"Figures," said Tanner, and the rest of the Rangers agreed.

"Liches!" exclaimed Kennedy suddenly as he racked his brain for imaginary monsters he'd once killed with his dice. "There could be those. Not likely though. They're super high level. But basically, they're wizards who went mad for power and turned themselves into eternal skeletons, in effect, so they could live for a really long time and conduct magical research for more power."

"You mean like... the *Ilner*," I said, interrupting the think-of-all-the-undead-you-can-or-die-fighting-the-one-you-missed lightning round Kennedy was currently being forced to play. "The *Ilner* who sought things that should not be known, according to Vandahar. The secrets to eternal life. The Not-Men. Could those be liches?"

Kennedy's delicate mouth formed a small *o* and I could tell from the faraway look in his eyes that he was adding up the data to see if my hypothesis was indeed correct.

"Yeah," he said softly. "That sounds like how it would go." And then he added, "And if that were the case... we'd be in pretty big trouble, Talker. We'd be in way over our heads if there were liches down here. If that was the case."

\*\*\*

If that checked anyone, made them stop and think, it didn't show. Kurtz didn't care about liches or were-ghouls who needed some kind of *Excalibur* to kill. Kurtz was gonna kill 'em all and let the rules sort it out.

And who said there were rules?

"If it bleeds, it can be killed," muttered Brumm. To which Tanner replied, "I don't think these things have blood anymore, Brumm. Look around. See any? Nope."

Brumm spat dip juice for a reply. It landed on the bones of another skeleton.

We were gonna make our hit time no matter what, according to Sergeant Kurtz.

"We're doin' it," he said, thumbing shells into his Rampage. The short-barreled shotgun he'd smuggled Oscar Mike. "Clock's runnin'. Everybody up."

We explosively breached the bronze doors a few minutes later. Headphones protected our hearing over a certain decibel level. We pulled back to protect from overpressure and gave Jabba and Autumn lots of extra hearing protection, wrapped and balled shemaghs, due to their crazy hearing and twitchy long ears. The four-man team went in first and I got a pretty good view of how it all went down in the seconds after they swarmed the entrance.

Oh, and the brass door rang from the explosion like a gong to signal the end of the world. We hadn't foreseen that part. Farewell, surprise on other parts of the complex.

It was wights. Or at least that's what PFC Kennedy the Wizard guessed on the other side of the brief and very violent fight we faced. Sergeant Kurtz had set the charge on the bronze doors. Giant and thick and inlaid with strange scrawling runes like Arabic, two slabs of bronze that barred our way. I cannot read Arabic. I can speak it, but reading it's a whole other thing. Kurtz had the charge planted at what we thought was a lock that looked like some kind of great seal made of twisting snakes in the form of a Celtic knot. Except it wasn't Celtic snakes. It was a river and it felt vaguely Egyptian.

"Here," said Last of Autumn, reading our thoughts through the Hunters' Fellowship. Following along with the conversation through our shared images and questions. She pointed to a space in the seams about three quarters of the way up the length of the two doors. "This is the sealing ward. Destroy this, and the door may become useless."

We walked through how it was going to go down, rehearsing our actions on the objective. Kurtz would blow it in from the number three team leader position. Tanner would sweep in and to the left in the number one slot. Brumm in the number four to the right. Thor to the left as two. Each covering their sector. Both teams were covered by blast blankets.

"Remember: surprise, speed, maximum violence," hissed Kurtz as we stacked.

No one needed to be told twice. We'd learned that in the shoot house. Except Kurtz had exchanged *controlled violence* for *maximum violence*. Because that was Kurtz's way of course. The assaulters would assert control of the room, killing everything as they did.

"Controlled pairs unless it doesn't have a heart. And if that doesn't work, shoot them until they change shape or catch fire," said Kurtz as we stacked. The rest of us would follow in once we got the clear, or come in to support if things got hairy. "If it's like the skeletons, no pairs to the chest. Work the skull."

The breaching charge, an eighteen-inch strip of 2400-grain explosive cutting tape, designed specifically to cut through metals extremely efficiently, went off... and destroyed the locking ward that was the seal of twisting snakes stamped into the ancient bronze of the door. But the two huge slabs that formed the rest of the portal didn't budge but an inch or so. A second later a sudden magical flash discharged like a thunderclap being played in reverse. Or at least that's what it felt like to me. All you could smell was something similar to burnt ozone.

Kurtz stepped up and tried to kick one of the doors open. It moved. A little.

"Talker, Soprano, on me!" he shouted.

We'd discussed this. In the event the doors didn't move well as we tried to breach, Soprano and I would rush forward from the stack and try to get them open physically so the assaulters could move in and clear the room.

In that second he called our names, I totally now understood "the fatal funnel" the vets had talked about regarding a breaching op. I'd done it as practice during RASP. Felt some kind of distant thrill that was tempered by the fact it was just training.

Now it was real.

Now...

... it was very real.

We heard the call of the sergeant and rushed forward. Not thinking. Heart not just beating, but hammering. It was thundering in my chest so hard I could feel blood rushing in my ears. If I'd had something to say, I doubted I could've spoken a word.

"Throw your back into it!" shouted Kurtz as we approached. He pointed with his assault gloves clearly where he wanted us. Then ordered, "Stay low!"

The guys with weapons and live rounds were going in over the top of us. Best not to be in the way.

We hit the two doors with our whole body weight. Tiny Soprano and a linguist who doesn't weigh much more. Time was of the essence and I felt myself literally perform a flying block on the door to try and thrust it forward. If there was an enemy in there, we only had a few seconds to get the Rangers in and kill them all before they, the enemy, figured out something was up. The question was... what was the enemy? What new horror was waiting for us that we hadn't planned for? You could only plan for so much. The unknown, that was the scariest part, was exactly that. Unknown. And that's what made it dangerous. And what made this the funnel on crack. Sorry, no pop-ups or even real live jihadis today. Today we were gonna find something no one else had ever seen before. Or at least... no one left alive.

No one from our world.

The doors were heavy. Incredibly heavy. Soprano and I leaned in and pushed and they slowly swung open on a low groaning moment that took forever.

Maybe two horrifying long seconds in which we felt completely exposed.

"Get down!" shouted Kurtz as the assaulters swept over and started firing into the room. I hit the floor and smelled nothing but ancient dust in my face and nostrils. Similar to the smell of old books in the stacks back at any ivory tower university's most venerable library. A smell I was very familiar with. But this had a rotten, foul... almost corruption to it as I lay there on the ground getting hit by hot expended brass. I sneezed as the suppressed gunfire started in pairs.

It had an almost rhythmic cadence. *Here's two. Here's two more for you in the face.*

There was surprise for sure. I just wasn't sure on whose side it fell.

There was speed. Surprised or not, the Rangers opened up on what Kennedy the Wizard would later tell us had to be tomb wights.

And maximum violence. Of course there was that. That's what Rangers did best.

As Kurtz and Brumm went right to our side of the room, maintaining their primary sectors of fire to cover the antechamber we were storming, weapons engaging from our side to the far wall, the crypt creatures did indeed look like rotting knights from some lost and elder bygone age. Horned helmets and desiccated armor. Toothless smiles in decomposing skulls with ragged pieces of leather flesh still clinging in places. Heavy, dark broadswords.

The explosive detonation of the breaching charge had woken them from their long slumber. That much was clear. They'd been lying inside what looked to be solid gold ancient sarcophagi arranged in two rows along the sunken floor of the crypt. Long stone rectangles with more of that strange twirling Arabic writing chiseled into the gold and then inlaid with turquoise and aquamarine stones. Heavy golden lids that had long ago been pushed aside and smashed to pieces on the surrounding floor.

I looked up to see the Rangers ballistically ventilating these monsters with solid hits. Ragged, papery bits of ancient mummified flesh flew away. Armor disintegrated from moldy corpses. Yet still the wights pulled themselves up from their golden coffins and stumble-rushed, red eyes glowing, toward the firing Rangers deep inside the musty old tomb.

Yeah. You heard that right. Their eyes glowed like hellish red embers. And for bonus points they hissed raspy, papery whisper-roars that sounded like the voices of drowning ghosts trying to pull you down into a moonlight whirlpool.

Outgoing rounds from the Rangers smashed into the wights, but they didn't seem to mind. Or at least three of them didn't. Brumm unloaded a full burst from the SAW and just disintegrated one, reducing it to scraps as it tried to reach for him.

Sergeant Thor dropped his primary as the one closing on him reached the five-meter mark. Letting his medium-engagement sniper rifle dangle, he whipped one tomahawk out and slashed it once, twice, three times in whirling back and forth cuts across the sleeping undead warrior that had made the mistake of getting close to him.

The cuts did little to the undead thing other than staggering its forward progress for a second. In no way, shape, or form did they prevent it from raising up the old chunk of steel I'd decided was some kind of ancient broadsword. The thing breathed out a breathy gasp of flies, or something, and then swung its heavy sword down at the Ranger sniper still raking it with the razor-sharp tomahawk.

But Sergeant Thor wasn't there. He was hacking and coughing as he dodged to the side, and the wight's crusty sword came down on the floor of the ancient crypt, striking old stone and causing sparks to fly.

Thor exploited the missed attack by hacking at one of the thing's arms, just jackhammering the tomahawk into the undead thing. Three quick chops and he was through the leathery mummified flesh and into the brittle bone beneath. One more and he was through that too, and the long-dead limb flopped to the floor of the burial tomb.

Off-balance, the wight tried to raise the heavy chunk of steel that was its sword off the floor and went stumbling away, gasping curses and promises I could barely translate from what to my ears was a hybridized Arabic as the blur of sudden gunfire echoed all around me.

*"Thief!"*

*"Interloper!"*

*"You will find only death here!"*

I was getting off the floor and Kurtz was in front of me, hacking at the wight as it went down, its remaining bony limbs impossibly flailing. Sergeant Thor wasn't seeing that more of the things were coming from out of the paintings of antique scenes along the wall. Secret doors were opening up all around us.

I had my rifle up and shouted "Engaging!" to clear one coming in at Sergeant Thor's blind side.

Best shooting I ever did.

Hunters' Fellowship?

Chief Rapp School of Good Marksmanship and Trick SF shooting?

Don't know. But I drilled that thing quick, aiming and sending fire right through the skull. I watched as one of my five-five-six rounds exploded out through the old war helm and brittle dry bone at the back of the wight's skull.

To my right I heard the deafening roar of Sergeant Kurtz slam-firing his Rampage, clearing off the newcomers, shredding ancient bone and armor with the concussive buckshot spray of the mini twelve-gauge. Later, after the battle, the wights on that side were plain ruined. He'd burned an entire mag putting down three and then gone to work with the Rampage when things started to get out of hand.

I don't know. Maybe… fifteen seconds. Probably thirty from when we fired the door with the breaching charge.

Ten ruined corpses around us. Ten at least.

The fight was over and the ruined messes of wights' corpses lay scattered across the ornate antechamber.

The funnel.

And then the other side of it…

The Hunters' Fellowship revealed everything within the room, even in the low light.

From inside the beautiful golden sarcophagi came the gleam of twinkling gems. Some of the weapons on the floor shimmered with an almost blue moonlight.

I heard Autumn's voice telling us in our heads, "There are mighty weapons of renown here." And we could tell from the Fellowship that she was indicating the softly glowing weapons on the floor.

But it was the scenes painted along the wall in dried paints mixed long ago that fascinated me. Like hieroglyphs and cave paintings. Telling me a story about the Ruin.

Telling us a story of what had happened to an SF detachment that had shown up way too early.

And became warlords in the long ago of the Ruin.

# CHAPTER FIFTY-FIVE

I would think often about what I saw on those walls within the subterranean chamber. The ochre and cerulean paint daubed there, depicting events from over eight thousand years ago when the *Ilner* walked the Ruin.

When an SF ODA— Special Forces Operational Detachment Alpha team—had arrived much too early to the party, and much too late at the same time. And what had become of them.

The rest of the team was busy securing the objective and getting us ready for the next breach. Kennedy and Soprano and one of the snipers got interested in what was in the bottoms of the fantastic golden sarcophagi. There was wealth untold just within this first room. Gems and tribal jewelry worked in silver and gold. The off-base pawn shops we weren't supposed to hawk our gear at would've paid top dollar for this stuff. Any Ranger would have been Charlie Potatoes that weekend. There were sacks full of coins stamped with the image of that same tribal-looking SF skull and crossed arrows.

The Lost Boys entered the room—Kurtz didn't want them involved in any fighting, so they were our perpetual tail. They stood, mouths agape, as they took in the treasure. But they made no move to touch any of it. That to me felt like a warning, but it was soon too late to voice the concern.

One of the snipers picked up a gem and died thirty seconds later, just falling over and going into sudden shock, his body convulsing for no discernible reason. Kurtz had no idea what was wrong with him but frantically worked to save the guy by hitting him with an anti-chemical agent injector to see if that would do anything. It didn't, and after a moment the man's body ceased its shaking and twitching.

It was Autumn who diagnosed the fatality.

"Poison," she whispered. "He has... been poisoned."

She was kneeling down, searching the treasure the sniper had been pulling out from the bottom of that sarcophagus. Using her small curved dagger, she separated one gem from the rest. It was the most vibrantly beautiful emerald I'd ever seen.

"This one has... a curse... on it," she informed me.

I looked over at the dead sniper on the floor. He had turned purple. Dead from an inability to consume oxygen. But not just through the lungs. All at once. Almost everywhere. As though his entire cellular structure had suddenly decided oxygen was poison. Every cell had been strangled. Individually.

"Maybe from the plague," said Tanner. "Saw stuff like that on YouTube before they shut it down. Could be something left over from the nano-plague."

"Leave all of it alone and let's get ready to move," said Kurtz angrily. "Sergeant Thor... your section good with leaving him until we're mission complete? Then we come back down here later to retrieve. I'll do it myself."

Thor, standing wide-legged near the body like some weightlifter priest getting ready to pronounce the Mass of

Rifle Blessing and Mass Gains, slung rifle hanging straight down across his massive chest and rig, large hands clasped over the deadly weapon, nodded that that would do for now.

The dead would be addressed. But they would be addressed later. After the killing and payback had been done.

I took in as much of the crypt wall frescoes as I could before it was time to move. Because what I was looking at was like looking at some future history of us. Of what the detachment could become.

If we made all the wrong choices.

Tanner agreed.

"We're lookin' at us, Talk," he murmured in the busy silence of objective-securing. Tanner. The guy who'd only come along for the ride because he thought it was a pretty solid way to ditch both ex-strippers and beat the inevitable Article 15 coming from that DUI last month and ten thousand years ago. Now he was waxing all philosophic at the dark art we were unraveling along the walls of a tomb.

It was clear that the dead in this chamber, the now dead again, the almost skeletal warriors PFC Kennedy had called wights, were servants of the *Ilner*. The pictures told their story.

Kings who'd ruled a seacoast to the frozen north.

Log houses like the hulls of ships against pack ice and jagged mountains.

Trade in grains with the south. Trade with dark-faced men wearing lion skins who carried shining spears. As though the men were actually lions who walked like men.

*That could be a problem*, I thought. *If we're all out of bullets.*

Then the *Ilner* came and made slaves of the Ice Kings. There was war and fire written on the walls. Battles that must've been huge, on the order of the old Civil War. The lower half of the wall was littered in stick-figure corpses done to death by the *Ilner* and their strange grim-faced warriors. And the host of warriors that answered their banner and call.

Study close enough and you began to see there were twelve recurring figures in all these scenes of conquest and violence. Twelve *Ilner*.

A Special Forces Alpha Detachment is made up of twelve guys. Tanner hipped me to that as we studied the drawings that were somewhere between Egyptian hieroglyphs and early Bronze Age cave paintings. Meanwhile, Kurtz kept up the hustle to get ready to crack the next door and keep moving. It was a simple door made of rotting wood that led deeper into the tomb. Whether we liked it or not, that was the only way to go.

Brumm was already on that door. Guarding it until we decided to give it a go.

There was a map on one section of the wall. A crude map of the world as they knew it then. The twelve recurring figures, the *Ilner*, had conquered far and wide throughout much of northern Europe eight thousand years ago before the Dragon Elves rose to power. Wars against some kind of ice men of the north. Wars against the orcs and trolls of the south. Orcs and trolls like savage pagans who worshipped an eight-armed god that otherwise looked like them. A battle in jagged mountains against huge slavering trolls with giant fangs.

Much death. Much fire.

But despite all this, they, the *Ilner*, carved out their own kingdom in the Bronze Age of the Early Ruin after all we had once known had gone the way of the dodo.

We followed the drawings around the wall, seeing where the Ice Kings, as the wights had once been in life, were defeated and sacrificed in battle to an almost Egyptian lizard that walked upright like a man.

I wondered if this was the Saur old Vandahar had told of. *Saura*. Foul. Evil. Contemptible.

"Talker!" It was Kurtz hissing at me. Getting everyone organized. "If there ain't a floor plan on that wall, then it ain't important."

Starting in the northwestern corner of the room, by the time I was halfway down the second wall of the fresco, the twelve *Ilner* not-men had gone from being what clearly looked like US Army personnel in contemporary gear similar to what we were wearing to sacrificing their enemies to the dark lizard pharaoh. Being rewarded with strange powers and weapons. Being treated like gods to the peoples they had put in chains and made slaves of.

There was time enough before Kurtz declared "guns up" for me to chance a glance at the third wall. Shadowy there. Or at least that's what I thought at first. But no, the paints and pigments there were darker in tone. And what I saw along that section of the wall was death, destruction, and what looked like hell on Earth. Or the Ruin, as it was now known.

The twelve gods presided over that wall like grim death watching a mad harvest of corpses and destruction. The story on that wall was not good.

*We're lookin' at us*, Tanner had said. Was that prophetic? A guess? Or just the wisdom of a grunt who'd been there, seen that, and gotten the scar to learn from it?

Wisdom can be acquired regardless of rank.

# CHAPTER FIFTY-SIX

"THAT was a tomb of slave kings," said Autumn as we moved swiftly along the next passage once Kurtz's team had cleared it of IEDs.

"How do you know?" I asked. We were talking about the room we'd just left. Where the wights had been done to death again. Undead zero, Rangers two.

"There were old... Dragon Elves Mist Markings in the room. You cannot read or... even see those kind of markings."

She pointed to her eyes. Indicating that somehow they were adapted in ways ours were not, to be able to see these "Mist Markings."

"What are they?" I asked.

She looked around trying to find the right words in *Grau Sprache*. Nothing fit, and so we slipped back into Shadow Cant, seeing as none of her people were around.

"The language of ghosts," she said simply. "It is everywhere... here."

Ahead, the team was getting ready to breach the next room at the end of the long hall. We were deep in the rock of the crag. It was silent and heavy down here under the earth. And best not to think about how much rock was on top of you.

There were more petroglyphs down here along the hall, but even with the Hunters' Fellowship in effect, it was way too dark to study them. I was just getting bizarre fragments that made no sense. But they tantalized me all the same. What can I say? I'm an information junkie. Add that to the coffee and the achievement thing I've got going and I'm actually a real mess. Thankfully, most of my addictions are positive. I quit smoking. Mostly.

The next door ahead was a simple door. But the hall was too narrow for a four-man breach. Instead Kurtz went in behind Brumm, guns up and following the SAW.

Almost instantly, short controlled bursts, hallmarks of Brumm's mastery of his weapon, began to bark out aggressively. Kurtz was calling out targets as the rest of the team moved in, and then the shooting started in earnest. Coming online to support Brumm's attack against the unseen foes.

Writing this all down, I sometimes have a hard time remembering what I was actually there for, and what I experienced via the Hunters' Fellowship. Like, I was right there when Kurtz and Brumm prepped to strangle an orc and knife him at the same time… except I actually wasn't. It's equally hard to recall perfectly what was spoken aloud, and what was communicated via the meld. We could hear each other's thoughts, see events others saw, but it's not easy to do much of that while focusing on your own personal tasks. That was going to take practice.

And then there was Kurtz, who was too Ranger to use anything other than tried and trained protocols.

Still, I do know that by the time I got there all the mummies were already dead. Apparently 5.56 works great on mummies. And it was Tanner, who had followed

Sergeant Thor, who let me know how it went down in there once they breached.

That I had become the official archivist of the Ranger detachment was clear now. Rangers had been coming up to download on me. Maybe it was just because the sergeant major had basically made me the de facto intel asset. But I think it was much more, or, now that I think about, much simpler, than that. The Rangers wanted a record kept. Their deeds put down. Or maybe it was just something had been hardwired into them living the Scroll Life and going to Ranger School. Something that had been just beaten into them so that they could fight and survive and do it again until everyone who opposed them was good and dead. They wanted a record kept, for the last and final AAR. After-action report. Rangers AAR everything they do, looking for ways to improve. This was no different, but with an added emphasis on recording the "who" part of the 5 W's—who, what, when, where, and why.

The *Who* of who they were was important.

The KIAs since we'd first arrived were starting to accumulate. And chances were, if things didn't radically change in our situation, there were going to be a lot more KIAs sooner rather than later. Getting it down, what happened to them, or what they wanted known if the worst should, had assumed a kind of informal importance on our hump south to hit the fortress. It had become my job, and I was cool with that.

So by now the download of intel, story, and personal account was just standard. They came to me. Told me something interesting and assumed when I was writing it down that night that it was going in the record of us. So there's a lot here, in this account, you're not getting. At least not just yet. It's all in kind of a shorthand notes section at the back of the journal my mom gave me as her kind of sarcastic indictment of my choice to be all I could be and join the military.

There are lots of stories and they'll go down in the record when we get someplace safe and I get more paper. Or papyrus. Maybe a clay tablet. Or a cave wall and some charcoal to draw on. Whatever.

Stuff like the story of Sergeant Kang slitting throats down in the dark beneath Sniper Hill. Which doesn't belong here in the middle of the tomb. But here it is.

He was one of the last to come to me and tell me his story of what happened. He's silent, even for a Ranger. But about three quarters of the way through the journey south, he came over one night and mumbled, "I want to tell you something."

Then he said nothing for a few minutes as we sat there. I could feel him working it out. Getting the story he had to tell just right. The story of what had happened to him, and what he'd done.

I waited. Because that's what you do.

And finally he began. It was a crazy story. He ran into some creatures we had no idea of during the battle. A thing that looked like a brain with tentacles. He could hear it screaming in his mind when he started jackhammering his tanto in where he thought its kidneys should be after he'd crept up on it. Yeah… it was a man with a brain for a head and tentacles coming out its mouth. It wore long wizardly robes. Kang said they were pretty fancy.

When it died it gave Sergeant Kang a vision. That's what he called it. A vision. A vision of a fiery plain where there was no love or kindness anymore and probably never had been. Kang said it was a burning, violent, lonely place and he could just feel it in his bones as he observed it in the sudden manifestation he'd been attacked with. He saw all this for just a moment with the thing's blood all over his gloves.

Again, Sergeant Kang's words: he knew it wasn't part of this world. And he said that there, in that vision place, across a dead sea that had become a volcanic plain where the bleaching skulls of prehistoric giants our world had never known lay baking under a red and dying sun, he said, "It was probably Hell... if there is such a place."

I listened. And then later, made notes. Promising I'd get it all down for him. He also told me he had a little sister who had become an actress in Hollywood. "She's a waitress and all. Hasn't got her big break yet but she's gonna. She's good. She's pretty too. Not like me."

Sergeant Kang is built like the Tasmanian Devil. The Looney Tunes character, not the animal. A squat inverted triangle of muscle and gear you don't want to meet if you're OpFor. He will flat out ruin you regardless of his looks. Yeah, he ain't pretty, but I saw him carry a wounded man through a battle while fighting off nightmare wraith riders on our six.

He didn't flinch. Just kept working the problem of desperate survival.

"If anyone ever gets back..." he continued. Whispering this part. "Just tell her... I'm sorry. Okay, Talker? The two of us just had each other. And I didn't mean to... leave her alone. I'm sorry about that."

He gave me her name.

Jade Kang.

So that's going in the journal everyone calls *The Log* now. That, and what's turning out to be a lot of other stories, last words, and things to be done upon demise.

Like the Ranger over in the rifle teams who tossed a fragmentation grenade, danger close, right into an ogre's gullet just as they were getting overrun on Phase Line Charlie that second night of the battle. He'd emptied his primary on the swollen raging creature in the night battle and there was no time to get a new mag in. It was either the grenade or his secondary as the thing closed to rip him to shreds. And if the MK18 he was working, as he told it, "wasn't doing it, then how was my sidearm gonna do a damn bit of good?"

So he pulled a frag, popped the spoon, and fast-balled it right into the thing's open mouth. The ogre was just getting ready to swing its huge, refrigerator-sized double-bladed battle axe dripping with blood and adorned with the skulls of goblins like voodoo charms. The Ranger got a strike, and the giant ogre gagged on the grenade. Then it just swallowed it and smiled.

Which apparently is not a pretty sight to behold in the dark during the middle of a fight for your life.

For half a second the war ogre looked just as surprised as the rifle team Ranger was. Then the awful smile, and it resumed its attack.

And *then* the grenade detonated down in its gullet, energetically separating its torso from its legs. Blowing the monster's swollen belly in every direction.

And that was that.

Those stories. The ones that separated the living from the dead. Which, in this kind of situation, and let's just call it *war*, is the only thing that matters, right?

And finally, for now, the one Tanner told me about the firefight inside the mummy chamber when Brumm and Sergeant Kurtz breached. This one is going in this portion of the record because it's part of Team Rogue's story beneath the fortress.

Later on, Last of Autumn put together the final piece of the puzzle to the room we were breaching. She told me that in Mist Writing it was called "the Chamber of the Chief Concubine" of someone she pronounced as *Raze*. But that could have been *Reyes*. And that could have easily been the name of some Special Forces operator eighteen series. But I didn't have enough info to confirm that bit of intel.

Just collecting.

For who knows when. Or who.

Best not to ask those questions. *Just keep picking 'em up and putting 'em down*, as Drill Sergeant Ward would've said a long, long time ago.

Except he meant boots during Basic during a long hot summer in July. He meant someday Basic would be done and we'd be off to fall and AIT and things would be different, if not better. That drill sergeant had trained enough young soldiers to know they needed the reassurance that "this too shall pass" during their season in the only hell they'd ever known.

He'd say that to you when some other wicked drill sergeant with a penchant for particularly torturous corrective punishment put you against a wall and went off to find someone else to torment. Left you sitting in an invisible chair for forty-five minutes as your legs and thighs burned and cried for mercy. Drill Sergeant Ward would ease on by, on his way to keep an eye on someone else, and just whisper in his thick Mississippi mud accent, "Dis too shall pass."

And then, somehow, you found a tiny bit more in you to just keep enduring a little longer. If just for the hope it would be over someday. Even if today was not that day.

So... this is what happened in the chamber of the chief concubine for *Raze* who may or may not have once been a special operator named Reyes. Probably an E-7 until he did a deal with the Lizard Devil and became an *Ilner*. A Not-Man. Who knows?

But now I am very curious to find out and I bet the story is on some wall down here within this massive subterranean complex beneath the fortress atop the crag above, where we are soon expected.

Brumm is following the front sight of his two-four-nine, according to Tanner, and he just starts ventilating mummies in short bursts. Mummies that are coming out of stone sarcophagi, the plural of the singular *sarcophagus*, a stone coffin, typically adorned with a sculpture or inscription and associated with the ancient civilizations of Egypt, Rome, and Greece. Except these final not-so-resting places are upright and set into the walls around the underground columned room. And though they are human-shaped, the mummies, they're large, but not ogre large. The occupants must've been maybe seven feet tall in life. And still so in death. They have lizard heads and claws. Like crosses between alligators and dinosaurs. Very reptilian. Wrapped in ancient and dirty bandages. Hiss-moaning slurs as they come forth to revenge themselves on those who have dared disturb their long, eons-long, sleep.

So, way ahead of you. These must be the Saur. Or at least, what they once were in life. Except wrapped in dingy bandages covered in scrawled Arabic. Wearing heavy gold bracelets and Egyptian-looking torqs about their thick reptilian necks.

Eight of them. Eight massive stone sarcophagi covered in arcane and magical symbols and strange curling writing that hurt the eyes to look at too long. They must have been waiting for the intrusion into the sanctum, because they come at Brumm from every corner of the room as soon as they're through the door. Specialist Brumm starts engaging as Kurtz peels off and starts to pick up the next sector, his rifle scanning.

Thor comes in, selects a target in his sector, and fires, practically disintegrating the first mummy he hits with his rifle. Brumm's brass is dribbling on the stone floor in intervals as the mummies take incoming and close regardless of effect of said incoming.

The only way to destroy them is to reduce them to nothing but grave whispers and rags. That quickly becomes apparent. Mummies are shot to pieces at close range. It's the only way to be sure.

Tanner, as the last man inside, picks up his sector of the room and starts engaging the mummified dead. Kurtz is yelling, "Keep firing until they're down!" Because controlled pairs ain't doin' it on lizard mummies.

There's a brazier, big and made of brass, gleaming in the firelight coming from its embrace. Yeah, there's a fire burning down here, and we smelled nothing. Where are they getting the fuel? How long has this thing been going? But compared to the dark horror of the rest of the room, it's almost a place you'd want to run to for safety. The rosy light coming from that fire, throwing itself out into the darkness and the fat hieroglyphed columns the lizard mummies are stumbling through to get at the Rangers, is almost like an oasis of safety.

"That's what it felt like when I first went in, Talk," said Tanner as he recounted the tale. "Like that was the safest place in the room and I wanted to just go there as those things came rushing out of the darkness. Then I started hearing them in my mind. And that woman who was crying."

That's correct. The Rangers are basically shooting these things to shreds before their outstretched claws can reach in and take a mummy-swipe. And just to make things more interesting, the mummies are attacking the Rangers' minds.

The mummies are roaring.

"But it ain't a roar you can hear, Talk. You know, it's just like a whisper... but how you can hear that with your hearing protection on and Kurtz shouting to put them down before you move to the next target, I don't know. But in your head, it's a roar. Like the ocean, or all the oceans in the world, all at once. Hitting the rocks below a cliff you know you shouldn't jump off... but... kinda want to. Or like a bottomless well that ain't got no end. It just fills up your mind with... y'know... despair. Like you got no reason to live anymore."

*Despair?*

Interesting word for Tanner, a usually lighthearted and easygoing Ranger, to use. Always quick with a joke if he can get away with it. Now he's talking about bad choices like they're as real as it ever gets.

"Like when Friday formation never ends because the safety briefing is inspired by whatever shenanigans happened last weekend. And you know the NCOs are gonna be all over the barracks all weekend long. That kind of... y'know, talk... hopelessness. The feeling there's never gonna be fun again."

Yeah. That kind of weekend for Rangers could be real hard on them. Due to deployments and training, they rarely got weekends. So when they did... they were important.

But the Rangers are on target in the mummy room and shooting like pros. No bag of bandages is going to stand up for long against excessively violent outgoing fire distributed generously.

Brumm doesn't relent. Hosing them just like he did that weird doppelgänger that attacked us back when we hit the HVT on the other side of the river. Which right now, seems like a million years ago.

The mummies went down even though the Rangers were under that psychic attack that felt like staring into a well of darkness and, as Sergeant Thor put it, injecting himself into Tanner's tale, "wanting to jump just to find out what was down there in the dark of a bottomless well."

Kurtz gave Sergeant Thor a look of bewildered disbelief when he said that, but nothing further passed between them.

And that was when the real trap inside the room got sprung. As the sound of gunfire in a tight confined space, the dribbling tinkle of brass on stone, the cavitating echo of thunder, faded, it was Brumm who heard her first.

"Got a live one, Sar'nt!" he shouted. His two-four-nine was back up and covering the figure he'd spotted in the shadows opposite the brightly burning brazier. Even I was hearing it and I was outside the door. Incredibly, it was the sound of a woman softly crying. Gently sobbing. Mourning.

Autumn heard it too.

"Tell them to wait!" she said urgently. And I told them, and she shouted her warning over the mind meld as well. But the Rangers were new to this. New to her. New to this strange and bizarre dark underworld we were completely marveling at. It was like walking through a haunted house. But a real one. One that would kill you.

And my warning and hers, they weren't fast enough.

One of the snipers had already gone in. They were on the objective. Securing the room. And that sniper, a guy named Marcos, went to cover the area around the brazier. Advancing right into its circle of light, and then… falling straight through the floor like it wasn't there. He screamed as he fell.

"I turned to look," said Tanner, recounting it all to me later. Smoking one of his last precious few cigarettes he'd brought along. The occasion warranted one. We shared it. He looked tired and dirty in the low light we found ourselves in as Kurtz tried to figure out if Marcos was gone forever. "I turned to look…" repeated Tanner distantly, seeing it all again, "and saw that the big old bonfire in that copper bowl…" He was describing the brazier. "… was just gone. It was a pit. There hadn't never been a light there. You knew it. It was all a trick. Right out of a horror movie where the main character realizes it was all just a lie. The things they saw weren't real."

An illusion.

After that—after Marcos—as we listened to the woman, a dark shadowy figure wrapped in a shroud, weeping in a shadowy corner, Autumn warned us again not to go near "her."

"Do not... bother... this thing," Last of Autumn cautioned. "She is... weeping dead. A spirit. A very angry spirit."

As the Rangers looked on in amazement at the otherworldly figure weeping in the dark corner and the pit on the other side of the chamber, I saw what would happen. What would happen if they tried to help her or comfort her. Autumn was showing me.

"Yes," said Last of Autumn within my mind. Seeing and commenting on what I was just working out. "She would drive you into the pit with fear... if you disturb her grief."

That was the trap the *Ilner* had left here, who knew how long ago. *Violate our tomb and our ghost concubine will scare you right into that pit, if the undead mummies don't make you want to jump in first.*

We left that horrible room.

Autumn had used the Fellowship's Mind Meld to assure Kurtz that the sniper Marcos was no longer among the living.

The pit was not bottomless, but it was a long fall. A *very* long fall.

"Well, that's just about the worst IED ever," said Tanner as we followed the path beyond, deeper into the tomb below the fortress.

"C'mon," said Kurtz bitterly. "Clock's burnin'."

# CHAPTER FIFTY-SEVEN

AS we proceeded farther into the underground tomb, we passed rooms that seemed pregnant with purposes we couldn't discern. Long gloomy halls that were like ossuaries. Vaults full of statues of strange mythical beasts and grim warriors presiding over the resting places of the dead. At points it was hard to tell if we were climbing up through the solid rock of the crag beneath the fortress, or heading deeper down into the fissures that had to lay farther below.

"Old Mother... told of a central well... into the upper levels," said Autumn as we took a break near midnight. "She said... she once went in and saw... a fantastic dome."

We knew that already of course. And she knew we knew. We'd thoroughly squeezed every last drop of intel about *Tumna Haudh* from the Old Mother and Last of Autumn and Vandahar. We even got what we could from Jabba, though the little gob knew nothing whatsoever. Vandahar and Autumn knew little more. But enough. It was the knowledge of that central well that had made us think this might work in the first place. A Back Door. If we could reach that central well, and use it... well, an express elevator to the penthouse suite that was a mad firefight behind enemy lines at the base of the Dark Spire sounded pretty good compared to what we were facing down here.

We'd had one other fight by then. Giant pulpy black spiders that looked oily in our Moon Vision. The massive arachnids had crawled into a ruined throne room right where we needed to pass. Some long-ago earthquake had opened a fissure within the room, and they had set up residence there, filling the place with their ghostly webbing, the ropy strands standing out in almost iridescent contrast to the darkness we found ourselves in.

Tanner, on point, creeping ahead silently, about twenty meters ahead of Kurtz, spotted the first strands of webs barring the way into the room. We probed but didn't get too close. That was when one of the big brutes, a shining-black-carapaced spider the size of a water buffalo, filled the entrance of the dusty and forgotten room and howled in anger at us.

Or in warning to its brood mates.

Tanner backed up fast, swearing, and alerted Kurtz to what we'd almost stumbled into. Though the giant black thing seemed to want to rush out from its webby holdfast, it stayed there in the webs and darkness, just waiting for us to be stupid enough to come in after it. Like it could think. Like it knew we had to go this way or risk a serious detour. There were other spiders back in the shadows behind it. Chattering and howling at one another. Strange, almost dog-like baying came from them, and then whispering chitters that bothered you on levels somewhere deep inside your brain.

*Imagine*, the darker parts of my mind mused. *Imagine getting trapped by them with no place to run.* That, as far as I was concerned, was a terrible way to go.

"They're smart. Could be pinning us down here if they're hunters," suggested Sergeant Thor as Kurtz assessed the situation tactically and tried to figure our next move, checking his cheap watch in the gloom. There was no clear way around them. The other passages we'd gone by all seemed to lead down into the depths. Which was definitely not the right way to go for what needed to be done in a few short hours.

It was close to midnight now. We had less than six hours to be in place before the attack at dawn began. Kurtz was right. The clock wasn't just burning. It was on fire.

"No idea how much ammo we'd burn just to get through," muttered Kurtz to himself. "And we can't afford nothin'."

Tanner kept his rifle trained on the big waiting spider inside the webs, challenging us, while Brumm watched our six with the two-four-nine. If fighting through was a no-go, it was looking like we'd have to backtrack to the last intersection, take a passage down into the darker lower levels we'd only glimpsed and not liked the sight of, and then see if somehow we could find some set of stairs going up and getting us where we needed to be.

PFC Kennedy inched along the narrow passage to come up with Kurtz. Pushing past the snipers and Autumn. Past Rico and Soprano with the two-forty. Kennedy held his gnarled old dragon-headed staff just like Vandahar had held his. Not just something to walk with. But some kind of arcane badge of office for wizards.

"Sar'nt…" whispered Kennedy. "Feel that breeze?"

Kurtz pulled off a tactical glove and held up one bare hand. He turned to look at Kennedy.

"Yeah?"

"If there's access to more air down here… then maybe I can burn 'em out of there and not suffocate us?"

It was phrased as a question. PFC Kennedy wasn't one to tell Kurtz what we were gonna do, or what a better plan might be. Best to let Kurtz make the call. Kennedy was getting wiser. I had a feeling some of his early troubles in the batt had been due to him assuming he was smarter than everyone else. Or it coming off that way.

Kurtz looked back toward the spider hold, thinking over PFC Kennedy's intentions. The giant thing lurking within eyed us like a hungry killer with all the time in the world to sit there and wait for its next meal. Time was a luxury we didn't have. And of course Kurtz was no doubt thinking about what Thor had just suggested—that we were being pinned down. Surrounded. Chances were the spiders had other ways of getting out of the room they owned and nested in. Even now they could be coming up from behind us, or out of some crack in the dark of the ceiling we'd missed. This was their world, and we were just guests.

"Not a full-on nape-strike like you did the giant with," warned Sergeant Kurtz, studying the ceiling above and testing that breath of air once more. "Just burn 'em out of there, or drive 'em off so we can get by."

PFC Kennedy nodded.

"Roger that, Sar'nt."

We pulled back toward a place where there was more space and air in the passage, and Kennedy went forward with Kurtz on his six. A few minutes later we smelled roasting spider.

It did not smell good.

Kennedy's torch-staff flogged the giant gross spiders with a whip of streaming flame. Webs caught and were consumed instantly. Later Kennedy told me that, once the spiders began to shriek, which was really disturbing, and backed off, he shot them with what he called *magic missiles*. Tiny comets of fire that erupted from his hands and fingertips—not the staff—and then side-windered into the hulking fear-struck arachnids he was roasting alive.

The old wizard had taught him that trick. Kennedy cackled when he told me that part. Snorting as he pushed his BCGs up onto his nose. Like some kid burning ants with a magnifying glass and reliving the lurid horror for his amusement.

But I try not to judge.

The spiders exploded in noxious gassy farts when the missiles hit. The smell was horrifying, and their poison, as it vaporized, made Kurtz's and Kennedy's eyes and throats burn because they were so close. They pulled back, and while we all waited for the nest to finish burning, the sergeant insisted they both get hit with atropine injections to counteract any side effects.

Eyes red and watering, Kurtz then led us into the blackened remains of the old throne room. The burnt husks of spiders, hairy legs upturned, charred and blackened, lay dead in a corner of the room where they had huddled to get away from the flames and nurse their injuries. The bodies of humanoid creatures also lay blackened everywhere. Perhaps these had been stored within the webs? Victims the spiders had dragged into their lair for later meals in times past.

"This tells us," said Sergeant Thor, down on one knee and studying the desiccated and burnt corpse of what was most likely an orc with a fanged overbite, "that we're headed in the right direction."

"How's that?" hissed Kurtz in the silence as we all stood there studying the damage and horror. His voice ragged from the burning poison he and Kennedy had gotten unhealthy doses of.

Not like mere poison would ever stop Kurtz.

"These orcs probably came down from the fortress above looking for treasure," said Sergeant Thor. He pulled a leg off of one of the larger still-smoking spider carcasses. It reminded me of a time when I'd eaten one of those Alaskan King Crabs. Far less appetizing, being what it was, though. "Adventuring. Ain't that what you do in your games, Kennedy? Go looking for treasure down in dungeons. That's the dungeon part of the game, right? You call it an adventure, don'tcha?"

"Right, Sar'nt," said Kennedy reluctantly. "You go on an adventure. That's what we call it."

"So yeah," continued Thor. "Why couldn't monsters do the same thing? Go on adventures. They want stuff. These guys just did a little off-duty trophy hunting when not watching the fortress walls. Or they got sent down here, maybe. Either way, this tells us we're on the right track. If they got here and got caught by these things, then we're heading in the right direction. That's what we're on, Rangers... an adventure."

Silence as we all just listened to Thor. He was right. It was a horrible place. But we were on an adventure.

*Wheeee*, I thought to myself. *What an adventure. Not what I signed up for.* And... *I bet coffee isn't a treasure we'll find down here.*

So there's me being selfish and all.

"Time to move," said Kurtz, and then we were on our way out of the room and through a maze of underground halls stretching off in every direction and into... a vast area devoid of anything. A cavern, like a giant bare and empty cistern filled with a strange green mist that was always distant. Buttresses reached up to support the ceiling high above. We'd entered through a hatch that had been torn off and cast aside long ago.

"This place is probably like a reservoir," said one of the snipers as we wandered and investigated it. "They could fill it up with water in times of siege if they had to. Or just to protect the tombs below."

No one dissented from the hypothesis.

We searched the whole space until we found rungs in the wall leading up to a trap door in the ceiling far above.

"Looks dangerous," said Tanner as we all sat there staring upward. "Glad I didn't go to the assault climber course."

The Rangers still had their heads on a swivel. We all did. The entire place so far was incredibly creepy. But as far as we could tell there was no other way out of this reservoir. If that was what it was. And straight up... well, that was the way we wanted to go.

"I'll go up top," said Private Soprano. The assistant gunner. He had been to the course and was an assault climber. "*Sergente?*"

Kurtz studied him. Soprano was the smallest and probably the most agile. Other than Jabba.

Kurtz okayed the plan, and Soprano shucked his extra ammo for the two-forty and gave it to me. He made ready to try the rungs, checking his gear and making sure his pistol was secured in the holster and his carbine was well placed and slung across his back. Barrel up. The rest of the

Rangers formed a perimeter to make sure we didn't get suddenly ambushed at any moment.

By ghosts.

The air felt tense down here. It was that kind of graveyard place where you know you shouldn't be. Anything bad could happen at any moment. But hey, that's the optimist in me talking. There was a breeze coming from somewhere, and despite spending over two hours searching the reservoir for a way out, we never did find the source of that dusty and foul air. Rotten, like it was coming from someplace down below instead of from above where we needed to go.

"You sure we're on the right path?" Tanner asked Sergeant Thor. But the big sniper didn't reply and only continued to watch the misty green darkness all around us. Waiting for those unquiet ghosts. Sure that by rifle or tomahawk, he'd get it done.

"Clock's burnin'," said Kurtz again as Private Soprano got ready to climb. Re-lacing his boots once again. "Now get up to that door, Ranger. When you're at the top drop a green ChemLight if it's all clear and we'll start our ascent. Drop a red one if for some reason the way is blocked or we can't assault up through there. Got it?"

Soprano nodded and turned to checking his gear one last time, whispering loudly to me as he finished.

"Hey. Know why I joined the Rangers, *mi amico*?" The son of Italian-immigrants-turned-Ranger's voice was rusty and he was breathing fast. I think he was nervous. And he should be. It was a pretty far climb up to the ceiling to reach the trap door, and if he fell from up there, it would be either death, worst case, or best case, pretty serious injury. And our situation, down here in the dark and crawling around a dusty old tomb full of otherworldly dead, wasn't the best for someone who was going to need a trauma team and an osteopath.

"I joined because *mia famiglia*... see, Talker, we are in... ah... how to put it... we're in the *family business*. Back in Sicilia."

Ah. I suddenly realized we were doing an info dump. The last will and testament the Rangers had been all about lately. I put on my listening face. But I prefaced that by saying, "You ain't gonna fall, Soprano. Don't think about it."

Because *I* sure wouldn't, I didn't add. When my turn came, if it did. Falling sucks. Physics don't care how bad you might get hurt. It's just math.

But I said it like I knew for sure he wouldn't. I didn't know that, of course. Still, it pays to think positively in dire circumstances down in deep tombs you never thought you'd find yourself in.

Now he started looping around his body all the climbing gear he could carry up. Rope. D-clips. 550 cord. All of it. The Rangers were always ready to climb. That was just second nature.

"I joined," he said breathily. His voice rasping in the hushed darkness. "Because my family is part of La Cosa Nostra. Not a big part. Kinda small, in fact. But, you know... back in Sicily we have some very nice action. But... ah... you see, *mi amico*, we need to expand. My uncles, who are the real bosses, well, it's like dis... they thought it would be nice if our family hadda some more skills. Violence. Combat. Ambush. That could go a real long way back home. We ain't so good at that right now. So... Uncle Andrea, he sees *Black Hawk Down*. The movie, y'know?"

Yeah. I'd seen that one.

"And he says to my old man one day, 'Let's-a send Giacomo to America and he learna ta be da Army Ranger. Then he come-a back and teacha us how to do the killing. Those guys are real tough.'"

Makes sense, I thought.

"Of course my old man was never in the mob. Came to America to escape it. Used to be a *carabinieri* in town. Ran the desk at the local precinct. He had dreams of me singin' opera. So he says to me… 'we come to America, Giacomo, and you learna to sing opera like-a Pavarotti. Okay? Then you never have to join the family business,' and he means La Cosa Nostra because if I'm a big opera singer and I ever come-a back to Sicily I get a pass. Only real way outta the family is to either be a priest or singa the opera. *Sì?*"

He looked up at me and smiled. Satisfied his gear was good to go.

"You can hear how I sound, Talker. I'm ain't a good singer, either. But truth is, I kind of *wanted* to join the family business. My Uncle is watching Blackhawk Down and having dreams, well, I'm watching Goodfellas and doin' the same thing. Nice suits. Good cars. Lotsa pretty girls. Travel. So I join the Army. Become a Ranger. I learn how to do all the stuff that's gonna put us on the map back home in Sicily. The family, that is."

Soprano pauses to fiddle with his gear. "That's why I'm doing this, Talker. I wanted go to Ranger School then go back and teach everyone how we can put those Scagliotti in their place. They're a rival family. Always gave us Sopranos a hard time. So… you know how it is."

He spits and then adds, "I can see the look on your face and you think I'm crazy. Put it down in the *registrare*, anyway, okay?"

The record.

I said that I would.

It didn't seem to occur to Soprano that the Scagliotti-Camilieri rivalry had probably wrapped up about ten thousand years ago. And for that matter so had the last cycle of Ranger School.

But why ruin a dream?

Kurtz was waiting at the bottom of the ancient rungs.

"This is gonna make-you recommend me for promotion, right, *Sergente* Kurtz?" asked Soprano as he pulled on the first rung in the wall. Testing it.

Sergeant Kurtz gave me a rare conspiratorial look and rolled his eyes behind Soprano's back.

"Yeah," he muttered. "Sure thing, Soprano."

The little man was about a quarter of the way up the rungs climbing toward the ceiling of the cistern, or whatever this place was, when Tanner whispered to me in the dark. "You know if he was in a regular line unit he'd'a been the guy fillin' out 4187s for Ranger School in the S-1 every month."

The rest of the climb wasn't hard for PFC Soprano. He moved like a monkey and when there were missing rungs, he had himself up to the next one based on sheer arm strength alone. Pulling himself upward. Impressive considering the amount of gear he was carrying.

He was way high up now, had to be at least five stories, when he made it underneath the trap door. We watched as he pulled a knife, reversed it, and tapped on the bottom of the lid.

The soft sound we heard far below had an odd quality to it. Later I'd put two and two together, but at that moment as the little Ranger hung beneath the trap door, balanced on rungs that had been set in the walls who knew how many thousands of years ago, the analysis of the sound wasn't the first thing on my mind.

"It's locked or something," Tanner suggested. Tanner had great eyes. "Now I think he's picking the lock."

"Where'd he get a lockpicking kit?" asked Kurtz.

If anyone would've asked, I had one. But that was supposed to be a secret. I had a pretty good idea where Soprano had gotten his though. Probably in a care package from back in Sicily. If his career track was leading toward the family business, well, I'd read a few Mediterranean Noir crime novels just to get a feel for French and Italian when I was studying them. Jean Claude Izzo was outstanding. Too bad he only wrote three crime novels before he died. But I was betting the lockpicking kit was courtesy of some Uncle Vito, or something similar.

*You be a good boy and come-a back after you learna everything the Rangers know. Black Hawk Down, mi bambino and all.*

Later I'd learn that most Rangers were skilled in lockpicking and hotwiring vehicles in accordance with the airfield capture missions. Soprano picked the lock in about thirty seconds. Five stories up, loaded with gear, and balanced on a couple of narrow rungs. No mean feat, to say the least.

"Got it!" he shout-whispered down below to the rest of us.

Kurtz shushed him.

Soprano slapped his forehead. Comically of course. Then a thick finger to his lips. But when he spoke again, it was in that same loud comic-whisper.

"*Sergente!*" he gestured for us to back away from below. "Sumting's not right about-a this door. Make-a space, *si prega?*"

*Please.*

We backed away and then he undid the bottom of the trap door.

Anyone else up there, and they would have died in what happened next. I was completely convinced of that as a sudden rockslide came pouring out of the trap door. And anyone up there except Soprano... and a bunch of us down below would be dead now too. Crushed by the falling rock that gushed out and onto the floor below where we'd been standing.

When the dust cleared, I fully expected to see Soprano's broken body lying among the rockfall. I didn't. Instead he was hanging by one hand from the ceiling above. He'd found, or made, some place to hang on in order to avoid falling to his sure death below.

We'd been warned. This place was filled with traps.

He swung into the trap door and climbed up, disappearing into the dark rectangle above. Two minutes later, a rope came down, dropping onto the floor. Then a green ChemLight tumbled down to us and Kurtz caught it with one gloved hand.

It was time for us to go up.

# CHAPTER FIFTY-EIGHT

ONCE the entire team was up and through the trap door in the ceiling of the cistern, which took a while, it was heading on toward 0300 in the morning. All of us were starting to feel the time crunch. If we didn't make our over-watch position to support the assault on the main gate, that attack was "going pear-shaped," in Tanner's words. The Rangers under Captain Knife Hand didn't have the ammo or manpower to push through. But that wouldn't stop them from trying.

The question was... how many more traps and enemies did we have to face down here?

The answer on the other side of the trap door in the ceiling was almost immediate. One by one, we came up the rope and hauled our gear up. I was one of the last because I'm not that important right now. Let's face it, no one is interested in starting up a dialogue on relations with anything creepy or crawly we're going to find down here. At least I was ahead of the Lost Boys in the pecking order.

As soon as I was through, I saw why the Rangers who'd gone before me were urging quiet and stealth as much as possible on the other side of the high trap door.

We had found the central well. The one spoken of by the Old Mother. The express elevator to the penthouse suite.

Or at least, we stood to one side of it. We were in a long hall that ran along one edge of the well, continuing as far as we could see with our enhanced vision. Less a hall and more a gallery. Like some sacred space of prayer one might find in an old monastery. Or some once-princely castle that had fallen into despair and ruin. Now bare and spartan, cloaked in shadow and gloom. Haunted and forgotten.

The inner side of the hall opened directly onto the well. The vast and massive well. A virtual canyon of underground dead space. But not round. More like an inverted pyramid of emptiness sunk underground. And across that canyon we could see more halls or galleries over there, layered one on the next like some enormous belowground cityscape. Some sections had caved in and crashed down onto others within the crawling necropolis, revealing the insides of tombs over there. Far away and forever out of reach. And far above, maybe six or seven stories up, loomed the dome described by the Old Mother. It was covered in paintings, like the Sistine Chapel or the Hagia Sophia. But the darkness was such that I, at least, couldn't make out any details up there, even with the Hunters' Fellowship.

It was all utterly fantastic, and bizarrely mesmerizing.

But none of this was the reason for our quiet and stealth. What had us cautious were the torches in the upper levels moving around the visible sides of the well. Many of them. Moving in masses. And it was here that the Moon Vision of the Hunters' Fellowship came in handy. It focused on the light sources bobbing up and down among the upper levels, focused and zoomed in, using those torches as anchor points.

Orcs. And lots of them.

Far too many of them for us to fight.

Kurtz was on that immediately.

He swore first. Then, "We cannot get into a fight down here. Clock's burnin' and we gotta make our time hack." He looked around at everyone, making sure we were reading him clearly. "We're gonna creep our way through as far as we can. We engage as a last resort. Repeat... only on a hard compromise situation."

He looked at me.

"You. You got that... ring thing. Turns you invisible and all. Right?"

I nodded.

"You comfortable using it?"

I said I was.

He nodded. Then made our plan. We were going to move up, following this gallery we were in. If it was like the ones we could see on the other side, we'd have opportunities to climb up to higher levels via stairs and long sloping ramps. And there would be tombs to hide in set within the walls of the sides of the inverted pyramid that was the well. Maybe, if the enemy had managed to get down into these levels, then maybe a lot of the tombs' nastier denizens had already been dealt with. Maybe.

In essence, Sergeant Kurtz was proposing a creep right through their lines and up into the library tower itself. Tanner would stay on point and I would follow close behind. If needed, I'd activate the ring while the team hid, and it would be up to me to find a route through the orc patrols ahead.

That made perfect sense if you just *said* it. Doing it sounded crazy. At least it did to me.

It was clear, as we studied the orcs, that they were looking for something up there above us in the top levels of the tomb.

"Mighta heard gunfire below," suggested Brumm, and then spat dip.

We started out.

The first hour was solid. We made good time as we passed the gloomy remains of tombs set in the walls. Skulls and carved runes adorned these places like warnings not to enter them on penalty of death. Or sometimes we made our way through rooms full of ancient weapons and chests like dusty old soldiers standing at attention. Kennedy pointed out that there was probably treasure in those chests if it was anything like the game.

"Probably traps too," someone muttered. "I thought wizards were supposed to be smart."

"You mean high on I-N-T," Kennedy responded. *Intelligence.* "Anyway if I'm the wizard... then Soprano's the thief."

"I'm no thief," Soprano protested from under his load of ammo for the two-forty. "Ain't never been caught stealin' nothin'."

"The thief," explained Kennedy patiently, "detects traps and disarms them. Like you did with the trap door."

Soprano nodded at this, then agreed. "Then I'm the thief. Okay. *Bene.*"

We bypassed our first swarm of orcs easily.

You could smell them from a long way off because they reeked. Real ripe. We faded into the ruins of a smaller tomb whose door had been pried open at some point in the past in order that it could be thoroughly looted. The Rangers stacked inside the tight tomb, weapons ready to do murder.

"If just one comes to investigate," whispered Kurtz as they approached, "I'll pull it inside and do it. Keep silent until I give the order to engage."

Kurtz had his garrote out. Brumm was ready to support with a folding seven-inch karambit knife that he was holding ready near the door to the tomb's darkness. His other gloved hand was free, ready to control Kurtz's would-be victim once the strangling began.

But the orcs passed without incident. There had to be at least thirty of them in that troop. We waited, checked the route forward, and then continued on our route up through the levels.

The next dodge happened midway up a set of titanic stairs. We were nearing the uppermost levels and the dome above. Now that we were getting close, the torches the orcs had left burning and our augmented vision showed me more of the fantastic dome above and the images that had been left to adorn its surface.

Twelve grim figures were featured. They looked less like time-lost special operators and more like Ringwraiths straight from the Lord of the Rings movies. They wore shadowy armor and dark cloaks. Their faces were lightless voids that felt wrong to look at. The only thing you could see in them, those voids now that you got close, were burning red eyes that stared down into the vast well below. At first I thought the red eyes must've been a fantastically vibrant pigment of paint used long ago with some technique that gave the glaring eyes a menacing, dismissive contempt for the viewer. But as my enhanced vision zoomed in, I could see that they were no mere tricks of paint and lighting. They were fantastically huge gems. Set in the dome sculpted above. Bigger than anything I'd ever seen before. And probably worth an untold fortune.

"Look at those," Tanner said halfway up the dusty gray stairs we were climbing along the edge of the well. We were near a fabulous giant bowl that was set in the railing and must have once served as some immense brazier to light the way for funerary processions bringing more heroes down into the dark of the tomb to sleep forever.

But somehow, even as I thought that, my mind told me that wasn't right. That wasn't what this place was.

There were no heroes down here.

This wasn't that kind of place.

*This is where*, some voice in my mind whispered, *evil goes to wait for its next chance.*

Chance at what? I wondered.

I was sure I didn't want to know the answer.

And then we heard the orcs coming toward the top of the stairs just above. Singing their marching songs. Yeah. I didn't mention that part, but the orcs had a kind of cadence of grunting and shouting and some words they sang as they moved. It was low, and harsh, and ominous.

The closest I can come to comparing it to something is that it was kind of like a demonic mumble rap. The orc troopers making the baseline *thumps* and *thuds* and other noises while one caller, their marching sergeant, did a kind of spoken-word poetry of violence, mayhem, and murder. Or at least that seemed to be the gist from the few words I could catch in Turkic and Arabic.

But like I said this orc swarm was coming straight at us from the top of the stairs, and there was no place the main body of our team could get to for a fade before the enemy topped the stairs, looked down, and saw a bunch of Rangers with murder in their hearts.

My mind saw an immediate firefight. Soprano and Rico were already down on the steps setting up the two-forty. Thor had his sniper rifle leveled on the big cold brazier. The other snipers were slinking into the shadows and getting ready to fire. Brumm was farther down with the SAW covering our backtrail.

But it would be loud, and there were at least ten other mobs of orcs all across the levels below and above us. There was no getting around that, or what would happen once we revealed our presence, and stealth was no longer an option.

We'd be surrounded and out of ammo in pretty short order. We would not reach our support position. The attack would fail.

I slipped the ring on. I'd had it ready. I ran by Tanner and said, "Keep down!" as I picked up a clay funeral urn.

I haven't mentioned that either. But there are ancient and dusty urns of all shapes and sizes everywhere, on every level. There's so many of them you don't see them after a while. And where there aren't urns there are grotesque candle holders that verge on the obscene. Scenes of rape and pillage. Twisting demons and snakes. Dragons. So I grabbed one medium-sized urn and ran to the top of the steps as fast as I could. Straight at the marching orcs who were about to spot us. One-handed, I chucked the urn off into the darkness to the left. Into a dark vaulted hall that intersected our own. I was almost on top of the lead orcs as I did it. I was face to face with a platoon of wild-eyed and snarling orcs who couldn't see me. Or so I hoped. Fangs. Darkly glittering malevolent eyes. Weapons. Spears. Short swords. Axes. Armor made of leather. Spikes. Scars and strange white tattoos. Horrific bad breath.

The urn crashed in the darkness of the hall off to our left. My left. Their right. And they stopped. Their war leader gave some shout. Instantly the orcs were spreading out, weapons ready to do instant violence.

"I'm here," whispered Autumn in my mind. She had come up to just below the level of the top stair. Almost invisible in her cloak and hidden behind a statue of a snarling minotaur with a giant battle axe at the top of the stairs. Golden coins and dead candles lay all around the base of the statue.

"I'll trick them now," she whispered.

I could hear her voice, and the voices of others, other Shadow Elves sounding like the Lost Boys, far off to the left and down that dark and shadowy hall filled with silent tombs. A moment later arrows came whistling out of the darkness and whipped past orcish heads. The orcs snarled and roared at the attack, bellowing war cries and pounding their thick chests.

Their war captain called out, "*Eifrit!*"

Which in Arabic is a diminutive form of a genie. *Efreeti.*

"It is their word for us," Autumn whispered in my mind. "It means little demons."

I watched as now the orcs, convinced elves were attacking from their right, organized loosely and charged the dark hall, shouting battle cries and giving war whoops. Their trumpeters blaring out *Uroo Uroo* to sound the alarm and call to battle across the great necropolis that was this tomb.

All around us other horns answered the urgent call. They were coming. The orc hordes were coming. But for the moment, the orcs who'd almost discovered us were off chasing rabbits. Shadow Elf rabbits. Which meant we had a moment to move forward and get ahead of what was about to happen.

Just a moment…

"It's clear," I told Tanner breathlessly, feeling my heart hammer in my chest as fear or adrenaline coursed through my body. "Have to move now."

Hand signals, and the team was up and moving. Hustling forward and interfacing with Kurtz for a bare-bones sitrep. Just a few more levels and we'd reach the dome. If we got lucky. And according to the Old Mother, the fortress was just above that dome.

We were close.

# CHAPTER FIFTY-NINE

WE were even closer when the shooting started.

"Use your secondaries!" shouted Kurtz as we breached the final level beneath the sprawling dome. We'd just ascended a line of twisting stairs that took us up through the last levels of the well, areas that seemed to be set aside for storage and construction. Lots of skulls, mummies, tools, and dead candles. The place reeked of something unholy.

And believe me, I'm usually a rational person of science. But some things are just *wrong*. And this whole place felt like one big that.

Somewhere, far down below, in some system of hidden rooms, secret tunnels, or unfound halls we'd never gotten close to accessing, lay the final resting places of the *Ilner*. The operators. But that discovery would have to wait for another day. Right now, we were in a running firefight and trying to make our way out and up into the tower in order to make our hit time.

The clock wasn't burning. It had burnt. Kurtz was no longer reminding us of that. He was just a desperate man doing his best to get us where we needed to be. His Rangers needed Team Rogue to be where it needed to be when the attack went down. And we weren't.

That was unacceptable. This was as close to mission failure as one of Kurtz's elements had ever been. The only positive was that at this point we were keeping the enemy tied up with us, which meant keeping at least some of them off the main gate.

The snipers were engaging teams of orcs trying to push us from the rear as the firefight made its way through the upper catacombs. Incoming crow-feathered arrows streaked through the shadows and firelight to land among us, striking walls and gear. Sergeant Thor had been hit, but it wasn't bad. Or so he said. Kurtz, Tanner, and Brumm were clearing the path forward. We'd hit dead ends twice and had barely gotten out of there as the enemy tried to close its forces about our necks like a noose you didn't want to get caught in.

It wasn't the dark and deep that made you feel claustrophobia's creep. It was the enemy. And for some reason that made you angry. Like all you wanted was a clear path to kill your way through and breathe some fresh air if there was any left in this ruined old world we ended up in.

At the last dead end we almost became just that. Dead. Suddenly going hand-to-hand as a group of orcs dressed in gray rags, probably six of them, came with knives from out of a secret door we hadn't spotted there in the nowhere-to-go space.

That was a common thing in Kennedy's games, according to the wizardly PFC. Secret doors. They were hidden and you could find them.

Kurtz and company were down to last mags. We'd need those for the fight in the fortress to keep the perimeter clear for the snipers to work once the attack started. So suddenly the Rangers and I were hacking at the orcs who'd come out of the secret door with our newly acquired "weapons of renown" we'd taken off the floor of the crypt far below. The crypt full of the wights who'd once been Ice Kings in the long-ago Ages of Forgotten Ruin.

Last of Autumn had told us the weapons were of Dragon Elf make. Shining and beautiful, broad, curved, leaf-shaped blades. They were light to handle, incredibly sharp, and hit with more force than they should have. That was the magic, apparently.

We'd just eluded a team of orcs following us up the last set of stairs and had come down this dark hall only to find a sudden torchlit dead end. I noticed our weapons beginning to glow with a soft blue cold light. The Dragon Elf weapons.

"Orcs!" shouted Last of Autumn in the little English she'd managed to pick up. Except it sounded like "Oaks!"

"Here they come," shouted Brumm. "We makin' a last stand here, Sar'nt." He was talking about the orcs to our rear, the ones who'd tracked us and followed us down this dead end.

Rico and Soprano wanted to use the two-forty to clear our way back to the stairs. But Sergeant Kurtz was trying to save the last two drums we had for the defense of the tower above. With the death machine that was a two-forty working inside the inner courtyard of the castle, we could keep the tower clear and work over the defenders forward of our position. Burning ammo now meant the snipers had to do all the work while the tower was vulnerable to counterattack. And that could get real messy.

It was a question of asset management. How best to employ combat assets given the current tactical situation.

That was when a seam in the rune-covered wall, those strange Egyptian hieroglyphics that were everywhere, just opened up, and out slipped these orc ninjas, because that's what I'll call them.

Orc ninjas.

They wore flowing dirty grey rags, even over their faces. All that could be seen were their glowering eyes and fangs. They moved silently, barefooted, and came swinging at us all at once. It was clearly a suicide attack. One of them whispered loud enough that I could hear and translate.

Effectively he said to his brother attackers, "My life for the Nether." And they all whispered back a reply in orc that I didn't understand.

Kurtz got his MK18 up and blocked a slash from the leader just in time. Then he kicked the thing in its balls, and apparently orcs had them because it went down groaning like a giant with severe intestinal distress. Kurtz fell back two steps, pulled the Dragon Elf blade he'd commandeered from out of his carrier where he'd stuck it, and jammed it right through the chest of the next fierce orc that decided to attack him. It was like the orc just impaled itself on Kurtz's new sword, it went in so smooth and effortlessly. The stunned orc gasped and died, and Kurtz pulled his blade back out just as easily.

The rest of the orcs came at the rest of us. Tanner fired once and drilled one right in the head, then shifted and fired again, nailing another right between its beady little eyes.

His shooting, like everyone else's, was on point. A polish of Hunters' Fellowship had been added to the skills honed in Chief Rapp's gunfighter school, resulting in some weird Matrix-level shooting even the Rangers were frankly amazed at.

"Hope it sticks," Tanner remarked.

"No luck. All skill. But don't jinx it," Brumm muttered.

Now we were fighting. Including the Lost Boys with their bows. And I was in it whether I liked it or not. I'd decided not to shoot unless I had to so I could redistribute my mags to the real killers if needed. Have I mentioned I just came along on this ride to do languages? I think I'd carried my weight. So, I already had the interesting little elven dagger out and ready to contribute in order to spare ammo. Again, not thinking I'd actually need to use it. The blade wasn't long. More on the order of a Roman gladius. And like I said, it felt light but when you swung it, it got heavier with increased momentum over the arc of the swing, or strike. Some kind of relativistic effect that counted as magic here in the Ruin.

I was near the dead end when the whispering orcs came for us out of secret door with their wicked daggers. Without thinking, I slashed the first one that got close to me and took off the side of its scalp just like that, cutting into brain and bone and then thin air.

That doesn't happen with regular knives and blades. Those have a tendency to bounce or just stick in cuts that deep.

But these were magic weapons.

The six orcs were dealt with in seconds, Kurtz getting two, Tanner two, me one, and I think Soprano shot one with his rifle. A couple had Lost Boy arrows in them, too. It all happened pretty quickly. And violently.

"These bad!" shouted Jabba as he cowered behind his ruck. This was his usual position when there was a fight going on. "Dark slayers. Not good. Not good." The little goblin shouted in his pidgin Ranger English and Turkic when he didn't have the right word. Jumping around and pointing as he did. "These from the Land of Nothing."

He said that last part in Arabic.

"What's he saying?" shouted Kurtz as more orcs came at us from the rear. The sergeant was looking to me for any kind of intel as to why the little gob was freaking out. But *Land of Nothing* had no context, sounded crazy, and didn't contribute to the immediate threat. So I went with, "He says we're in trouble."

"No shit, Talker." Kurtz then shouted at Thor. "Clear us a way back to the stairs. We gotta backtrack our way out of here."

Two snipers had died on the way in. One from a… curse. The other from a fall. That left four. What happened next was amazing because as I turned away from the bloody remains of the orcs we'd just hacked to death, adrenaline surging through my body and making me feel like I was going to have a heart attack, fall into a pit I'd never get out of, or win some incredible prize, still hard to tell which, I could see dozens of orcs running down the dark, column-lined hall that had led us to the dead end.

"Copy that!" roared Thor. "Snipers, *Kill First, Die Last*. Move and cover."

The snipers had already been covering our six, two on each side of the corridor with Brumm anchoring from the left. Now Thor had them firing and moving in teams up the columns and right into the face of the enemy, covering and rapid-firing precise shots with their big rifles into the oncoming orcs. They weren't gonna burn ammo staying and getting pinned down. Each round would buy a few more meters to reach the stairs we needed to get back to.

No, it wasn't an ideal situation for snipers. They did not like to get cornered. But when they did, they went full honey badger.

The snipers didn't just hold the corridor, they moved up, shooting as they went. Covering and reloading while the sniper to their rear stepped in and started sending rounds through the next wave of orcs. Big rifle rounds that ruined snarling orcs at near point-blank range and continued on to wreck the next beast in line. Smashed twisted faces and lumpy skulls exploded while other rounds landed center mass in smelly bulky bodies and sent them twisting away, only to be replaced by another even more vicious fiend with a gutful of nasty intentions.

Thor was running his team when Kurtz shouted, "Stairs ahead. Bravo. Use your secondaries!" That meant for us to let our low-ammo rifles hang by their slings and move to our sidearms to clear our way up and out. Which everyone had a lot of ammunition for. The truth was you rarely ever used your pistol.

"Except for going to the chow hall when you're in the sandbox," Tanner remarked later.

Or wasting Deep State noncontributors, I didn't add.

Ahead of us, the snipers moved into position on the body-littered stairs looking out over the vast space of the tomb well. They would pivot left and control our rear while the assaulters, myself, Kennedy, Autumn, Jabba and the Lost Boys hustled up to the next level, still looking for a way out of this madhouse.

Bad news. There were a ton of orcs coming up the stairs from every level below us.

"We're gonna get pushed from behind, Sar'nt, when we take the tower!" shouted Brumm as he covered the snipers who were now pulling back.

"Heads down!" shouted Kennedy, and sent a volley of magic missiles into a group of orcs firing more arrows at the snipers. The shooting stars streaked away with all kinds of light show pyrotechnics before ravaging those orcs, exploding them and setting fires down there.

Autumn turned and fired three fast arrows, nailing one of the bigger war leaders rallying his troops below for a big push against our rear. One arrow through his eye. Two stuck and quivering in his chest. The lesser orcs around him bellowed in rage and gnashed their teeth up at us.

Confusion reigned, and that bought us a few minutes. We were killing our way out of there, but we were definitely in trouble.

And then Kurtz made the top of the stairs and shouted, "I see daylight! This is the way!"

I felt myself wanting to run faster for the exit. We'd gained the top of the stairs and Kurtz was back, pushing the snipers into the final chamber ahead of us. I was in there a couple of seconds later and there were indeed wide stairs leading sharply up into what looked like very early morning light.

We'd made it.

The snipers went past us, getting quickly organized to take position in the tower above this basement. Kurtz was on the comm and trying to raise Captain Knife Hand. Our watches said we were late to the party. But just.

"No comm with Intruder!" shouted Kurtz.

"I can hear gunfire!" one of the snipers shouted from the bottom of the stairs. They were stacked there and waiting for the order to take the tower above once the weapons sergeant was satisfied with the situation.

"Now's our turn, *Sergente*," announced Soprano, almost excited to get the two-forty ready. They would set up on the ground floor while the snipers went higher into the ruined upper levels.

"Get a visual on the courtyard!" ordered Kurtz, and one of the snipers went off to take a peek. By the time he got back, the *Uroo Uroo* horns were sounding while ominous drums got walloped from down below where we'd just come. Over that, I could now hear the sound of distant gunfire from up in the fortress.

The attack was underway.

"Can't tell what's going on," said the sniper when he got back from the scout, "but it looks like they're moving against the secondary defenses and the defenders there are on the forward lines of defense. We get up there, it'll be a shooting gallery, Sar'nt."

Brumm spat from his position guarding the narrow hall to our rear that gave access to the stairs below. Where the horns and drums were getting louder. "They're comin', Sar'nt Kurtz."

The look in his eyes wasn't fear. But it was serious. And that was saying something for the SAW gunner who'd looked a charging giant in the eyes and fired a Carl G.

"How much you got, Brumm?" asked Kurtz.

Brumm tilted his weapon and studied it.

"Hunnert-fifty rounds, a grenade, my elf knife, and a half can of Copenhagen. I can hold 'em… Sergeant."

Kurtz made a face. A sick face. And then there was some look between them that passed, and I had no idea what it meant. But later, I would.

"Go, Sar'nt," said Brumm, nodding to his sergeant. "I got this. Switching to on."

Kurtz hesitated and then nodded back as he gave the order for Team Rogue to take the tower of the Lost Library and bring fire against the rear of the enemy. But not before unslinging his MK18 and leaving it with its last mag for Specialist Brumm. Leaning it against the wall. Then Team Rogue got the order to move.

We were in the game now.

Snipers. Autumn, her eyes fierce with revenge. Kennedy serene but breathing deeply through his nose like he was trying to draw in oxygen—or arcane power. Rico and Soprano, hustling workmanlike to get their beast into play now that the order had been given. Kurtz had already gone, and I could hear the sound of his Rampage slam-firing to clear someone unlucky enough to happen to be where the angry Rangers wanted to go next.

Kurtz had gone first. Because Rangers lead the way.

I pulled my remaining magazines. Two left. And handed them to Brumm.

"You want me to stay?" I asked.

Brumm shook his head. He was intently watching the hall he had been left to secure. Not ready to go for the high score like Thor might. That wasn't the look in his eyes. I could read that there. But because his brother Rangers needed him to hold the line down here where it was thin and most needed. And so the rest could save the others out there pinned down at the gatehouse and trying to move forward under fire and against overwhelming odds.

"Thanks, Talk," he croaked dryly at me. "Get up there now... help Kurtz. Gonna be crazy. Take care of him."

He took the mags and then I was gone.

Things looked bad from the moment I saw the whole battle going down just after dawn. Up there and underway with both sides doing their best to annihilate the other side. But now the Rangers were about to do what they did best. Which was to be exactly where you didn't want them to be.

# CHAPTER SIXTY

*Tyger Tyger, burning bright,*
*In the forests of the night;*
*What immortal hand or eye,*
*Could frame thy fearful symmetry?*

THINGS were a mess once I made it up out of the ruined tower basement and into the actual battle for the fortress. But apparently things were even worse for the Rangers pinned down at the gatehouse. Worse and getting worse by the second.

The Rangers could not move forward across the first courtyard and into the next line of defenses. Arrow fire from the Black Hawk Orc archers was finding its way into the gatehouse and keeping several Rangers stuck inside. The Black Hawks were excellent and relentless marksmen. Or marks-orcs. Vandahar had unleashed a powerful lightning bolt against the next gate in the second line, but some kind of magical warding had caused the bolt to reflect and dart off into the morning sky with a sudden thunderclap.

"Hmm," the indignant old hedge wizard was reported to have murmured as he hunkered with the assaulters under heavy incoming. "That doesn't bode well."

The assault teams were down to trying the Carl Gustaf and the last 84mm round the detachment was carrying. The sergeant major and his group were looking for an opening in the gatehouse to fire from where they wouldn't get nailed by the monkish archers King Triton was throwing against them.

And there was a problem with that last round itself. It was an FFV441 HE round. Or an airburst round used as anti-personnel munition. Fire it into a group of enemies, or their positions, just above their heads, and it exploded steel balls in every direction. It could be devastating against lightly armored personnel, but chances were, it wasn't going to do much against structures like the wall of the next line of defenses within the fortress where the Rangers needed to create a breach.

That was where Team Rogue was supposed to come in. We were supposed to be hitting the enemy defenses from behind and causing them to pull enough assets away from the main defenses to deal with us, thus allowing the assaulters at the front gate to start moving up through the lines of defense.

But, as I've said, we were late to the party.

The Rangers were pinned and doing their best just to avoid being turned into pincushions by incoming arrow fire. They were down to one mag for primaries and firing back when they could get a shot on the shadowy orc defenders. Wounded men were being dragged out from under fire, arrows embedded in their bodies where the ESAPI plates hadn't protected them, clinging to the hope that the poison they'd been warned about wasn't as bad as they'd heard. A few mags for their secondaries and then the found weapons they'd scoured from the battlefield back at Ranger Alamo was what was coming next.

"This is it, boys," the sergeant major was heard to say as he moved among the hunkering teams who were just moments from being given the order to assault across open ground and try to get under the next wall, scale it, and overcome the defenders regardless of a secondary attack that wasn't going off as planned. No diversion, follow the plan because that was all that was left. And of course heavy arrow fire was everywhere. Streaking in through the breaches and windows. Whistling into the furniture and architecture. Thudding and snapping on plate carriers. Sinking into flesh as Rangers swore and returned fire with their dwindling ammo.

Someone opened up with a half a pouch on their SAW, all they had left, and ruined a cluster of archers who'd gotten a good angle into the gatehouse and had already shot several Rangers.

"That'll learn 'em," the Ranger said, tossing aside the two-four-nine and pulling out his tomahawk. He was one of the true believers. And it seemed he'd been waiting for this moment all his life whether he'd known it or not.

It would be a massacre. Crossing open ground under fire. No two ways about it. But if they got against the wall on the other side of the open ground kill zone, then there were a few breaching charges left, and someone might get in.

"That Valhalla y'all are always on about is callin', Rangers," the sergeant major muttered as he moved from cover to cover inside the ruined gatehouse. Organizing who could go forward and who had too many arrows sticking out of 'em.

"One way or the other," finished the sergeant major. Now they were just waiting on the captain's final order to move.

Near the main assault point out of the gatehouse, the scouts and Captain Knife Hand's security team were set to go first and lead the charge across open ground. Sergeant Hardt chanced a glance at the commander and saw that his captain didn't look too good. One of the scouts told me later, "Hell, Talk. Looked like he was gonna be sick all over the place right there."

But no one thought that Knife Hand was looking horrible due to fear. That wasn't even considered. Everyone knew he'd been sick with some kind of bug none of the rest had picked up.

"We was all scared, Talk," continued the scout. "I'll admit that right here. Ain't no shame. But when you Ranger, you still do it and all whether the fear's there or it ain't. Ain't nothin' if the Knife Hand was scared. He'd still go even if he was. But he wasn't. He was just real sick. Like he had bad food poisoning or something. And now, at the worst possible time, he was real sick like he was just gonna die right there, Talk."

But that's not what happened.

Knife Hand was sick. He did look like he was going to hurl everywhere, and according to those close to him he was sweating like a pig and looked pale to the point of gray.

"He was mad and getting angrier by the second because everything was going wrong inside the gatehouse," said the scout. "His team sergeant had taken an arrow right in the throat. Man was down and probably dying but Chief was all bloody and trying to save the team leader. It was bad, Talker. Really bad in there.

"Then Captain says, just to himself like, 'I'm gonna be sick.' But it don't sound like him at all. It's like... I don't know. Like a growl and all. Like an animal that ain't so happy. I turned around to find the XO because he was probably gonna have to take us out across that kill zone where we were all gonna die in a few seconds, and when I look back at the captain, who'd stumbled off to find a corner to get sick in, I'm looking at a damn werewolf, Talker!

"'Cept it ain't no werewolf, man. It's like a... a were*tiger*. Like if a man suddenly became a tiger. Orange stripes, white fur. Tiger face. Big white fangs. But walking like a man with huge claws. And I swear he's comin' straight at me and he's got pure murder eyes like one of them big cats. So things just got worse and we're done. Then the captain just takes off running right straight through the breach regardless of the incoming, right where we were about to go through, moving faster than anything I've ever seen, and he's up on the wall of the next defenses in a bound or two. Moving like a cat and a man at the same time, using his claws to gain the top o' the defenses where the orcs are shooting from. He just goes straight up the wall like a cat. You ever seen 'em do it? I have. And guess what, the orcs, they're as surprised as I am and the rest of us, as suddenly the captain, and I know it's still him because there's shreds of his gear hanging off all over his new tiger body, is just ripping them to shreds like Wolverine in the X-Men. Claws and jaws and everything.

"He just goes Cro-Mag on them like some running back who cannot, I repeat cannot, be stopped. Not that I ever got one o' them on my fantasy team, mind. He's slashing their throats with these big-ass claws, bites a guy's head off. I mean an orc. And one time, right there in all that chaos as he's just ruining their defensive line, I seen him pick up two swords and just start running at some of the orcs and then straight through them up there like he's a spinning top. Except with two really sharp swords because there's blood spray and I tell you... he's takin' limbs off with one slice.

"Everybody's like... y'know, 'what the...' and that's when the sergeant major keys his mike and sends out, 'Net call, all elements, assault, assault, assault.'

"Then it was really on. Assault teams breached the next wall no problem because the orcs with bows and arrows are either trying to shoot the captain now, impossible, or save their asses by getting out of the way. So we had enough time to get over the wall and in among them. After that I lost sight of the captain 'cause we were fighting room to room, but I heard the orcs in other parts of the defended wall screaming for their lives.

"It was awesome, Talk. Barely heard their screams over the tiger roaring and growling, which, honestly, is just about the scariest thing I've ever heard in my whole life. Ain't like at the zoo when it's behind a cage. Ain't like that at all. When you're out there in the jungle with it, and there ain't no wire, Talker, it's real scary as real gets, man."

# CHAPTER SIXTY-ONE

ONCE I got out of the basement of the ruined tower that was the Lost Library, the snipers were already working over the orc archers and staged infantry within the fortress, and Sergeant Thor was working *Mjölnir*. Shooting steadily in a target-rich environment. The poor dumb savage orcs had no idea what was happening to them as their heads began to explode.

One of their war chiefs finally figured out what was going on and ordered a massed charge of the staged orc infantry, some force lying in reserve to support the forward defenses, against the Lost Library adjacent to the rising dark spike that was the formidable *Barad Nulla* itself. That charge ended badly when Rico and Soprano methodically cut down the entire element. It was a machine-gun team's dream engagement scenario. Organized groups with little to no maneuver space and almost no cover, giving the team the perfect chance to do search and traverse fire, maximizing the machine guns' capability. It was literally what machine guns are made for.

Kennedy fired a volley of magic missiles at orc archers attempting to target our snipers in the upper reaches of the Lost Library, which like the other "towers," Dark Spire excluded, was little more than a ruined shell open to the sun and sky. Those archers caught fire and burned, flaming and trailing black smoke as they fell from their perch. Kennedy moved to support Rico and Soprano on the ground level.

Another orc charge was coming now as *Uroo Uroo* horns bellowed out and orc captains rallied their lessers to the attack once more. Soprano and Rico were in the middle of a barrel change, having fired heavily to wipe out the first charge, and something went wrong as they did so, allowing a large group of orcs to make the edges and openings of the tower. Kurtz and Tanner were fighting from the entrance arch just to keep them back. Exchanging firing positions as they tried to hold the perimeter and give whatever malfunction had plagued the two-forty the time it needed to be corrected.

Tanner, dry on 5.56, pulled his secondary as a huge orc thundered through the opening. He red-misted the orc's skull instantly. The next two got the rest of the mag as Tanner backpedaled to get a new one in. Kurtz began slam-firing like a machine, ruining the orcs that dared to exploit the sudden opening. Shredding them with shotgun slugs.

Rico requested a position change on the two-forty to clear the attack, and Kurtz waved him off. I was there, with Tanner and Sergeant Kurtz. I burnt my last mag and transitioned to my pistol. Rico and Soprano fired short bursts at a group of orcs who were trying to come through the remains of the last wave that had been torn apart in the courtyard. And Last of Autumn and her younger brothers were with us, taking shots with their bows when they could. Getting kills every time. The courtyard out there was littered with dead bodies. Orc bodies.

The plan had been for me to slip on the ring and link up with the captain and the assaulters at the gate to coordinate the attack. But the enemy had basically just turned toward us en masse, either to fight us or flee through our defense. There was no way for me to get through, even invisible, to link up with the main element.

"Hold here," Kurtz shouted at me as the orcs charged again. "Main element can probably hear the snipers now anyway."

Looking out through a fracture in the ruined tower, I could see a fire had broken out in one of the towers closer to the main gate. Thick black smoke was belching up and into the morning sky.

That was when I spotted McCluskey.

The SEAL was in his black-rider-Ren-Faire-tragedian getup, dark cloak flying as he crossed from the last line of defenses and ran for the tower of *Barad Nulla*.

I'd almost shouted "Look" or some equally stupid thing when Autumn casually turned, focused her currently nocked arrow, and fired right into the running SEAL.

She turned to me as she set down her bow and drew her ninja sword from its scabbard.

"I have a request now, Talker," she said calmly, as though we were anywhere but in the middle of a battle. Out there in the central courtyard that overlooked the valley below, in the shadow of the ominous spectacle that was the ancient tower, the wounded SEAL in his villain getup was bent over double from the silver-feathered arrow she'd just put in him.

Numbly, I nodded to her. My mind was moving slowly, but I was processing what was about to happen. She was going to get him. And I needed to tell her no. *Wait. Let's do this as a team.*

"If I perish…" She was speaking to me in Shadow Cant. "Your Rangers must… go down into ruined Tarragon and

591

destroy the dragon. So no one else from the tribe will ever need to... face S'sruth the Cruel. The little elves you call Lost Boys... my brother is their leader. He will rule one day... when I am no more. And he will die before the dragon, as we all do... confronting the wyrm's evil. Kill S'sruth and you will save the Elves of Shadow... and our fault... will become untrue. Even if I am gone then."

Before I could say "no" or "stop" she was gone, leaping out of a ruined window within the wall of the Lost Library, racing to meet the vampire who was even now pulling her ashwood and silver-feathered arrow from his body. He shouted at the sun, arched his back, and saw Last of Autumn coming for him. Then he smiled and drew his own blade. *Coldfire.*

And I heard Last of Autumn shout as she charged, "I am Queen of the Shadow Elves, low man. I am revenge, Triton. I am revenge!"

# CHAPTER SIXTY-TWO

THE next wave of orcs came against the tower as I just stood there getting hit by the occasional hot brass from the nearby blaring two-forty. It was going to be close, and right at that moment it was starting to look like we'd get overrun. An arrow streaked through the main opening, past Tanner and Kurtz who were defending there, and barely missed me. It shattered on stone behind me.

"Get down, Talker!" shouted Tanner. "They're coming through."

But all I could do was watch Last of Autumn run out into the shadow of *Barad Nulla* to meet her death against the powerful vampire who'd been one of us. Once and long ago.

"Get him down!" shouted Kurtz. And as he moved into the doorway, firing and ejecting spent shotgun shells from his weapon, Tanner dashed at me and knocked me down.

"You don't wanna die today, Talk!" said the wily PFC who was, when I really thought about it, my best friend in the detachment. "Need you here, brother."

That brought me back to life. Told me what I needed to do. We, all of us, were in this together. We were brothers. And we had a sister. She'd gotten us off that island, Last Queen of the Elves or not.

For a moment I turned over on my back and watched the snipers higher up in the tower, its central floors and roof collapsed long ago, still engaging the defenders at the forward defenses. Then I got to my feet and searched for Autumn.

What I saw was the most amazing sword fight I've ever seen in my life. Better than pirates or ninjas or superheroes. If the Rangers were going to stay here in the Ruin, they'd definitely need to get good at combat with hand weapons. They'd need to be trained by her, or whoever had taught her.

The SEAL, Mike McCluskey from Michigan, King Triton servant of the Nether Sorcerer, or *whatevs*, moved like living smoke as he fought the elf to the death. Last of Autumn. Queen of the Shadow Elves. She shouted as she went out to meet him sword to sword. His black rogue's cape twirled, misdirecting his movements as his body turned to a living liquid-like smoke and suddenly exploded another step forward in their battle. Then he corporealized into McCluskey and his dark-bladed weapon lashed out in savage fury, hammering at her. He was controlled chaos, but he fought like a wild beast cornered.

Then there was Autumn. As fast, if not faster, than the vampire SEAL. Her movements were darts in one constant direction, slashing at the shifting vampire in the morning light with her bright weapon. Her blade like sudden lightning strikes should have ruined the vampire, but instead all she did was slice smoke as the battle raged closer and closer to the tower.

That was his goal. I could tell. McCluskey was retreating toward the tower even as he attacked relentlessly.

I could see his strategy.

And I understood.

I remembered him talking about how he didn't do well in sunlight and that he had charms and wards to protect him, but even still he felt like he had the flu in daylight.

Was that true? I didn't know. But it was the only intel I had to make the call.

Inside the ancient and formidable tower, he would have darkness. Utter darkness. Something close to night, or at least far better than direct sunlight. He might even lock it and wait for night.

And right now, it looked as though he was using Autumn's vengeful fury to pull her into the tower. Into his web. Into a trap.

McCluskey unleashed a series of dizzying attacks against Autumn, shifting the balance of power in the battle and driving her back and to her knees as she flashed her blade back and forth doing everything she could to protect herself. Then McCluskey turned to smoke and streaked off toward the open black door of darkness that was the entrance to *Barad Nulla*.

Last of Autumn needed help.

I went out the same ruined opening she had and raced toward their battle, pulling my sidearm as I ran. At the last second McCluskey rematerialized into his dark rogue form, turning from black smoke thing to man, and I fired, unsure if I was even getting hits. He laughed like he'd won and ducked inside the tower.

"Don't go in there!" shouted Autumn at me from the stones of the courtyard. He'd knocked her down and almost run her through. Maybe he had. I couldn't tell. I was blind with rage.

A gate was coming down to seal the tower and I was running into the darkness beyond it. Into *Barad Nulla* itself.

This probably wouldn't be good.

I slipped the ring on and got under the gate as it fell. Then I turned saw Last of Autumn slide in too at the last second just before the gate sealed us in and we found ourselves in the total darkness of the other side.

And silence. Except it wasn't. Insane whispers in the darkness and the sounds of things with claws scrabbling up and away. I felt webs, old and hot and dusty. I slapped at my carrier, sure I'd felt some black pulpy spider scurrying across it.

I heard her in my mind. Autumn.

*It's magic, Talker. The darkness is. It negates the Hunters' Fellowship. The Moon Vision. But I can see a little.*

*Why did you attack him all alone?* I asked her. *The Rangers could have helped you. And if the Fellowship is negated, how come I can still talk to you?*

The vampire laughed at us in the darkness. It was a cruel laugh made by an unhinged mind. He sounded high above us. Far up and away in the tall and massive tower. But at the same time, the smoke in the dry laughter was present and close in the thick darkness.

This was a very strange place.

"Gonna kill you, little linguist," whispered McCluskey. He snorted derisively. "Knew you were a problem from the get-go. Didn't know why. Couldn't put my thumb on it. But y'know, instincts. It's what separates people like me from the amateurs. Pros from the rest of you sheep. Know what I mean, little soldier boy playing at Ranger?"

I wanted to tell him he wasn't *people* anymore. He'd crossed a line a long time ago and left his humanity somewhere lonely and awful. My guess was there were probably a bunch of dead SEALs there, wherever that lonely place was, wondering why they'd been done by one of their own. But my voice was dry and it didn't want to say anything tough or brave.

I focused on getting a new magazine in my pistol. Or at least, it was my pistol now. It had once been the sergeant major's. Now it was mine. After it had... cleaned Deep State Volman... I guess we decided without saying anything that it was mine to keep. And I wasn't here to have a conversation with him anyway. I was here to remove yet another obstacle to mission success. And a fully topped-off pistol was gonna make that a lot easier even if the suck was ramping up.

"Fine," I muttered, feeling myself embrace it. "I'm more than fine with that."

*You are special, Talker.* It was Autumn inside my head. Her voice calm and cool. And intimate. Like we knew each other in ways we hadn't when using our voices. *They call what you can do, Talker of the Rangers... sainikku. A power of the mind that crosses realms. Vandahar sensed it. You have a rare power. Most aren't even sure what it is, or what it does. There is much to fear about it, and not just because it is unknown. But sometimes in the Ruin... sometimes... even good things are revealed here. Some of your Rangers are becoming the thing they will be in time. That is the Ruin and what it does. It reveals, Talker. It reveals us for what we truly are.*

And...

*I came after him because it was he who hunted my people after the betrayal at the gates of Barad Nulla long ago. He owes a debt, and I have come to collect for my people.*

Okay. *Sainikku.* That sounded close enough to the Japanese word, *Saionikku.* So... *psionics.* Whatever. No time for that right now. I'll get Vandahar to explain it but that's probably what he meant when he was being all cryptic. But first I've got to get us out of here. Get her out of here without both of us dying.

Suddenly the urge to kill the vampire wasn't as strong as the urge to save Autumn. I could tell she knew she was going to die today. And she knew that if she could get in a fatal strike against her people's enemy before that happened...

... well, that was big for her. That was something worth dying for.

Maybe that was the psionics talking. I had no idea. I could just tell that was what she was thinking. That her death might provide an opportunity for a better tomorrow for someone else. The way all heroes think.

But I didn't want her to die. I didn't want anyone to die today.

I had other plans.

Make the other guy die. Everyone goes home today. Those were *my* plans. Those were my thoughts.

I had a flare. Five in fact, on my carrier.

*Don't,* she said, reading my mind and seeing my plan.

I pulled the flare and ignited it, tossing it onto the floor with my M18 out and scanning the darkness all around us. The weapon the sergeant major had given me. His weapon.

I hoped I was still invisible.

A large piece of pottery came flying out of the darkness above and landed nowhere near me. He was aiming for Autumn. She moved fast toward the base of a long stair that curved around the wall of the massive and empty tower.

Although, now that the flare was lit, I could see that it was not totally empty.

The Forge was here. Sitting dead center in the main room. Revealed by the hissing red light of the smoking flare.

McCluskey opened fire with some kind of automatic weapon. He'd had the Forge for two weeks. It was to be expected. We'd figured he'd try to gin up a weapon for himself.

He fired at Autumn because he could see her. I was still invisible. Rounds smashed into her armor and threw her against the wall along the curving stairs climbing up into the gloom. In the guttering light of the hissing flare I saw her face go pale as she slid down the wall and slumped on the stairs.

And I saw McCluskey too, up there in the dark, leering over a high balcony ledge and laughing down at her. His fangs making him look like a hideous monster. A man no more.

I fired the sergeant major's sidearm at a stupidly ridiculous distance for a high-percentage pistol shot, but the front sight was crisp when I broke the trigger and for some reason that I couldn't explain, I felt pretty good about it. Or the Hunters' Fellowship still worked on some level. Or Chief Rapp's school of SF shooting had made me just that good.

What had Brumm said? *All skill. No luck. Don't jinx it.*

McCluskey dropped the weapon and grabbed for his head, disappearing back into the darkness and blocked from my view by the high balcony. Swearing as I heard him stumble away from that ledge. His heavy black boots scraping against the stone as he groaned in pain and screamed.

At that moment I wished I had silver bullets. Was that vampires or werewolves?

"Damn you!" he shouted down at me, and his enraged bellow echoed off the high walls.

I raced up the stairs to Autumn and knelt next to her, checking for wounds.

"I don't think... it's serious," she gasped.

I popped a flare and ran my hands across her armor, near her heart and lungs.

"What about him?" she tried to say. But she couldn't seem to catch her breath.

"He's hit," I said. "Don't know how bad."

I remembered McCluskey saying he healed fast. And that he'd died before and come back. Wasn't that what vampires did?

My gloves came away with a little blood. I pulled one off and checked that area. It was red. But not dark red. No artery hit or nicked. I pulled back her cloak and inspected the wound. The round hadn't penetrated her fine silvery armor; it had just destroyed the delicately made chain linkage that felt like silk. Her armor had acted like bulletproof Kevlar plates. I suspected it was magical. Still, the two rounds that had hit her had probably fractured some ribs. Magic armor or not, physics still gonna physics.

"Lie down," I told her. "Just try to breathe, Autumn."

Her eyes fluttered for a second like she was going to pass out right there as I tried to make her more comfortable. Then they were back. Watching me. Just the way they had in that vision I'd had of us in a small sailboat, heading south toward the Cities of Men.

She swallowed thickly and found some inner resolve to hang on.

"I gotta go kill him now, Autumn," I told her, ejecting a mag and sliding in a new one. "Wait here now."

# CHAPTER SIXTY-THREE

"I hear you… so c'mon up, little soldier boy," said the vampire in the darkness as I climbed the curving stairs inside the tower of *Barad Nulla*. "Got something real nice for you when you get here."

I was invisible. But that didn't mean I was inaudible.

McCluskey didn't sound good. He sounded like a junkie coming down off a bad spike. I could hear him groaning and coughing. I still had the ring on. And I was climbing the stairs. Pistol out and in the high ready position I'd learned in RASP. Finger straight and out of the trigger until McCluskey gave me another chance at a solid sight picture. Then I'd punch his ticket again until he changed shape, or caught fire. His voice was getting close as he talked and I climbed. I wouldn't miss at this range. And apparently you didn't need silver bullets, or stakes to the heart, to kill a vampire in the Ruin. Apparently, firearms worked just fine.

"You got me good. I'll give you that, little soldier boy," he said as though we were old friends discussing some pleasant remembrance. "Think I lost my eye. Bullet's still in my skull."

He laughed like a man dying.

"But I've had worse." His voice was so close as I neared the top of the steps, I was sure I'd see him in a step or two. "I'll be fine. But you, on the other hand..."

I heard him pop the spoon on a grenade. Then I heard it roll across the floor right toward me at the top step.

"... won't be," he finished.

Thanks, Captain Obvious.

I flung myself down the stairs, face first, and kissed old dusty stone as the grenade went off behind me. If it had made it down the first few steps, I would have been done for. Instead it detonated on the balcony I had just arrived at seconds earlier.

I was on my feet again even as the dull roar of the blast still echoed within the tower, pushing off stone and following my barrel up into the darkness, ripping another flare and tossing it ahead of me.

I spotted him in the hellish orange light. Just for a second. His pale face ruined by the bullet in his skull. He was laughing like a lunatic.

"So you wanna play with the big boys now!" he screamed at me.

He turned to smoke and rushed for my weapon. Still smoke. Still McCluskey.

I felt his cold hands around my throat and I was bent over the balcony. I'd jerked the sidearm back to keep it away from him and he'd gone for my throat instead. Which meant...

*He could see me.*

Maybe some side effect of the grenade blast had disabled the ring. Temporarily? Or permanently.

"How do ya like me now, soldier boy?" said the ghoul luridly leering in my face. Fangs out and wide hungry smile to boot. He was choking the life out of me with claws that were as cold as ice.

I jammed the M18 into his midsection and squeezed. Three shots and he turned to smoke and streaked away from me. I sucked in a gasping breath of air as a trap door opened in the ceiling. He howled like a wounded animal as bright daylight shot down into the darkness.

The thing I saw moving up the ladder, screaming and smoking in pain, was like a cross between a demon and McCluskey. Leering, obscene. And utterly tormented by the sun.

I gasped for more air that wouldn't easily come and launched myself at the ladder. I wasn't going to let him get away. I was going to finish this now.

That was when I heard the titanic cry of something from the age of dinosaurs shriek and roar beyond the thick walls of *Barad Nulla*. Something so unnatural and bone-chilling, my legs literally stopped and said climbing up into the light to follow McCluskey wasn't a great idea.

A huge shadow blocked out the sunlight on the ladder, and McCluskey disappeared up into the darkness there as some great storm passed close to the tower and its very walls shuddered all around me.

But he had to die. Had to, if just to save Autumn. He'd betrayed us all. Not just the Shadow Elves long before we ever showed up. The Rangers too. And the dead require an answer for such abuses. The dead Rangers I'd written the names of in the journal that had followed me from all the known to this unknown. To the Ruin of everything that once was.

To the Ruin of now.

I looked up and saw the huge tail of a lizard cross the open sky above the trap door. Just one brief flash of the completely impossible. I'm smart. I could put two and two together pretty fast.

"Come on up and meet my friend S'sruth, soldier boy," laughed McCluskey wildly up there and out of sight.

*No thanks*, my mind said as my arms and legs began to climb once again. Gripping the M18 and trying to remember how many rounds I'd fired. Reminding myself I'd gassed up with a fresh mag.

McCluskey, when I found him at the top of the Barad Nulla, was half done for. He was leaning against the parapet. His sword, *Coldfire*, was out, but it hung limply from his pale and trembling claw, and he didn't look in any kind of shape to use it against anyone any time soon.

I would have raised my weapon and emptied it into McCluskey, but of course there was the giant dragon, green and gold, undulating across the sky all around us. It was completely unlike anything I'd ever seen before. Its triangular horned head was pure malevolent evil, its eyes like bright burning emeralds that glared with some kind of blazing bonfire at the center. Its belly was shimmering gold and shining and immense, the scales along its back and sides like massive plates of green armor that glittered in the morning sun. Two huge leathery wings spanned away from it, catching the air and keeping the massive lizard aloft.

It howled in triumph, and I felt everything I thought of as strength go right out of me. I was surprised I was even standing. I looked down at the sergeant major's M18. It felt small and useless at that moment.

McCluskey laughed like a madman being strangled and enjoying it nonetheless.

The dragon was coming straight for us, roaring tyrannically like some elder beast from the ages of darkness before man had ever walked the earth. Insulted at our presence.

I was cooked.

I felt the edge of the parapet opposite the laughing maniacal SEAL at the top of the strange tower. The edge was against my back. I wondered at that moment if I should just keep backing up and fall to my death before I died by dragon.

"Back blast area clear!" someone shouted, a voice from below and behind me in the courtyard where the battle still raged. I turned to see the sergeant major, way down there and just inside the body-littered courtyard of stone, surrounded by his team. They were engaging fleeing orcs in every direction.

The sergeant major had the Carl G on his shoulder and was stoically aiming it upward in our direction. Solid. Just like the little drawing in the manual on how to properly aim and fire the weapon no matter what's going on around you. I threw myself to the deck of the tower, and a second later the HE round from the Carl Gustaf streaked overhead, shrieking and smoking as it went, and exploded near the incoming dragon.

The dragon screeched in rage as its armor and flesh was ruined by the anti-personnel round. Eardrums, hearing protection or not, cried bloody murder at the dragon's howl of wounded rage.

The giant thing was hurt, its body riddled, wings torn and shredded, by tons of small balls meant to ruin human combatants.

It hovered in closer, glaring at me with its purely alien eyes as it snatched McCluskey off the roof in one grab, turned with a flap of its giant leathery wings, and pulled its glittering green-and-gold bulk away and off into the morning sky. Bellowing in rage at the hundreds of wounds it had just received. Flying nonetheless.

I lay there, watching the dragon go.

Knowing I should be dead.

But I wasn't.

# CHAPTER SIXTY-FOUR

ME helping Autumn as much as she was helping me, the both of us limped from the tower of *Barad Nulla*. The orcs were dead. Or leaping to their death from the open edges of the crag that supported the Dark Spire. The Rangers were giving no quarter. No mercy. And the orcs, warriors in their own way, chose no mercy.

It was like something out of the Bronze Age.

The Lost Boys were there, taking Autumn away from me, glaring at me as they pulled her away. And just before she was gone, she gave me a look.

It was that look in the vision of the sailboat. I don't know what to call it. But it's the look that says there is more than duty, service, and this life we are prisoners of. Something that's just us. One time, before I'd read the books written by Stephen King, a fellow scholar had been bemoaning the institution we were both at. He was leaving to go do charity work in the third world. Giving up everything for a river upcountry in the Stone Age and some people to lose himself in. I suspected there was more to it. When I asked him why he was going, he simply replied, *There are other worlds than these.*

He told me to read the Dark Tower series. Then I would understand. I didn't. But I read the books anyway and I knew the phrase. And now, watching her being led away by the Lost Boys, I knew what she was telling me. If we were other people, it could be different. She wouldn't be their queen, destined to face the dragon that had almost just killed me. Alone. Instead we'd be those people in the boat. Sailing to the Cities of Men. It was the opposite of the David Bowie song "Heroes."

*We could just be us, if just for one day on a boat.*

And maybe that last look said, *All things are possible, Talker. Things dreamt, and things never dreamed of.*

\*\*\*

It was Tanner who found me as I crossed toward the ruined tower of the Lost Library. He was pretty rough to look at and broken up. Tears ran away from his angry eyes. And there was all the pain the world can ever know in there. No one needed to tell me it was bad. I knew.

"He's dead, Talk," he shouted at me, sobbing and bellowing. "And I don't want any of this anymore!"

I didn't need to ask who. I knew. But I did anyway.

"Brumm," wailed Tanner, wiping the dirty sleeve of his fatigues across his red-rimmed eyes. Unashamed. Tanner, the least of all the Rangers. The one who'd been there and done that. The three-DUI, two-stripper-marriage, lifetime PFC. The one who thought you didn't have to be hard to be a Ranger. You just had to Ranger, and you could be funny too. And you could cry when your buddy didn't make it.

"They got him down there," sobbed Tanner as he came close.

"No," I think I mumbled as I pushed past Tanner, making for the tower and the crowd of tired Rangers gathering there. I felt like the world was going to fling me off it once more. Because a lot of people, me most of all, should have died before Brumm. Brumm who killed the giant and said *Carl G don't care* like it wasn't anything special. Brumm who wasn't afraid when the rest of us were.

"Yeah," said Tanner, and swore at something, someone. Everything. "He killed most of 'em but he was out of ammo. Just whatever he could get his hands on at the end. They cut him up. Bad, Talk."

"No."

No.

I was still moving to the Lost Library when Kurtz came out. Holding Brumm in both arms. Brumm stared skyward seeing nothing. He was indeed cut up bad. He was dead.

No.

Because... you don't want it to be like this.

Kurtz was shaking. But he wasn't crying. He looked like a man who was trying to hold on while the world spun him off in every direction it could. He looked like he was being carried away by a flood.

"They were brothers, Talk," shouted Tanner as I stumbled toward the scene, Tanner unable to control his crying as he swore at himself.

Kurtz began to walk away from the tower, carrying his dead soldier like a good NCO. Like a Ranger. And I knew he'd keep walking until he hit the front gate and he'd go out and maybe never come back to the Rangers.

"Same dad," wailed Tanner. "Just different moms."

I turned toward Tanner. I'd had no idea. No idea Kurtz and Brumm were actual blood brothers. That Brumm wasn't a mini Sergeant Kurtz trying to Ranger hard. But that he was his little brother. Trying to...

"They joined the Rangers to be together. Lived in separate states when they were kids. Only got to get together once a year during the summer when they was growing up. That..." And Tanner started crying so hard I could barely understand what he was saying as he followed me and I followed Kurtz. But what Tanner said was something to the effect that they kept in touch with each other. Every day. By ham radios. "Switching to on" had been some kind of code for that between them. Between brothers.

Some kind of message that no matter what—having different moms who change your last name out of spite, alimony and divorce, just terrible parents, poverty, life, and other states—they were still brothers no matter what.

*Switching to on.*

Every family has those. Words and phrases I'll never understand no matter how much I try. Words that mean nothing. Words that mean everything.

I felt useless.

And then I was crying too. And I couldn't look anymore because it was too much. Because we were supposed to have won.

And it felt like we'd lost.

Other Rangers, now that the fighting was over, were coming to watch Kurtz carry Brumm out for the last time. Silence as they watched the best of them carrying his dead brother away to bury him alone.

And then... Chief Rapp happened.

He came into the courtyard, his sleeves and carrier covered in blood. Ranger blood. I heard his big resonant voice bellow. Whether it was grief or something I don't know. It was just a cry that said, "Oh no!" He let his high-speed SF weapon go, dangling from his sling, and he moved swiftly toward Kurtz, holding out his massive arms and hands, saying "Oh no!" over and over again.

"Lemme see him, Sergeant," bellowed the giant SF operator. But Kurtz, who was much smaller, was just shaking his head and the tears were starting to come but his mouth was shut tight. Sealed. It would stay shut forever. His lips pressed tight. Pure rage and anger and endless grief. Forever.

Someone told the chief that Brumm was dead.

"Maybe!" shouted the chief. "Maybe," he said again, his rich voice echoing out over the courtyard. Somewhere there was shooting as some last holdout of orcs was done in by Rangers still securing the fortress. "Or maybe," said the chief, now speaking to all of us, "maybe this place here is different than where we come from. Maybe there is some kinda magic here. And maybe something more."

He tried to take Brumm's lifeless corpse away from Kurtz, but Kurtz jerked his dead kid brother from another mother away and held him like he was a treasure he'd never part with. Roaring something unintelligible in his strangled rage.

"Nooooooooooarrrgggggh!"

"I know," soothed Chief Rapp in his Mississippi mud accent, towering over Sergeant Kurtz, the chief's bulk and muscle double the size of the tough-as-nails Rangers weapons team sergeant.

"Set 'im down and lemme try one mo' time, son."

He took hold of the body and eased it down onto the stones of the courtyard. Kurtz was still enraged and yet hoping the universe had got this one wrong. Just this once. Maybe he had a little faith left.

Oh please, I thought. Just this one time. Let me be… wrong.

*So it can be right.*

The chief studied the body of Brumm for a long moment as he knelt down next to it on the bloody stones of the courtyard. Then he pulled off his helmet and rifle, undoing his carrier as he raised his hands to the sky and started to speak. Speaking like a black preacher on the last Sunday of all Sundays. Powerful. Rich. Awesome.

"There's magic!" he shouted. At all of us. "Always was! Now I believe in it more than ever."

He lowered his hands and stared at Brumm's lifeless body. We were all silent. Unsure what was going to happen next.

"He got this!" shouted the chief, and slammed his hands down onto Brumm. Slammed them down like he was forcing something that wouldn't fit… back into a place it had to go.

Had to.

And then he resurrected Brumm from the dead.

Brumm came back to life like he'd been hit by the shock paddles. Gasping and staring around wild-eyed at every Ranger standing around him in stunned silence.

The chief backed away, raising his hands and praying. Or praising. Thanking Jesus. The Rangers began to shout and cheer.

Kurtz held his brother, whispering something.

*Switch to on, little brother.*

*Switch to on.*

We'd won. The fortress was ours. The Forge was back in our hands.

And death had been cheated. If just for today. If just for one man.

# EPILOGUE

SOME of the Rangers started to eat their MREs right there in the body-littered courtyard where orc blood collected among the stones. Vandahar was there and the old wizard swept off his crazy wizard's hat and laughed good-naturedly at what had been done. The orcs driven out. The dragon driven off. Brumm coming back. The old man's laugh was good and genuine. And made you want more of it in this world.

Word was Captain Knife Hand had disappeared. But the wounded were being attended to. And the dead. There were dead beyond the power of Chief Rapp. Who insisted it wasn't him who had the power.

Maybe Brumm was a miracle.

Maybe it was magic.

Maybe it was a one-time shot. A gift from the universe. Or… whomever.

Whatever. We'd take what we were given where we found it. But I couldn't say we wouldn't ask questions.

I had a ton.

But now wasn't the time.

It was the sergeant major who found me.

"C'mon, Talker. Time to debrief. And I got something to show you."

He led me away. Me following that long-legged road march stride. I had seen many weird things. A dragon. A resurrection. Ghosts and death. Tombs filled with treasure. A vampire. A beautiful elf girl who gave me a look that said… *all things are possible*.

And that was just today. And it was only a bit after 0700 in the morning.

We held the fortress. It was ours now. The Lost Boys and their queen, Last of Autumn, were setting up camp near the Lost Library. Claiming it as their own.

The sergeant major led me to a small tower that hung over the ledge of the crag. It was near the inner defenses and not defensive in nature. We walked into it, and I realized it was a kitchen. A normal medieval kitchen with a cooking hearth, pots and pans of beaten copper, an old rough table, and a few odd chairs. A giant open window looked out over the beautiful valley below the crag. The day was turning green and golden, and I could see the hawks out there catching the first thermals of the day. Crying out to one another that today would be a good day.

I tried to forget the image of the dragon looming above me at the top of the tower. And how close I'd been to death at that moment.

The sergeant major rummaged around in his ruck, and instantly I recognized his camp percolator.

He had coffee?

He'd been holding out on me?

"Look at this…" he said, opening a small wooden door at the back of the kitchen. Rough steps led down into a small cellar. There were hams hanging, breads in baskets. Things in jars. Food, I hoped. But no, better than food.

There was coffee.

Sacks of it.

I couldn't see it yet, but I could smell it. 'Cause I'm an addict.

Turned out there were five sacks. Five large sacks. All stamped crudely with something that basically equated to *Product of Portugon* in Portuguese. I could translate that. That's also one of my languages.

I hauled the sack up while the sergeant major found some eggs and cut some ham off the hanging shanks. Thick slices.

For a while we worked at getting the kitchen up. Firewood. Water from a nearby well. I made the coffee using a strange little grinder I found in the kitchen. The sergeant major cooked eggs and bacon in a copper skillet. Finally we moved the chairs and sat down around the rough table right there in the tiny medieval kitchen. Next to the open window.

I tasted the coffee and watched the hawks hunt.

It was... the best coffee. Real coffee. Ground and brewed right here. By me.

"Good?" asked the sergeant major in his Texan mumble as he scooped up his eggs. "Guess we coulda made toast," he added.

"Yes, Sergeant Major. This is... real good. And it means..."

"Means a lot. Means a lot, Talker. Means people out there with a civilization we can relate to. But that's for another day."

I kept thinking about Brumm being dead. And then not being dead. I asked the sergeant major about that.

He continued to eat, and then, as he finished his food faster than me, he took a sip of his coffee and sat back for a moment watching the hawks. He fished his Kindle out of his cargo pocket and set it down on the rough table in the rustic fortress kitchen. I could tell this would be his reading place. This was where we'd be able to find him. Just like his little circle of stones and fire out on the island that had almost been our Alamo.

"Man could get used to this," the command sergeant major said to himself, staring out the window at the valley and the golden sunlight as the day began to heat up. "That's for sure."

He looked at me. I was still waiting for an answer. But I wasn't going to prompt a sergeant major for one.

"You know what Ol' Shakespeare would've said, PFC Talker?"

I did not, so I said nothing. Shakespeare said a lotta stuff. Chances were I'd get it wrong. I like to be right. I'm sick that way.

"He said… *There are more things in heaven and earth, Horatio, than are dreamt of in your philosophy.* That's from *Hamlet*. It was a play. But I been thinking about this since we spotted our first orcs back on the LZ. This world's a strange place. Maybe it isn't even ours. Maybe it is. But I've been having strange dreams ever since we got here."

He paused. And for a long time we just drank our coffee. Finally, he leaned forward and I could tell our pause was coming to an end. There would be a lot to do today. The fortress would need to be scoured. Blood washed. Defenses and watches set up. Quarters organized. Forge restored to working order. More of the Orc tossing game. That and a lot of other things for a lot of days to come.

"You know that… meme," continued the sergeant major as he studied the hawks out there. "Those pictures and words you young guys like to communicate by instead of just pickin' up the phone. You know that one where it shows a buncha studs in high-altitude drop gear coming in at dusk or dawn or whatever. And it says someone is praying right now and asking for help. And help is on the way. Two minutes to insertion. You know that one, Talker?"

I did.

"Well, maybe that's all that happened. What Shakespeare was trying to say. Someone here in whatever this place is... they needed help, Talker. And the universe, or whatever, decided to send Rangers. That's what I think about all of it. I've been that guy. Droppin' into some hellhole to try to croak a tyrant and make things a little easier on the oppressed. So maybe this... this is just that. But all like ol' Shakespeare was tryin' to say 'bout the nature of the universe and stuff. There's mysteries we ain't even thought of, Talker. Reasons we don't understand yet, know what I mean?"

I took a deep breath.

I had coffee. That was actually all I needed when I got right down to it. Everything else was just a *want*. But coffee. Coffee was a *need*.

I could face what came next. Dragons, vampires, were-captain-knife-hand-tigers. Whatever the Ruin had. I was sure there was more to come. I was sure the captain would come back to lead us. He'd lead us even when he'd become something else. Something terrible. And he'd continued to lead in the only way he could at that moment. By attacking our enemies like a wild and berserk animal.

"Talker..." said the sergeant major as I got up to go and find some way to be useful and help the Rangers stay alive one more day here in the Ruin.

I looked back at him. He held my gaze for a moment to tell me that what he was giving me was the truth. That I could measure by it. That I could survive with it.

"You done good, Ranger."

\*\*\*

That night, I dreamt in Elvish.

# THE END

# RANGER CREED

Recognizing that I volunteered as a Ranger, fully knowing the hazards of my chosen profession, I will always endeavor to uphold the prestige, honor, and high esprit de corps of the Rangers.

Acknowledging the fact that a Ranger is a more elite Soldier who arrives at the cutting edge of battle by land, sea, or air, I accept the fact that as a Ranger my country expects me to move further, faster and fight harder than any other Soldier.

Never shall I fail my comrades. I will always keep myself mentally alert, physically strong and morally straight and I will shoulder more than my share of the task whatever it may be, one-hundred-percent and then some.

Gallantly will I show the world that I am a specially selected and well-trained Soldier. My courtesy to superior officers, neatness of dress and care of equipment shall set the example for others to follow.

Energetically will I meet the enemies of my country. I shall defeat them on the field of battle for I am better trained and will fight with all my might. Surrender is not a Ranger word. I will never leave a fallen comrade to fall into the hands of the enemy and under no circumstances will I ever embarrass my country.

Readily will I display the intestinal fortitude required to fight on to the Ranger objective and complete the mission though I be the lone survivor.

Rangers lead the way!

# ALSO BY JASON ANSPACH & NICK COLE

Galaxy's Edge: Legionnaire
Galaxy's Edge: Savage Wars
Galaxy's Edge: Requiem For Medusa
Galaxy's Edge: Order of the Centurion

# ALSO BY JASON ANSPACH

Wayward Galaxy
King's League
'til Death

# ALSO BY NICK COLE

American Wasteland:
The Complete Wasteland Trilogy
SodaPop Soldier
Strange Company